LER FO

Qty

Qty

Cut By:

Scanned By:

Scanned B

PRAISE FOR *FAMILY SECRETS 2 – DOUBLE DESTINIES*

Having been blessed by Nancy Petrey's first novel, *Family Secrets – Divine Destinies*, I was eager to read her sequel to it, *Family Secrets 2 – Double Destinies*. I found the sequel to be an even greater blessing. The captivating plot of this delightful romance novel kept me eager to learn what would happen next. One moment you have a terrorist throwing a knife at a young woman in a church in Mississippi. Weeks later the story takes an unpredictable and dramatic turn during a concert in Budapest. As the story unfolds in many exciting events, you begin to admire, and identify with, two young couples who fall madly in love and try to figure out how to arrange a double wedding. Very cleverly Nancy uses the dialogue to teach Christians about their Jewish roots, the meaning of Yiddish words and traditions that help us understand Christian values. Lovers of music will be blessed by the way the author uses her extensive knowledge of music to enrich this enthralling love story. If you want to get lost in a book filled with suspense, conflict, tenderness, joy and inspiring examples of the power of prayer, I heartily recommend this book! It is a book you will commend to your friends.

Rev. Walter Matthew Albritton, Jr.
Pastor Emeritus of St. James United Methodist Church, Montgomery, AL
Assistant Pastor of New Walk of Life Church, Montgomery, AL
Pastor of United Methodist churches for 70 years
Author of over 20 books

Family Secrets 2: Double Destinies is first a love story, but it carries the reader on a journey of many dimensions. Two college couples (both engaged to be married) drive the story and deal with the temptations of young love, conviction and life calling,

Christian and Jewish heritage. Life is mostly smooth sailing, but conflict interrupts with themes of rape, demon possession, dangerous "friends," and a terrorist assault.

Randall Murphree
Editor of *The Stand* magazine, American Family Association

PRAISE FOR FIRST NOVEL: *FAMILY SECRETS – DIVINE DESTINIES*

"Family Secrets is another win for Nancy Petrey and her fans. A romance with enough twists and turns to keep me turning page after page until I finished. Enjoyable, encouraging, historical and educational as I learned quite a bit about the Jewish faith. I did a speed read while visiting my daughter, left it for her to read and can't wait to get it back and read again!" – Judy Hood, Mississippi

"Captivating novel where suspense, mystery, and intrigue converge. Filled with adventure and faith. Not only is it entertaining but educational as well. Who knew a quiet college town could have so much action which is revealed with the turn of every page. Highly recommend." – **Richard Street**, Illinois

"After reading *Family Secrets – Divine Destinies,* I feel like I've been on a whirlwind adventure! Nancy is a gifted writer and teacher. Her historical knowledge of Israel from her own studies, as well as her many trips there are interwoven into the narrative in a way that brought back memories for me of my own trip years ago. Her characters meet in the Deep South, beginning their journey together, and ultimately walking in the paths of Jesus in Israel. They are completely lovable and are on the ride of their lives as they come together in a divinely orchestrated way. She drives home the point that life with Yeshua/Jesus is an adventure and you don't want to miss it! Looking forward to the sequel." -- **T. A. May**, Florida

"Characters come to life in Nancy Petrey's book, with fast moving interwoven story lines of romance, discovery, intrigue, persecution, and faith with an overriding theme of divine purpose—often described as 'God incidents' in her book. The author, a lover of Israel and a teacher about the Jewish roots of Christians, pours her knowledge into the accounts of four main characters, their families, and their adversaries. Scripture, Jewish and Christian historical references, and facts about anti-Semitism are clearly related by and for her characters who found understanding, peace, and joy as a result. Readers have that opportunity as well. I highly recommend *Family Secrets, Divine Destinies.*" – **Ann Tate**, Alabama

"I enjoyed this book. I felt right at home. It was not only enjoyable but very educational concerning so much about the Jewish religion and customs. It was so impressive to be reminded of how important and meaningful it is to pray about every and ALL things and not just the certain things that we normally might pray about. It's important to remember to include Jesus in our thoughts throughout each day and not just concerning certain or special things. I do that pretty much but I will be more thoughtful and intentional thanks to this book." – **Mack Howard**, Arizona

FAMILY SECRETS 2
DOUBLE DESTINIES

NANCY PETREY

Energion Publications
Gonzalez, Florida
2022

Cover Design:

ISBN: 978-1-63199-797-6
eISBN: 978-1-63199-798-3

Energion Publications
P. O. Box 841
Gonzalez, Florida 32560

energion.com
pubs@energion.com

DEDICATION

I dedicate this novel to my heavenly Father who directed me and reassured me through His many God incidences in my life as I wrote. He spoke in various ways to confirm me. I delight to call Him, "Abba."

May the Scriptural and historical lessons woven through the plot by His Holy Spirit bring understanding and honor and glory to Him. And may the great Lover of our souls receive from readers the love and gratitude due Him.

ACKNOWLEDGEMENTS

I thank my friends on Facebook and other friends who have encouraged me to write a sequel to my first novel, *Family Secrets: Divine Destinies*. Janice Bell-Lewis, my Messianic Jewish friend, volunteered to proofread as I was writing it. She continued to express her enjoyment of the story along the way and also offered valuable suggestions. My son Jim Petrey, who inspired me to write the first book and was my primary proofreader, offered his services again as a proofreader for this sequel. He was close to college age in the time setting of 1997-1998, so that was helpful and his input vital. I am very grateful for the ways Janice and Jim have assisted me.

The prayers of my friends, Debra Little, Holly Shelton, and others were invaluable, and I thank them. Kay Verrall and Richard Street answered questions for me regarding names of places, flight information, and other facts. I appreciate their help.

Lee Ann Williamson of Starkville, who has a world evangelism ministry, as well as a singing ministry, graciously consented to appearing in this novel as a singer. Thank you, Lee Ann, my friend of many years.

I am greatly appreciative of my endorsers and friends, Randall Murphree of Tupelo and Rev. Walter Albritton of Montgomery. Randall endorsed the first novel, so I am doubly thankful to him for his reading and endorsing the sequel. Walter is a long-time friend who has been preaching for 70 years and is approaching 90. His newest work is assisting the pastor of a black congregation in Montgomery, AL. He had never read a book of Christian fiction until he read my first novel, and he loved it! He says this sequel is even better. I am so grateful for his efforts in proofreading and writing an endorsement.

As always, I am greatly indebted to my publishers, Henry and Jody Neufeld of Energion Publications. They do excellent work. I am blessed by their confidence in me. This novel is the seventh of my eight books they have published.

My greatest thanks and praise goes to the Lord for giving me such **joy** as I wrote this novel and for affirming me in many God incidences along the way. I pray He is glorified, and souls are brought into His kingdom through God's use of this book.

TABLE OF CONTENTS

ACKNOWLEDGEMENTS...v
CAST OF CHARACTERS ix
INTRODUCTION xi

1   Safe Landing...1
2   Sharing Time with Parents.................................5
3   New Year's Eve Plans.......................................11
4   Pete's Dilemma...17
5   Comfort Food and Sharing...............................25
6   Watch Night Services..31
7   The Rock..37
8   Another Family Secret.......................................43
9   Time Apart - Comparing Notes 51
10   An Interruption at Dinner 59
11   A Soul Set Free...65
12   Together Again 71
13   Boot Camp...79
14   Britt's Testimony...89
15   Adaton Baptist Church.....................................97
16   Testifying of God's Love 105
17   Heart to Heart Talks..111
18   Church with the Carson Family 121
19   Pete's Surprise...127
20   Sarah's Surprise...133
21   Game Changer...139
22   Double Destinies..145
23   Three Exciting Phone Calls.............................151
24   Loving Your Enemies......................................159
25   Plans Settled..165
26   Teaching Jewish Roots....................................171
27   Prayer Time..179
28   A Muslim's Life Changed.................................185

29 A Plot Uncovered 191
30 Drama in the Classroom 199
31 All Things Work Together for Good............................209
32 Fruit...219
33 Beauty 223
34 Mrs. Pagani's Protégé 229
35 Change of Plans..237
36 Vienna...245
37 Together Again in Budapest............................251
38 His Nail-Pierced Hand 259
39 Leaving Prague 267
40 Making Wedding Plans 273
41 Passover Seder 281
42 Jehovah Jireh 287
43 More Fruit 293
44 Walter and Jenny's Wedding 299
45 Double Wedding..303
46 Honeymoon 311

    END NOTES...319

CAST OF CHARACTERS

JEFF M. QUENTIN, JR., son of Jeffrey M. and Leah Quentin, Tupelo, Mississippi

  Jeffrey M. Quentin, Sr., owner of Jeffrey M. Quentin Wholesale Grocery

  Leah Quentin, daughter of Rabbi John and Rachel Cohen, Chicago (deceased)

  Grandparents – Everett and Joyce M. Quentin (deceased)

GLORIA ANNA SONDHEIM, daughter of Alvin and Sylvia Sondheim, New York

  Grandparents - Samuel and Anna Berkowitz Sondheim, Chicago

  Great-Grandparents - Isaac and Ruth Levin Sondheim, Chicago (deceased)

SARAH ZIPPORAH BERNSTEIN, daughter of Dr. Nathan and Naomi Bernstein, New York/Israel (deceased)

CHAYA AND MAX BIRNBAUM, sister and brother-in-law of Sarah Bernstein, New York

PETER ("PETE") CARSON, roommate of Jeff Quentin, Columbus, Mississippi

  Parents – Lars and Elsa Carson, owners of Carson Travel Agency

  Siblings – Britt (and Camille) Carson, Melvin (and Carola) Carson, Edwin, and Elinor Carson

JENNY SIMMONS AND REBECCA NORTH, roommates together, formerly roommates of Sarah and Gloria, respectively

PASTOR JEFF JAMES – Pastor of Adaton Baptist Church outside Starkville, Mississippi

PRISCILLA CALDWELL, desk clerk in Hamlin Hall, from Tupelo, Mississippi

GARY GRAYSON, friend of Priscilla Caldwell, Tupelo, Mississippi

BRYAN GREEN – high school friend of Pete Carson, Columbus, Mississippi

LAURA HENDERSON – girl whom Pete dated in high school, Columbus, Mississippi

BIANCA PAGANI – Gloria's piano teacher at Mississippi State University

EDSEL GRUBER – concert manager for Bianca Pagani, New York City, New York

ARTURO ZAPPALA – piano accompanist for Gloria Sondheim, Mississippi State University

WALTER SESSIONS – student at Mississippi State University, friend of Jeff and Gloria

AHMAD AND FADWA HAFEEZ – friends of Britt Carson on Columbus Air Force Base

JULIE – friend of Elinor Carson, high school student

INTRODUCTION

This novel is the sequel to my first novel, *Family Secrets: Divine Destinies*, which was published August 2021. So many readers insisted on a sequel that I felt inspired to write one, and my first draft was completed less than two months later! The setting for both novels is Mississippi State University in Starkville. Frequent "God incidences" (there are many in both books) that happened to me while writing provided God's confirmation for this sequel.

In the first novel Gloria and Jeff fall in love, and their roommates, Pete and Sarah, fall in love. All but Pete become Messianic Jews, meaning they meet and embrace their Messiah, Jesus/Yeshua. In both novels, their adventures are varied, and Scriptural and historical lessons are woven into the plot lines. In this sequel the story continues in their sophomore year on campus, then moves to Europe, next to Chicago, back to MSU, and ends as they are about to fly to Israel.

More family secrets are revealed in this sequel, as the story advances to the fulfillment of the couples' double destinies. Romance is the overriding theme, and the couples grow in their faith and live it out in different scenarios.

In the parts about the characters' ministry, I included in the fictional stories actual events based on my husband's experiences of setting people free from demonic bondage and his use of the supernatural gifts of the Spirit.

In my first novel Dr. Michael Brown, foremost worldwide Messianic Jewish apologist, author, and radio show host, was featured as a conference speaker at Trinity Church near Starkville. In the plot he profoundly affected the life of Jeff Quentin. In the sequel there is another real-life Christian minister inserted in the narrative, Lee Ann Williamson of Starkville. She is an evangelist and leader of Christian World Ministries, which she inherited from her father, Rev. Cecil Williamson, a worldwide evangelist. Lee Ann is also an outstanding singer and recording artist. I am grateful she gave me permission to use her as a character in the novel.

It has been one of the greatest joys of my life to write these two novels. My prayer is that Christians will grow in their faith and biblical understanding, Jewish people will receive their Messiah, and my Heavenly Father will be glorified.

Shalom and love,
Nancy Petrey

CHAPTER ONE

SAFE LANDING

TUPELO, MISSISSIPPI
DECEMBER 30, 1997

"Oh, Jeff, it is so good to finally have you home, all safe and sound. I'm sorry you missed Christmas, but we never observe it that much anyway. Yesterday I took down what little decorations I had. Your dad does have a present for you. He'll give it to you later. He has to talk to you about it. You will be happy to know that Jeffrey and I lit the candles for Hanukkah for the first time. I am eager to hear how they celebrated in Israel. As you know, Hanukkah, the same as Christmas, is also a time for gift-giving." Leah rushed to unlock the house. Jeffrey lifted a heavy suitcase out of the trunk, and Jeff hastened to get the other big suitcase out and bring it into the back hall. Leah continued, "Son, I have never been so glad to see your face. I was uneasy the whole time you were in Israel. Jeffrey and I stayed on the internet, checking the news in Israel, afraid we would hear of a suicide bombing."

Jeffrey added, "Only three months ago there were five killed, including one American teenager. And 181 were injured by **three** suicide bombings in the Ben-Yehuda pedestrian mall in Jerusalem.[1] Just horrible! The fax that Pete sent brought waves of relief to Leah and me, but then we didn't hear from you for another few days."

Leah couldn't wait to share something she knew Jeff wanted to hear. "I have been learning to pray ever since our visit to the synagogue in Columbus with you and your friends back in October.

Being so worried about your flights and your time in Israel, my knees really got a workout these last few days."

"Mom and Dad, I can't wait to tell you some of the answers to your prayers. You didn't pray in vain. There's a whole lot more than what I said coming from the airport. But let me get settled in first." Jeff went back to the car to get his carryon, his heart rejoicing to hear about his mother spending so much time in prayer. He closed the garage door and joined his parents in his bedroom upstairs where they had already gone to help him unpack. "Mom, I told you before, that letting your heart be troubled and afraid is an exercise in futility. That's what Jesus said, and He also said, 'My peace I leave with you.' Another time he taught that worry will not add one inch to your height. That's really funny that He put it that way, but He knew how to get His point across."

"Now, Jeff, your dad and I have made our peace with your new belief in Jesus, that he is the Messiah, but do you have to talk about him all the time? Come here, son, and let me hug you tight. I have missed you so much. Besides your dad, I don't have anyone else to lavish my love on but my only child. I bet you feel the same way, don't you, Jeffrey?"

"You bet I do, Jeff. Give me a big hug, too." Jeff loved being embraced by his dad, because he wasn't a naturally affectionate person and didn't hug him that often. Maybe his overpowering hunger for intimacy with Gloria was partly a result of being shown so little affection from his dad.

All the bags were soon unpacked with the three of them working, and they went down into the den to relax and finish their conversation.

"Mom and Dad, it won't be long until you will have a daughter-in-law to lavish your love on. June will be here before you know it. Also, Gloria may come here to visit for spring break. We haven't fully decided yet, however. She is an only child, too, as you know, and her parents want her in New York. I can hardly wait to hear her play our piano again and sing like the last time she was here.

She will be featured on her piano teacher's television program in February. Please say you will come to MSU and hear her play. The program will be televised in the concert hall. I will let you know the date and time."

Jeffrey looked at Jeff sternly. "Son, we want you to come home more often. You spent the entire Thanksgiving holidays in Port Jefferson with Gloria's family, and you returned to school from there. We only got a glimpse of you when you came home to pack for Israel. We do appreciate the phone calls, but it is not the same as seeing you in person. We haven't seen Gloria and the ring you gave her since you were engaged either. I guess my comment to you at the synagogue that night must have spurred you on to propose to her. It makes me feel good that I am still having an influence on you at this stage in your life."

"Well, of course you are, Dad. I remember your exact words: 'We are proud of you. The girl you have chosen is high quality. If you continue in your relationship, we would be honored to welcome her into the family.' And it just so happened that it was that very night I proposed to her!"

Hearing this, Jeffery Quentin began to gain confidence that his long hoped-for destiny for his son would surely come to fruition. "That was a whirlwind courtship for sure. Your mother and I want to offer you and Gloria our house, including the back lawn, for your wedding in June. We will spare no expense in making it the most glorious wedding of the year in the State of Mississippi. Isn't that right, Leah? And we will help you and Gloria find a beautiful home in Tupelo after you graduate and begin working for me. Then when I retire, you will take the helm of Jeffrey M. Quentin Wholesale Grocery. How does that sound?"

Leah was ecstatic. "Oh, Jeff, you have chosen a wonderful girl, and I agree wholeheartedly with everything your father has said. Let me add that we will make sure that Gloria's parents and grandparents will have the best accommodations possible in Tupelo for the week of the wedding."

There was a pause in the conversation as Jeff considered these plans his parents had for Gloria and him. "Excuse me just a minute, Mom and Dad. I'll be right back, but I have to run to the bathroom, and also I need a big glass of cold water right now." As he walked to the bathroom he began to pray silently. *Oh, Lord, what can I say to them? I love them with all my heart, but there's no way I can make them understand that their plans for my life's work are not YOUR plans. I've got to stall them somehow... Oh! I know what to do. You must have just given me this idea – I will call Pete and ask him to call me on the house phone. Please, Lord, put the words in my mouth after I talk to Pete. Thank You.* As soon as Jeff was out of the bathroom he called Pete and was relieved that he answered. Pete was glad to do as Jeff asked. While Jeff was using the icemaker and pouring himself a glass of water, the phone rang.

Leah came in the kitchen and answered the phone. "Oh, hello, Pete. I am glad I got to meet your parents at the airport... Yes, Jeff is available. He isn't resting yet, and we have been having a great conversation... He's right here." She handed the phone to Jeff.

CHAPTER TWO

SHARING TIME WITH PARENTS

After Jeff hung up the phone, Leah came back in the kitchen. "Honey, I know you are ready to climb into your comfortable bed after such a long flight. But wait to retire until after we have supper. Earlier I fixed us a chicken casserole, tossed salad and your favorite, pecan pie. It will only take me a short while to get it all on the table. Now you can go back and talk to your dad, and I will call you in a few minutes."

Jeff was thankful his mother hadn't pursued the conversation they were having, but what would he say to his dad? *Lord, I am going to open wide my mouth, and you will fill it,[2] just like you have done for both Gloria and me many times. Please keep the love flowing between Dad and me.*

"Dad, I am so glad I don't have jet lag like I did my first day in Jerusalem. Jet lag isn't as bad on the return trip, thank the Lord. But still I am really looking forward to getting in my bed after supper. Mom said supper would be on the table in a few minutes. Pete was calling me to say that I must go to Columbus to his house and meet all of his family. Mr. and Mrs. Carson have planned a dinner on Friday night, and Pete is going to share his experiences in Israel with his whole family. It's a big deal. They have a large family. Pete has three brothers and a sister. She is the youngest, then a brother is next to her, and Pete is right in the middle. His two oldest brothers are married. So, on Friday night, Pete will be the star of the show, as they say. They want me to share a little also."

"That's great, Jeff. I enjoyed getting to know Pete the night we all went to the synagogue in Columbus. Your mother has been a different person since then. I had no idea the toll it was taking on her to hide her Jewishness all those years and especially to hide it from **you.** It blessed my heart when you, Gloria, Sarah, and Pete visited us back in October, and the whole misunderstanding was cleared up about her parents' death. I am not one to cry very much, but I surely cried that day, when your wounded heart was healed and your relationship with your mother was made right. She is like a bird out of a cage. We go to the synagogue almost every Friday night. She and Delia Green attended a conference last month, and she is all into Jewish roots now and so proud of her identity."

"Praise the Lord! You remember Pete's girlfriend, Sarah Bernstein. She is an Orthodox Jew, and she is teaching Gloria and me about our Jewish roots. And I have to tell you this – ever since Gloria and I gave our hearts to Jesus as our Messiah, we have been seeing so many prayers answered. When we were on the Golan Heights in a town named Katzrin, Sarah was born again! We really had prayed for that. Her parents were killed in a suicide bombing in Jerusalem. They lived in Katzrin, and we actually went in their house. A Jewish rabbi and his wife live there now, and they told Sarah that her parents became believers in Jesus – they call him by His Hebrew name, Yeshua – and they attended Rabbi Katz's congregation. It's what we call a 'God incidence' that our tour guide **happened** to choose Katzrin on the Golan Heights for our first stop on the tour. Hearing about her parents believing in Yeshua was all the proof she needed. Then she followed their example and professed **her** belief in Yeshua as **her** Messiah! And you will never guess what triggered her realization that Yeshua is the Messiah. Pete was commenting on Miriam Katz's Christmas candies, and Gloria reminded us that it was December 25th, Christmas Day. No one had even thought of it. It hit Sarah, and she started crying. She said, 'You keep saying you were **born again**, and Christmas is about Jesus being BORN! You say you are **saved**. I read in the Book of Matthew that the angel told Joseph to name the baby Yeshua, because He would **save** His people from their sins. His Hebrew name means '**salvation**.' I see it now. I want to be **saved**!" Jeffrey didn't have time to respond before Leah came into the den to tell him and Jeff that supper was ready. Jeffrey felt he was rescued just in the nick of time. His son's religious conversation was making him uncomfortable.

Jeff knew his father could only absorb so much at one time, and there would be another time to witness to him. "Your little simple meals always turn out to be scrumptious feasts, Mom. My taste buds are watering. Hmm, hmm!" Jeff was not disappointed. His mom was truly a good cook. It got him to thinking about what it would be like for Gloria to cook for him. *Well, so far she has been perfect in every way. Dare I hope that her culinary skills will match her skills in singing and playing the piano? Will she be as awesome in the kitchen as I am sure she will be in the bedroom? Wait, Jeff, don't go there. Keep your mind on this delicious meal set before you and having satisfying conversation with your parents.*

No one felt like talking because the casserole, salad, and pie occupied their undivided attention. Jeff demonstrated his pleasure by licking his lips. "Delicious! Mom, how do you do it? You have a maid, but the times I have eaten Jetty's food were nothing to compare with **your** cooking. I don't ever want to take you for granted. Would you please do me a favor and write down a few recipes for Gloria? I have no idea if she is skilled in preparing meals."

"Of course, I will. It took me several months after we were married to get the hang of it, but now I have quite a large selection of dishes I can prepare. It won't take Gloria long to learn. Be patient with her, son. And **you** must learn to cook, too. Your father is pretty good in the kitchen."

"Thanks again, Mom, for this exquisite meal. I am feeling sleepy now, so I am going upstairs and get ready for bed. I will call Gloria first, and then I'm off to dreamland. I love y'all. There are no better parents in the world." He kissed his mom and hugged his dad.

Jeff bounded up the stairs, his heart racing. As much as he loved good food, Jeff loved his sweetheart more, and he could hardly wait to hear her voice on the phone. He dialed the number. *Please, please, Lord, let Gloria answer. She is an hour ahead of us, but don't let her be asleep yet, please.*

Gloria was not about to go to sleep until she heard from her beloved. She would patiently wait. She knew he would call. It was a good time to continue writing in her diary about the experiences they had in Israel and the things the Lord showed her all along the way. When the phone rang, her heart jumped. The diary fell on the floor as she grabbed the phone. It was just the voice she wanted to hear. "Hello, my dear fiancé. Erev tov. Ani ohevet otcha. Can you hear me kissing you?"

"Hello, my gorgeous Gloria, the love of my life. I am kissing you back. My heart is about to beat out of my chest with longing for you, for your lips, to hold you close. How will I ever survive without seeing you for six more days? It seems like an eternity. Wait, what were those funny words?"

"Jeff, I have learned how to say 'I love you' in Hebrew, but I first said, 'Good evening.' That's *erev tov*. In Hebrew the adjective comes after the noun, so I said 'evening good.' Ha! Then I said *Ani* which means 'I' and *ohevet* which means 'love,' and *otcha* which means 'you.' But it is different when you say it to me because Hebrew pronouns are both masculine and feminine. Complicated, isn't it? Anyway, for you to say 'I love you' to me, here is what you say: 'Ani ohev **otakh.**' Did you get that? The ending letter of the last word is guttural-sounding. Say it to me."

Jeff was about to roll on the floor laughing. "My awesome fiancée, I love you." Now if that didn't give you chills, I will try to say it in Hebrew. I LOVE YOU!"

"Okay, funny man. I got the message. You give me chills no matter what the words are. The sound of your voice melts my heart.

What are you doing down there in the Deep South? Wait, don't tell me. Mrs. Quentin just loaded you up with a gourmet meal, didn't she? And your dad is trying to get you to run his company and have a huge office. Am I right?"

"You hit the nail on the head, but there's more – they offered their house and lawn for our wedding venue. What do you say to that?"

"You know I showed you the church where we are going to be married, First United Methodist Church of Port Jefferson. And remember my mother said, 'Alvin and I will give you a wedding the likes of which no one around here has ever seen before!' Jeff, I would love for Mr. and Mrs. Quentin to come up here, so we can wine and dine them. Or should I say, 'Miss Leah and Mr. Jeffrey,' like you call my parents, 'Miss Sylvia and Mr. Alvin'? Keep reminding me that Mrs. Gloria Quentin will be a southern belle and must talk accordingly. Ha! Anyway, your parents will know their daughter-in-law better after being in the place I grew up and having time to relax and get to know my parents, as well as my grandparents, Papa Sam and Mama Anna. I feel like it is the better place to have our wedding, all things considered."

"Well, you are the bride, and I want you to have your way. Anyway, I am not as interested in the wedding as I am interested in what comes after."

"Oh, you mean the reception? My dad will see to it that it will surpass all wedding receptions that have ever been in history."

"Now, honey, I was talking about what happens when we spend our first night together. Mmm, mmm. Oh, the thought of it!"

"Yes, you are absolutely right. We must plan our honeymoon and get the reservations made right away."

"Gloria, you know that is not what I am talking about."

Gloria sighed. "Jeff, I am trying not to think about it, okay? It is almost six months away. Don't get me hyped up, please. I can hardly get you out of my mind to do the simplest task these days.

Jeff, I love you, love you, love you! I must hang up and go to bed. You need to rest, too. Lila tov. That means 'good night.' Mwah! I am kissing you, my beloved." And Gloria hung up the phone.

CHAPTER THREE

NEW YEAR'S EVE PLANS

Fatigue set in before Jeff had even taken the time to brush his teeth.

He laid his head on the pillow, and he was out like a light. Instead of "sugar plums dancing in his head," he had visions of Gloria holding him in her arms most of the night. In the morning, sunlight streaming through his window woke him up. He turned over and looked at his watch. It was 8:30 a.m. "This is the day that the Lord has made. I will rejoice and be glad in it," he weakly croaked out as he sat upright and stretched. "Oh, great God, I thank You for that fantastic night's sleep, ten solid hours. I smell bacon and eggs cooking, and I thank You for that, too, and for my sweet mother. My father, too. Also, I thank You for those delightful images of Gloria during my sleep. How can life be more fulfilling? And it is all because of YOU."

Jeff had been learning during the Bible studies back at college that he needed to begin each day with Bible reading and prayer, so he turned to the Book of Acts, chapter 10, where he had left off reading on the plane. He noticed the footnote which said that Cornelius, a Roman centurion who loved the God of Israel, was the **first** Gentile to believe in Yeshua as Messiah. For about the first ten years of the Church before that, the only believers were Jews. Jeff got excited, reading about Peter's preaching. As Peter was telling about Jesus' healing people, then being killed on the cross, and raised from the dead, Cornelius and his household were baptized in the Holy Spirit and spoke in tongues. Peter had not even prayed for them. *God just did it! Peter was amazed. And that is the very thing*

11

*that happened to Gloria and me when Rabbi Katz and Miriam prayed for **us**. It happened to us before we really understood what it was all about. So these people were Gentiles, but God treated them just like the Jewish people, no different. I want my dad to understand this. In our growing family, he will be outnumbered by us Jews. Wait. Oh, my -- he and my mother aren't even saved yet. Lord, please use **me** like you used Peter that day.*

Jeff's dad opened the door and walked in. "Son, I waited as long as I could, but our breakfast is going to get cold. Come on now, and let's not make your mother wait any longer. She has put on the dog once again," laughed Jeffrey.

Jeff threw on a robe he found hanging in the closet and bounded down the stairs after his dad. His eyes got big when he saw the table. "Whooee! This spread looks like that of an upscale New York restaurant. Mrs. Jeffrey Quentin, the matriarch of our family, has surpassed herself in preparing this culinary delight."

"Enough said. Let's eat, son." And Mr. Quentin began to pass the plate of eggs and bacon to Jeff.

Jeff didn't want to make a big deal out of it, but he could see that his parents weren't used to saying a blessing. "Thanks, Dad, and let's thank the Giver of all good gifts, our great Father God who provides all our needs, and Who worked through my talented Mom to give us a delicious breakfast." Quickly bowing his head, Jeff prayed, "Thank You, Father. We love You. In Jesus' name. Amen." Jeff's prayer only paused the conversation for a minute. Then the three of them dived in. The spread included banana nut bread, French toast, link sausage, bacon, scrambled eggs, biscuits with honey, toast with jelly, orange juice, and hot coffee. The men ate with gusto, and Leah mostly smiled as she ate a small serving of several things. Her satisfaction was in observing the empty plates and serving dishes after the meal.

"Well, Jeff, what are your plans for the day?" asked Leah.

"First, I think I will go down in the basement to work out with weights, so I won't get flabby and be short-winded, climbing the stairs. Sitting on an airplane and in a touring van for days and eating **your** cooking just now, 'Aunt Jemima,' has put me completely out of shape. Gloria may lose interest in me if I turn into a butterball, rolling down the steps. Ha!"

"Oh, Jeff, you are a mess! Seriously, how are you going to spend this week?"

"You know what? I didn't think about it being New Year's Eve until this very minute. Let me see now… Who can I get to ring in the New Year with me? I've already planned to see Pete on Friday, but who is here in Tupelo? …. Oh, I just remembered – Gary Grayson lives here. I didn't know him until that night when we stopped at the scene of the accident, and the Lord had me pray for him. Did I ever tell you and Dad about that?"

"No, you didn't. What happened?"

"We had just left a church service and were driving toward Starkville on Highway 82 West when the road was blocked by a two-car accident. We pulled over, and I got out of the car, when I saw a victim of the accident lying in the grass. It was Gary Grayson. Mom, I know you won't understand this, but at the church service I invited Jesus to be my Lord and Savior, and I experienced a total change on the inside. The power of the Holy Spirit was on me, and when I prayed for Gary and asked him a question, he opened up and confessed all his sins. We were both crying hard. Then he asked Jesus to forgive him. He went from crying to laughing in just a few minutes! But the most spectacular thing of all was that he stood up. When I first saw him, he had blood coming from his leg, and it appeared to be almost severed from his body. But now he was walking on it. Mom, I'm telling you, it was a miracle! And God used ME to bring it about, flowing His healing power through ME!"

"Son, are you sure? That is shocking. I don't know what to say. What do you think about it, Jeffrey?"

Mr. Quentin had a blank look on his face. Hesitatingly, he ventured to comment. "Jeff, I hardly know you anymore. It makes me think you've joined some kind of cult. Wait... no, it can't be that. You look so happy, and so... sure. I don't want to throw cold water on any of these experiences you are having. It's just so new to me. Miracles don't happen in this day and time, do they?"

Jeff's heart went out to his parents. He remembered what he had told Gloria right before they got off the plane at Thanksgiving, and he was about to be introduced to her parents. He said they should let their lights shine for Jesus, but not so brightly that her parents would see searchlights and be afraid they were about to be captured. He and Gloria should turn their wattage down."

Leah intervened before Jeff could answer. "Yes, Jeff, go ahead and call your friend. It seems like just the way to spend your evening. I need to clean up the kitchen, and I better get started on your laundry. It looks like you have two weeks' worth, even though you were only in Israel nine days, including the flights."

"But Mom, why don't you let Jetty do it? Isn't that what maids are for?"

"I gave her two days off. She will be back Friday."

"Well, you are an angel. You are setting the bar pretty high for Gloria, however. But even if she can't reach it, I won't be disappointed. She is a prize! And I love her unconditionally. Okay, I will see if I can get in touch with Gary."

After about five minutes Jeff went in the laundry room to tell his mother his plans. "I found the number in the phone book, called, and Gary answered. He was taken aback that it was me. I asked him how he was spending New Year's Eve. To my surprise, he and his friend, Priscilla Caldwell, are going to church. Whadya know about that? St. Luke United Methodist is her church, and since the accident, when he's home, Gary has started going with her to nearly every service. He invited me to meet them there and was overjoyed when I agreed."

"What? How odd. College students don't go to church in the middle of the week, do they?"

"Well, this is not an ordinary church meeting. They call it a 'watch night' service. They light candles and pray mostly, he said. But they also have sharing of Scripture and testimonies. I was excited to hear that Gary will be giving his testimony. What a God incidence that I happened to call him and find out he will be telling about how he met Jesus and was saved and healed. And I am part of his story because God used me as sort of a sparkplug. It starts at ten-thirty. They have a young people's choir kicking it off. At midnight they are going to celebrate big time with firecrackers and noise makers. What a perfect way to usher in the year 1998. Finally, the refreshments will be served. Doesn't all that sound great? Only one thing missing – Gloria won't be there."

"Jeff, are you sure you are up to it? Jet lag can hit you when you least expect it."

"Of course, I am up to it. I will have plenty of time to get a nap before I go. Now I am going upstairs to get some reading done in the new books I bought. Would you like to hear the titles?"

Both parents had guarded expressions on their faces. "Is one of them about miracles?" asked his dad. "If so, I hope it is an objective, impartial account. We don't want you falling for anything written by quacks or imposters. I hope you read the endorsements to see if they are by people of impeccable reputations."

Jeff couldn't help but chuckle. "Dad, you don't need to worry. The first one is written by Dr. Michael Brown, the world's foremost Messianic Jewish apologist. He has a doctorate in Near East languages, has written over 35 books, and is host of the daily nationally syndicated radio talk show, the Line of Fire.[3] The title of his book is *Our Hands are Stained with Blood: the Tragic Story of the "Church" and the Jewish People.*[4] It is mostly a history book of the church, as the title indicates. And Gloria, Pete, Sarah, and I heard Dr. Brown preach at Trinity Church near Columbus. He is the one who prayed with me, and I was born again. I am now a Messianic Jew like Dr. Brown and like Gloria because I also believe Jesus is the Messiah."

"Okay, son. That one sounds safe and educational. What about the others?" asked Mr. Quentin.

"I started that one on the plane and also another one, a real page turner, *The Hiding Place* by Corrie ten Boom.[5] She was a Dutch Christian whose family hid Jews from the Nazis during World War II. Then I bought two books in Emmanuel Book Shop in the Old City in Jerusalem – *Operation Exodus* by Gustav Scheller[6] and *Appointment in Jerusalem* by Lydia Prince.[7] Hey, I just now realized that these books aren't about theology. They are true stories. Surely you can't object to any of these. I know you won't worry about me any longer, Mom and Dad."

Jeffrey and Leah were all smiles now. "No son, we aren't worried at all. We love to see you so alive and learning new things, even if these new things are foreign to us. But I promise we will keep an open mind, son," declared Leah, and Jeffrey agreed.

Jeff climbed the stairs, looking forward to reading all he could while he was out of school. "I will be back downstairs whenever you call me for another one of your delicious meals, Mom," shouted Jeff at the top of the stairs.

CHAPTER FOUR

PETE'S DILEMMA

NEW YEAR'S DAY 1998
AMORY, MISSISSIPPI

Jeff and Pete drove up to the Coffee Pot restaurant in downtown Amory simultaneously at 11:00 a.m. "Happy new year!" they exclaimed at the same time as they got out of their cars and grabbed each other in a bear hug.

"Thanks for inviting me, Pete. This is the perfect halfway point between Tupelo and Columbus for our 'emergency' meeting, as you described on the phone last night. If you are like me, you haven't been out of the bed long, and you won't survive another five minutes without a slug of black coffee, as strong as they can make it. Let's get a table. Thank goodness they are open. I need toothpicks for my eyes!" Jeff was in a jovial mood, but he could tell that Pete certainly was not, and he was puzzled.

"Yes, buddy. Let's take that table over in the back corner, so we can talk privately without having to whisper," responded Pete.

The waitress was glad to see some customers. She was wondering if it was worth getting out of bed to come to work on New Year's Day, since she wouldn't be getting many tips. "Well, good morning, guys. Here's a menu. What can I get you?"

"I will order for us both, Jeff. I know exactly what you want, and I want the same." Handing the menu back to the waitress, Pete said, "We will take two very large black coffees with Danish pastries."

The waitress was back in only five minutes. Jeff and Pete were already deep in conversation, with Pete taking the lead. "Jeff, you are the best friend I have ever had, and I know I can count on you to give me advice about this awful situation I have been thrown into. I am going to be brutally honest, and I trust you won't write me off after I tell you what has happened. What I need is the truth, even if it devastates me. I don't see how I can feel any worse than I do now."

Jeff had prayed all the way as he drove to Amory, but now he silently prayed even more earnestly. Pete understood and waited. *Oh, Lord, I can tell this may be a turning point in Pete's life. May my words be exactly what he needs to hear. And please let him feel my love for him and Your love for him. Give him courage to obey You.* Jeff looked at Pete and reached out for his hands across the table. "Well, there are two of us together here, and you know what Jesus promised – 'Where two or three are gathered together in My name, there am I in the midst of them.'[8] Okay, Pete, He is here, and He is the best Counselor you could have. Lay it all out before Him, and I will be His human mouthpiece."

Pete squeezed Jeff's hands. Tears came to both their eyes. Then Pete sat back in his chair, relaxed as much as he could and began his story. "I got a call from Bryan Green yesterday, asking me if I would meet him at the Depot for a beer like we used to do when I was in high school. You remember we met him at B'nai Israel Temple that night, and I was surprised he was Jewish."

"Yes, I remember him. He said you and he used to party on Friday nights. But that was the old Pete, not the new one." Jeff cut into his Danish and had a deep gulp of coffee before it cooled off.

Pete's eyes were downcast. "Before I even considered the implications of revisiting my former life as a party guy, I found myself saying yes. I realized it was New Year's Eve, and I surely didn't want to spend it alone. My parents had been invited out for the evening, so all of a sudden I felt stuck."

"Oh, my goodness, forgive me, but I should have called and invited you to go with me to the Watch Service with Gary Grayson and Priscilla Caldwell at St. Luke United Methodist Church. Gary asked me to come share my testimony after he shared his about that awesome miracle that happened. I was looking forward to seeing you tomorrow night at your house, and it didn't dawn on me that you would be available to go with us last night. So sorry."

"Well, we have been together almost non-stop since we met Gloria and Sarah back in October, so you certainly can't be faulted for not inviting me last night. I do want to hear all about it, but I need to tell you what happened at the Depot. First of all, when we got there, we were not alone. A lot of our high school crowd was present, and it was obvious that most of them had already consumed many mugs of beer and other drinks. Of course, they raucously greeted us with slaps on the back, glazed eyes and 'Welcome back!' in slurred speech. Suddenly, it hit me like a ton of bricks that I was in the wrong place, and I felt an urgency to escape. I was not the same guy they once knew, and my conscience was telling me I better get out of there."

"That is welcome news. I knew when I saw you come up out of the baptismal waters at the Jordan River last week that you were brand new. You were squeaky clean. The old Pete was buried with Jesus, and the new Pete was raised to life by the power of the Holy Spirit."[9] Jeff was smiling, but Pete still looked downcast. He stopped and took a big swallow of coffee and several bites of the Danish.

"But wait till you hear what happened next. Laura Henderson, a girl that I dated only once, came up close to me at the bar. I had not yet ordered a beer, but I had plenty sloshed on me. She had a stronger drink in her hand, and before I could stop her, she ordered me a beer. When the bartender slid it toward me, she put down the money, pushed the beer in my hand, and pulled me over to a booth on the far side of the room. She didn't sit across from me. She sat beside me. Then she got right up in my face and began her little seductive speech, probably one she had used with other guys. She told me how handsome I was, how she would never forget the night we spent together. Then she began to caress my face. I tried to back up, but she planted her lips on mine. Talk about feeling trapped! I quickly grabbed the beer and raised it to my mouth, so she would back off. My mind went in high gear about how I could get away from her without making a scene."

"Hey, buddy, I gotta break in here. I can't help but ask, weren't you sending up silent prayers to the One who could deliver you from that trap?" Jeff felt distressed.

"Actually, no, and that is what grieves me. The Lord was not in my thoughts at all. I had walked right into the devil's lair, so to speak. This girl, who was dressed so scantily that almost her whole body was exposed, began to take my hands and put them where they ought not to be. That set me off, and I became like a tiger. I slapped her!"

Jeff's eyes got wide. "You slapped her? Wow! As you were talking, I was beginning to dread what you would say next, and on the inside I was deeply disappointed, thinking you had fallen away from God. But now I am rejoicing! Praise God you did not respond to her."

Pete managed a half-smile, but he knew Jeff had not yet heard the whole story. "Wait, dear member of our Holy Roller squad. There's more to tell, and this is actually the worst part. Let me continue. Okay, this female tempter had an ace up her sleeve, and she played it. She told me that the night we went out together, she got pregnant. And when she knew for sure, she made an appointment with an abortionist in Starkville and took care of the 'blob of tissue,' as she called it." Pete sat back, drained, and waited for Jeff to absorb this new revelation.

Jeff couldn't say anything for several minutes. He silently prayed about what he should say. Pete drew a deep breath. "Well, I can see you are as shocked as I was, and I didn't know what to say either. But I was still boiling from the anger stirred up in me when

I slapped her, so I struck out at her with my words. I said, 'Laura Henderson, I did NOT get you pregnant, and you know it! Yes, I admit I went too far in our love-making, but not that far. If you found out later you were pregnant, then it was from another guy, not from ME.' Her claws came out then, and she actually spit in my face! Then she dropped the bomb. She was breathing fire, and in a demonic voice she growled, 'Well, I say you did it. You raped me! And you owe me $400 for that abortion. If you don't give it to me, I will call your parents and tell them. Then I will give them an option to pay me $400, or I will file a charge of rape against you. If you think I am making an empty threat, try me.' I was devastated. All I could think of was getting out of that bar as fast as I could. I shoved her aside, got out of the booth, and found Bryan. I told him I needed to hurry home. I lied and said that I had promised my parents I would only be gone an hour." Pete put his head in his hands and sobbed.

Jeff got his billfold out and left money for their order plus a tip on the table. He stood up, locked his arm around Pete's arm, then pulled him to his feet. "Let's go sit in my car. I will turn on the heater, and we can talk and pray. Come on." Pete took some napkins with him and followed Jeff to his SUV. They got comfortably seated, and Jeff began to sing. Pete was surprised. He dried his eyes and face and eventually joined in – *Amazing grace, how sweet the sound, that saved a wretch like me. I once was lost, but now am found, was blind, but now I see. Through many dangers, toils, and snares, I have already come. Tis grace has led me safe thus far, and grace will lead me home.*[10]

Singing was way out of Jeff's comfort zone, but he felt that the Lord was directing him to get "in the Spirit," so his counsel to Pete would be from the Lord and not from Jeff's own reasoning. Being around Gloria and joining her in worshiping the Lord this way had sharpened his spiritual senses. He was ready now to counsel Pete. "I think I have the mind of the Lord on this, Pete. First, a quick prayer." Jeff grabbed Pete's hands and bowed his head. "Dear Jesus, Wonderful Counselor, Everlasting Father, Almighty God, and Prince of Peace, Pete and I come before Your throne of grace right now, seeking wisdom. We are confident that when we ask, we will receive. Show Pete what to say and do. Thank You in advance. In Your name. Amen."

"Okay, Pete, the first thing I am hearing from the Lord is that you are not to fear. Did you hear me? DO NOT FEAR. That is the opposite of faith. The devil wants to push you into doing something out of fear, and you will later regret it. Whether or not this girl carries through with her threat, your response should not be out of fear of what might happen."

"Thanks, Jeff. I am feeling calmer now. I think the fear is leaving. I know Jesus said He gave us His peace. So I accept it. I am going to do absolutely nothing about that girl's threat. I am going to live my life and let God deal with her. Hey, wait! Wait!" Pete grabbed Jeff's arm. "I just remembered what I saw! When she was putting her hands on my face, I noticed her arms. They had scars on them right where her lines of veins were showing. You know what that means? That girl is on drugs! She is shooting up with something. She was desperate to get some money out of me. I know it! I know it!"

"Whew!" Jeff let out a big sigh. Then he started to laugh, and Pete joined in laughing. "I have to tell you, all the time I was telling you not to fear, I myself was letting fear nibble at the edges of my mind. My imagination started going wild, thinking how in the world this would play out. You see, Pete, both of us have a lot of growing to do. We have not arrived. Oh, how we need Gloria and Sarah with us to keep us steady, us Holy Rollers balanced on all four wheels. And that's the truth!"

Pete's laughter died down. "Not so fast, buddy. Yes, you and I can see she was not pregnant, at least not from me. That is a big relief. Also, I know now I will probably never see this girl again, and I am not gonna have to pay for that night of lustful indulgence, but I am not out of the woods yet." Pete's expression of joy changed to sadness.

Jeff didn't respond for several minutes. "Yeah, I think I know what you are thinking. Why did you go to that bar in the first place? Is your commitment to follow Jesus real or not? Also, you are probably thinking about your past and how your selfish quest for pleasure has hurt other people. Maybe you are having a hard time forgiving yourself. Is that it?"

"My brother in the Lord, you are exactly right, but you left out one thing. Why don't I care about Laura Henderson and the pain she is suffering from drug addiction and the miserable life of an unsaved person? Isn't one of the reasons I have my sin problem solved and my death question answered to tell other people about Jesus? They can be set free, too."

CHAPTER FIVE

Comfort Food and Sharing

J eff convinced Pete they needed to have more time together, so Pete drove his car and followed Jeff in his SUV to Tupelo. Having another one of Mrs. Quentin's home-cooked meals gave Pete another reason for going with Jeff to Tupelo. When they walked in the door, they smelled Italian food.

"Mom, I talked Pete into spending the rest of the day at our house. I was sure you would have one of your spectacular meals ready about this time, and I see that you do. Ah, spaghetti! Praise the Lord!"

Jeffrey and Leah greeted Pete with warm handshakes. "I hope you like spaghetti, Pete. Jeff can really put it away, and judging from your massive height, I bet you can do the same," laughed Leah.

"And there is much more to go with it. She has fixed a fruit salad, garlic rolls, and strawberry shortcake, as well as the usual iced sweet tea and coffee," added Mr. Quentin.

"Oh, Mr. and Mrs. Quentin, you excel in southern hospitality. I still remember that awesome turkey and dressing with all the trimmings and pecan pie you served the four of us back in October," exclaimed Pete.

"That was a memorable visit with you, Jeff, Gloria, and Sarah," said Mr. Quentin. "Well, our son has blessed our hearts with his engagement to Gloria, and I could see when we visited the temple in Columbus that night that you and Sarah may be headed in that direction, too. Am I right?"

"Now, Jeffrey, please don't put Pete on the spot," pleaded Leah. "Let's all be seated and enjoy our meal. I know it's a bit unusual to have Italian food on New Year's Day, but I was not about to serve pork and black eyed peas now that I have reconnected to my Jewish roots." Everyone joined in the laughter.

Pete dug in, realizing it was the Lord's "comfort food" for him and no coincidence that this meal came on the heels of his traumatic experience of the night before. He was content to just eat and continually express his delight to Mrs. Quentin as the meal time passed. Verses from Psalm 23 invaded his thoughts: *You prepare a table before me in the presence of my enemies. You anoint my head with oil. My cup runneth over. Surely goodness and mercy shall follow me all the days of my life, and I will dwell in the house of the Lord forever.*

They were having a second cup of coffee when Leah asked, "Boys, I have not heard nearly enough about your trip to Israel. Let's go in the den, and you can tell me more about it. I will clean up the table and the kitchen later. Jeff has only skimmed the surface in his report so far. Okay?"

"Yes, Mom. Let's go now, before Pete and I fall asleep. We both were out so late on New Year's Eve, and our lack of sleep might hit us any time now."

They got seated comfortably, and Pete began the sharing time. "I don't know what Jeff has already told you, but I will share first. Probably the highlight of the whole trip was seeing Sarah meet her Messiah in the very house where her parents lived. God used me in what I said, when I mentioned the word 'Christmas.' And after Gloria pointed out that it was Christmas Day, a light went on in Sarah's mind! She realized that Jesus was BORN on Christmas Day, that He had come to SAVE us from our sins. Suddenly, she had an overpowering desire to be BORN AGAIN, to be SAVED, like the three of us had been, as well as her own parents. The Rabbi and his wife prayed for both of us, and we collapsed on the floor. I am telling you, I felt like I was actually in heaven, and a whole hour passed before we woke up. Jeff and Gloria passed out, too, when they were prayed for!"

Jeff spoke up. "I'm glad you told your version, Pete. I already told mine to Dad, but Mom is hearing it from you now. Yes, that really was the highlight of our trip."

"Well, I wasn't through," Pete continued. "Then we went to the Jordan River to be baptized. I felt so clean, really washed from all my sins. Believe me, I had plenty to be washed from." Pete realized anew how true that was, in light of what happened the night before.

Jeffrey and Leah looked at each other. They were puzzled about what all this meant. Jeffrey wanted to know more about the security aspect of the trip. "Well, I haven't heard either of you say anything about your flight there and back. It's common knowledge that El Al has the best security of any airline, so I didn't worry about your trip. I did think about the suicide bombings in Israel and the never-ending conflict between the Palestinians and the Israelis. Did any attacks happen while you were there? I tried to keep up on the news daily, and I didn't hear anything."

Pete decided he was the one to tell Jeff's parents about their apprehension of the terrorist at JFK Airport. Jeff figured he would, so he sat back and silently prayed, knowing this was a sensitive subject with his Mom. "When we were here last, Mrs. Quentin, Sarah got upset as you talked about your parents being killed when Islamic terrorists planted a bomb in their car. Sarah's parents had recently been killed in Jerusalem by a suicide bomber. And not only that, a guy who had the appearance of a terrorist attacked her on campus. He put a gun in her side, but she called his bluff, and he ran away. That's how we met. I saw it happen and tried to comfort her, offering myself as her 'shadow' or 'a shield' to protect her. She told me that her father had been a witness in the 1993 World Trade Center Bombing and was called on to testify in the trials of the suspects. She felt sure the terrorist network that did it had traced her, the youngest and most vulnerable one of the family, to Mississippi State University. Thus the attack on campus."

Jeff interrupted. "This is background, Mom and Dad, for what happened at JFK Airport prior to our takeoff. Now brace yourself, Mom, and don't let fear come into your heart. You are about to hear how our Heavenly Father has His hand of protection on us four friends since we have given our lives to Him. Pete is telling you this, not to show our bravery, but to show how Jesus delivers His followers."

"Well said, buddy. We were waiting for Sarah's brother-in-law Max to join us in the departure lounge. Suddenly, Sarah saw that same man who attacked her on campus, sitting behind us. She described him in detail to me; it was definitely the same one who had attacked her. After we held hands, and Gloria prayed, we cornered him in the rest room with the help of Max and a security guard. Jeff found the man's gun in the adjoining stall. Then he was handcuffed and led away to the airport jail."

"Best part coming up!" Jeff crowed. "As we walked toward the gate, people in the adjoining lounges stood and clapped. Gloria and Sarah were already on the plane. When we entered the plane, the whole cabin erupted in applause. Everyone rejoiced as they watched Pete and me kiss our sweethearts. And two sweet middle-aged Jewish ladies kissed Max on both cheeks."

Jeff and Pete were giving each other "high-fives," as Leah and Jeffrey stood and clapped. "Okay, boys, that happy ending has put my mind at ease. I have to agree that God is certainly watching over you. Jeffrey and I will continue to pray for you, and we won't let fear steal our joy."

"Way to go, Mom," exclaimed Jeff. "As I said before, Pete and I need a nap about now. The adrenaline that has kept us afloat is running low. New Year's Eve took its toll."

"Okay, go on upstairs and take your nap. Pete, I don't think Jeff's double bed will accommodate Jeff and you with your six foot seven inches frame. You better use the bed in the guest room next to Jeff's room. Your dad and I are going to nap also after I clean up the table and kitchen. We will have hot dogs, not pork but beef, tonight whenever you are ready. We can sit together and enjoy an old movie on T.V. afterward, unless you have other plans. See you later," said Leah. "Oh, and let me say that I really appreciate your sharing with us about Sarah meeting her Messiah, about the baptism, and about the terrorist incident at the airport. I can see that God has heard my prayers for your safety, and I praise Him."

"Yes, son. Your mom and I are not the same since you were here last. Praying together and reading the Bible together is getting to be a regular thing now," added Jeffrey, shyly.

Jeff couldn't go upstairs without giving his parents the most loving hug he had ever given them. "I love you both so much. There are no better parents in the world." He kissed them on the cheek, then hurriedly bounded up the stairs with Pete.

CHAPTER SIX

Watch Night Services

Jeff was overjoyed that he had his bedroom to himself because he couldn't wait any longer to have a private conversation with his girl. Gloria's phone only rang once before she picked it up. She had been waiting somewhat impatiently for Jeff to call. "Hello. This is Gloria."

"Ah, music to my ears, my Gloria, my fiancée, the most beautiful woman in the world."

"Oh, Jeff, I had just about given up, waiting on you to call. I was so tempted to call **you**, but they taught us at The Knox School that the girl never calls the boy first. She has to wait on **him** to call **her.** I was sorely tested, honey. Is there some reason it has taken you this long?"

"Gloria, you won't believe all that has been going on with me in Tupelo. There's way too much to tell, but I will hit the highlights, and then you tell me what **you** have been doing, okay? We have only been apart two days, but I feel like half a person without you. There's an old song my mom and dad liked back in the 1980s that has been going over and over in my mind. Actually, it is a graphic picture of my deep love for you and the phases of my emotions apart from you. The name of it is 'The Rose.' I won't sing it, but here are the words, and I bet you know it – *Some say love, it is a river that drowns the tender reed. Some say love, it is a razor that leaves your soul to bleed. Some say love, it is a **hunger, an endless aching need*** (Jeff's voice was filled with passion). ***I say love, it is a flower and you, its only seed***.[11] Oh, Gloria, the longing I have for you is so intense it actually feels like a **hunger, a pain** until I can hold you in my arms again."

"Sweet Jeff, my husband-to-be, I know Romeo and Juliet did not feel half the love I have for you and that you just expressed for me." Gloria's voice was husky, filled with emotion. "Jeff, let's don't wait till June. Let's get married on spring break in March."

"If only that were possible, but let's just concentrate on school and at least finishing our sophomore year before we embark on something as major and life-changing as marriage. Now, I must change the subject, before I get more inflamed. First, tell me what time is your arrival at Golden Triangle Airport? I assume you and Sarah are flying in on Saturday, right? Pete and I will be there to pick you up and drive us all back to Mississippi State. We will have the rest of the day to get settled in, and we can go to church together on Sunday. What do you say?"

"Yes, Sarah and I have our tickets. We will be arriving at 4:00 p.m. on Saturday. And that's a great idea about church. I can't wait to see our friends at Adaton Baptist. They have not stopped praying for us ever since we left, and I have already had a phone conversation with Grace Thomas. After what I told her about our trip, she wants to go to Israel!"

"That's great. Now let's talk about what you have been doing. Please tell Miss Sylvia and Mr. Alvin hello for me, and that I can't wait until they meet my parents at the wedding. Also, I can't wait for Mom and Dad to meet Papa Sam and Mama Anna. I think all of us have so much in common that the conversation will really flow."

"Yes, it will. I will always cherish the time we had together at Thanksgiving – Mom, Dad, Papa Sam, Mama Anna, Pete, Sarah, you, and me – sharing about so many subjects. The conversation was rich, not to mention we announced our engagement, and you proposed to me with a beautiful ring. But I have been making **more** memories with Mom and Dad in the last two days. Jeff, I got them to go with me to a watch night service at First United Methodist Church in Port Jefferson. They had been there a few times, but last night was totally different from what they had experienced before. That church has changed a lot. They have a new pastor, and he gave us a powerful message. Mom and Dad were squirming in their seats. When we first arrived, and Pastor Reynolds greeted us at the door, I could see that our name Sondheim made an impression on him. I think it affected his sermon, because he kept talking about the Messiah and about Jesus being a Jew and longing for His people to accept Him. Jeff, it's only a matter of time until Mom and Dad take the leap of faith that **we** did. I am so happy!"

"That is awesome, Gloria. You will never believe how I spent New Year's Eve. I attended a watch night service just like you. And at a Methodist church. I know what you are thinking – a God incidence. Amen, it was. Gary Grayson and Priscilla Caldwell invited me to St. Luke United Methodist Church. Can you believe it? Ever since Gary was saved and healed, and Priscilla was saved, they never miss a church service. Gary gave his testimony, and he asked me to give my testimony, too. It really scared me to stand up in front of all those people – and they were mostly young people – and tell them what happened the night we visited Trinity Church. I didn't leave out the supernatural part, how Dr. Michael Brown had a 'word of knowledge' for me and 'read my mail.' Then how he prayed with me to invite Jesus into my heart. The fear left me as I continued to tell the story of the way God used me to pray for Gary and be God's mouthpiece for bringing salvation and healing to him. And Gary had them on the edge of their seats as he told the details of his repentance, faith in Jesus, and the miraculous healing of his almost-severed leg! But here is the most exciting thing that happened at the service. Are you ready for this?"

"Darling, I have chills all over me, hearing you speak with such authority right now. Please go on."

"Okay, the service closed out with prayer at the altar. The pianist played, and the song leader led the song, 'In His Time.' That was the subject of the pastor's message, 'Time,' because we were about to celebrate the New Year coming in at midnight. He kept saying, 'The time of salvation is **now**, and salvation doesn't only mean getting your ticket for heaven, but it means being healed and delivered.' He told Gary and me to come stand beside him at the altar, and people could come ask us to pray for a specific need."

"Wow! I like that pastor. He wasn't afraid to do something different, to be led by the Spirit. What a blessing you had, Jeff, to participate in that service."

"Yes, Gloria. The young people and some of their parents, and even old people, began to come to the altar. The ones that came up to **me** and whispered their request in my ear were mostly the young people. It was like what happened with Gary that night at the accident scene. The Lord would give me something to say to them, and then they would pour out their hearts, confessing specific sins. Then the Lord would give me the words to pray as I laid my hands on their heads. First, there were a lot of tears, and then there were expressions of joy. Oh, me! I could hardly stand up there, the power was so strong. I knew I couldn't fall down, so I leaned against the altar rail behind me and kept praying for people, one after the other. Gary and Pastor Jordan were doing the same thing. I think every single person attending came for prayer."

"Jeff, you are blowing my mind! Tell me if you could see anybody getting some kind of physical healing like Gary had."

"I only saw one person have a big outward change. It was a teenage girl who had a very bad stuttering problem. First, I had a word from the Lord about the reason for her stuttering, something that happened in her childhood. I told her what the Lord said, and she got the biggest smile on her face and then began to hug my neck and tell me in a loud, steady voice that she was healed! She raised her hands and praised the Lord for knowing and caring about the trauma she had suffered. She was truly set free. I watched her walk over to her friends and start talking non-stop, saying the Lord healed her. They were flabbergasted to see the change. I didn't even pray for her, but God did His thing just like He did that night with Gary. I think we were at the altar for maybe twenty minutes with people coming to the pastor, Gary, and me with their prayer requests. And then, suddenly, a siren went off and scared us half to death! People came out of the kitchen and said, 'Come on, folks. Let's eat. And then we will go outside for fireworks.'"

Jeff was winding down now and began to look longingly at his bed, knowing he better get a nap before Pete came barreling into the room. "Gloria, I hate to tell you, but I have run out of steam, and I must get a nap and get one quick. I haven't told you yet that Pete is here. He is in the guestroom getting a nap. My Mom put on a spread for us just like she did when the four of us visited back in October. I feel so sluggish. Sorry, my love. I want to hear more about what you have been doing, but Pete will be barging into my room very soon now, and I need that nap. I will call you back later."

"I understand. My mom and dad have been filling me with exquisite food also. I do have something important to tell you though, so don't wait too long to call again. In the meantime, keep these Hebrew words in your mind – I say to you, 'Ani ohevet otcha,' and you say to me 'Ani ohev otakh,' I LOVE YOU. I have been adding other words and phrases to my vocabulary, and I want you to catch up with me. It is almost evening, so 'Erev tov,' darling. I will tell you when you call back about a certain book that we must study together. I am kissing you now – can you feel it? I love you so much, Jeff."

"I love you with all my being, adorable wife-to-be. I am kissing you back and holding you very, very close. Can you feel it?" Kissing sounds were exchanged over the air waves. Jeff hung up and then hit the bed and went into a deep sleep immediately.

CHAPTER SEVEN

THE ROCK

Pete woke up about 4:30, stretched, and sat on the edge of the bed, trying to remember the dream he just had. *Boy, what a great nap. I feel so much better. Pouring out my heart to Jeff was just what I needed. And followed by a delicious meal and now a nap, I feel like a new man. Lord, I need to talk to You. I think you were trying to tell me something in that dream. It was exhilarating, standing on top of a mountain and looking down to see dark smoke swirling up from chimneys, but being far away from its smothering effects. I know I heard You call me "Rock!" I heard you say, "Matthew sixteen, eighteen." Do You want me to go find that in the Bible? What does it mean, Lord?*

Pete straightened up the bed, put on his shoes, and went to find Jeff. He knocked on his bedroom door. "Hey, Jeff. Let me in. I've got to tell you about the dream I just had."

Jeff rolled over, sat on the edge of the bed, and said, groggily, "Come on in. Man, couldn't you give me a few more minutes? I was in the middle of dancing with Gloria at our wedding reception."

Pete came in and sat in the chair by the bed. "I don't have any sympathy for you. You had the same amount of time as I did to sleep. Oh, let me guess. You called Gloria, didn't you? I should have known. You poor, sleep deprived thing."

"You guessed it, Pal. I hadn't talked to her since yesterday, and I was wild with loneliness. But what about you? Have you called Sarah?"

"As a matter of fact, I have. I called her yesterday morning. She was having a great time with Chaya and Max and filling them in on our experiences in Israel. Max had different experiences, of course, so he and Sarah were both sharing. Sarah told me that she gave them the unvarnished truth about meeting the Messiah in Katzrin and about their parents also believing in Yeshua! Chaya had a hard time taking it in, and Max sort of sulled up, she said. But she was determined not to hide anything from them. I told her I was proud of her. Then she told me how Chaya had been putting the final touches on their new house and had already decorated Sarah's bedroom. You remember that Sarah had lived with them in Queens after their parents died. But when they moved to Stony Brook, Sarah moved in the dorm at MSU. Chaya told Sarah that she hoped she would be available to help her when the baby came in late May, saying surely school would be out by then."

"Uh oh. Gloria and I haven't set the date of the wedding yet, but we think it will be in June. I want you as my best man, and Gloria will certainly want Sarah as her maid of honor. I hope Chaya and Max's baby will cooperate. Hey, wait a minute, maybe you have given us an excuse to move the date up. Gloria said a few minutes ago, that she couldn't wait until June but would love it if we could get married during spring break in March. Hmm, what do you think, friend?"

"Well, offhand, I say the four of us should elope in March!" Pete had a laughing fit, and it made him feel so good. "Don't comment, buddy. I had something on my mind when I came in here. Have you got a Bible in this room?"

"Sure, right here on the nightstand. I have started having a morning devotional time, and I am in the Book of Acts right now. Here it is. What's going on?"

"Well, I had a dream during my nap. I was standing on the top of a mountain looking down at dark smoke swirling out of chimneys and feeling glad the air was clear where I was standing. Then I heard the Lord call me 'Rock!' He said, 'Matthew sixteen, eighteen.' Let me look up that verse.... Okay, here it is: 'Now I say to you that you are Peter (which means ***rock***), and upon this rock I will build my church, and all the powers of hell will not conquer it.'"[12]

"That's your name, Peter. Yes, there is no doubt that God is speaking to you. I remember reading about that. It was at Caesarea Philippi when Jesus asked His disciples who men said He was. Then He said to them, 'Who do YOU say I am?' And Peter – but he was called Simon before this happened – said, 'You are the Christ, the Son of the Living God.' Jesus then said He would build His church on the truth of that statement that came out of Peter's mouth. Jesus told Peter that he didn't know that truth himself, but the Father had revealed it to him. What Peter said, his confession of faith, was like a rock, strong and immovable, that Jesus could build on."[13]

"Whoa! I am humbled by this. How could Jesus think I am strong and stable enough to be called a rock? He has a much higher opinion of me than I do of myself. And He knows what I have done and the kind of person I have been."

"Hey, friend, don't belittle yourself. Peter was weaker than you are. He denied he even **knew** Jesus, when the rubber hit the road. After Jesus had been arrested and was being taken before the Jewish religious leaders, a little maid in the High Priest's courtyard intimidated that rough fisherman, accusing him of being with Jesus. Peter even used a curse word to declare for the third time that he did not know Jesus!"[14]

"Thanks, Jeff, for reminding me of that. Okay, so God is calling me a rock. The rest of the story is that Jesus forgave Peter and reinstated him to go and feed His sheep. And Peter said he loved Jesus three times. Jesus said to feed His sheep three times.[15] And just to think, Peter was the one that God picked out to preach a sermon on the Day of Pentecost, and it kicked off a revival that was the birth of the church."

"Now that's what you call REDEMPTION, friend. God's affirmation **three times** after Peter struck out **three times.** And 50 days later at the feast of Pentecost, that redeemed fisherman caught

5,000 fish for Jesus in **one day**! Really, **more** souls were saved than 5,000 because they only counted the men."

"What would I do without you, Jeff? I'm not being mushy, but I love you. You can call on me for anything. After all, I am THE ROCK! You got that?" Pete laughed, and they gave each other high fives and stood to their feet.

"Let's go downstairs and have some conversation with Mom and Dad," said Jeff.

Jeffrey was sitting in the den, reading a book, and Leah was beside him, doing some embroidery work. Jeff and Pete sat down across from them. "Pete and I had a great nap and also a great conversation. We have been exploring the meaning of Pete's name. Did you know that Jesus called Simon, one of His disciples, the name Peter? He told him that it meant 'rock.' And we discovered that the meaning of a name has a powerful effect on a person. You probably don't know that story in the New Testament. Most Jews have the Tanakh, which doesn't include a New Testament, but I am happy to see that your Bible does have it. If you ever want to read about that story, go to Matthew 16 and John 21. It makes some good reading, Mom and Dad."

"I'm sure it does, son," said Leah. "I wonder what my name means."

Pete spoke up. "In the Book of Genesis, Leah is the first wife of Jacob, who was the grandson of Abraham. She had six sons. I studied this in Sunday School when I was growing up, so I will give you the benefit of my vast knowledge of Scripture." Pete winked at Jeff.

"Now that's a funny one, you man of the world. You don't have any vast knowledge of Scripture any more that I am the King of England!" Jeff laughed.

"How dare you doubt me, roommate. You don't realize you are talking to THE ROCK! Now, I will proceed to enlighten you, a scripture-challenged person, Mr. Jeff Quentin." They all laughed. "Seriously, Mrs. Quentin, it is an honor that you are named Leah. Out of the six sons she bore to Jacob, the fourth one was Judah, and the Jews came from Judah. Jeff and I are excited that Jesus is called 'the Lion of the tribe of Judah' because that means He is able to protect us. But let me go on. Leah had a maid who bore Jacob two more sons. Jacob's second wife Rachel was barren for a long time, so she gave **her** maid to Jacob, and the maid gave birth to two sons. Then Rachel had her own two sons, Joseph and Benjamin.[16] I'm sure you know that God renamed Jacob. He became Israel, and his twelve sons became the twelve tribes of Israel." Pete sat back with his chest puffed out, proud of his Bible knowledge.

"Thank you, Pete. Jeffrey and I have a new habit of reading the Bible and praying together, and we are past Genesis, but for some reason, I wasn't paying attention when we read that part about Jacob's wives and children," apologized Leah. "What you have said has truly made me feel special. Thank you."

Mr. Quentin had put down his book and was concentrating on Pete's explanation of who Leah was in the Bible. "Yes, names are important. When Leah and I were pondering over what to name our baby boy, we both agreed that you should be named after me, Jeff. And the way people could keep us separate is that I am Jeffrey, and you are Jeff, an abbreviation of Jeffrey. We discovered that my name means 'divinely peaceful.' Your mother commented that it was a perfect name for me because of my temperament. I am a good balance for Leah. I am the calm one, and she is more emotional. Anyway, Jeff, your name has the same meaning, 'divinely peaceful.' Our names are obviously a gift from God, for which I thank Him."

"Dad, when you started talking about your name, I was waiting for you to explain the initial M. in both your name and mine. I have never known what the M. stands for."

"I have been curious about that, too, Mr. Quentin. It surprises me to hear that Jeff doesn't know what it means. I figured he just didn't want to say." Pete was puzzled.

"Jeffrey, do we really want to talk about this right now? I think it is time for supper," Leah said as she headed toward the kitchen.

CHAPTER EIGHT

ANOTHER FAMILY SECRET

"Leah, come back in here. This is important, and this involves our Christmas gift to Jeff," demanded Jeffrey.

"Okay, honey. I don't know why, but it feels like you are about to open a can of worms," said Leah, sadly.

"No, darling. This is not a can of worms. This is a timely unveiling of our son's heritage."

Jeff and Pete looked at each other. "Dad, what in the world do you have to tell me?" Jeff was on edge with anticipation.

"Son, I will start with that piano that your beautiful fiancée played for us back in October. That piano belonged to my mother, your Granny, Joyce M. Quentin. She played it beautifully. When she became sick, she had it moved in our house, knowing her days were numbered. She told me to give it to you, Jeff, whenever you married and established a home. Little did she know that you would marry a songbird who could get such glorious music out of her piano." Jeffrey motioned his son to sit beside him on the sofa.

"I think we are about to find out about the initial M. in our names. I myself have never known what it stood for. When my mother became very ill, I visited her in the hospital, and she could hardly talk fast enough, trying to fill me in on the family history. I took notes, because this was precious information, and it would change our lives. She had instructed your granddaddy, Everett Quentin, to go to their house, look under the bed, and bring a memorabilia box back to the hospital. When she handed it to me, I gasped! It was gold-plated, encrusted with small jewels, and it was large. Mother had told me I would find out my middle name and many other things about the family inside the box. She said to give you this box, Jeff, along with the piano when you married."

"What? Dad, this sounds like a movie. Don't leave out anything about what Granny said." Jeff was breathless. "Where is it? I have never seen it, and I was fourteen when Granny and Granddaddy died, six months apart. That was five years ago, and you have never mentioned this important family history. You and Mom are just alike. She never told me the truth about the death of **her** parents when I was only five years old. And now I see you have been hiding something about **your** parents, too!" Jeff was getting angry, and so was his mother.

"Jeffrey, I am trying to stay calm, but I can empathize with Jeff. You showed me the beautiful box when you first brought it home, but you said we wouldn't open it just yet. You did say that the contents included information about your middle initial. I never go up into the attic, and I guess that is where the box is. I was wondering what Christmas present you had for Jeff that I didn't know about. Just to think, all these years we could have found out your middle name. But we never opened the box!" Leah's voice was getting louder and louder.

Pete could see he was the only objective person in the room, and he felt an obligation to solve the mystery as quickly as possible. "No worries. Pete the Rock is here! Point me to the attic. Mr. Quentin can enlighten us, and I bet it is going to make every one of us very happy. In fact I am sure of it."

Jeffrey rose to his feet, reached in his pocket for the key to unlock the attic, rushed to the carport, retrieved a step ladder beside the back door, and said, "Follow me. Prepare for some heat and dust. I myself haven't been up in the attic for five years. And don't hate me when I tell you I have NOT looked inside the box. I can't explain why. At this point, I am as curious as all of you are, believe it or not."

Leah's frustration had not abated. "Okay, Jeffrey M. Quentin, Sr., you need to live up to your name, 'divinely peaceful' one." Everybody laughed, and the air was cleared.

"Give me the key, please, Mr. Quentin. I am the Rock, an unbiased spectator, and I must be first up the ladder, folks. Okay?" Laughter continued as Pete turned the key in the attic lock. "Fear not, the Rock will push all the spider webs aside. I have my penlight right here. I will case the joint and make sure, Mr. Quentin, that you do not stumble over the carcass of a dead rat. When the coast is clear, it will be time for you to locate the box. Everyone else, stay on the ground. This is the Rock talking." Leah giggled.

Jeffrey climbed up after Pete and told him where to shine the light, so he could flip the switch for the attic ceiling light. "It should be right about here, to the right. I am looking for a bigger cardboard box that the gold box is in, along with a few other things…. Okay, I see it. It's not heavy. I will bring it down."

"After you, Mr. Quentin," said Pete, as they descended the ladder. Everyone hurried back to the den, while Pete closed up the attic and locked it.

"Pull your chairs up close to the sofa," Mr. Quentin directed. "Jeff, you sit by me. This tape is easy to cut through with my pocket knife."

"Wait, Dad, wait. I feel the gravity of this moment and of the family secret that is about to be revealed. I need to feel God's presence. I need to know how to respond. I am going to pray. Please join me…. Dear Father, God of Abraham, Isaac, and Jacob, and the God and Father of our Lord Jesus, my Messiah, we ask You to direct this holy moment and to direct the responses of each of us. For some reason, this secret has not been revealed until NOW. Please show us why. And I thank You for my wonderful Granny and the gifts of this beautiful box and the excellent grand piano. In Jesus' name. Amen."

Jeffrey lifted the gold box out of the cardboard box. Oohs and ahs filled the room. The jewels were sparkling. They looked like diamonds, rubies, emeralds, and sapphires, but no one said a word. Jeffrey opened the box and drew out a small leather-bound book with words engraved in gold on the cover. He read, "Mendelssohn Family History." Still, no one said a word. Jeffrey opened the book and began to read. "I, Joyce Mendelssohn Quentin, am a direct descendant of the famous 19ᵗʰ century composer, Felix Mendelssohn, and his wife, Cecile Jeanrenaud, of Germany. Felix was the grandson of Moses Mendelssohn, the preeminent Jewish philosopher of the German Enlightenment. Moses' son Abraham was a banker. He was the father of Felix, who was born in 1809 and died in 1847 at 38 years of age. Felix and Cecile had five children. I am descended from their second oldest son Paul."[17]

Jeff felt short of breath. "Is there more history, Dad? Keep reading."

"Yes. My mother wrote, 'Our family hid their Jewish heritage, because they wanted to advance professionally and not be subject to anti-Semitism. Nevertheless, they did not escape it entirely. But as an added measure, they adopted the Christian faith. Felix and his siblings were baptized as Lutherans in 1816.'[18] Jeffrey read silently a few minutes. "Now comes the part about me, why my middle name is only represented by an initial."

"That's the part we all want to hear Dad. Please keep reading," urged Jeff.

"Here are Mother's words: 'Everett and I had never told anyone about my Jewish heritage, and over the years I grew more and more ashamed that I was such a coward. I could at least give a Jewish name to our only child, I argued. Everett said no, but I told him I would give Jeffrey the middle initial of M., and in due time, I would reveal to him his Jewish ancestry. Everett agreed. We both knew that some famous people had middle initials that didn't stand for anything, so it was a good compromise in order to pass on my ethnic identity." Jeffrey closed the box, sat back, and breathed a sigh of relief. "Now the cat is out of the bag, as they say. Finally! I am at peace about all this." No one felt like talking.

Jeff was thinking of his prayer earlier. *Okay, Lord, how should I respond? Help me say the right thing to Dad. Show me how this affects my life. I already know I am Jewish through my mother. And help me to be sensitive to Dad right now. He says he is at peace. Is he really? I bet Gloria will love to know that I have a famous composer in my genealogy. I wish the name rang a bell, but it doesn't. Probably she will know Felix Mendelssohn. Maybe she has even performed some of his music. I can't wait to tell her.*

Pete knew it was time for him to speak up and bring a kind of closure to this mystery being solved. "Goodness, what an interesting story. These family secrets keep being revealed. I knew it was going to make everybody happy. As for the middle initial thing, it's obvious to me why you, Mr. Quentin, and you, Jeff, haven't thought that much about it. After all, lots of famous people have middle initials, and they don't stand for anything. Look at President Harry S. Truman. When he was born, his parents didn't even give him a name until he was a month old. Unable to decide between a middle name honoring Harry's maternal grandfather, Solomon Young, or his paternal grandfather, Anderson Shipp Truman, John and Martha opted not to give little Harry a middle name at all and settled on something that could represent either grandparent: the letter 'S' by itself.[19] The 'S' didn't stand for anything, you see."

Leah was feeling better and better. "That's right. Jeffrey's middle initial hasn't really bothered me anyway. Years ago it popped into my head that Michael J. Fox had a made-up middle initial. He was born Michael A. Fox, but for several reasons he didn't like it, so he changed his name to Michael J. Fox.[20] I just figured Jeffrey's parents gave him a middle initial that probably didn't stand for anything."

Jeff's wrinkled brow smoothed out, and a huge grin spread over his face. "Well, I don't know about the rest of you, but I am going to celebrate. Both my parents are Jewish. My fiancée is Jewish, and our children will be Jewish. Whoo! Hallelujah! We are the Chosen People, the natural brothers and sisters of the Messiah of Israel, the

King of the Universe, Yeshua-Jesus, my Lord and Savior. Glory!" Jeff picked his mother up off the floor and whirled her around in a circle. She loved it. Then he grabbed his dad in the strongest embrace he had ever given him and even kissed him on the cheek. Jeffrey kissed him back! Then he went for broke, grabbed Pete's hands and led him in a happy dance, both kicking up their heels. The four of them continued celebrating with Jeffrey and Leah ending up locked in each other's arms and passionately kissing. Jeff and Pete looked on with delight and winked at each other, knowing what the other one was thinking.

"Sarah, here I come!" shouted Pete. And Jeff shouted, "Gloria, here I come!" Together they shouted, "Only two more days!"

"Hey, Mr. Rock, how did you know I was going to say that?" asked Jeff.

"Because we are on the same wave length, buddy, when it comes to our girls."

Leah caught her breath, and holding Jeffrey's hand, she walked toward the kitchen. "Come on in the kitchen, fellas. I will serve you hot dogs, chips, and brownies with ice cream at the kitchen table in fifteen minutes max."

"Mrs. Quentin, you are truly the hostess with the mostest, but after we eat, I need to get on back home. I left the house this morning before my parents woke up. They haven't seen me all day. I have to say 'Happy New Year' to them before they go to bed. And by the way, I don't think any of us here have said 'Happy New Year' today, the first day of 1998. It reminds me of when we were in Israel. We almost forgot it was Christmas Day when we were driving up to the Golan Heights. But then God reminded us in a dramatic way when Sarah met her Messiah. Jeff and I have already told you about it."

Jeffrey was overflowing with joy. "This is the happiest New Year's Day I have had in my whole life. I have never felt the love of God like I do now. It may shock you for me to act so uninhibited, but I have to say 'Praise the Lord, praise the Lord, praise the Lord!'"

"Honey, I just love the NEW YOU. You have been loving on me and letting the Lord love on you. I join you in saying, 'Praise the Lord!'" Leah stopped what she was doing, went over to Jeffrey, and planted another kiss on his lips, hugging him tight.

"I have to say one thing before we eat, Mom and Dad. The Spirit of the Lord is all over this place and all over us, working out His purposes in our lives. Each of us has a divine destiny, and that includes Sarah and Gloria. The way He orchestrates things is magnificent. Yes, magnificent!"

The four had a group hug, and then sat down to eat supper.

CHAPTER NINE

TIME APART -
COMPARING NOTES

After Pete left, Jeff excused himself from the table, saying, "Thanks again, Mom, for another good meal. Nobody's hot dogs are as good as yours, and the dessert was delicious. I don't think I will join you to watch a movie on T.V. I have so many good books to read. I promised myself that I would finish *The Hiding Place* tonight and read some more in *Appointment in Jerusalem*. With Dad finding out he is Jewish, it seems more urgent than ever to read as much as I can about the Jews in these autobiographical books, which are also enlightening me about the history of World War II."

"We understand, Jeff. Your dad and I may skip the movie, too, because now we feel more drawn than ever to study the history of the Jews in the Bible. My heart is flowing over to know that my sweet husband is also Jewish, and he's even the descendant of a famous Jewish musical genius."

Jeff hurried up the stairs, brushed his teeth, and got ready for bed. He was determined he would not fall asleep until he finished Corrie ten Boom's book. As he finished reading the last paragraph, the phone rang. *Oh, that must be Gloria. She beat me to it. I was about to call and tell her I had finished Corrie's book but also that I know what my middle initial means now.*

"Hello, this is Gloria." Leah had picked up the phone in the den. "Hello, Gloria. Happy New Year!" Jeff came on the line as soon as his mother did. "Happy New Year, Gloria!"

Leah laughed. "Jeff, ya'll go ahead. We love you, Gloria."

"Oh, I love you, too, Miss Leah, and please tell Mr. Jeffrey I said, 'Happy New Year.'"

Jeff waited till he heard a click. "Oh, my precious Gloria, I LOVE YOU. You will be amazed at what has happened here today. Dad really shocked us, when he gave me my Christmas present. It had been in the attic for five years." Jeff knew he better not play with Gloria's emotions. He would tell it straightforward as fast as he could. "We were talking about the meaning of names, starting with 'Peter' meaning 'Rock.' Then Mom asked about her name Leah. Pete gave a Bible summary of the names of Jacob's wives and sons and emphasized that Jacob's first wife's name was Leah. Mom said she felt honored to have that name. Then Mom and Dad told me my name has the same meaning as Dad's – 'divinely peaceful.' Don't you like that? Oh, Gloria, I am trying to get to the point. Here it is: Everyone wanted to know the meaning of the middle initial 'M.' in mine and Dad's names. You won't believe what happened. This is so exciting. My heart is about to beat out of my chest. I hope I don't die before I tell you!"

Gloria laughed and began to sing, "*I've got peace like a river. I've got peace like a river. I've got peace like a river in my soul.…* Darling, one of the fruits of the Spirit is peace, and that's what your name means. Take three deep breaths and proceed. Now MY heart is racing." Gloria chuckled and could hear Jeff chuckling also.

"Okay, I will talk a little slower. Dad uncovered his own family secret. He said he visited his mother, my Granny, Joyce M. Quentin, in the hospital, when she was very ill. She knew she would die soon, so she asked my Granddaddy, Everett Quentin, to go to their house, look under the bed, find a cardboard box with her memorabilia box inside and bring it to the hospital. He brought it to her. Dad said she lifted a large gold box out. It was encrusted with small jewels, like rubies, diamonds, emeralds, and sapphires! His mother told my dad to give it to ME when I am married and get settled. She said my dad was also to give me her grand piano that sits in our living room. It's the one you played on Gloria."

"Oh, fantastic! I love that piano. It's bigger than a baby grand and has a really beautiful tone. The keys have an easy action, so fun to play. I am thrilled, honey. And the gold box sounds very mysterious. Did you all open it? What was inside? Oh, my, I am impatient for you to tell me."

"As I said, the box was in the attic. Dad had not even opened it ever since he put it there five years ago. Can you believe it? When Pete and Dad got it down, we sat in the living room, and Dad opened it. He read from a little book in which Granny had written her story…" Jeff paused. "Gloria, are you ready for this?"

"Oh, Jeff, please don't keep me in suspense."

"Okay, but don't let your heart race away. Granny wrote about being **JEWISH** and wanting to hide it, just like my mom." Jeff waited for Gloria's response. The phone was silent.

"Jeff, your dad is Jewish? He really is?" Gloria let out a little squeal.

"Does that make you happy? It surely does make ME happy! Let me continue Granny's story. Because of anti-Semitism, Granny's ancestors had adopted the Christian faith. They did not want their Jewishness to hinder their professional lives in the midst of an intolerant society. Now hold on to your hat, and you will see what my middle initial 'M' stands for. Granny was a direct descendant of Felix Mendelssohn, the famous composer!"

Gloria gasped so loud, Jeff could feel it over the phone. "OH, GLORY! Felix Mendelssohn! No wonder my song grabbed you so hard that night when out of the blue I sang a hymn to you. You have those musical genes in **you**, Jeff. I bet you could become a great singer or play most any instrument you want to. Do you realize what an honor it is to be a descendant of that great composer? He was a child prodigy and first performed at the age of nine. At the age of 13, he wrote a piano quartet, but he wrote over 100 compositions in his early years. At 15, he wrote his first symphony for full orchestra. He composed all kinds of orchestral music and, besides being a pianist, he was also a conductor and a teacher. I learned all this in my Music Appreciation class. Besides that, in my chorus class, we are singing the great oratorio he wrote, *Elijah*. Oh, I love it! Also, one of my favorite Christmas carols is 'Hark! The Herald Angels Sing,' and he wrote the music to that, too. But, Jeff, the wedding march that will be used in our wedding for the recessional is music written by him! It is from his most famous composition, 'Midsummer Night's Dream Overture.' And can you believe that Felix was friends with Queen Victoria and Prince Albert and played the organ for them as they sang? Their daughter used his "Wedding March" in her wedding!"[21]

"I knew you would know this Mendelssohn guy, I knew it. I love it that he wrote that Christmas music. You never heard my Granny play the piano, but she was really good, maybe as good as you."

"Thanks for that compliment. Let me tell you more. Anti-Semitism had a profound effect on Mendelssohn's family. For instance the name Bartholdy was added as part of his last name. His father Abraham wrote Felix, 'The Bartholdy name was meant to demonstrate a decisive break with the traditions of your grandfather Moses, who was proud of being Jewish. Moses said, 'There can no more be a Christian Mendelssohn than there can be a Jewish Confucius.' Abraham wanted his son to drop the name Mendelssohn entirely. The Mendelssohn Bank in Berlin was closed by the Nazis in 1938. Another hurtful thing I learned in my class is what the famous composer, Richard Wagner, did. He is the one who composed the Wedding March that is used for the bridal **PROcessional**. Remember, Felix wrote the Wedding March that is used for the **REcessional** music. Three years after Mendelssohn died, Wagner wrote an anonymous essay, 'Jewishness in Music,' attacking Jews in general, and specifically Mendelssohn. It marred his legacy, sadly. And the Nazis stopped a scholarship and destroyed his statues.[22] So it's easy to see that your grandmother wanted to protect your father from anti-Semitism, giving him only the middle initial M.

for the Jewish name, Mendelssohn. And your grandfather helped her keep the secret."

"Right, Gloria. She wrote that she was ashamed of her cowardice, so she wanted to reveal the name to her son and grandson in order that our ancestral heritage could be passed down. The box is mine, but I will leave it here, until we have a home of our own. In the morning Dad and I are going to examine all the contents of the box. Also, Dad made notes of what Granny shared in the hospital about her own life, not just her genealogy, personal things that would be a blessing to us."

"Oh, I can hardly wait to see the box and read the little book myself, as well as play the piano again. I hope we will be visiting them soon, maybe for spring break."

"That's a possibility. We need to pray about our plans for spring break. I have loved being with them these last few days. Before I leave there tomorrow evening to go to Pete's house, I am going to present Mom and Day with the beautiful tallits[23] I bought for them in Israel. They are praying together now, so it's the perfect gift. But it doesn't match their gift of the gold box and the revelation of my middle name. Okay, it's your turn to share. Tell me how you have spent New Year's Day."

"**My** report will be an anti-climax coming after **your** report, Jeff, but I am still eager to share. I presented my mom and dad with their tallits also. They expressed genuine appreciation. You said you were going to do some reading. Well, I have also been reading. I have a book on modern Hebrew, and I am adding to my vocabulary. I want you to practice the words and phrases I have been giving you, please. If our destiny is to one day become Israeli citizens, learning the language won't be a waste of time. The Old Testament was written in Hebrew except for a small part in Aramaic. All the New Testament books were translated into Greek, but Matthew, Mark, and Luke, plus the first fifteen chapters of Acts are highly Hebraic. And then if you add the New Testament quotations of the Old Testament verses, you will see that possibly over 90 per cent of the Bible was originally composed in Hebrew. Just think, God spoke Hebrew when He created the world! We've got to get started, learning the 'parent language' of earth. So here are two more Hebrew phrases for you to learn. Do you want to get something to write on?"

"Gloria, this is out of my comfort zone. I almost failed Spanish, for goodness sake!"

"Don't worry, sweetheart. Languages are not hard for me. I will teach you. Ready? Say 'ToDA raBA.' That means 'many thanks.'" Jeff repeated it several times. "Two more, and we are finished for the day. Say 'BevakaSHA.' That means 'Please.' Now say, 'YaFAY.' That means 'Lovely.'"

"Hey, that's a piece of cake. I will ask you to kiss me, saying 'BevakaSHA.' Then after five minutes of kissing I will say, 'ToDA raBA, YaFAY!' You are lighting my fire in Hebrew, baby!"

"Ooh, I can see that honeymoon in Israel coming, my adorable man. Hmm…. Now let's see, where were we in this conversation? Oh, yes. Let me tell you that the book I am reading is *Shock Absorption: A Survival Guide for Living in Israel* by Esther Rivka.[24] It tells about making aliyah, going to an 'ulpan' to learn Hebrew, becoming a citizen, driving, serving in the IDF, shopping, and every topic you can imagine. Something else I have been doing is talking to Papa Sam and Mama Anna. I gave them the details of our wonderful Hanukkah tour in Israel, and I thanked them profusely for making it possible. They told me all about their aliyah plans."

"Well, they better not move away until we have our wedding. I can't wait for my parents to meet them. Of course, my parents and your parents meeting will be glorious. I know they will love each other. Can you believe it? Every one of us is Jewish. What a wedding it will be. I have asked Pete to be my best man – he will be the only person in the wedding party who isn't Jewish, but he knows there are no favorites with God. Besides that, He is a wild branch that has been grafted into the Jewish olive tree, growing right beside Sarah, a natural branch. That discovery in Romans, the eleventh chapter, has blessed his socks off. I know Sarah will be your maid of honor, right?"

"Of course. She and I have talked a lot. I drove over to Stony Brook and visited with her, Chaya, and Max. I love Sarah's bedroom, the way Chaya has decorated it. Chaya is a little fatter since we saw her at Thanksgiving. The baby is kicking, and she feels wonderful. The delivery date is May 14th, can you believe it? That is the 50th anniversary of the State of Israel. When we were there for Hanukkah, it was the **beginning** of the celebration, and they haven't stopped celebrating, I hear."

"Baby, I have to tell you that Pete talked to Sarah also. He said she is a little worried that her promise to be with Chaya during the birth, and taking care of the baby afterward may keep her from coming to our wedding. I think this is a matter for prayer, don't you? As soon as school is out, Sarah plans to fly to New York. Maybe one week is all the time Chaya will need Sarah's help to care for the baby. I know we haven't set the date yet, but if our wedding is on the second weekend in June, Sarah won't miss the wedding, in my opinion. However, if the baby arrives late, it may throw a monkey wrench in our plans. You can see, I have been thinking ahead."

"Well, I am going to cool it. Remember what Jesus said, 'Therefore do not worry about tomorrow, for tomorrow will worry about itself. Each day has enough trouble of its own.'25 Anything can happen between now and then. We have got to trust God, Jeff. He is orchestrating our lives, and everything will be beautiful 'in His time.' I have been studying the Book of Ecclesiastes, of all things. The part I am reading now, Chapter Three, is about God having a time for all things. Oh, how I love Jesus. What an awesome Shepherd He is. I am learning not to worry. Everything that has happened since I gave my heart to Him has been perfect. I could never have planned my life to be so beautiful. Who could have guessed what a gorgeous man God would give to me? I love you with all my being, Jeffrey Mendelssohn Quentin, Jr. You light my fire. I am mad for you, almost out of my mind for you. And I can't wait to see you in just two days. Two days! Please say a prayer for us, and I will get that good night's sleep awaiting me."

"Right now my heart is so full, I may start to cry, but I will pray. Dearest Father, I worship You. I praise You. I love You. Thank You for giving me Gloria for a wife. Thank You for the precious gift of knowing that my whole family is Jewish, like my Savior is Jewish. Gloria and I lift up all these concerns I just voiced. Yes, we both trust You to lead us step by step in our lives together. We receive Your peace. May we fulfill the destinies that You have for us. In Jesus' name. Amen."

CHAPTER TEN

AN INTERRUPTION AT DINNER

FRIDAY NIGHT, JANUARY 2, 1998
HOME OF MR. AND MRS. CARSON

Jeff left Tupelo at 5:00 p.m., so he would arrive at Pete's home in Columbus right at 6:00 p.m., the time the Carson family dinner would begin. *I am glad to finally be able to spend time with Pete's wonderful parents. Bless them, Lord, for going out of their way on Thanksgiving weekend to arrange our flights to New York to get the El Al flight to Israel at such a busy time as Hanukkah. You have given them an outstanding travel agency. I am not used to such a large family gathering, Lord. Please help me to quickly memorize the names of everyone, and help me to fit in and offer something positive to the mix. Okay, here is the address. Pete misrepresented his parents' economic status, I see. This is no "humble home." It's not an antebellum mansion, but it is really beautiful, and this neighborhood could be considered upper class. But if Pete had come from a poor family, it wouldn't make any difference to me. I really thank You for my outstanding friend, Lord.*

Pete was all smiles as he opened Jeff's car door. "Good to see you, pal. I can't wait for my whole family to meet you. Come on in. We are about to sit down and eat. Afterward, I will take the stage and share all about our trip to Israel. I want you to say something, too."

Mrs. Carson, dressed in a multi-colored, sparkling holiday dress with a fancy white apron, opened the door and reached for

Jeff's hand, giving him a warm handshake. "Oh, Jeff, we are all excited you have come. Our time at the airport was so brief, I need to introduce myself again. I am Elsa, wife of Lars Carson, parents of Pete and four more children. Oh, and we are of Swedish descent, hence the blonde hair."

"Mrs. Carson, let me give you a hug. Gloria and I are indebted to you and Mr. Carson for getting us connecting flights with El Al for Hanukkah in Israel. You had your own Thanksgiving plans, and we must have kept you away from your family. But you stayed on our case, until you got us the tickets. Thank you. Also, may I call you Miss Elsa?"

"You certainly may, and you can also say Mr. Lars. Pete told me you are 'double Jewish,' having just discovered that not only is your mom Jewish, but so is your dad. Congratulations. Our family feels honored to host you today, one of God's chosen people."

Lars Carson joined them in the entry hall. "Welcome Jeff. Come right in. I want to introduce you to the rest of the family. We are truly honored to have you join us this evening and to add to the Israel trip report that Pete will give us."

"Miss Elsa said I could call you Mr. Lars. I hope that's okay. I just have to comment on your appearance and say, 'No wonder Pete is tall!' It looks like to me that you are even taller than he is at six feet seven. I am preparing myself to meet the rest of the family and trying not to get an inferiority complex about being a dwarf." Everybody had a good laugh.

"My roommate buddy, Mom and Dad, is much taller than I am on the inside, I assure you. He is doing 'mighty exploits' for the Lord. Remember, I told you about that night at the accident scene on Highway 82. Tomorrow we pick up Jeff's fiancée, Gloria Sondheim, at the airport, as well as my girlfriend, Sarah Bernstein. The four of us call ourselves the 'Holy Rollers,' and I don't feel complete until we are all together and 'rolling' again. It has been three long days since we have seen our girls, and tomorrow is the fourth day.

You may not remember what young love feels like, but I can tell you it feels like an eternity since we last saw them."

"I can't think about that right now, Pete. I am getting ready to do another 'mighty exploit.' I am faced with learning six more names. I am an only child, Miss Elsa and Mr. Lars, so your large family is, hopefully, not going to intimidate me. Please say their names slowly." Jeff chuckled nervously.

Mr. Carson put his arm around Jeff's shoulder and led him into the dining room where his family was seated. Everyone stood up. "Okay, family. We have an outstanding guest today, one of the chosen race, and we are highly honored to have him in our midst. He is eager to learn your names and to get acquainted because he and Pete are fast friends, and you already know they have been to Israel together with their girlfriends. Actually, Jeff is engaged. I tell you what, please introduce yourself in order of your ages, oldest first, after Jeff introduces himself."

"I am the one who is honored to be here with all of you. My name is Jeff Mendelssohn Quentin, Junior, son of Jeffrey Mendelssohn Quentin, Senior, and Leah, daughter of Rabbi John and Rachel Cohen. My mom grew up in Chicago. My Quentin grandparents passed away five years ago. I was born and bred in Tupelo. Now it's your turn."

Pete's family introduced themselves – Britt and Camille, Melvin and Carola, Edward, and Elinor. All shook hands, but Britt reached out and embraced Jeff and pumped his hand up and down. Elinor was sixteen. She and her brothers all had blond hair, but hers was nearly white. The two wives were short brunettes which made a neat contrast with their tall husbands. The married couples lived in Columbus. Edward was seventeen, and he and Elinor both lived with their parents. Elinor was probably five feet nine inches tall, Jeff guessed, and quite a beauty. They were all seated, except for Elinor. She and her parents went to the kitchen and brought in numerous dishes.

Mrs. Carson named the dishes, for the sake of Jeff, since it was all Swedish food. "Jeff, today we wanted to give you a new experience. You probably haven't enjoyed Swedish dishes before. Normally, our diet consists of American food – you know, junk food!" Everyone laughed. "Seriously, here is the menu: Swedish meatballs in spicy sauce, shrimp sandwiches, Swedish hash – that's meat and vegetables – and later for dessert we will have cheesecake with whipped cream and jam, and mud cake."

"Miss Elsa, I really love Swedish meatballs, and I bet everything else suits my palate, too," exclaimed Jeff. "Besides, I am a college guy and need the education. Ha!"

Mr. Carson said the blessing, and the food was passed around the huge table. Everyone was silent as the meal progressed. Jeff was making mental notes of each one's appearance. *Miss Elsa is a beautiful lady, almost as beautiful as my mother. She is very feminine but still looks as strong as an ox. Mr. Lars looks like Pete and is handsome, but he doesn't have that 'lady-killer' appearance like Pete. Pete's older brothers look almost like wrestlers, but they have dainty little wives who appear to be very submissive, and they're pretty. Edward has a studious look and is probably a scholar, not athletic, but attractive. Elinor is flirtatious. Surely she knows I am already taken. I think her parents better watch her closely. I wonder how all of them are sizing me up. Dear Father, I am reminded that You said in Your Word that 'man looks at the outward appearance, but the Lord looks at the heart.'*[26] *Please help me not to judge people by their physical appearance.* Jeff's plate was soon empty. "Miss Elsa, I like every one of these Swedish dishes. You are a good cook."

"Thank you, Jeff. Elinor and I will serve the desserts now. Come help me, Elinor."

The doorbell rang. Pete pulled his chair back and went to see who it was. Jeff could see the entry hall from the dining room, as Pete opened the door to a sexy blonde who looked drugged. Jeff quickly realized it must be Laura Henderson. He figured Pete might need some help and joined him at the door. *Help, Lord! This girl is up to no good. Show Pete and me how to handle her.* Laura was demanding to see Mr. and Mrs. Carson. Pete took her arm roughly and got her in the front seat of his car. Jeff went back in the dining room and explained that Pete had forgotten about his promise to help a high school friend with her brother, who had just gotten out of drug rehab. "I need to go with them because this guy will be hard to handle. He told his sister Laura that he was going to the drug store to get some cough medicine. She couldn't stop him, so she came here to get Pete's help. I am going with them. We will try to be back within the hour. Please pray for us." Jeff got in the back seat of Pete's car, and Pete pulled out of the driveway. *Please forgive me, Lord, for telling that big fat lie. Help Pete know what to do. Talk to him, and please talk to me about our course of action. In Jesus' name. Amen.*

Laura grabbed the steering wheel and bit Pete's arm. She scratched his face and cursed him. "Stop this car and turn around right now! I am going to tell your parents that you raped me! If I don't get to tell them in person, I will call them on the phone!"

Jeff jerked her back in her seat and held her shoulders to the seat. Pete speeded up and headed out of town, trying to think where to go. "Laura, I already told you I did not get you pregnant. We did some heavy petting that night, but we did not go all the way, and you know it. Let me repeat myself – if you got pregnant, it was by some other guy, not me. Besides, how do I know you need the payback money for the abortion and not for drugs? Your arms look like you've been shooting up." Laura got loose from Jeff's grip and slapped Pete. Jeff grabbed her again and didn't let go.

Pete had no idea what to do. He felt helpless. Jeff kept praying silently that God would put words in Pete's mouth. He knew this was primarily Pete's battle. He was glad to assist, but it was important that Pete get the victory over this satanic attack. His past should never have power again to come back and haunt him. Pete kept driving, going west on Highway 82.

Laura saw she was fighting a losing battle and changed her strategy. In a seductive voice she said, "Oh, honey, I am so sorry

I bit you and scratched you and talked ugly to you. When you accused me of being a druggie, it set me off. I will never be like my brother, never! But I am desperate to have you love me like you once did. We could have had a baby together, but you didn't want me. I couldn't go on without you, and I had to do what any girl would do who found herself pregnant and had no man in sight. Besides, if my daddy found out, he would beat me half to death. Don't you see, I had to get an abortion. I stole money from my daddy's payroll bag and paid the $400. Later, I needed $100 more. It was so easy the first time, so I stole from Daddy again. This time he caught me. He knew I had also stolen the $400. He was drunk, and he balled up his fist and knocked me out! He is demanding that I pay him back, and I don't have it. Darling, I have a part-time job now, and if you'll give it to me, I will save from my paycheck and pay you back in a month's time. I promise." Jeff couldn't keep Laura from leaning over and kissing Pete on the cheek.

Pete was disgusted. "I don't believe you. You may have gotten an abortion, but I also know you are taking drugs. You will not get any money out of me. You need Jesus!" Pete pulled in the empty parking lot of Trinity Church and drove around back. Suddenly, a plan formed in his mind. He knew it had to be the Lord's plan, and it seemed like the perfect solution. *Jeff has been praying. I know it. Thank You, Lord. I could never have thought this up myself.*

"Jeff, we are going back to my house and talk to Britt and Camille. We need Camille's help with Laura. She is a licensed family counselor, as well as a practical nurse. If Britt thinks it's a good idea, and Camille agrees to go with us, we will drive back out here. This is a secluded place. It's quiet and will be the perfect place for dealing with Laura."

"Okay, Pete. I agree. I think you have heard from the Lord. I am praying as you drive."

Laura struggled to escape Jeff's grasp. "I hate Camille! I hate you, Pete!"

CHAPTER ELEVEN

A Soul Set Free

Soon Jeff was at the Carsons' front door. Pete parked his car a little way back in the driveway, so whoever answered the door wouldn't see him struggling with Laura. Jeff felt composed and fortified with God's presence. Elsa answered the door. "Oh, Miss Elsa, we are having a problem with this drug-addicted person. Please ask Britt and Camille to come out here, so I can get their advice. And I want to apologize to you and Mr. Lars for interrupting your dinner. We don't think this will take much longer, and we do want be back here soon to share with the family about our trip to Israel."

"Oh, that's all right, Jeff. Mr. Carson and I have had our share of interruptions at dinnertime, raising five lively kids. I will get Britt and Camille. And don't worry, I am saving the dessert for you and Pete."

Britt and Camille came to see what Jeff wanted, and they walked outside. "Pete thinks you can help us deal with this drug-addicted person, Camille, since you are a family counselor and a practical nurse. If it is okay with you both, could you go with us, Camille, and help Pete and me with this situation?"

Britt spoke up. Well, if it has anything to do with drugs, Camille can help you. She encounters that issue with families all the time. If you are willing to go, Camille, I will support you in prayer. Go ahead. I see Pete parked back there in the driveway with someone. Where are you going?"

"We plan to go to the parking lot of Trinity Church out on Highway 82 West. It is totally private, so it's a good place to deal with this person. Thank you so much, both of you." Camille went back inside to get her purse and then got in the back seat with Jeff. Pete introduced her to Laura Henderson.

On the drive back to the church, Laura was quiet. In fact, no one spoke. Jeff was tuning into God's Spirit and listening. He felt like Pete had truly heard from the Lord and that Camille was the key to solving this crisis. He also sensed that Laura was sizing her up and planning a strategy to get the money she needed. Pete drove behind the church. As soon as they got out of the car and Pete gripped Laura's hand, it became obvious that the tiger had not been tamed yet. Pete had to lock Laura's arms behind her, as she cursed and screamed.

Camille had not been told the nature of the problem, but she knew immediately what was wrong. Pete told Jeff to hold on to Laura while he briefed Camille. They walked away, and Pete quickly summarized the whole story, as he watched Camille's face. It was a relief to see that she was not shocked and showed no trace of fear or disgust.

Camille talked calmly to Pete. "This girl has demons and needs deliverance. Yes, it is obvious she has been taking drugs and is lying to you. She will do anything to get more drugs. Somehow I knew when Jeff told us that you were leaving to help this friend's brother that it was not the brother, but the friend, who needed help. Also, I knew it was a girl, possibly an old girlfriend of yours, Pete. I don't understand it, but God shows me things I could not possibly know unless He had revealed it to me by His Spirit. In the Bible it's called a 'word of knowledge.'"[27]

Pete remembered what Jeff said about Dr. Brown, who "read his mail" at this very church. That must have been a "word of knowledge." And then shortly afterward God used Jeff in the same way with Gary Grayson, an accident victim. Salvation came in Jeff's case, and both healing **and** salvation came in Gary's case. This spiritual gift made all the difference, thought Pete.

"I will talk to her, Pete," said Camille. Be ready for a violent response. Camille sat down on the bench beside Laura and began speaking in a calm, placating voice. "Laura, what do you need $400 for? Maybe I can lend it to you. I want to help you, but I need you to answer some questions for me, okay?"

Laura relaxed, and Jeff cautiously released her from his grip, slowly moving away. He and Pete sat on another bench close by and watched intently. Camille held Laura's hand and continued talking to her in a conciliatory tone. "Laura, I know you think that having $400 will solve your immediate problem, but if you get that money, another problem, maybe worse, will present itself. I help families with severe problems, and the way they are solved is by getting to the root of the **main** problem. I have seen love and joy replace hate and anger when just **one** person in the family does this **one specific thing**. The change doesn't come overnight, but it surely comes. Would you like to know what the 'one specific thing' is? And once I tell you, will you be willing to do it?"

Laura's face gradually changed from a desperate expression to an expression of hope, and her body language also expressed hope. But mixed in with the hope was a sly smile. Jeff and Pete saw it. They both continued praying but with more intensity. Camille remained silent until Laura gave her an answer.

"My home has become a dangerous place for me. My mother died last year, and my father has grieved so deeply, he doesn't care about anything but getting another bottle of whiskey. After he gets good and drunk, the smallest thing will set him off. I am afraid of him. He beats me for no reason. He makes enough money to buy the food we need, but he spends it on alcohol, and my brother and I don't have enough to eat. The grocery store where we have an account won't let me have any more groceries until we pay them what we owe, $400. They are looking to me, because I am more responsible than my father, and I have a part-time job."

Pete could hardly restrain himself. Anger boiled up within him. This was a different made-up story to get money for drugs.

He was more convinced than ever now, that she had **not** had an abortion, but he would be silent. Camille seemed to know what she was doing. He couldn't quell his anger though. Jeff grabbed his arm to keep him from interfering.

Camille changed her tone from soft to firm. "Laura, you need Jesus. You are addicted to drugs. You lied to Pete, and you are lying to me. You will do anything, yes, anything to get money for drugs. If you get the money and get another fix, it will only last a short time, and you will be right back to the pain, the craving, and the degradation. Listen to me." Camille got right up into Laura's face and spoke with the full authority of the Holy Spirit. "The one specific thing you can do right now is to **confess** that you are hooked on drugs, and that you have lied to get more drugs. You can ask God to forgive you. You can ask Jesus to save you and give you a brand new life. Do you want to do it right now? What have you got to lose? I will lead you in a prayer. Laura, you can be **free** this very night."

Laura suddenly got up and began to run like a wild animal. She hoped the keys were in Pete's car. She would get away, she thought. Pete easily caught her and took her back to Camille, clamping her arms behind her. Striving to control his anger, he spoke forcefully, "Laura, your whole life can be changed **right now, tonight**. Do it!" He forced her back down on the bench by Camille, and Camille gripped her hands tightly. She waited until Laura realized she could not get away and relaxed. Camille could feel the Holy Spirit empowering her and speaking through her.

"Let's kneel here in the grass in front of the bench, Laura. Will you pray with me?"

Laura knew she was trapped. In utter despair, she fell to her knees and began to cry like a child. As Camille put her arms around her, she cried harder. Then she sobbed violently, hardly able to get her breath. Angrily, she shouted, "Okay, okay! I'll do it! I am tired of the horrible pit I am in." Then she pleaded as one without hope. "But do you think God will have mercy on me? I have never given him the time of day. I said a few prayers as a child, and I went to church a few times as a teenager, trying to fit in with the nicer kids. I don't even have a Bible, and I can't say one Bible verse. Why would God care about me? My family sure doesn't. The only attention I get is when I dress sexy and go to bars, and guys pick me up for their own pleasure. I feel so used, so dirty." Laura felt deep shame and began to cry from the depths of her being.

Camille held Laura closer and stroked her hair and assured her of God's love. "Honey, that's why Jesus had to die. He died for your sins and for the sins of all of us. He had **no** sin, so He was qualified to be a sacrifice for **our** sins. Not one person in the world is good enough to approach a holy and perfect God. But since God loves all His creation, everyone He has made, He planned a way for people to come to Him. He had to give up His only Son to die in our place. He went to hell for us, the place we deserve to go. Jesus **paid** for our sins, so we can be forgiven and live in heaven with Him and the Father forever. Let's pray now. You can ask Jesus to forgive you, to come into your heart, to purge away your uncleanness, to deliver you from drugs, to give you eternal life, and to give you the **power** to stay clean and to bring honor and glory to Him."

Pete and Jeff were praying almost audibly now for Laura to make a confession of faith and be saved. They could feel the moving of the Holy Spirit. As Camille and Laura stood, they stood. It was obvious that they were standing on holy ground. Camille led the prayer, and Laura made an effort to repeat the words after her, but she couldn't get the words out! She stuttered, and then she gritted her teeth. Without warning, she wrenched free of Camille's hands, and threw herself on the ground. She shouted in a guttural, unnatural voice, "NO! Lucifer, help me! They are trying to get us! NO!"[28]

Fear overcame Pete and Jeff, but Camille had confidence that these demons in Laura were on the way out.[29] She reached down and grabbed Laura's face in her hands, speaking with the authority of the Holy Spirit, not to Laura, but to the demons within her. "Come out of her, you foul spirits! Come out right now, and do not harm her. I command you in the mighty name of Jesus Christ, Son of God, and Lord of heaven and earth. Come out! Go back to the pit you came out of, and never touch this girl again."

Then Camille stood back and watched them leave, as Laura heaved and vomited on the ground. Camille reached in her purse that was hanging over her shoulder and drew out a packet of wipes. She wiped Laura's lips, her hands, and her clothes. Then she gently pulled her back on the bench beside her, speaking softly, "Dear child of God. You are free. They will never torment you again as soon as you give your life to Jesus Christ, the One who has just delivered you from Satan's control. Jesus did this because He loves you. He has paid for all of your sins, and He will put His own robe of righteousness on you. What we are about to do is almost like a wedding, where you say 'I do' to Jesus. Repeat this prayer after me."

Pete and Jeff looked on in awe. As they heard Laura repeat the prayer after Camille, they knew she meant it. She was not playacting. This was real. Pete felt like shouting, but he waited.

The prayer ended, and Laura echoed Camille's 'amen' in a loud voice. "Amen!" Then she went over to Pete and thanked him for not giving her the $400 and for helping her get free. She thanked him for bringing Camille. She thanked Camille, and she thanked Jeff, too. With her arms upraised, she shouted aloud, "Thank YOU, Jesus. I love You. I want to serve You. The joy You are putting in my heart right now is awesome. I know I'm saved, I can **feel** it, and it is a much greater **high** than I ever got from drugs."

Pete had an idea. He led them all back to his car and said, "Let's go to my house and continue to celebrate with Laura. Jeff, we never did eat our dessert. Laura can have a full plate with us. Then we can gather with my family and share about our trip to the Holy Land. I have never seen anything like this before in my life. I am learning that not only is Jesus the Redeemer who brings us salvation and the Great Physician who brings us healing, but he is also the DELIVERER who frees us from Satan. I feel like we have just won a championship football game. Time to celebrate, I say."

CHAPTER TWELVE

TOGETHER AGAIN

"Great idea, Jeff. Here we are back in our dorm room, getting the unpacking behind us, so we can go **together** in your SUV to the airport to get our girls. How long has it been since us Holy Rollers have been apart?"

"Only four days. I can't believe it. So much has happened to us in that short time, both in Tupelo and in Columbus, life-changing stuff. I find out my dad is Jewish, and we are descended from one of the most marvelous musicians of all time. You find out how powerful the Holy Spirit is in dealing with your past and a demon-possessed girl who represented your past. We both see her changed life and the power of God in casting out demons. Our lives would make a good movie!"

"Jeff, I had no idea that Camille was such a powerhouse in the Spirit. She is a true servant of God. Even with all her responsibilities in her job, she has committed to discipling Laura by taking her to Bible study weekly and talking to her daily. Camille has lots of friends who also do mentoring, so it won't be long before Laura has a whole new circle of friends, Christian friends. This feeling of satisfaction I have in taking part in a changed life certainly gives me a greater high than any worldly pleasure."

"I feel the same way, although my part was very small. I was impressed with her testimony in front of your family. She was once bold for the devil, and now she is bold for the Lord."

"I have got to talk to Britt and find out if he lets God use him the way Camille does. It really makes me feel guilty that my relationship with my own brother and the rest of my family is on a superficial level. I think that is coming to an end after last night though. Laura standing before them and giving her testimony felt like a real ice-breaker. Actually, I don't know where my family members stand with God. They are all church-goers and live moral lives, as far as I know. But that's all I know about them on a spiritual level. It's funny that I have always been the wild one in the family, but it seems God is moving in my life more than in their lives. However, I didn't know about Camille until last night. I wonder what else I have yet to find out. What family secrets does the Carson family have?"

"Pete, I have to say this. I am thrilled that you are my roommate and that God has brought us together in a friendship with our beloved girls. It's a good thing I like surprises because there's no telling what God has up His sleeve in our future adventures together. And another thing – how great that we have **already** shared with Gloria and Sarah by phone what has been happening with us these four days. And they have shared with us, too. That leaves the rest of the time we are with them today for plenty of hugs and kisses."

"You said it. Let's hurry to the airport. I am envisioning Sarah in my arms."

They were about to leave and lock their dormitory room when the phone rang. Pete answered. "What a surprise, Britt. You never call me on campus. Jeff and I were headed out the door to pick up Sarah and Gloria at the airport. What's happening?" Pete listened for about five minutes, then concluded the conversation – "That is a fabulous idea, bro. I know Jeff will agree. What time did you say? … Okay, if Sarah and Gloria give a thumbs up, the four of us will be there. Thanks a lot for inviting us. See you then." Pete hung up the phone.

"Now, Pete, before you say anything, I want you to know that I do not have an open mind to any plans that would circumvent the plans I have with Gloria, and you know what I mean. To use an old-fashioned term, I'm talking about **smooching.**"

"And you think that's **not** on my mind with Sarah, dear room-mate? I thought you knew me better than that. Let's talk in the car. We need to get going if we want to make it in time for the 3:30 landing."

Jeff cranked up the Ford before Pete could scramble in the front seat. "On our way at last. I will stop at that convenience store up the road to pick us up some snacks. I am starving. Then after we pick up the girls, we will bring the girls back to get unpacked. Then we can go to our favorite place, Harvey's. After that, **it's every man for himself**! And this man is going to get **alone** with my bride-to-be. Pete Carson, you better not have made any plans with Britt that will derail **my** plans."

Pete remained silent a few minutes, teasing Jeff, then surprised himself when he said, "Yep, no plans to derail **your** plans. I will be doing the **same** with Sarah, my gorgeous doll."

Jeff was getting anxious. "Then why did you say to Britt that if our girls agreed, we would be there, and 'thanks for inviting us'? You are trying my patience, Pete Carson."

Pete laughed. "Now, Jeff, don't you trust me? Here's what Britt said. He wants the four of us to come to their house at 7:30 tonight for dessert. See? We can still have our dinner at Harvey's, but we can't linger. Then we will go to their house, and after that...."

"There's more to it than that, Pete. You better tell me the rest of it, or I will lock you and Sarah out of my Ford at the airport and take Gloria off for a romantic reunion. Then I will come back and get y'all after I am good and ready."

"Calm down, bro. I'll tell you. This is important. Since Gloria and Sarah have been filled in on what happened last night with Laura, Britt and Camille want to share Scripture with us to show how deliverance of demons is a vital part of ministry. They know we are 'all in' with bringing people to the Messiah, and they want to help equip us. Remember when we were on the Golan Heights, after Rabbi Katz prayed for you and Gloria, she said she felt like Jesus was commissioning y'all to be His witnesses and bring people into His kingdom. God is setting it up with my own brother and sister-in-law to provide training for the four of us. I can't think of a better way to begin the new year, can you?"

"How can I say 'no' to that? It is really timely. Not to mention that Gloria and Sarah have never met your family, Pete, and it's time they did." Jeff breathed a sigh of belief. "Well, God knows that the four of us need some smooching time, so He will somehow fit it in tonight with these plans, don't you think?"

"That's the only thing that has me worried, Jeff. Sometimes in the Bible, God wanted people to fast, you know, like the men having no relations with their wives right before He gave them the Ten Commandments.[30] That alarming thought just came to my mind, my **carnal** mind. At least **you** are the one driving, buddy, with Sarah and me in the back seat. As the saying goes, I am going to 'make hay while the sun shines.'" Pete slapped Jeff on the back and laughed.

Jeff and Pete were soon sitting in the waiting area for arriving flights, staring at the gate, and not saying anything. Both were envisioning that magic moment when Gloria and Sarah would be in their arms. Jeff had his handkerchief ready to wipe off Gloria's lipstick. "Here they come, **Pete**. My heart is skipping a **beat.** Hey, that rhymed. What are you thinking?"

"I am actually thinking, when is the perfect time and when is the perfect place for me to get on my knees and ask Sarah to be my wife? There, I said it out loud. I know you have been wondering about it, too. Oh, I see her. She is a little behind Gloria. I am coming baby, I am coming."

The travelers streamed in, and soon Gloria was in Jeff's welcoming arms, exclaiming, "Oh, how I have missed you, handsome man. You have not left my thoughts, day and night." Several travelers stopped to observe the young couple, who appeared to have been separated for a very long time. Jeff didn't waste even a moment with words. His warm, tight embrace and his lips said it all. Some of the travelers chuckled and finally moved on. Jeff and Gloria were oblivious to anything or anyone.

Pete and Sarah went into each other's arms with wild abandon. Sarah could not contain her delight, and she quietly squealed, as Pete kissed her hands and face over and over.

A traveler who had the seat in front of Gloria and Sarah on the plane and had heard their conversation touched Sarah on the shoulder. Sarah turned around. The man said, "My dear, you better go claim your baggage. I am sure you can continue your greetings in the vehicle your young man has parked outside." He winked at Pete and continued on.

Jeff urged, "Hey, guys, let's go to the baggage claim and get this show on the road. Pete and I have some exciting news to share with you."

Jeff and Pete hauled Gloria's and Sarah's luggage up to the third floor of the dorm. They saw only a few girls around, so they figured they beat everybody back after the holidays. When they got all of the luggage and tote bags in the room, Jeff shut the door. Then he plopped down on Gloria's bed, pretending he was exhausted. The other three stood around, looking at him. Pete spoke up. "Well, we guys will go down to the lobby and wait on you ladies to unpack. Those lounging chairs look really comfortable. I feel a nap coming on." Pete left, expecting Jeff to follow him.

Sarah began unpacking, but Gloria stood there looking at Jeff. "Jeff, I can see you are so tired and need a nap, like Pete. She reached over and ruffled up Jeff's hair. Jeff grabbed her and pulled her down beside him on the bed.

Gloria jumped up quickly. "Oh, no you don't, dear fiancé. We aren't married yet. And even if we were, Sarah is in the room. Are you blind? My, how you have changed, you wolf! I thought

you knew that God wants us to avoid even the appearance of evil."
Gloria's impatient expression was enough reprimand for Jeff.

"My sweet lovebird, please don't fly away," pleaded Jeff, until
he saw that Gloria had begun to unpack her bags, ignoring him.
"Oh, well, a fella can try, can't he?" Jeff kissed her on the neck as
he left the room, feigning sorrow.

Gloria turned to Sarah and threw up her hands. "Absence
makes the heart grow fonder – now that is certainly an understate-
ment in our case. Sarah, I apologize for Jeff. He has not acted that
way before, and I am determined he will control himself from now
on. I don't want us to do anything to compromise our witness for
Jesus, because Jesus is the only reason we found each other in the
first place! I will never forget that night in the library when I was
drawn to him like a magnet. It was the first time I had told another
person about my faith in Jesus Christ. The words just flowed, and
the Holy Spirit used my humble attempt at witnessing to bring Jeff
into the fold. And the way He fanned the flames of love in us is
the most awesome thing. Also, I have seen the Spirit at work in the
relationship you and Pete have. Falling in love with Jesus, meeting
you and your becoming my best friend and roommate, falling in
love with Jeff, our going to Israel together with you and Pete, and
our upcoming marriage – how can life be any more abundant? I
guess the icing on the cake would be if you and Pete got married,
too, and the four of us still continued to be the fabulous four Holy
Rollers!"

"Gloria, I have to admit I was shocked by Jeff's behavior just
now. But also I must confess that my thoughts about Pete have
not been entirely holy. I hope with all my heart that Pete and I can
be joined together in the bonds of marriage fairly soon, and I am
praying so hard about it. It has to be HaShem's decision, and He
has to orchestrate the whole thing. Yeshua will surely guide us. I
am depending on Him."

"Okay, friend, we need to stop this girl talk and go downstairs
to our men. The plans they have for us tonight at Britt and Ca-

mille's house sound exciting. I can't wait to meet them and learn from them. That experience with Pete's friend, Laura Henderson, is the most way-out thing I have ever heard of. But if it's in the Bible, I want to learn more. I know Jesus cast out demons. He did it a lot, and He gave His disciples the power to do the same. It looks like the four of us may be doing it, too, and that scares me. But everything so far in my walk with Jesus has been fulfilling and wonderful. We can trust Him, Sarah. He won't lead us into anything that He won't enable us to handle. There. I'm standing on faith. Now let's go downstairs. Our room is in order."

CHAPTER THIRTEEN

BOOT CAMP

The meal at Harvey's was excellent, as usual. Pete paid the bill, and the others contributed to a nice-size tip. Then they were on their way in Jeff's golden Ford Expedition SUV to Britt and Camille's house. As it came in sight, all were impressed with the perfectly manicured lawn, the two-story brick house with stately white pillars, and the beautiful banner emblazoned with a Bible verse: "As for me and my house, we will serve the Lord – Josh. 24.15." They knocked on the door at precisely 7:30. Their hosts met them with smiles and hugs, took their coats, and ushered them into the living room. Pete introduced Gloria and Sarah. "Britt and Camille, these are the two most beautiful girls on the MSU campus. Jeff and I are amazed they would even look at us twice. But it has to be a 'God thing,' that they think Jeff and I are the two handsomest men on campus." Pete grinned broadly as Sarah squeezed his hand.

Camille hugged Gloria and Sarah. "The Carson family has heard so much about your Holy Roller group, as you call it. God has a sense of humor, putting two New York Yankees with two Mississippi southerners. He is really the consummate Matchmaker, isn't He?"

Britt shook their hands. "I heard Mom and Dad say they wanted to meet you both. They are delighted that Pete has chosen a Jewish girl and a pretty one at that. And it's really something that you girls live close together in New York. You became roommates before you even knew you were practically neighbors. And Jeff met you, Gloria, and afterward Sarah, before Pete met either one of you. I have enjoyed hearing all about it from Pete."

Sarah couldn't resist mentioning Britt and Pete's blond hair, saying, "Pete told me of your Swedish descent, Britt, which accounts for your blonde hair, but Camille is a brunette, and so are Gloria and me, as well as Jeff and his parents. I am eager to meet the rest of the Carson family." Gloria agreed with Sarah.

"Well, you **are** going to meet them. Mom already told me to invite you girls next Sunday, a week from tomorrow. We can go to our church, First Baptist, then go to Mom and Dad's for dinner and fellowship. What do you say? And, of course, that includes you, too, Jeff." The four were all smiles, saying they were looking forward to it.

The two couples sat on plush, blue velvet loveseats. Camille and Britt drew up two chairs close to them and then went to the kitchen. Camille brought out a tray with six plates of pie and silver forks and spoons. Britt brought china cups and a coffee pot. Each person had a small lap tray. There were two slices of pie on each plate, pecan pie and lemon icebox pie. Silence reigned as the dessert was finished off and the trays and dishes taken back to the kitchen.

Camille and Britt sat down with their Bibles. "Welcome to boot camp," exclaimed Britt. "I have been looking forward to this. Thanks, Pete, for suggesting a Bible study." Gloria had brought her Bible, a notepad, and pen. She moved over closer to Jeff and shared her Bible. Sarah reached in her purse and drew out her Tanakh and Brit Hadasha. She handed the Brit Hadasha to Pete. Britt took the lead. "It's good to see you brought your swords."

"Swords? I have no idea what you are talking about, brother," said Pete.

"Okay, I will show you, but first I have a question. I count three swords for sure, but what are those other two you brought, Sarah?" asked Britt.

Sarah held up her big book. "This is the Tanakh that I have used since I was a teenager. It is the original Hebrew Scriptures, except mine is English, and it has the same books as the Christians' Old Testament. 'Tanakh' is an acronym for the three sections of it."

As Sarah began to explain, Camille made notes on the back of the teaching she had prepared. "Well, Sarah, it looks like Britt and I are students tonight also. I love this."

Sarah smiled. "Okay. The 'T' stands for 'Torah,' the first section of the Tanakh. Christians usually call this section by its Greek name, 'Pentateuch,' which includes the first five books in both our Bibles. The word 'Torah' simply means 'instruction,' but Christians always call it the 'law.' Got that?"

"We got it, Sarah. Keep going," said Britt.

Sarah resumed. "The 'N' stands for 'Neviim,' the Hebrew word for 'Prophets.' And the third section is 'K' for 'Ketuvim,' the Hebrew word for 'Writings.' This last section of books begins with the Psalms. So you see, the **arrangement** of your Old Testament books and the Jews' Tanakh are quite different, especially in the third section."

Camille thanked Sarah. "I guess your question has been answered, Pete, about what our 'swords' are. The Bible is a 'sword.' And we are going to do battle with our unseen enemies with our swords. But, one more thing, Sarah. I am going to guess that the book you gave Pete is your Hebrew New Testament, right?"

Gloria broke in. "Yes. It is called the Brit Hadasha. In the Hebrew language, the adjective comes **after** the noun, so 'Brit' means 'Covenant,' and 'Hadasha' means 'New.' Sarah knows this, but the rest of you may not. Our Messiah Yeshua used the Tanakh, and so did His disciples. There was no New Testament then. If you will turn in your Bibles to Luke 24:44-45, I will show you how He validated the three sections of the Scriptures that Sarah just told you about. This happened when Jesus appeared to the disciples after He rose from the dead. Listen. 'Then He said to them, 'These are the words which I spoke to you while I was still with you, that all things must be fulfilled which were written in the **Law of Moses** [first section] and the **Prophets** [second section] and the **Psalms** [third section] concerning Me. And He opened their understanding, that they might comprehend the Scriptures.'"

Gloria waited until the note-taking was done. "So you see, Jesus was Jewish, the Apostles were Jewish, and the Scriptures were written by Jewish people, with the exception of Luke."

Camille responded. "You know what? There is a lady in our church who is teaching a Jewish Roots class. I wasn't interested in it, but I am now. Britt, we must sign up for it." Britt agreed.

Britt began. "Here is the teaching we have for you tonight. Turn to Ephesians, the sixth chapter, starting at verse ten. To save time I will paraphrase, but please read it word for word when you get back to your dorms. In this life we are in enemy territory. Adam sinned, and the devil took control of our planet. Jesus called him 'the ruler of this world.'[31] When Jesus comes back, it will be curtains for the devil and his demons. Jesus will rule from Jerusalem, and we will rule with Him. In the beginning the devil was cast out of heaven, and a third of the angels followed him.[32] Make a note to read Revelation, the twelfth chapter, later. So, in the Ephesians passage, the Apostle Paul is telling us how to do spiritual warfare against the devil and his demons, the fallen angels. We have to put on the **armor of God**. Say that … 'armor of God.' The **helmet** of salvation protects your mind from Satan's lies. The **belt of truth** keeps the rest of the armor in place. The **breastplate of righteousness** keeps your heart protected from loving anything more than God. The **shoes of peace** keep you moving out to share the gospel. The **shield of faith** stops the fiery darts of doubt and condemnation from the devil. Now here it is, the **offensive weapon** – it is the **sword of the Spirit, which is the Word of God.** If you put on the full armor of God, and put it on with prayer, you will be perfectly equipped to fight the devil in your daily lives and not be defeated. But remember this, your enemies are **not** human beings, but they are the wicked spirits who are acting **through** human beings."

Camille interrupted. "Pete and Jeff, I know you have told Sarah and Gloria what happened last night with Laura Henderson, right?" Sarah and Gloria said they knew. "Now that Britt has given you basic instructions for every Christian in enemy territory, as he put it, I want to tell you about the **gifts** that God has provided when you are in the heat of battle. These word gifts and power gifts are useful in both encounters with demon-possessed or oppressed people and also with Christians who need to be set free. Turn to First Corinthians, chapter twelve."

Jeff spoke up. "Pete and I know a little about that. One night we discussed it. These kinds of gifts were used by Dr. Michael Brown when he talked to me about my past. He knew things that he could not have known unless God told him. And I knew how to talk to Gary Grayson when he was the victim of an accident. God put a question in my mouth to ask him, and it sliced open his heart. He poured forth a confession of sin. Also through my prayer Gary was physically healed! I was amazed that God used me so soon after I was saved. God did it again at a Watch Night Service at Gary's church in Tupelo. We both gave our testimonies. After the pastor preached, he asked us to join him at the altar and pray for the people coming with specific needs. One girl had a stuttering problem. The Lord showed me an incident in her childhood that caused it. She was immediately healed. I didn't even pray for her. Then she began talking to her friends a mile a minute!"

"That is wonderful, Jeff. God has put you in action before we even study about it." Camille continued, "Let's start with verse eight – we see 'the word of wisdom' and 'the word of knowledge.' Jeff, what you described with Dr. Brown and also with the girl who had a stuttering problem was a 'word of knowledge.' This gift helped me when Laura was making up a story. I knew it was a lie. Of course, you can tell when people are addicted to drugs just by their appearance without a supernatural word of knowledge. But the Lord had already been talking to me about Pete's friend Laura before I saw her. She said that she needed help for her brother, but God showed me before I saw her that it was the girl **herself** who needed help from drug addiction. As for you knowing how to talk to Gary Grayson, that was 'the word of wisdom.' In verse nine, we see the gifts of **faith** and the **gifts of healings.** Those gifts were working in you, too, Jeff. Wow! You were a powerhouse of the Spirit those two nights."

"Well, I certainly didn't know what I was doing. I was a brand new Christian. The only thing I can tell you is I felt the anointing of the Spirit so strong that I couldn't stop myself from getting out of the car and going over to help Gary. I had no idea what I was going to say or do, but I trusted God to fill my mouth with His words. And I trusted Him to give me words for the people at the Watch Night service. And He did. Praise God!"

Gloria also praised God, as she thought back to that night of the accident. "I see that after 'faith' and 'healings' comes 'working of miracles' in verse ten. The healing of Gary's leg just had to be a 'miracle,' it had to be! His leg was almost **severed**, and then he came **walking** over to our car with Jeff."

Camille was clearly moved with Jeff's testimony. "This is one of the most marvelous testimonies of healing I have heard. And if this happened when you had just been saved, I can only imagine what your ministry is going to accomplish from here on, Jeff Quentin. Please stay humble though. When God uses us in a big way, we must give Him **all**, and I mean **all,** the glory. It is such a privilege to participate in God's kingdom work."

Pete felt like he had to offer something to the teaching. "I see the gift of 'prophecy' in verse ten. I hate to show my ignorance, but isn't that when someone predicts the future?"

Britt answered. "Yes, the Bible is filled with prophecies, many in great detail, that were fulfilled exactly. Jesus fulfilled hundreds of prophecies about His birth, His ministry, His suffering, His betrayal, His crucifixion, and His resurrection. There are also **more** prophecies in the Old Testament that will be fulfilled in His **Second** Coming. I have been reading the Book of Acts, and I can think of two prophecies off the top of my head. One was by the prophet Agabus who predicted a famine.[33] This same prophet predicted

Paul's arrest, too.[34] But back to the 'word of knowledge' – that was the gift Peter had when he knew that Ananias and Sapphira had lied to the Holy Spirit, and he called them out on it. Then God judged them on the spot and they died.[35] Prophecy really turns me on."

Jeff got excited. "I love this Bible study. It just came to mind that Dr. Brown used the gift of prophecy that night at Trinity Church when he told me about my future. I have his words permanently imprinted in my brain cells. I can quote it to you. Listen to this: 'You will be seeing your parents soon, and the Lord is preparing you for a painful encounter, but your friends will help you weather the storm. The Lord will give you an understanding heart for your mother, and He will use you to bring her into His sheepfold. The Lord has given you power to get wealth in order to establish His covenant.' Well, the four of us can testify that God has fulfilled most of this prophecy. That gives me confidence that He will fulfill the rest."

"And I, Pete Carson, am glad to be your roommate and close friend. I know you will need some help to establish God's covenant, right? I can be real helpful with the wealth part. And Sarah is studying accounting. Now won't that come in handy? We'll divide the loot four ways, whadya say?" Pete found that he was laughing all by himself. Sheepishly, he apologized, "Sorry, folks. I didn't mean to revert to my old carnal nature. I admit I have a lot of changing to do yet. Thank the Lord I have a patient girlfriend who loves me unconditionally."

Sarah patted Pete's arm and smiled up at him. "I am learning a lot tonight. Yes, I have to agree, Jeff, that Dr. Brown gave you a true prophecy. Now I want to keep learning. We have three more to go, 'discerning of spirits,' 'different kinds of tongues,' and 'interpretation of tongues.'"

Camille continued the teaching. "The reason we started this study was to address the ministry of deliverance, casting out of demons. I want to warn you not to dabble in the occult. Sometimes people open themselves up to demons by doing that. For instance, do not, I repeat – do not, read horoscopes or have anything to do with astrology and the signs of the Zodiac. Also, have nothing to do with fortune tellers or spiritualists. These mediums think they have power to contact the dead, but the spirits they summon are not the spirits of someone's 'dearly departed.' They are demons who are masquerading as their deceased loved ones. Any activity, such as Ouija boards, handwriting analysis, et cetera, which people engage in to get guidance, is an open door for the devil to invade their lives. Stay out of the devil's territory, and get your knowledge, guidance, and comfort from the Holy Word and the Holy Spirit. All other spirits are unholy! Besides the occult, the other major avenue by which Satan can enter a person's life is the use of drugs and alcohol. These lower a person's defenses, and the devil takes advantage of it. As for the gifts of the Spirit, there is so much more we can learn about them, but we need another session for it. Jot this down for further study – I Corinthians 14, which shows the **way** the spiritual gifts are used in the church, Ephesians 4: 11-13, which shows ministers **themselves** as gifts to the church, and Romans 12: 4-8."

Britt spoke up. "Before we leave tonight I have a personal testimony, and also we need to look at the ministry of Jesus in casting out demons. Write this down, Matthew, chapter ten, and Luke, chapter ten. In Matthew ten, Jesus sent out His twelve disciples with specific commands. In Luke ten, He sent out seventy, yes, I said seventy, with instructions. I will paraphrase. Right off the bat, Jesus gave His disciples power over unclean spirits, to cast them out, and to heal all kinds of sickness and all kinds of disease. Matthew records that **first**, and after that, he lists the names of the disciples. That makes me think that casting out evil spirits was a top priority for Jesus. On down in the chapter, he gives practical instructions for them as they preach, heal, cleanse lepers, raise the dead, and cast out demons. Wow! Do you know anyone doing that today?"

"I certainly don't. But I want to do it. I want to do the real stuff. I don't care if nobody else is doing it today." Gloria had a pained expression on her face.

Britt felt Gloria's frustration. "I am reminded of what my English teacher said, 'A little learning is a dangerous thing; drink deep; or taste not the Pierian spring …,' a poem by Alexander Pope. It means that a person may make costly mistakes from his limited knowledge and may mislead others."

"Oh, I guess I sounded juvenile. You are right. I don't want to go off half-cocked. I want to study for God's approval, and He will send me forth when I am ready." Gloria relaxed.

"Yes, God sets things up so beautifully when we are ready. Then He pushes us out of the nest. Ha!" Britt was really enjoying himself. "Let me continue. Jesus sent out the seventy to **everybody**, Jews **and** Gentiles. The twelve disciples had been sent **only** to the Jews. The report that the seventy had when they came back was the way I felt when I first cast out a demon. Here it is in the Bible – 'Then the seventy returned with joy, saying, 'Lord, even the demons are subject to us in Your name.' And He said to them, 'I saw Satan fall like lightning from heaven. Behold, I give you the authority to trample on serpents and scorpions, and over all the power of the enemy, and nothing shall by any means hurt you. Nevertheless do not rejoice in this, that the spirits are subject to you, but rather rejoice because your names are written in heaven.'"[36]

"I have to interrupt," said Gloria. "Earlier you told us that Satan was cast out of heaven, and a third of the angels were cast out with him. I think it was in Revelation twelve. That fits with Jesus saying, 'I saw Satan fall like lightning from heaven.'"

"Right, Gloria. The Bible explains itself. Sometimes people think they have found a contradiction, but if they will get familiar with the **entire** Bible, their doubts can be settled. Now to continue with this passage – as you probably know, the 'serpents and scorpions' Jesus referred to are demons, and we can take authority over them in Jesus' name. But I want to stress what Camille said. When God's power is on us to cast out demons or do any other supernatural works, we have to remain humble and realize we are only **vessels** of His Holy Spirit. And when we **feel** God's authority and power, we don't need to lose our perspective. It's more important to know our names are written in heaven than to see our names in lights on some church marquee because we are great 'demon chasers!'"

"That's funny, Britt. I agree that belonging to Jesus has to be much more fulfilling and exciting than chasing demons, although I haven't chased one yet." Gloria chuckled. "I think my favorite story in the Bible about demons is when Jesus cast seven devils out of Mary Magdalene.[37] Can you imagine how she must have felt? One minute she was tormented and dirty inside. The next minute she was gloriously **clean** and filled with love and laughter. I wish some artist would paint that, the before and after effects of deliverance from demons. Maybe there will be a movie about it. But there is more to the story. Mary Magdalene was the FIRST person to see Jesus alive after His resurrection.[38] And, Britt and Camille, us four Holy Rollers went there and SAW the place where it happened – the Garden Tomb in Jerusalem![39] Can you believe it? And not only did Jesus talk to her there after His resurrection, but He made her the FIRST evangelist. He told her to go and tell His disciples that she saw Him ALIVE! Women were not trusted to be faithful witnesses at that time in history, but Jesus broke tradition. He welcomed her and the other women who wanted to follow him through the land. I think some of them may have supported him financially.[40] Oh, I love Him so much. He is so tender and understanding and kind and loving. He loved Mary Magdalene, but no more than He loved everyone else. I have heard that some people believe they got married. Hogwash! People just need to read the Bible and not listen to fairytales. We have the truth in this marvelous book, the Holy Bible. End of sermon." Gloria laughed, and everyone joined her.

CHAPTER FOURTEEN

BRITT'S TESTIMONY

All eyes were on Britt. "Now I will tell you what happened to me. Sarah, my testimony will include the other sign gifts you asked about in I Corinthians 12, discerning of spirits, speaking in tongues, and interpretation of tongues. I had an encounter with a demonized person at Columbus Air Force Base, where I work. I am in the 14th Security Forces Squadron, which maintains 24-hour law enforcement, security and antiterrorism protection for a base community of 10,000 personnel. Part of what I do is to investigate on-base criminal activity associated with military, civilian and Department of Defense personnel.

Camille was smiling. She was proud of her man. Britt was obviously in excellent physical shape for his job. The expressions on the four friends' faces showed how impressed they were. "No wonder you were not afraid last night, Camille, when the demon in Laura started calling on Lucifer!" Pete remarked, in wonder. "I'm sure that being around Britt has made you feel invincible."

"No, Pete. I was not afraid because I have complete confidence in my Commander-in-Chief, and I was acting under His authority. Satan is no match for Him," Camille declared.

Britt said, "Pete, it IS true, however, that Camille is under my protection, since I am her husband. She submitted to my decision for her to go out there last night and help that young girl. I didn't have to be there. Well, let me continue. One of the flyers who was being trained at the base attacked his wife in their apartment. I happened to be patrolling that area one night when it happened.

I heard her screams and saw through the window a man standing over her with a knife and yelling at her. I knocked the door down to get inside. The woman had already been cut on her face, and the blood was pouring out. Her eyes were filled with terror. The man backed up when he saw me, but he still had the knife in his hand, and it looked like he was about to lunge at me. I kicked the knife out of his hand and quickly jerked his hands behind him and forced his head, face first, on the floor. Then I pressed my knee in his back until I could handcuff him. The woman slowly stood up and fell on the sofa. Her screams turned to crying. Between sobs she told me what had happened."

The friends were on the edge of their seats. Sarah was breathing fast. "Was that man a terrorist that had infiltrated the base?"

"That was the first thought I had, Sarah, because he looked like someone from the Middle East, and his yelling was not in English. Neither were his wife's words that she screamed at him. She gave me the story. 'This is my husband Ahmad, and I am Fadwa. We are Muslims and immigrated to the United States five years ago. We became naturalized citizens. Then Ahmad enlisted in the U.S. Air Force. He was a pilot in Bahrain where we came from, and he wanted to become a pilot here in the Air Force. His high test scores and performance showed such an aptitude for flying that he was accepted. We were living in New Jersey, but the military sent Ahmad here to get the pilot training. I have been meeting with some of the other pilots' wives for a Bible study, but I did it secretly, knowing Ahmad would not allow it. I was reading my Bible and praying, when he came through the door and caught me tonight. You may not know it, but Muslim husbands can beat their wives, and nothing is said about it. I have been beaten many times since our marriage, but this was the first time he has threatened to kill me! I knew he meant it. His eyes were full of fire, and his voice changed to a guttural sound. He was like a monster coming at me!' Then the woman broke down crying again."

"Well, what did you do?" Pete wanted to know.

"I called on God to give me understanding. I didn't know what to do. This woman may be on the verge of giving her life to Jesus, I thought. I didn't want to mess up God's plan. Maybe the man was **not** a terrorist. But even if he was, and he had evil purposes against our country, he still needed to be saved. I looked over at him, praying hard for God to give me wisdom and give me compassion for this Muslim man. He had become calm, but he looked very worried. I decided to talk to him, depending on the Holy Spirit to put the words in my mouth. 'Ahmad, were you actually going to kill your wife? Don't you have any love for her? Don't you want to have children with her and a family? Do you want to be kicked out of the pilot training program? What will you do then?' I waited for him to answer."

"Ahmad struggled to get in a sitting position, and I helped him sit on the floor, not removing the handcuffs. The wild look in his eyes was gone, but his expression showed he was still angry. He said, 'My wife knows that the Christians' Bible is a book of lies. Our prophet Muhammed was visited by the angel Gabriel, who gave him the Quran. That is our holy book, and it has the true words of Allah. Fadwa, bring me our Quran, and also bring me your Bible. Mr. Policeman, you must remove these handcuffs, so I can demonstrate the power of Allah, our god.' I honestly did not know whether I should do that or not, but I sensed the Holy Spirit directing me to allow his demonstration. As soon as he had both books in his hands, he stood up. I stood up, too, and patted my gun in its holster. Ahmad saw me do that and stepped back. I had no idea what he was about to do. I prayed in tongues quietly. He took a deep breath and said, 'Don't listen to lies, Fadwa! Then he held up the Bible in his right hand, shouting, 'This is the TRUTH!' He quickly held up the Quran in his left hand, and shouted, 'This is a LIE!' Confusion covered his face. I kept praying in tongues. Ahmad shook his head and said, 'No, no! I didn't mean that! THIS is a LIE!' and he held up the Quran again. He was sweating as he held up the Bible and shouted, 'THIS is the TRUTH!' Three times he tried to call the Bible a lie and the Quran the truth, and he COULD NOT DO IT. He got it backwards every time. His eyes grew wide. His chest was heaving. Then, suddenly, he threw both books down on the floor, charged out the door, and ran into the darkness. I clearly heard the Holy Spirit say, 'Do not follow him. He is coming back.' The minute he rushed toward the door, the windows started rattling, and the door kept banging loudly for several minutes! I knew it was demonic activity."[41]

Pete and the others were breathing hard. They dared not interrupt, but all began to silently pray for understanding. Britt continued, "Fadwa was scared, but after everything got quiet, she went to the door to look out. She began to cry and say, 'I have prayed so hard for him. I am finding peace by reading the Bible. The other wives are praying with me. I am feeling love, **real love,** for the first time. I want Ahmad to feel this love. He has abused me often during our marriage, but I still love him. I think the real truth is in the Bible, not in the Quran. Thank you for being here tonight, Mr. Policeman. What is your name?' I told her, 'Britt Carson.' She relaxed and smiled. I could tell she felt safe with me. This whole scene was obviously a work of God, and I began to believe with my whole heart that she and her husband would be saved that very night."

"Oh, Britt, this is better than any Hollywood movie. I am so in suspense to hear the rest of the story," Pete blurted out. "Please go on. I don't care if it takes till midnight or longer." Everyone agreed.

"Well, it wasn't long before two of my security colleagues came to the door, and they were carrying Ahmad on a stretcher. After they found him passed out on the ground behind the next apartment complex, they did some checking and found out where he lived and the name of his wife. They were coming to tell her that they would take him to the base hospital. Ahmad was lying there, motionless, and looked catatonic. Fadwa fell on him, kissing him, and trying to get him to wake up. He didn't respond. She insisted that she knew what to do, and they must not take him to the hospital. I still can't understand why they obeyed her, but, reluctantly, they put him on the bed in the bedroom. They told me to report to them later about his condition. After they left, Fadwa looked me straight in the eye and said, 'I know you are a Christian. All the time you have been here I have felt the same presence around you that I feel when I go to Bible study. And I saw you praying a while ago. Somehow I know you can pray for Ahmad, and he will wake up. Would you do that?'"

"You mean you never gave her any indication that you were a Christian?" asked Jeff.

"No, but I felt Jesus BIG on the inside of me the whole time I was there. That is what she felt, too. Here is what happened. I put my hands on Ahmad and began to pray. Out of my mouth came a language I did not know. I was shocked, but I kept praying, thinking that this must be the gift of speaking in tongues. I had been praying privately in my prayer language for a year, but this was not the same. It didn't last long, and the flow stopped. Then I opened my mouth to interpret, and out came English words. I instinctively knew it was a translation of the tongues I had just uttered. I heard Fadwa gasp, and I turned around to look at her. Her jaw had dropped. The message I interpreted was a simple statement of the gospel, how Jesus died for our sins and was raised from the dead in three days to give us eternal life and was now in heaven, praying for us. Fadwa started bawling, and she fell to her knees. She cried out, 'Jesus, I know You are the Savior of the world, You love me, and You died for my sins. You have given me eternal life. Please come inside my heart like you are inside Mr. Carson's heart. I will follow You all the days of my life.' Then she stood up and hugged me and thanked me over and over."

Sarah was excited. "But what about Ahmad? You were praying for **him**, but his wife got saved!"

"What happened next is that Fadwa and I both laid our hands on Ahmad and prayed for him to wake up and to know what Jesus did for him and to ask Jesus to save him. And that is exactly what happened! Those two embraced and cried for the longest time. I went and sat down on the sofa, trying to get my strength back. I was totally drained of energy. It came to me that Jesus had the same feeling when a sick woman touched his garment, and he felt power go out of Him. The human side of him needed rest. Before this, I had no idea how strenuous it is to do the ministry of deliverance. There were lots of demons inside Ahmad. When he unwittingly proclaimed that the Bible was true and the Quran was false, those demons came out of him. But they followed him when he ran out the door, and since Ahmad wasn't protected by the blood of Jesus, they went back inside him and made him catatonic."

Pete remarked, "Those demons made a racket when they left, didn't they? That makes me think of the Gadarene demoniac that Jesus cast demons out of. The demons went inside the pigs, 2,000 of them, and they caused the pigs to plunge down the cliff into the sea and drown![42]

Camille looked at her watch. "Folks, this study has taken much longer than I thought it would. It has been quite a full day for you girls, flying to Columbus, going to the college to unpack, and then coming back to Columbus. All of you probably are looking forward to a good night's rest before church in the morning. The Christmas holidays are drawing to a close. Also, you still have your drive back to Starkville tonight. What a whirlwind of a day."

Britt stood. "Let's make a circle and have a closing prayer. Then you can be on your way." Everyone joined hands. "But wait, I have to bring you up to date on these two Muslims. Only a few days after Ahmad and Fadwa were saved, they invited Fadwa's Bible study friends and their husbands to a Bible study in their apartment. This happened about six weeks ago, and Ahmad tells me they are still going strong. Their bonds of friendship are growing, they feel God's love as they study, and they want to share with others the salvation they have found." Gloria started clapping and praising the Lord, and everybody joined her.

Britt laughed. "Oh, I almost forgot to tell you that I prayed for Ahmad in the ARABIC language! Of course, Fadwa knew every word I said before I interpreted it in English. I thought I was praying in an unknown tongue, but it turned out to be a **known** tongue. It was just like the Day of Pentecost in Acts, chapter two, when the 120 people prayed in tongues, and the thousands of people who heard them understood 'the mighty works of God' in their own languages. It wasn't gibberish. It was real languages. I felt so honored, and it humbled me to know that God had used me to bring salvation to two Muslim people. Oh, Lord, let's pray!" Britt broke down crying. Pete squeezed his hand and looked at his brother, admiringly.

Camille began the prayer, and around the circle each one prayed. Gloria led out in singing, "I Love You, Lord." The Holy Spirit enveloped them, and their hearts were filled with love, joy, and thanksgiving. After many warm embraces, the four friends reluctantly got in Jeff's Ford and drove away.

CHAPTER FIFTEEN

ADATON BAPTIST CHURCH

On Sunday morning, January 5th, Jeff and Pete were still sleepy when they drove up to Hamlin Hall in Pete's yellow Chevy. They went inside to wait in the lobby for Gloria and Sarah. Priscilla was at the desk and greeted them cheerily. "Hey, fellas, I betcha I am going where you are going this morning, Adaton Baptist. Gary will be here shortly to pick me up. Isn't it great to be back at school and have the opportunity to hear Brother James preach again, as well as see friends we haven't seen since we left for Christmas?"

Jeff went up to the desk. "You bet. I am so glad y'all will be at Adaton today. But we need to get together with just the six of us sometime."

"Yes, we do. Oh, Jeff, that ministry time on New Year's Eve at St. Luke was fantastic! I loved seeing the Lord use you and Gary, as well as Pastor Jordan, to minister to people. I wish that kind of thing would happen at Adaton Baptist."

"Jeff, we are ready to go," said Gloria, as she and Sarah came down the stairs.

Jeff and Pete stood up and were now wide awake. Pete let out a wolf whistle. Both stood there and gaped. Gloria's medium-length dark hair framed her beautiful, smiling face in curls. Her dress was royal blue, and the soft material flowed as she walked. "What a striking figure," Jeff thought. Her shiny black shoes had very high heels, and her diamond-like earrings and necklace were beautiful. Sarah's makeup was subdued but perfect with gold earrings and necklace. She wore a bright, rust-colored tailored dress with brown alligator pumps. Before Jeff or Pete could say anything, they both explained that these were new clothes given to them at Christmas. They felt obligated to dress up, even though the college girls attending church rarely got any dressier than slacks and blouses with flats. The girls invited warm embraces from their men but said they were saving their kisses until they were on the way back to the dorm after lunch. Jeff and Pete helped them put on their dress coats.

Pete had to say something. "Gazing at you all dressed up, Sarah, is making my heart beat fast. You are always beautiful, but today you look like a model."

"Thanks, Pete. Chaya and Max were amazed that my Hanukkah gift fit me so perfectly. They were praising HaShem they got the right size. And they loved the tallits I brought them, saying they were much more ornate than the ones they had, and they treasured them because they came from Israel."

Jeff nuzzled Gloria's neck. "Honey, I promise I won't kiss you and mess up your lipstick, but I only want to inhale your fragrance deeply. My heart is doing flip flops, observing your new dress and shoes, and the sublime beauty of your face and figure. I wish Pete and I had known what you two would look like, so we could have dressed more in keeping with our top-class models."

Now how can I graciously deflect that compliment? thought Gloria. "Clothes certainly don't make the man. You are so good-looking you put the brilliance of a peacock to shame." Gloria covered her mouth to keep from laughing out loud.

Pete wanted to stop the idle chatter. "We belong to a mutual admiration society, but these accolades are getting cornier and cornier. Stop it, you guys, and let's go." Pete held Sarah's hand and led the way to his car.

Gloria could hardly wait to see Grace Thomas and ask her what she thought about the faxes they had sent to the church in her care while they were in Israel. As soon as the Holy Rollers came in the door, Grace ran up to Gloria with welcoming arms. "You won't believe what Brother James has planned, y'all. He wants Gloria to give a short report during our service today. Isn't that great?"

The friends looked at Gloria. "Oh, my, I don't know if I can do that. I am not good at public speaking, especially when I haven't prepared." Her smile disappeared, and a frown took its place.

Jeff lifted her chin and stared right into her eyes. "I have no doubt whatsoever, that you will do a perfect job. As you have always said, Jesus will put the words in your mouth. I have seen Him do it for me, so I am sure of it. We will all be backing you up in prayer when you go up on the stage." Pete, Sarah, and Grace nodded their heads and offered words of assurance.

Pastor James came down the aisle to Gloria. "I want you all to know that nothing has excited me in a long time as much as the faxes you four sent us here at the church. We have prayed faithfully for you while you were in Israel. Now, Gloria, we want to get a taste of the answer to our prayers. Please bless us with a five-minute report. Say anything you want to, and we will lap it up." Jeff James squeezed Gloria's hand and walked back to the stage, not waiting for her reply.

The organ and piano began a lively prelude of "Victory in Jesus," as everyone took their seats. Grace sat by Gloria with Sarah on her other side. She reached over and patted Gloria's hand. "You can do it, sister." Gloria's mind went blank. As the announcements were being made, she had butterflies in her stomach, but then a deep peace came over her, and, suddenly, she was at the Garden Tomb in Jerusalem. It was like a movie, and she was in it. She heard a voice behind her say, 'Mary.' She turned and said, 'Rabboni,'[43] and fell to her knees. She wanted to put her arms around Jesus, but He had to leave. He said, 'Go and tell my disciples I am alive.'"

Jeff elbowed her on one side, and Grace pulled at her, saying, "Get up, Gloria. Go up there. It's time for your report. Pastor James is calling you."

Gloria began to move toward the stage. She was still in a dream-like trance, but she was putting one foot in front of the other. She walked up to the pulpit, still enveloped in a deep peace, and looked out at the audience. She remembered she must open her mouth and expect the Lord to fill it. The congregation was waiting. Jeff prayed harder. Gloria's face was wreathed in smiles, and she finally spoke. "HE'S ALIVE! HE'S ALIVE! I was there. I talked to Him. He was ascending back to heaven, but He told me to tell you He has risen from the dead. I am a witness. I was there, right there in the Garden Tomb in Jerusalem." The congregation was murmuring. Then the murmuring turned to quiet wonder as Gloria raised her hands and began to sing, *I come to the garden alone, while the dew is still on the roses. And the voice I hear, falling on my ear, the Son of God discloses* ... The congregation began to sing with Gloria: *And He walks with me, and He talks with me, and He tells me I am His own. And the joy we share as we tarry there, none other has ever known.*[44] There was not a dry eye in the building. Gloria put her hands on the pulpit and explained, "Oh, people, honestly I was so scared to come up here and speak to you, but somehow the Spirit took me back in time to that awesome moment when Mary Magdalene saw the risen Christ, and He commissioned her to go and tell the good news of His resurrection and His offer of eternal life. For a moment I thought I was actually Mary Magdalene!" The congregation stood and applauded.

Gloria smiled and indicated they should sit back down. "I want to tell you one more thing about our trip, and I hope I don't take up too much of Brother James' time because he always has a stirring sermon. Well, we were up on the Golan Heights, the northernmost part of Israel. An extremely dramatic thing happened to us, especially to Sarah, while we were up there, but it is her story to tell. As we left that place, I remarked that I felt strongly that the Lord was commissioning us like He did His disciples on the Day of Pentecost to go and be His witnesses and to make disciples. And He was sending us out from the highest point in Israel. That's all

I wanted to say right now. Thank you for being patient and listening to me. And THANK YOU so much for your prayers. They meant everything to the four of us in Israel." Gloria blew kisses to the audience. As she walked back to her seat, she noticed Gary Grayson and Priscilla Caldwell seated several rows back from them and waved. Gary gave her a big thumbs-up.

Jeff James came to the pulpit. "I have an announcement to make. As I speak, my wife is in the fellowship hall, putting together a light lunch for anyone who wants to stay and hear more from Gloria, Jeff, Sarah, and Pete. I know they may have been planning to eat at a restaurant, as most of you may be planning to do, but we hope you all will be willing to enjoy this simple food in order to have some more spiritual food from these travelers to Israel. What we just heard is an enticing sample, don't you agree?" The congregation stood and applauded a long time. A few couples left to go pick up some fast food to supplement Celeste's sandwiches, as it looked like the whole church would be staying for lunch. Jeff James realized that God had changed his agenda, so he streamlined his sermon, cutting it down to twenty minutes. He could feel God's approval and rejoiced inside, realizing that "little is much when God is in it."[45]

DRIVING BACK TO MSU CAMPUS

"Wow! We really **have** been commissioned, like you said, Gloria." Pete was excited. "You may not find my church very interesting next Sunday, friends, after what happened here today. I loved their questions and getting the opportunity to share our experiences in Israel."

"And wasn't it great to have Gary and Priscilla there? From the number of questions they asked and the looks on their faces,

I think they are serious about planning a trip to Israel. Did y'all notice that?" Jeff asked.

"I certainly did," answered Pete. "Grace Thomas was drinking it all in, too. And did you see Pastor James' face and the way he wrote things down? It wouldn't surprise me if he got up a trip for the whole church. Of course, most people couldn't afford it, but he may be able to get six or seven people. That's my guess. You know what, I felt my heart about to burst as I contemplated that God may be giving the four of us a ministry **together**. Let's recapture that feeling we had in Israel, singing 'Days of Elijah.' Lead us in our theme song, Gloria."

Gloria started singing, and the others joined in, belting out "Days of Elijah."[46] The men were uninhibited and sang louder and louder. Gloria and Sarah looked admiringly at them, thinking how they were really "men of God."

"Pastor James touched my heart with that sermon about Abraham and how God called him and made a covenant with him for the land of Israel," marveled Sarah. "All those passages in Genesis and in the New Testament about Abraham make so much sense to me now, since I have been born again. I would give anything if Max and Chaya would let me talk to them about Yeshua and the New Covenant. Would you all help me pray that they will have ears to hear and a heart to understand?"

"Of course, baby doll," assured Pete, as he leaned over and kissed Sarah on the cheek. "You and Gloria are both like Mary Magdalene, messengers of the good news."

"Gloria, you gave an out-of-this-world witness in the Adaton pulpit this morning," said Jeff, drawing Gloria into his arms in the back seat. "I am so proud of you, but you had me scared for a minute. I thought you weren't coming out of your trance, and then you wowed us!"

"Thank you, Jeff. All of your prayers pulled me through. I was the scared one, at least until the Holy Spirit calmed me and took me to the Garden Tomb. I really did feel like I was there. And sharing with the church members at lunch was something special. I could sense a deep hunger in the people for the things of the Spirit. Quite a few people said they wanted us to come back and teach them. What do you all think about that?"

Jeff leaned forward, saying earnestly, "I think I have a revelation from God. Remember last night at Britt and Camille's when they taught us? They said they were equipping us for ministry. What happened today at lunch was an **example** of the ministry they were equipping us for. It was not a coincidence that Pastor James sprung it on us today. It was a God incidence – you know it! This is our destiny. But I have no idea how this will play out. Should we bounce around some ideas about our ministry together?"

No one said anything for a few minutes. Then Sarah spoke in a tentative tone. "When I look back and see what has happened to me since I enrolled at MSU, a mere four months ago, I am astonished. Did I plan it? Did I have even an inkling that I would meet you all, that we would go to Israel together, that I would be saved, and that people would be looking to us for answers today? NO, I did not. Why should we be concerned about the future? It is obvious that HaShem has been orchestrating all the details of our lives, and I think it started with Gloria the night she gave her heart to Yeshua at the Baptist Student Union meeting. Then the rest of us were impacted, and here we are today. We should not have **one care** in the world about our future. Our Lord has all the plans, and what He has started, He will complete. Agreed?"

"Oh, Sarah, you are an angel," exclaimed Gloria. "I agree, wholeheartedly. It is actually a **sin** to worry. I know just the Bible verse that will put the 'Amen' on what you said, Sarah. It's from First Peter 5:7. 'Casting all your care on Him, for He cares for you.' I will sing a song about it. It is very comforting, and we need comfort. We have no idea where God is leading us, but we know He loves us and would not put us in needless danger. He takes pleasure in blessing us. I believe that. Now I will sing it: *I cast all my cares upon*

You. I lay all of my burdens down at Your feet. And anytime I don't know what to do, I will cast all of my cares upon You."[47]

"That is beautiful, Gloria," said Pete. "Sing it again, and we will try to join in." They kept singing the song until MSU came in sight. Pete pulled up in front of Hamlin Hall and turned off the ignition. Then he leaned across the bucket seat and enveloped Sarah in his arms, kissing her until she opened the door and hopped out. "Bye now, my Romeo. 'Your kisses are sweeter than wine,' and I may get drunk as I dream of you in my nap. Don't laugh. I'm serious."

Gloria and Jeff delighted in each other in the back seat, murmuring tender words in each other's ears and kissing, until they heard Sarah open the car door. Gloria got out of the car and looked longingly at Jeff, until they drove away.

CHAPTER SIXTEEN

TESTIFYING OF GOD'S LOVE

LOBBY OF HAMLIN HALL
WEDNESDAY NIGHT

"I really enjoyed the BSU meeting tonight," said Jeff. It was very different, but the Lord must have inspired the format. The question Grace Thomas asked to kick off the meeting was perfect – 'Out of all that happened to you over the holidays, what **one thing** made you feel the love of God more than at any other time?' So many astounding things happened to me, that I didn't see how I could narrow it down to only one thing. Right away I knew I was not to speak until everyone else shared. I prayed hard to say only what God told me to. And I think I did that."

Gloria agreed. "You did, honey. I could feel it. Your story about the love flowing between you and your dad when your family discovered that your dad was Jewish and a descendant of the famous composer, Felix Mendelssohn, touched my heart. His not being affectionate toward you in the past suddenly changed. I like the way you said that his joy was like the high striker at a carnival who hit the lever so hard, the puck knocked off the mounted bell at the top. You said Mr. Quentin was really uninhibited, praising the Lord, and you and he hugged and kissed!"

Pete commented, "It almost makes me jealous that now my three friends are 'double Jewish.' And here I am, the only 'goy' in the group."

"But none of us have the honor of being called '**the rock**,' the namesake of the Apostle Peter. That oughta make you feel loved, bro." encouraged Jeff.

"Well, as a matter of fact, it does. I wish I could have told the group more of the details of the morning in Amory when we met for coffee, Jeff. Your love for me really carried me through, when I was facing a possible lawsuit. You helped me get back to the Lord after I had given in to temptation. You set me back on my feet, and together we heard the truth about the situation I was in. Because of your love and your prayers, I was delivered from fear and shame. How can I ever thank you enough, bro?"

Pete and Jeff had a good bear hug. Sarah was silently thanking God that Pete had not hidden that awful episode at the bar from her. Her man had been tested, and he passed the test. Not only that, but God used Pete to set that poor girl free from Satan. Sarah's heart filled with love for Pete, and she sat back and basked in HaShem's love.

"My turn to share," said Gloria. "Jeff, I had the same reaction you did. What would I say? But God was faithful to put the words in my mouth, finally. At first I thought it was impossible because of the abundance of awesome experiences I had, most of them with you all. Then I could hear the Lord whisper to me that I was to listen very carefully to what the other students were sharing. And He wanted me to put myself in their shoes and try to feel what they were feeling. At first, I couldn't concentrate, and that's when the Lord showed me how self-centered I am. Oh, it hurt. It really hurt! What came to my mind from Scripture was the widow who had only two mites to give at the temple. She was dirt poor, but Jesus treated her with the greatest of respect and said she had given **more** than all the rich people who made a show of giving a **big** offering. He said she had given **all** she had.[48] I can't comprehend it. All of us are wealthy. Trying to feel what the poor woman felt seems impossible. But as I pondered it, the Holy Spirit comforted me and brought a verse to my mind, 'To whom much is given, much is required.'[49] And I enjoyed sharing how the 'much' is you, Jeff. I felt so secure and loved when you took charge of our tour of Israel and even paid for the guide and the hotel in Tiberias. Being the one to hold you in the Jordan River as you lay back in the water sent a thrill through my soul. Oh, glory! I can feel it again," exclaimed Gloria.

"I'll tell you how I felt when Grace gave us that question. I felt overwhelmed," exclaimed Sarah. "I could **not** pick out one instance of feeling God's love more than at other times. The feeling of HaShem's love has accumulated in my heart for months now. In my bed every night I think back over my life here at MSU and in New York and in Israel, and I feel like His love permeates everything, even the little things. However, I can't get around the fact of that dramatic moment when I realized that I wanted to be **born again.** I understood that Yeshua was born on that very day that we call Christmas, and my **eyes were opened to see Him as my Messiah** at last. Right there His LOVE flooded every inch of my being! Okay, that's it. That's the 'one thing' that made me feel HaShem's love more than at any other time. But I am glad the meeting was over before I could give my answer tonight, because at some future meeting I would like to tell my whole life story. But wait. Don't say anything about it, okay? It's got to be totally orchestrated by HaShem."

"I think we should pray about that right here right now." Jeff reached out for Gloria and Pete's hands, and the four made a circle of prayer. Jeff led. "Father God, we all want to thank You for allowing us to give our testimonies tonight. We are in full agreement with Sarah that You, HaShem, will set up a time for Sarah to give her testimony. We feel honored to have been there the moment the veil was removed from her eyes to see her Messiah, Yeshua, the Savior of the world and the King of the universe. Toda raba, Avi – thank You, Father – for the awesome things you are doing in our lives. Please show us, now that we are back at MSU, what You want us to do. We know You will orchestrate it, so we are not worried. Just help us to be sensitive to Your voice and to be obedient to follow, however You lead us. We all love You and thank You for letting us feel Your love so strongly. In Jesus' name, Amen."

The four friends said their 'amens' and hugged each other. Gloria spoke up. "Before we part our ways, I think I just heard God say that we are to be praying for our visit with Pete's parents in Columbus on Sunday. He said we should lift up in prayer each member of his family, as well as each of us. Ooh! I can feel chill bumps! Ooh! God is up to something. I have no doubt. How will we be able to concentrate in our classes and do homework the rest of the week?"

"Wait, I have a question, Jeff," said Sarah. "Are we still going to be helping you with birthday cake deliveries on Fridays? As we make our plans this week, I just wanted you to know that we don't have to attend temple, unless you all want to. But your parents may be attending, Jeff, so you may want to go. As for me, now that I have been born again, I really do prefer going to a church regularly. I like Adaton Baptist and Pastor James, as well as the people who attend there. Do you all think that should be our church home, and maybe we should take a more active part?"

Pete lit up. "I was thinking the same thing, Sarah. Except for attending my church in Columbus, First Baptist, this coming Sunday, I am in agreement. Jeff and Gloria, do you agree?"

Gloria wanted to make a sort of schedule for the Holy Rollers. "Yes, I do. If it's okay with you guys, I will use one of my new 1998 calendars and fill in dates for our activities as a ministry group."

"That sounds exciting. We already have a name, and now we will have a calendar of ministry," said Jeff. "Someone pulled me aside at Adaton last Sunday and asked if we would come to his church to speak. He is a senior, and he usually attends an interde-nominational church. I can't remember the name of the church, but he asked if we could come some Friday night. The guy is Walter Sessions. Do y'all know him?"

No one knew him, but they agreed to accept his invitation. "Jeff, you find out all the details, and tell me, so we can put it on the calendar," said Gloria. "And I want to put my piano performance on the calendar. It's in February. Okay with you all?"

Pete chuckled. "Do you think we should list all our classes on the calendar? After all, that's why we came to MSU, to get an education!"

Sarah punched Pete in the arm. "You are trying to be funny. You know if we did that, there would not be any room for our ministry dates. Oh, Gloria, remember to save Wednesday nights for BSU meetings. I love going there. And let me say that I think that in ALL of the ministry we do together we should testify of God's love. That's the bottom line." Loud 'amens' erupted from the four.

"Holy Rollers, it is time to keep our appointments with our comfortable dormitory beds. I am in need of some sound sleep so I can keep operating at the high speed of this crazy group." quipped Jeff. All agreed and went their separate ways.

CHAPTER SEVENTEEN

HEART TO HEART TALKS

I t was 9:30 when Jeff and Pete got back to their room at Suttle Hall. "I can't believe we are back so early, Jeff. It's a good thing, because I need to hit the sack. I've got to get up early in the morning and study for my Criminal Justice Class. However, I can't put off talking to you about something that has been weighing on my heart heavily ever since we got back from Israel. Do you have some studying to do, or can you be a sounding board for me and give me some advice? It's about Sarah and me."

"Of course, I will do anything to help, but I may not have any advice. What's it about?"

"I will come right out and say it. It's about sex. I am having a very hard time keeping my hands off Sarah. I am a real Christian now, so I know we have to save ourselves until marriage, but it's getting so I can't sleep. I lie awake at night, picturing the fulfillment of my desires."

"You mean you are fantasizing about sex?" Jeff asked.

"Yes, bro. Do you ever do that?"

"No, I don't. Of course, I have had zero experience with women in that way, and I know you have indulged yourself. You have had quite a reputation as a womanizer. One thing I know is that if you have lusted for Sarah, you have already sinned. That's what Jesus said about adultery in the Sermon on the Mount.[50] Pete, this is serious, even though it's not technically adultery. You need to be delivered from those unclean thoughts. That's the 'old man,' and now you have to 'put on the new man,'[51] as the Apostle Paul says. Satan was unsuccessful in his attempts to make you fall to sexual temptation, when he sent Laura Henderson to you that night. You didn't have any trouble rejecting her advances, and that's commendable. But how much more should you have self-control when it comes to Sarah, whom you love with all your heart. Can't you see that?"

"Yes, I see that, Jeff, but I burn with desire for her, all of her."

"Well, then, why don't you get married? Have you said anything to Sarah about marriage?"

"We hinted at it on the plane coming back from Israel. Yes, I know my destiny is to be the husband of Sarah Zipporah Bernstein. She is the girl of my dreams, and no other girl compares with her. I have been with many. Sarah is the one, and I know it."

"Then what are you waiting for? Don't you have the money to buy a ring? But that's not an excuse anyway. I proposed to Gloria before I gave her a ring."

"I am scared. Okay, I said it. I am scared. What if I make a lousy husband? What if Sarah decides I am not the kind of guy she wants to spend her life with? Others may think I am self-assured, but I can tell you I have very little self-confidence. Maybe that is why I have seduced so many women, thinking it will make me more of a man. Oh, I feel ashamed right now. I am finally facing up to myself in that area. Jeff, tell me what you are thinking," begged Pete.

"I am thinking there is something in the Bible about your dilemma. I read it the other day, but I can't remember exactly what it says. I will look on the internet about marriage and what Paul said. Maybe I can find it. I think God's Word will settle the issue."

Jeff didn't search long until he found the Scripture. "Pete, this is God's answer for you. It is in First Corinthians 7: 8-9. 'But I say to the unmarried and to the widows: It is good for them if they remain even as I am [Paul was single]; but if they cannot exercise self-control, let them marry. For **it is better to marry than to burn with passion**.'"

"Whoa! That is certainly my answer. Okay, I'll do it. I will go buy a ring, and I will propose to Sarah at Sunday dinner at my parents' house in front of all my family and friends. That's what **you** did, Jeff, when we were at the Sondheims' house on Thanksgiving weekend. Thanks to you, I have a model to follow."

"Problem solved. Let's hit the hay. Life goes on, friend, and there are four more days until you pop the question. Proud of you, buddy. Let's get some zzzzzs."

THURSDAY NIGHT
OFFICE OF PASTOR JEFF JAMES

"Come on in, Jeff and Pete. I will sit at my desk, and you can pull up those two chairs over there. What is the nature of your visit? If it has something to do with helping me plan a trip to Israel for our church, I am all ears. In fact, I have been thinking about approaching the four of you. But I see just you two men have come." Pastor James got a note pad out of his desk, ready to take notes.

Pete began, "We are thankful you could meet with us on this short notice. We didn't want to tell you what it's about until we got here, because what I am looking for is your answers 'off the top of your head,' so to speak. And I know that will be Bible answers. As three guys talking, two single and one married, we wanted to have a heart-to-heart talk about sex." Pete settled back in his chair, enjoying the pastor's raised eyebrows and the corners of his mouth turning up into a nervous grin.

Jeff added, "I am along for moral support mainly, although I need to learn also."

The pastor looked at Pete. "So you are the one, Pete, who needs answers about sex, huh? Why would that be, and why at this time? Judging from your handsome masculinity, my instincts tell me you have had some experience already. Am I right?"

Pete decided to bare his heart and get right to the point. "Pastor James, sad to say, yes, I have had experience, and I am ashamed of it. I have called myself a Christian since I came down front in my church and shook my pastor's hand at the age of fourteen. I confessed my sins and got saved. But I didn't become a **real** Christian until Sarah and I gave our lives to Jesus when we were in Israel. Living this real Christian life with my friends is more fun than all the worldly pleasures I have had since my early teens. Okay, let me get to the point. Sarah is an Orthodox Jew who has been born again. She is as pure as can be and always has been. She lets me kiss her and hold her, but I know that is the limit. Pastor, I am burning with such desire for her, I can't even sleep at night. What can I do? I am happy, and yet I am miserable!"

"Well, you have come to see me at an opportune time because I have been preparing a teaching for the youth at Adaton this coming Sunday night, and guess what the subject is?"

"The subject wouldn't be sex, would it, Pastor?" Pete ventured to guess. The pastor smiled and nodded his head. Pete looked at Jeff.

"Another God-incidence," Jeff exclaimed. "Well, we are on the right track, coming here tonight, aren't we Pete?" Pete grinned.

"Before I even get out the notes I was preparing, I will declare this 'off the top of my head,' as you say, Pete. In the first chapter of Genesis we find that SEX IS GOD'S IDEA. His very first command to Adam and Eve after He created them was to '**be fruitful and multiply.**' You know what that means, don't you? It means sex! Reproduce, have kids. The Bible doesn't say, but most likely they probably began to obey after the sun set that night. Ha!"

Jeff and Pete were both wide-eyed. Jeff laughed. "I can't believe I never even thought of that before. I thought when the devil came into the Garden of Eden and tempted them, and they sinned – THAT was where sex originated."

"Yeah, I guess I thought that, too," agreed Pete. "It seems like whenever we find something that gives such pleasure, we automatically think that God has called it off-limits. That's stupid, isn't it?"

"Wait a minute, Pete. God **does** set up limits, but He doesn't do it to be a killjoy. He does it for our own protection. Since God's gift of sex is so powerful, more powerful than the atomic bomb, it must have boundaries. Our Father God provided the boundary for sex – marriage between one man and one woman."

Jeff brightened. "Oh, I know all about that. We friends have talked about it, the story of God making Eve and giving her to Adam. I have it memorized. 'Then the rib which the Lord God had taken from man He made into a woman, and He brought her to the man. And Adam said, 'This is now bone of my bones and flesh of my flesh; she shall be called Woman, because she was taken out of Man.' Therefore a man shall leave his father and mother and be joined to his wife, and **they shall become one flesh**.' Pastor James, Gloria and I are engaged, and we are both looking forward to fulfilling that Scripture, the last line, I mean."

Pastor James almost laughed, but he saw how serious Jeff was. "So you and Gloria are engaged. That's great. Well, Pete, that can be an answer to your problem. I have a verse for that. Let me find it."

Jeff interrupted. "Oh, I already found it on the internet, Pastor James. Paul said it was better to marry than to burn with passion. When Pete heard that last night, he made up his mind to propose to Sarah this coming Sunday. Then he relaxed. This morning he said he finally had a good night's sleep."

"Yeah, I did, but the minute I lay eyes on Sarah tomorrow, I know that burning will ignite again." Pete looked hopeless.

Pastor James' brow furrowed, and he started flipping pages in his Bible. "Pete, because you have had previous sexual experiences, it is entirely possible that you have picked up a demon of lust. I would say this demon hides most of the time, because you now have a greater power living inside you. The Holy Spirit has taken up residence in your human spirit, which is called 'the candle of the

115

Lord.'[52] He is working from the inside out as a searchlight to make you like Jesus. Paul taught us that we should not be 'conformed to the world but be **transformed** by the renewing of our minds.'[53] Sorry, fellas, I don't want to get in a long study, but I think I need to give you a little more understanding in order to deal with this spirit of lust that has entered you, Pete, and is tormenting you. You yielded to temptation one too many times, and it provided an opening for the devil. You may want to jot this down." Pastor James slid two note pads and pens across his desk to Pete and Jeff.

Pete said, "If you have the time, so do we. I don't want any demon spirit inside me, no way!"

"Okay. Here goes. Just like God is a Trinity – the Father, the Son, and the Holy Spirit – so is man. You are a spirit, you have a soul, and you live in a body. How do I know this? Jot down First Thessalonians 5:23. 'Now may the God of peace Himself **sanctify you completely**; and may your whole **spirit, soul, and body** be preserved blameless at the coming of our Lord Jesus Christ.' Got that? Now write this down. Your soul is made up of **your mind, will, and emotions**. Your soul is your personality; it's who you are. People know you over the telephone, even when they can't see you. So, you see, the Holy Spirit is sanctifying you from the inside out, and it's a lifelong process. He is making you holy, transforming your soul so you will carry out the will of God for your life. Remember that is what Paul says at the beginning of Romans, twelfth chapter. He starts out saying, 'Present your **body**, a living sacrifice.' As the Holy Spirit works on you, eventually, even your **body** will be transformed. It will happen in the twinkling of an eye at the last trumpet, when God raises up the dead to meet Jesus in the air. If you are alive at that time, your body will be transformed on the way up to meet Him."[54]

"Let me get this straight, Pastor. Going back to what you said about the Holy Spirit living in my human spirit, and He begins doing an inside job on my soul. You think that a demon is lodging in my soul somewhere, maybe in my mind?" Pete was serious.

"Well, the battleground is the mind, Pete. You are fantasizing about sex and can't sleep at night, you say. The Holy Spirit shows His presence in our lives through the fruit He produces – love, joy, peace, longsuffering, kindness, goodness, faithfulness, gentleness, and **self control**.[55] It is a good sign that you **desire** to have self-control. The Spirit is working on you, and you want to be free of this spirit of lust instead of giving into it. That's good. I can see it is painful for you though."

"Yes, Pastor. Can't you just cast it out of me? Jeff and I have heard from my brother Britt about how he cast demons out of a Muslim man. It wasn't a spirit of lust. I guess it was a spirit of murder, but he had lots of demons. Anyway, I want to be FREE!"

"To be honest, Pete, I have not had experience in the deliverance ministry, but I have heard others tell of their experiences. I know the Lord will show me what to do. After all, we have the Scriptural record of Jesus and the Apostles casting out demons. But let me finish sharing some more on sexuality. Pete and Jeff, please keep in mind that your bodies are **temples** of the Holy Spirit. Meditate on that. The Corinthian church had trouble with sexual sins, and Paul had a lot to say to them.

"Pastor, I need to learn from the Bible all about this subject, but I want to get delivered today, if at all possible. However, I do know how God values the virtue of patience and waiting on Him. He wants me to practice developing self-control, I guess." Pete slid down in his chair. He was afraid to hope.

Jeff reminded himself he was there for moral support. "Hey, buddy, remember how God used me to get Gary saved and to heal his leg when I was a brand new Christian? Remember how that girl was healed from stuttering. You have nothing to worry about. If Pastor Gary doesn't get you delivered, Britt can do it. And if he can't do it, I will do it. No worries, buddy."

Pastor James smiled. He loved these guys. They were so transparent. They had youthful zeal, and it was refreshing. "Okay, here is the last of my teaching. This is a long passage, but I want to make sure I have faithfully discharged my duties in ministering to two of the finest young men I have ever met."

"Now that makes me want to take it all in, pastor. Please proceed. I will be ready for prayer as soon as you finish." Pete was smelling victory ahead.

"This passage is to the Corinthian Church – 'Do you not know that your bodies are members of Christ? Shall I then take the members of Christ and make them members of a harlot? Certainly not! Or do you not know that he who is joined to a harlot is **one body with her**? For 'the two,' He says, 'shall become **one flesh.**' But he who is joined to the Lord is one spirit with Him. Flee sexual immorality. Every sin that a man does is **outside the body**, but he who commits sexual immorality **sins against his own body**. Or do you not know that your body is the temple of the Holy Spirit who is in you, whom you have from God, and you are not your own? For you were bought at a price; therefore glorify God in your body and in your spirit, which are God's.'"

"I never heard that before," exclaimed Jeff. That sounds like sexual sin is the most serious of sins, because it is a sin against your own body."

"I know it's serious, Pastor, and that is why I am here. When I am with Sarah, I don't want to be thinking about sex. After we are married I will be rewarded. But now I want to have pure thoughts about her. She deserves it. I want to be a husband she respects and trusts."

"Pete, push your chair back. Let's get on with it. Jeff, we are both going to lay hands on Pete and cast the spirit of lust out of him. Jesus told His disciples to cast out demons, and He gave them the power to do it. We have His Holy Spirit, and we have the power to do it, too. Jesus is the same today, yesterday, and forever. Amen."

"Wait a minute, Brother James. I brought some holy anointing oil back from Israel. Let me put some on Pete before we pray." Jeff reached in his pocket for the oil, poured it on his finger, and made a cross with the oil on Pete's forehead. The fragrance was sweet. They all closed their eyes and enjoyed feeling the presence of the Lord.

Pastor James began the prayer, "Jesus, You taught us to pray, 'deliver us from evil.' I ask You now to deliver Pete from this evil spirit of lust. He has confessed his sin. Your Word tells us that if we confess our sins, You are faithful and just to forgive us our sins, and to **cleanse us from all unrighteousness**.[56] You said Your disciples would know the truth, and the truth would set them free. Pete knows the truth. YOU are THE TRUTH, and we believe that You are setting Pete FREE. In Your mighty and powerful name, we pray, Lord Jesus."

"Look at me, Pete," said Pastor James. "I am going to address the demon inside you. I won't be talking to you. Relax." Pastor James was obviously anointed by the Holy Spirit as he looked in Pete's eyes and in a loud voice said, "I command you, foul spirit, demon of lust, come out of Pete right now! Come out!"

Pete's eyes got wide, and he coughed hard for several minutes. Then he slumped down in his chair, taking deep breaths. After his heart stopped racing, he put his head in his hands, and cried tears of joy and relief. Jeff and Pastor James waited, giving Pete time to savor his freedom. He was cleansed. Jeff got the oil out of his pocket again. "Pete, I know the demon is gone. The Lord told me, as I was silently praying in tongues. Now I am going to anoint you with oil again. It is the symbol of the Holy Spirit. I will pray for you to be baptized in the Holy Spirit like the Apostles were on the Day of Pentecost and like Gloria and I were at Rabbi and Miriam Katz' house in Israel. You will have the power to keep your thoughts focused on Him and resist temptation."

The pastor added his final admonition. "Pete, God has promised that no temptation will overtake you but what is common to man, but with it He will give you a way of escape that you can bear it.[57] Look for that way of escape."

Pete lifted his hands to heaven. After Jeff prayed, he praised the Lord in a new dimension he had never experienced before, profusely thanking the Lord for setting him free.

CHAPTER EIGHTEEN

CHURCH WITH THE CARSON FAMILY

"**O**n the road again, fair lady." Jeff smiled at Gloria, as he held the door of the Ford open for her on Sunday morning.

Pete bowed with a sweeping hand of welcome, as he opened the back door for Sarah and scrambled in close to her. "Nothing more exciting than the Holy Rollers traveling again!"

"You guys look really spiffy, a lot more dressed up than last Sunday when we went to Adaton," said Gloria.

Jeff grinned. "Well, I didn't think you could be any lovelier than you were last Sunday in your new dress, but you are more of a knockout than ever in this frock, babe. Your parents surely don't spare any expense, buying you clothes. Pete and I knew we had to do some shopping to come even close to matching you and Sarah, our MSU fashion plates. After all, we are going to First Baptist Church, the big downtown church in Columbus."

"That's right, Jeff. When I was growing up, my mother made sure all us Carson kids were 'keeping up with the Joneses' in the way we dressed. We may not live in a mansion like yours and Gloria's, but in every other respect, we were rubbing elbows with the bluebloods. I love your outfit, Sarah. What do you think of my new suit?"

"I think you are more handsome than ever in that suit, but what I like best is your after-shave lotion or whatever that manly scent is. I can't believe you have not tried to kiss me this morning. I guess I will have to take the initiative, sweetie." Sarah put her arms around Pete's neck, inhaled his fragrance, and pressed her lips against his. She was surprised when Pete failed to display his usual passion and wondered why.

Pete squeezed her hand, looked deep into her eyes, and said, "The day is not over yet, my love." He sat back in his seat and smiled, totally relaxed.

Jeff looked in the back seat to see how Pete was doing since the deliverance session in Pastor James' office. He could tell that he was completely different. Pete's expression was that of a satisfied soul, nothing to prove and full of confidence. *Wow! That demon is really gone. Lord, You used Pastor and me in a powerful way, and Pete is free. Please let all four of us do this kind of ministry. So many people are tormented, and you want them to know that in Jesus there is salvation, healing, and also deliverance.*

Gloria sensed that they needed to change the subject. "Jeff, I am sorry that Sarah and I couldn't go with you and Pete to deliver birthday cakes at MUW on Friday. You did go, didn't you?"

"No, there were not enough orders to justify driving there. The birthday cakes I have orders for can wait until next Friday. Pete and I delivered a few on our campus. I must confess I don't have the drive for my business, Quentin Services Unlimited, like I had before we went to Israel. Ministry is the thing on my mind now, and it is encouraging that we have already had some calls since we shared at Adaton, as you know. You and Sarah are filling in our calendar, aren't you?"

"I am the one keeping up with it, Jeff," replied Sarah. "Gloria has been spending a lot of time at the music building, practicing the piano, so she lets me do the calendar and call people back with dates. Also, it seems the professors are really piling on the home-work this second semester. I have missed being with you all the last few days, but I have made great progress in my accounting course and the other classes."

"And I don't know when I've had so much fun in my Chorus class and at voice lessons as I had on Thursday and Friday. Dr. Johnson is the greatest director. Practicing Mendelssohn's oratorio,

Elijah, is a thrilling experience. I can't wait till we perform it. And you all, don't forget about my television performance in February, playing two pieces written by Chopin and Liszt. You must be in the audience, praying for me. Okay, your turn, guys. Sarah and I have told you about our classes. Now you tell us about yours."

Jeff spoke first. "My economics class is a breeze, as usual. It's something I understand without even trying. I guess that's the way God made me. I inherited that business sense from my dad. And I am enjoying my history class. It used to bore me, but now I always look for God's hand in the people and events back in time. Of course, since our education at MSU is a secular education, we believers need to do some researching on our own to really understand the course of history. As we learned at BSU, the Bible is history. It is the history of the Jewish people. It is HIS STORY, the story of Jesus, really Yeshua, His Hebrew name. After Noah's flood, God populated the world again. He divided people into nations through the three sons of Noah. The people had one language, and they gathered in one place. They wanted to make a name for themselves and began building a tower to heaven for pagan worship. They did not scatter over the world like God told them to, so God had to come down and scatter them by confusing their languages. They couldn't continue building the tower. That is found in Genesis, chapters ten and eleven. Then God started with one man and his family with whom He would make covenant and through whom He would reveal Himself to the world. Abraham and his descendants through his son Isaac and grandson Jacob were chosen. Starting with Genesis, chapter twelve, God records His program for world redemption through this family. HIS STORY continues through sixty-five succeeding books of the Bible and ends in Revelation. Now we are waiting for the appearance of our Messiah from heaven to defeat evil and to rule and reign. God prepared the Jewish people for the first coming of the Messiah, and He is now preparing them for the second coming of the Messiah. And the story is written by all Jewish people except for Luke. THAT is the summary of the REAL history of the world. The best is yet to come." The friends were spellbound, listening to Jeff scope out the Bible.

"Hey, you ought to be a preacher, dude." exclaimed Pete. "Talk about keeping it simple. Even little children can understand it the way you tell it. That means I can understand it. Ha!"

Gloria had to know the schedule. "Pete, tell us what to expect today. I know we are meeting your family at the church. Then exactly what happens next?"

"I have to tell you my mom is really excited about meeting the love of my life, Sarah Zipporah Bernstein, and also meeting you, Gloria. My dad is, too. Mom is going to do like your mother did, Jeff. She is going to 'put on the dog' for our noon meal, which in the South we call 'dinner,' not 'lunch.' Even though she works full time in the travel agency with Dad, she is a great housewife, too. All week she has been preparing dishes and putting them in the freezer. She will get a little help from Camille and Carola. Carola is the wife of Melvin. Elinor, the youngest, will help her, too. We have a banquet-sized table, so the twelve of us can be together. As for the schedule today, we will arrive at church early and get seats close to the front. One pew won't hold us all. Mom gave permission to Edward and Elinor to sit with their friends. You will like the music, Gloria. We have a great choir, and the organist will probably blow us out of there. There aren't too many preliminaries, because our preacher is 'chomping at the bits' every Sunday to preach. His name is Brother Gene Wagner. He grabs your attention, spitting out his words like a gatling gun!"

Sarah held Pete's hand. "This is so new to me. But what I am looking forward to the most is being with your family, Pete. You have met my sister Chaya, and you were with Max in Israel. You seemed to feel comfortable around them, and I hope I have the same experience with your family. I have enjoyed the Adaton services, too, but I am a little nervous about a big formal downtown church. My family would be shocked to know how I am moving in thoroughly Gentile circles these days. Pete, I hope we can go back to temple before long. I don't want to forget my roots."

"Aw, you know I want you to feel comfortable. Of course, we will attend the temple services whenever you want to. I want to make you happy, sweetheart."

"Here we are, folks," said Jeff, as he pulled in a parking spot at the church. Pete led them to the front door, so they could get a bulletin and be greeted by some of the deacons. Pete and Jeff noticed the people who were already seated, craning their necks to give the four attractive young people the once over. Faces broke out in smiles, as the four friends made their way down the aisle to join Pete's family on the third middle row. Gloria flashed her brilliant smile, and some of the women nodded their heads in recognition. It was truly impressive to see all those blonde heads of the Carson family, thought Sarah, as they approached.

The sanctuary was bustling, with people coming in and making loud conversation. Pete introduced his friends. Each one of his family members stood to shake hands. Britt and Camille hugged Sarah and Gloria. Elsa Carson also reached out and hugged them. Edward and Elinor walked across the aisle from where they were seated to meet Sarah and Gloria. Since Jeff had already met the entire family, he stood back and enjoyed watching the greetings. Pete's friends made oohs and ahs over the huge, gorgeous sanctuary. The majestic organ startled everyone with a Bach prelude played at maximum volume. All were seated. The Sunday morning worship service at First Baptist Church of Columbus, Mississippi, was now in progress. Sarah reached for Pete's hand and looked up at him for comfort. She was scared.

CHAPTER NINETEEN

PETE'S SURPRISE

I t was 12:30, and everyone was seated at the big dining table in the Carson home, with Lars Carson at the head and Elsa, the Carson matriarch, at the other end. Mr. Carson stood and made a formal welcome to Pete's guests. "Dear Jeff, Gloria, and Sarah, we are delighted you joined us for church this morning and now are having dinner with the Carson clan. We are an even twelve, and I think that is significant. Three of us are Jewish, reminding us of the **twelve** tribes of Israel. This is a high honor to have the descendants of Abraham, Isaac, and Jacob sharing a meal with us. I am also reminded of the **twelve** disciples of Jesus, our Lord and Savior. In the last book of the Bible and in the next to last chapter, we read about the Holy City, the New Jerusalem, which has **twelve** gates of pearl with the **twelve** tribes' names inscribed. The **twelve** foundations of the City wall have the names of the **twelve** apostles, who were also Jewish."[58] Mr. Carson paused. "Amazing! I did not know I was going to say that. God must have put the words in my mouth. I am not a preacher, but I want to say something else and then say the blessing before our food gets cold. Ever since Melvin was in high school and had an assignment to read Corrie ten Boom's book, *The Hiding Place*, every member of our family has read it. We all are well aware that our Messiah came through the Jews, and we have memorized the verses of Abraham's call in Genesis, the **twelfth** chapter. Hey! There is another **twelve**." The whole group smiled. No one minded that Mr. Carson was taking so long. "Anyway, we know that whoever blesses Abraham's descendants, the Jews, like

Corrie ten Boom's family did, will **receive** a blessing, so I want to hold my hands out to Jeff, Gloria, and Sarah right now and bless them." The rest of the family did likewise, saying, 'We bless you, our new Jewish friends.' "Okay, I will conclude with praising the Lord that through the Jews all the families of the earth are blessed, according to God's promise to Abraham. And we know that fulfillment is in our Messiah Jesus, the Seed of Abraham, who was born of Mary, a Jewish girl."

Carola, Melvin's wife, stood up and applauded. Everyone joined her, smiling at Mr. Carson and clapping. She said, "Now let's give a special embrace to Jeff, Gloria, and Sarah, as a way of honoring them, and then Mr. Lars can say the blessing over the food." Love flowed throughout the room with the embracing and kind words.

Lars said a short blessing. All were seated, except for Elsa, Camille, Carola, and Elinor, who headed for the kitchen and then brought the food out. Dishes were passed around the table until everyone's plate was full. Elinor, having already asked about choice of drinks, poured iced sweet tea and water. The food was delicious, but more attention was paid to the interesting conversation. Elsa began, "Sarah, Pete has filled us in a little on your life, and Jeff has told us about himself and Gloria when he visited us recently. But we would like to hear **you** tell about **your** family and how you decided to come to Mississippi State University."

Pete gave Sarah's hand a squeeze. "Before Sarah speaks, I think it should be pointed out that she has the distinct privilege of having the same name as Abraham's wife, and her name means 'princess.' If Abraham is the 'Father of faith' as the Apostle Paul writes about, that makes Sarah the 'Mother of faith,' don't you think? And Sarah had a baby at ninety years of age! Not only that, but she was gorgeous, because two kings took her for their harems."

Sarah was embarrassed but still couldn't help but laugh at her adorable man who was 'pitching' her to his family. What better advocate could she have? "My goodness, Pete has a biased opinion, showing the truth that love is blind." Pete was beaming, hanging on every word of Sarah's. "I have a large family, but I am closest to my sister Chaya, who lives fairly close to Gloria's parents in Long Island, New York. I am living with them now when I'm not at school. Chaya has her first baby due in May. Max, my brother-in-law, is a dear man. He and Pete became friends on the flight to Israel. I think Pete already told you that my parents, Dr. Nathan and Naomi Bernstein, were killed in a suicide bombing in Jerusalem. That's why I am at MSU. Being the youngest in the family and the most vulnerable concerning anti-Semitism and terrorism in New York City, my family sent me South. On two specific occasions Pete has protected me from attacks over the last months."

The Carsons gasped, but no one ventured to ask for an explanation. Jeff decided to change the subject, taking a cue from the Holy Spirit. "Gloria and I are indebted to Sarah, because it was through her that I learned I am Jewish, and Gloria learned why her parents are not showing their Jewishness to any degree. I told you some of my story, when you had me for dinner that night. We four have had a fast friendship ever since Gloria and Sarah became roommates. As you know, Pete is my roommate. We call our group the 'Holy Rollers,' one reason being that we are always traveling and having adventures for the Lord. He has directed and 'set us apart' for His purposes. That's the meaning of the word 'holy.' Sarah took us to worship at B'nai Israel temple here, and she really has taught us a lot about our Jewish roots. The most recent thing I have learned from her is that there are basically three kinds of faith groups in Judaism – orthodox, conservative, and reform. Sarah was brought up in the Orthodox Jewish group, the most biblical of the groups, which adheres to the Law of Moses. The temple here in Columbus is in the reform group, which is the most liberal. Conservative is in the middle. Did I say it right, Sarah?"

"You surely did, Jeff. I will say one more thing about my heritage. I am of the Ashkenazi Jews, which come from Germany and central and eastern Europe. The Sephardic Jews are basically from the Middle Eastern countries. In Israel, the modern Hebrew language form everybody speaks is Sephardic. In New York, we from Ashkenazi roots call the Sabbath, 'Shabbos.' It's a Yiddish pronunciation. Yiddish is more like a German dialect, but it uses a Hebrew alphabet, and it has three million speakers today.[59] The Sephardic pronunciation of the Sabbath is 'Shabbat.' We had a glorious time in Israel, saying 'Shabbat shalom,' on the Saturday we were there. Oh, by the way, since you Carsons are of Swedish descent, you may be interested to know that Yiddish is an official minority language in Sweden. And Sweden is a major source of children's literature, cartoons, and music videos in Yiddish. Now, I will end my little speech. Thanks for being patient, but I really do enjoy sharing my heritage with Gentiles."

Jeff had to set the record straight. "Pete and I have been working on our Yankee sweethearts, trying to teach them redneck dialect. Gloria and Sarah keep saying 'you guys,' when it is so much easier to say *y'all*. In Israel every time they said, 'Shabbat shalom,' Pete and I would respond, 'Yes, shalom y'all.'" Pete and Jeff laughed, while Gloria and Sarah rolled their eyes.

Melvin spoke up. "Sarah, your roots are from eastern and central Europe, you said. Do you know which country the Bernsteins came from?"

"We came from Hungary," Sarah answered.

Pete stood up. "Folks, I love all this sharing, but I have to interrupt. Let me say, Mom, your meal was exquisite. See, my plate is clean. Can we all give a round of applause to Mom for working so hard to provide this good meal today?" All obliged with prolonged clapping. Elsa grinned from ear to ear. "And now, I have something to share that cannot wait another minute. Mom, will it be all right for us to have our dessert and coffee a little later?"

"Sure, son. We are on tiptoe to hear what you are about to share. Go ahead."

Pete stood in front of Sarah. "Please come over here so everyone can see us, Sarah." Jeff, Gloria, and the Carson family moved their chairs in order to have a full view. Pete brought Sarah side by side with him, his arm encircling her. "The Lord showed me that now is the time to make public the divine destiny He has for Sarah and me, and He wants it to be shown in front of my family and closest friends." Sarah put her hand over her mouth, and hot tears began to pour down her cheeks. Gloria began to cry. Lars and Elsa's eyes got big, and a collective gasp went up from Pete's siblings and the two wives. Jeff's chest puffed out in pride. Pete's heart was about to thump out of his chest. He took a deep breath and began his speech to Sarah, looking tenderly into her wet eyes. "My darling Sarah, you are the joy of my life. Ever since I met you, every day is worth living. You have brought out the best in me, and because of your influence and the fact that Jesus is living inside of me, I am becoming the man God created me to be. I cannot imagine ever being apart from you. Just like God told Adam that Eve would be 'bone of his bone and flesh of his flesh, and the two would become one,' I am hoping you will say 'yes' to that destiny." Pete already had the little ring box in his hand. He got down on one knee, held out the diamond ring to Sarah, and asked in a broken voice, with love pouring from his eyes, "Will you marry me?"

Sarah was sobbing and couldn't speak. Jeff, Gloria, and Pete were silently praying that she would find her voice and say "yes." Sarah took the ring, and Pete slid it on her finger. Sarah leaped into his arms, and buried her face in his neck. Pete said, "Honey, I can't hear you. Did you say yes?"

Sarah yelled, "Yes! Yes! Yes! I will marry you. I love you with all my heart. You are my *BASHERT!*" No one had a clue what the word *bashert* meant, but they knew it was good, very good. "This is a gorgeous ring, Pete. Thank you, thank you. It shines brightly like my love for you."

Jeff remembered the night he proposed to Gloria, and how Pete urged him to kiss her. Now he would return the favor: "Kiss her, Pete! Now is the time. **There's no better time**. Kiss her!" Only Pete and Jeff knew the significance of Jeff's words. And Pete was very glad to oblige. Not caring who may be embarrassed, he gripped Sarah so hard in his arms that her feet left the floor, and he kissed her more passionately than he ever had before. Sarah could not stop the delightful squeal slipping out of her mouth. Everyone in the room had chill bumps and vicariously felt the kiss.

Elsa was exhilarated. There could not have been a more successful family dinner with this startling proposal of marriage in their midst. She went over to Lars, and they stood together. After waiting for the newly-engaged young couple to savor each other, Lars said, "Son, we heartily approve of your choice for a wife, and Elsa and I give you and Sarah our unreserved blessing. Elsa added, "Yes, we are so happy for you. Let us continue celebrating with dessert and coffee in the living room."

Each member of the family lined up to congratulate Pete and Sarah and to hug them both. Soon everyone was comfortably seated in the living room. Elsa, Elinor, Camille, and Carola brought little lap trays out and the pie and coffee.

CHAPTER TWENTY

SARAH'S SURPRISE

Intimate conversation and adoring looks between Pete and Sarah as they ate the pie drew the attention of the family, as each looked for an opportune moment to ask a question. Melvin could hold back no longer. "Sarah, I have a question, actually two questions. The first one is probably what everybody here wants an answer for. Please tell us what that word means that you said when Pete proposed. You said he was your **bashert**."

Sarah's laughter was melodious. Sheer joy had flooded her heart, and she felt drunk. It took an effort to return to her usual serious disposition. "Oh, that word came right out of my heart, not my head. I should have realized none of you understood. I will be glad to tell you. Pete is my 'soul mate.' I know you understand that phrase. But I will tell you more. In the Talmud we learn that forty days before a male child is conceived, a voice from heaven announces whose daughter he is going to marry, literally a match made in heaven. In Yiddish, this perfect match is called 'bashert,' a word meaning *fate* or **destiny**. In the New York newspapers you can often see in the listing of Jewish personal ads one that reads, 'Looking for my bashert.'"[60] Sarah felt so drunk, she got tickled and couldn't stop laughing for a while.

Pete intervened. "Folks, this is not the Sarah I know. And I swear she has not had a drop of any alcohol. But I, for one, am deliriously happy that she is this full of joy. You know, sometimes Orthodox Jews can be so serious, afraid that they will break one little law in the Torah. But she and I are both learning that 'Where the Spirit of the Lord is, there is liberty'[61] and also, 'If the Son makes you free, you shall be free indeed.'[62] Yep, marrying Sarah is my divine destiny. I am her **bashert**, and she is mine!"

Gloria looked at Jeff and winked. "Thanks for explaining, Sarah. Now I know my second Yiddish word, and that is what Jeff and I are to each other. He is my *bashert*, and I am his. Also, I want to correct something you said, Pete. Jeff and I are calling ourselves Messianic Jews, since we met our Messiah Yeshua; so even though Sarah has an Orthodox Jewish background, she is now a Messianic Jew, having also believed in Jesus."

Sarah had such peace in her heart that her normal inhibitions were suspended. She went over to Jeff and Gloria and kissed both of them on the cheek and embraced them. "Dearest friends, yes, I do have a new identity as the bride of Messiah. I and all Jews who believe in Yeshua are considered to be Messianic Jews. Another description could be *Hebrew Christians*. Now I want to teach you more. I am happy to inform you, Jeff, Gloria, and Pete, that the four of us have begun the process of marriage. The Jewish engagement or betrothal period is called *kiddushin*. In the Orthodox tradition we are considered legally married right now. This is the time that we are being sanctified, or set apart. The betrothal period used to last a full year, but, thankfully, in modern times the first and second part are now combined in one ceremony. The **second** part of the marriage process is called *nisuin*. We will stand under the *chuppah*, a tallit stretched over four poles, symbolizing our house. Under this wedding canopy we say seven blessings. The groom will smash a glass with his foot, which is a remembrance of the destruction of the temple. Oh, there is much, much more, but I will tell about it at another time. Anyway, then the couple goes to a private room to consummate the marriage, after which there is a great celebration of food, music, and dancing. Jewish weddings are spine-tingling events!"

Gloria was elated and had to share. "Sarah, your description is fantastic and fits with what Jesus said to His disciples about his upcoming departure back to heaven, 'Let not your hearts be troubled…. In my Father's house are many mansions, or rooms,… and **I go to prepare a place for you**… and **I will come again** and receive you unto Myself, that where I am you may be also.'[63] I looked it up on the internet and found a teaching about the Jewish wedding. After the betrothal, the groom usually went away for about a year. During that time he would build on to his father's house. He was '**preparing a place**,' like Jesus said. Since he was eager to go get his bride and bring her back there to start their marriage, he was liable to cut corners. So the father had to be the one to decide when the room or the house was ready. That is why, in speaking about the time of His return for His bride, Jesus said, 'Of that day and hour no one knows, not even the angels in heaven, nor the Son, but only the Father.'[64]

All in the room were amazed at what they were hearing. Talking about the subject of the Jewish wedding continued for about fifteen minutes, with Gloria and Sarah fielding the questions and sharing their knowledge. Even Elinor was drawn in and asked questions.

Melvin knew it was time to change the subject. "Sarah, all this is very interesting, and I have learned a lot, but I have a second question for you, concerning the origin of your family in Hungary. First, let me say that your laughing jag really got me going. I am finding out what a fun person you can be, and how perfect you are for Pete, also a fun-loving person. It certainly is true that 'a merry heart doeth good like a medicine.' That's from Proverbs 17:22. Okay, here goes. You said you were from Hungary. Do you know if any of your ancestors went through the Holocaust?"

Sarah sat back and thought a minute, composing herself. "Melvin, it's true that laughter is like a medicine. Thank you for allowing me to 'let down my hair,' so to speak. I truly am happier than I have ever been in my life. But I see it's time to 'come back down to earth.' This question gets me sober fast. Yes, Melvin, I had family members who went through the Holocaust. One of my relatives had his diary published. He was fortunate that he escaped."

"Oh, he escaped? Did his whole family escape? Please give me some of the details. Then I will tell you why I am so interested."

"Melvin, to tell you all the contents of my relative's diary would take not only today but maybe a week or two. But I happen to have a copy of his diary in my purse. Here, I will read you a part of this very dramatic account that centers around one man, about whom books have been written, a Swedish hero. I have been reminded of him lately because of your family's Swedish descent. Let's see… Okay, here's an exciting part. This man helped my great-uncle and many in his family to escape death. Uncle Boris has written, 'The Russians were closing in on Budapest. In January 1945, the Red Army had taken the last road out of the city. Trapped inside were Nazi and Arrow Cross gunmen, the Jewish captives, and this Swedish hero. The Arrow Cross was a Hungarian anti-Semitic group, which began a reign of terror at that point. One of their number, Father Andras Kun, directed a mass execution of Jewish patients in a hospital. A woman of the Arrow Cross used a sub-machine gun. Father Kun pointed his pistol at the Jews and said, 'In the holy name of Jesus Christ, fire!'"[65]

Camille couldn't stop herself. She practically screamed, "That man, Father Kun, was a devil, definitely not a Christian! I have read about the Nazis claiming to be exterminating the Jews in the name of Christ. That is a lie from the pit of hell. They were Satanists, not Christians!"

Britt explained, "Maybe all of you don't know the tragic history of the church, beginning in the third and fourth centuries, and continuing even today in sermons from mainline churches that are filled with replacement theology."

Jeff interrupted, "Oh, yes, I know about it. Last October I bought Dr. Michael Brown's book, *Our Hands are Stained with Blood: the Tragic Story about the Church and the Jewish People.*[66] What I have read so far will curl your hair. Even Martin Luther, the 'Father of the Reformation,' joined the Jew-haters. Replacement theology says that God is finished with the Jews as His chosen people and has transferred all His promises to the Church. He has left the Jews with the curses! Isn't that awful? They need to realize that if God doesn't keep His promises to the Jewish people, He may not keep His promises to the Church. Thankfully, none of the churches we have attended so far have been deceived by replacement theology. In fact, Adaton Baptist, the church we attend the most, has a deep love for the Jewish people and Israel. They have welcomed us with open arms. But, I didn't mean to interrupt Sarah's story. Please continue, Sarah."

"Well, it needed to be said, because this anti-Semitism within the church has been a stumbling block, keeping the Jews from recognizing Yeshua as their Messiah. But I will go on. I am not ready yet to tell you the name of the Swedish hero who saved my family, so bear with me. I will resume reading. 'Father Kun had a dead or alive poster made up for this hero. The person who found him and shot him on sight would receive a reward.' Okay, I will use his first name, Raoul."

Melvin became agitated, and Sarah noticed. "I know you want to say something, Melvin, but please wait until I have finished reading." Melvin nodded his head, but he had a wondrous expression on his face. "'Budapest was going to fall to the Russians. Adolph Eichmann escaped, but he left an order for the SS to annihilate the 70,000 Jews in the central ghetto before the Red Army arrived. Ten to fifteen thousand Jews not in the ghetto were murdered in the final siege. Raoul had left his office in the Swedish legation and was hiding all over the city, making all kinds of deals to keep the Jews safe. He had stored food in a warehouse and was feeding the Jewish community. Food was also the only bargaining chip he had left with which to bribe the Arrow Cross. He demanded they stop attacks on his 'protected Jews,' and for food they agreed. But the Nazi soldiers had not forgotten Eichmann's final command. Raoul had an informant inside the Arrow Cross who sent him a message through a Christian go-between by the name of Szabo. He found Raoul in his hiding place and told him that all the Jews in the central ghetto would be killed within the hour. It was too late to do anything. However, Raoul's former successes gave him confidence that it was never too late. He had a brilliant idea. It was one minute to midnight. He hurriedly wrote a letter with the Swedish royal seal and said to Szabo, 'Only one man can stop this.' Raoul sent Szabo with the letter to SS General August Schmidstuber. He said, 'Tell Schmidstuber if this pogrom proceeds and the Jews die, I will personally testify at the War Crimes Tribunal and see that he is hanged for murder.' Nazi and fascist gunmen continued to assemble in front of the central ghetto. Finally, Schmidstuber ended the suspense by picking up his telephone and cancelling the slaughter. Two days later the Russian troops arrived and found that all 70,000 Jews in the central ghetto had survived!' My great-uncle, Boris Bernstein, was one of them! And he, some of his family members, and all the Jews were indebted to one man from Sweden, Raoul Wallenberg."[67]

Everyone began to talk at once. Sarah couldn't field all the questions. She looked at Melvin. "Melvin, I could see you were itching to tell us something when I mentioned the name Raoul. Are you ready to share?"

Melvin was exhilarated, and he moved forward to the edge of his seat. "I certainly am. I haven't even told Carola all the things I have discovered in my Carson family genealogical research. Thank you for the perfect introduction, Sarah. I am excited to broadcast the news. Carson family, Jeff, Gloria, and Sarah – and you Sarah will soon be a Carson, too – here is the revelation of the hour! Ta da! **Our family is kin to the famous Swedish hero, Raoul Wallenberg!** I planned to share this news, but not necessarily today. Then when Sarah told how her relative was saved by the actions of our ancestor, I knew this was the perfect time."

The four friends looked at each other and grinned. Gloria blurted out, "This is a **God-incidence**, and one of the highest order. The tapestry that our Lord is weaving of our lives and showing His divine destinies for all our families represented in this room is **staggering!**"

CHAPTER TWENTY-ONE

GAME CHANGER

All in the room were rapt with attention as Melvin spoke. "First of
all, Raoul Wallenberg was a blond like us." Melvin paused
to let that sink in. Everyone smiled. "He never married, and at 33
years of age, in Budapest, he was arrested by the Russians and sent
to the Gulag, never to be seen again. So he had no descendants. But
the Carsons are descended from someone **else** in his family. Listen,
I have even more startling news. In my research I found this quote
by Wallenberg himself, and I was floored. He bragged, 'A person
like me, who is both a Wallenberg and **half-Jewish,** can never be
defeated.'[68] Raoul was blonde, and he was a Lutheran, so he didn't
appear to be Jewish, no matter what he said. He was considered to
be a Gentile because Yad VaShem, the Holocaust Museum in Jerusalem, in 1963, recognized him as 'righteous among the nations,'
and 'nations' in Hebrew means goyim – Gentiles. Remember
that Corrie ten Boom also was recognized as a 'righteous Gentile'
by Yad VaShem in 1967. I read in another place that Wallenberg
was **one-quarter** Jewish. In Wikipedia, it is claimed that he was
one-sixteenth Jewish through his great-great grandfather on his
mother's side. He could have been exaggerating when he claimed
to be half-Jewish. Either way, he was very proud of his Jewishness."

Edward had listened to every word that Sarah and Melvin had
said, and his interest was growing by the minute. "So, if Wallenberg
was part-Jewish, and we are kin to him, does that mean that we, the
Carsons, are also part-Jewish? Anyway, we can't be related to him

directly, so hurry and tell us who we are related to in the Wallenberg family. Please tell us more about that family in Sweden."

"Thanks for your question, Edward. If a trace of Jewish ancestry makes one Jewish, then the answer is yes, the Carsons are Jewish. I will let you all decide." said Melvin. "I am not nearly through with my research, but I will tell you what I have found out so far. Our family line comes through Raoul Wallenberg's mother, Maria "Maj" Sofia Wising, who was born in 1891 and died in 1979. Maj's great grandfather was a Jew named Michael Benedicks who settled in Sweden in 1780 and converted to Christianity. He became a jeweler and eventually the financial advisor to the king.[69] I was tracing our family lines through Mother and Dad and found the Benedicks name on Dad's side. I kept looking, and it led me to the name Raoul Wallenberg. I am ashamed to say that his name did not ring a bell. But as I kept reading, I realized what an honor it is that we are related to him. At first, when I stumbled upon these facts, I was shaken. I had to examine my heart to see if I had a prejudice against the Jews." Melvin became very emotional and looked at Pete and Sarah. "You know what, I had no interaction with Jewish people, Pete, until you invited Jeff over for dinner last Friday, a week ago. And now today, as I am getting to know you, Sarah and Gloria, and also you, Jeff, I have been really impressed with the high caliber of you Jewish people. Whatever trace of prejudice I may have had, it is totally gone." Tears came to Melvin's eyes.

Carola gave Melvin a tissue and held his hand. "I have to echo what Melvin said. It is a real honor for the Carson family to be part-Jewish, even if it is only a trace. Whenever we have our first child, Melvin, if it is a boy, maybe we could name him 'Raoul.'"

"Hold it, Carola" Pete interjected. "I think Sarah and I should have first dibs on that name. It would make more sense for a hundred per cent Jewish mother to give her son that name, in my opinion. But, I tell you what, whoever gives birth to a baby boy **first** can have the name."

"Deal, little brother," said Melvin. That's magnanimous of you. However, Carola and I have a head start on you and Sarah. So start choosing your alternate name." Everyone had a good laugh. "Now, let me continue with our ancestor's story. Here is something astounding. The Wallenbergs were nicknamed the 'Rockefellers of Sweden.' That alone proves they were Jewish, because God has given the Jewish people a talent for making money."

Jeff had to interrupt again. "I know something about that. My dad, Jeffrey Mendelssohn Quentin Senior, recently found out he was Jewish. As a matter of fact, he had never known what his middle initial stood for until about two weeks ago, and I was present at the time. Y'all may know that Felix Mendelssohn was a famous composer, and we are descended from him. His family was Jewish but chose to hide it because of wanting to advance professionally in an anti-Semitic environment. Anyway, not only does Dad have a talent for making money, but **I do also.** I found this out when Dr. Michael Brown, the foremost Messianic Jewish apologist in the world, ministered to me. I felt so honored. He said, and he was quoting from Deuteronomy 8:18, that God has given me the power to get wealth in order to establish his covenant. I was bowled over!"

Pete was eager to put his two-cents worth in. "Roommate, since you are a Jew who knows how to make money, and I am a Swedish 'Rockefeller,' I think you should bring me in as a partner in your Quentin Unlimited Services. Don't you agree?" Jeff playfully punched Pete in the arm.

Elinor was also becoming more interested in the conversation and had her own question. "So if I am Jewish, and it gets out at school, how do you think it will affect my popularity? In case you didn't know it, I have quite a following, and I don't think Jews have such a good reputation around these parts, know what I mean? In fact, I overheard two girls talking at lunch the other day about the Jews. Something in the news had caught their attention. Dorothy said, 'My parents call them 'Christ-killers.' Joann chimed in, 'Yeah, and they have horns!' I was horrified, since I knew that my brother had a Jewish roommate and was going with a Jewish girl. I kept quiet, but it did make me angry!"

Lars tried to bring closure to this subject, but first he wanted to correct something. "Rabbi Boruch Clinton said this: 'It began with a mistranslation of Exodus 34:29 – '... and Moses didn't know that his face shone when God spoke with him.' The Hebrew word for the verb 'shone' is *karan* and is phonetically close to the word *keren,* which can mean **horn**. The error was compounded by the Italian artist, Michelangelo, in his sculpture of Moses, which portrays our leader with two horns.'" [70]

Melvin resumed sharing information about Raoul Wallenberg. "I want to tell you more about this heroic man. The Wallenbergs had a banking empire. Raoul's cousins, Jacob and Marcus Wallenberg, founded the Enskilda Bank in Sweden, and they had trade relations with the German government. Claims have been made that they collaborated with the Nazis in the war effort. [71] But Raoul did not participate in their banking business. The Americans, specifically President Roosevelt, requested that Raoul Wallenberg be assigned by the Swedish Ministry for Foreign Affairs to its legation in Budapest. There was a condition. Sweden would do this in exchange for a lessening of American diplomatic pressure on neutral Sweden to curtail their nation's free-trade policies toward Germany. [72] I don't want to give a history lesson here. Hey, Elinor, don't fall asleep!"

Elinor snapped to attention. "Melvin the professor, you need to quit boring us. I have to get on the phone with Julie. May I be excused?" Elsa moved over to Elinor and whispered in her ear. Elinor huffed and puffed, then pasted a smile on her face.

"Elinor, I promise I am only going to share one more short story about Raoul Wallenberg. Then you can go call Julie," cajoled Melvin. "Well, everyone, let me finish. If you want to read a good book about Raoul, I recommend *Lost Hero* by Dannie Smith. Anyway, you know what first inspired Raoul to rescue the Jews in Hungary? It was a movie, *"Pimpernel" Smith,* a 1941 British anti-Nazi thriller, produced and directed by its star Leslie Howard.[73] It was shown to Raoul and his sister Nina in a private screening. Raoul said that kind of rescue effort is what he wanted to do. As far as a movie being a prime motivator in Wallenberg's life, I say we should never underestimate the power of drama to shape lives. Well, I am through. What I have shared shows the significance of the marriage proposal we have witnessed here today. Pete now knows his ancestral link with the Jews, making him Sarah's true *bashert*, and she is his. I agree with Gloria that it was their destiny to be drawn to each other. And I love her description of God weaving a tapestry of our lives together. And now the unveiling of the Carson family roots makes this an even bigger **God incidence.**"

Gloria had been mesmerized, hearing what Sarah and what Melvin shared. Now she came out of her reverie, declaring, "The music that fits in here today is Handel's 'Hallelujah Chorus' from the *Messiah*. It is blasting forth inside my head, but we need a choir and an orchestra to perform it. Nevertheless, I will sing the last few lines, if you won't think I am *meshuganah.*" Gloria laughed and laughed. "I see question marks on every one of your faces except Sarah. Tell them, Sarah."

Sarah started laughing, too. "Yes, I was thinking that very same thing, Gloria. You ARE 'meshuganah.' You have done impossible feats, but there is no way you can sing that music as a solo. People, Gloria is not **crazy**, which is the meaning of the first Yiddish word I taught her – 'meshuganah.' She simply has that much faith. Go for it, Gloria."

"Oh, don't mind me, everyone. I'm over it now. Instead of singing, I will simply 'amen' what has been shared here today with one word, a word that is the same in every language. It is Hebrew for 'Praise the Lord!' I am going to count to three, and let's all shout it together. Ready? One, two, threeeee – **HALLELUJAH!**"

Elinor was the only one in the room who did not join in. Her dad noticed it, went over to her, and encircled her with his arms, hugging her tightly. She looked up in his face with a grateful smile.

CHAPTER TWENTY-TWO

DOUBLE DESTINIES

UNION BUILDING
WEDNESDAY, JANUARY 15

Jeff and Pete found a private area in the Union Building and waited on Gloria and Sarah to join them. The lunch crowd had cleared out, but the food bar was still open. "How have your classes been this week?" asked Jeff.

"What classes?" joked Pete. "I have been walking on air since we left my house on Sunday, rehearsing all the things that transpired and savoring mine and Sarah's new identity as an engaged couple. Some very big decisions are ahead of us, but I am enjoying having my head in the clouds and do not want to come back down to earth. So, to answer your question, I have to say that every class has been a triumph. Wait, change that. My days of lying are over now. I will rephrase it – every day has been a blur."

"Now, roommate, I can certainly identify with you. We have hardly talked all week, and we haven't been with Gloria and Sarah, abiding by their wishes that we give first place to our education. You said yourself, that's why we are at MSU, to get an education."

"Well, Jeff, the classes have been painless, and I have done the work required, making notes in class, turning in homework, et cetera. But my heart has been consumed with Sarah, thinking ahead to our marriage, where we will live after college, and the kind of livelihood I might provide her."

"I have to say that I am like you. I have attended class in the body, but I am not there in spirit. My heart is wrapped up in my glorious fiancée, thinking ahead just like you. Isn't that something? Let me ask you, does Israel enter your thoughts as a place y'all might live? I'm talking about after we graduate from college."

"Yes, bro. I have turned that over in my mind. Now that I may have the proof of Jewish heritage, I could qualify for citizenship. You know, we really are very young to be making a radical decision like that. Speaking of being young, I haven't found out Sarah's birthday yet, but my twentieth birthday is coming up in March. When is your birthday, and have you found out Gloria's birthday? Right now the four of us are still teenagers. Now **that** is hard to believe. I certainly do not feel like a teenager. At least becoming twenty will take us out of that category."

"I turn twenty in April. I think Gloria's birthday is in May. That is hardly a factor, however. I have another question. Since we have been doing everything together, do you think we will continue our Holy Roller group after we are married? I know you haven't had time to talk to Sarah about it. I guess you don't have a projected date for the wedding either, do you? Wait... here come Gloria and Sarah. We need to talk over these things with them. I am sure they have been talking together about it."

Gloria and Sarah are all smiles as they meet Jeff and Pete with outstretched arms. "Hey, fellas. Oh, how I have missed you guys. Oops, I meant to say 'Y'ALL,' not 'you guys,' now that I am in training to be Mrs. Jeff Quentin, a southern belle wife," beamed Gloria.

Pete picked Sarah up off the floor and hugged her tightly. "Well, I do believe that you have grown more beautiful since I last saw you, babe."

The four friends went to the buffet to get dessert and coffee. The Union was practically deserted. Jeff opened the conversation. "I am so glad we don't have classes this afternoon. We have plenty of time to talk about our future before we go to BSU tonight. Pete and I have hardly spoken since Sunday, trying to concentrate on our courses, but we were just talking now about our future with

146

y'all as married couples. I will launch out with the first question to consider. Have you girls been talking about our weddings and where you would like to set up housekeeping?"

Sarah began. "Well, the first order of business for me after you guys dropped us off Sunday was to call Chaya and tell her that you proposed to me and gave me a beautiful ring, Pete."

"Of course, that's exactly what you should have done. I hope she was happy about it. Was she?" asked Pete.

"To be honest, I knew she might not be fully in agreement. Max was standing there, and she told him in a somber voice. I could hear their conversation. I was surprised that Max said he was glad, and he encouraged Chaya to say, 'Congratulations.' Then she came back on the line and did that, but still her voice didn't sound very happy. I said, 'Chaya, I am convinced that Pete is my *bashert*, and I am his. After he proposed to me his brother Melvin told us he had found Jewish ancestry in the Carson family line.' When I said that, her voice changed. She said, 'That's wonderful! I can't wait to hear more about it.' Then she said, 'Well, if you are going to get married, we must arrange for Pete to meet our whole family.' I agreed and said that maybe it would be possible for us to come to New York during our spring break. She said she would talk to all our siblings and see what could be arranged. I told her that Pete and I would pray about it and ask HaShem to work it out within His plans for us. She paused a few minutes and relayed our conversation to Max. I could hear him saying, 'That is GREAT!' Then she came back on the line, and her voice had lost every trace of disappointment. She said she loved me and to give Pete their love." Sarah's face was wreathed in smiles, and her friends rejoiced with her.

"And after that, Sarah and I turned cartwheels all up and down the hall on the third floor!" joked Gloria. "God is giving us favor, you all… I mean 'y'all.' Our lives are unfolding within God's divine destinies for us. This has happened to Sarah, but we are together as the Holy Rollers, so it has happened to all four of us. Do you agree?"

"Well, we have talked about it before, when we first began to call ourselves that," said Jeff. "We said 'All for one, and one for all.' We have seen God orchestrating our lives. That doesn't mean we don't have decisions to make individually and also as couples, but when we submit our plans to Him, He causes it all to work out. And so far our lives have been intertwined. Maybe the Lord wants us to keep our group going as two married couples **together**. Pete and I were talking about that possibility before you walked in."

"Hey, I have an idea," said Pete, thoughtfully. "Could it be we have **DOUBLE destinies**? Maybe we are supposed to have a **double** wedding." Pete sat back and looked to see how his comment had affected the others.

Gloria cleared her throat, and began to speak quietly, almost conspiratorially. "You won't believe it, guys, but Sarah and I talked about the four of us having a **double** wedding. Jeff, what do **you** think about it?"

"Honey, do you remember when we visited your parents last Thanksgiving, and one day we were sitting in your bedroom, talking about getting married? I remember exactly what you said. You said, 'I envisioned us marrying this summer and applying for married housing on the campus.' Then I said I was thinking the same thing, but I added to the vision. I said, 'Let's do it, and let's go on our honeymoon to Israel!' You were thrilled and said, 'Let's call Sarah and Pete right now, and let's contact a travel agent and plan it.' I said, 'Wait a minute. You don't take other people with you on a honeymoon.' Then you pondered about our starting out together alone and later Pete and Sarah joining us, but they would have to get separate rooms. Then you claimed to have an **epiphany.** I didn't know what that was. You said, 'It's a revelation. Maybe Sarah and Pete will get married, too. It surely would cut down on the cost of our trip. Double occupancy price is cheaper for the rooms.' You adorable girl, so naïve and so **wonderful!** Come here. I've got to kiss you right now."

Gloria gladly went to Jeff, and they connected like magnets. Pete and Sarah were not to be outdone and fell into each other's arms. Pete's mind was flooded with ideas. "I think I just had an epiphany, too," chuckled Pete. "If all are in agreement, we should proceed with the vision you two had last Thanksgiving. Is there any reason we can't have a double wedding in June and go to Israel for our **honeymoons**? Notice I used the plural, 'honeymoons.'" Everyone laughed. "Then we could apply for married housing on the campus, if we find two suitable apartments next to each other. Or we could rent a duplex apartment off campus. That may be the best arrangement. I know of several we could look at."

"Whoa, roommate, you are making my head spin. This life-changing event of a wedding, especially a double wedding, with family and friends present is something we have got to spend a lot of time praying about. Don't y'all agree?" pleaded Jeff.

Gloria was excited. "I have to tell you something about the vision Jeff and I had that day in my house in New York. I know now it was a **true** vision. Jeff and I knew we were going to get married, but we did **not** know for sure that you, Pete and Sarah, would also be getting married. And at the time we had the vision, we did not even know we would be going to Israel **together** in only three weeks. Holy Rollers, pay attention! To me it is obvious that the Lord God is orchestrating our lives **together**. Let me hasten to add – that definitely does not mean that we won't do some things separately as couples, as well as individuals. Our group is **not** a commune. We are different so we can **make** a difference. But God has already shown us that we have a ministry together. I am going to pray about it some more, but a double wedding looks good to me. Besides, it would cut down on the enormous expense of two separate weddings. Of course, choosing the location is a serious matter when you consider how widely separated New York and Mississippi are. But you know what? I am getting more and more excited to see how the Lord will work it out. I have a feeling that it will not only be unique and maybe a 'first' in wedding history, but everyone involved will be magnificently blessed by HaShem."

Jeff took charge. "Okay, friends, this was a very fruitful discussion. Let's go back to our dorms, get our homework done and get ready to go to the Baptist Student Union tonight. I heard someone say about last week's meeting, "If that didn't bless you, then your blesser is broken!"

CHAPTER TWENTY-THREE

THREE EXCITING PHONE CALLS

Gloria and Sarah were getting ready for bed, both exuberant after the BSU meeting. "I have to quote Jeff and say, 'My blesser is certainly not broken because that meeting blessed my socks off!' Oh, Sarah, isn't it an awesome experience to testify about what God is doing in our lives? The four of us took up practically the whole hour."

"You are right, and I could have gone on and on another hour. Everyone was on the edge of their seats, and chills were all over me as I told about Pete proposing to me. And when Pete dramatically revealed his part-Jewish heritage, it looked like Gary Grayson's jaw was about to hit the floor!"

"Yes, I heard gasps going up all over the room. And when Grace Thomas said she hoped Adaton Baptist would get up a trip to Israel, I felt the Holy Spirit envelope me with His love, showing me God's approval of our Holy Rollers in a stronger way than ever. Sarah, isn't it exciting the way God is using us with our peers? We are no longer just a curiosity to them as Jewish couples, and I am including Pete in our ethnic identity. The hunger for the things of God in that room was palpable."

"Okay, roommate. What does the word 'palpable' mean?" asked Sarah.

"It means 'tangible, unmistakable or visible'. In other words it is **obvious** that our friends at the BSU want to learn more about the Holy Spirit, God's Word, and about the Jewish roots of the church, about Israel, about everything that I am bubbling over to tell them." Gloria got so emotional that she fell on the bed and dissolved into tears.

Sarah went over to her, thinking she would comfort her, but when she touched Gloria, she broke out into laughter. "Gloria, what is happening to us? Are we going crazy? Are we meshuganah? You are crying, and I am laughing!"

"Oh, think nothing of it, Sarah. We are living the normal Christian, or should I say 'Messianic Jewish,' life! **WE** are not the ones who are crazy. **Normal** Christians should be excited about life **in the Spirit.** It's the only way to live, if our Messiah Yeshua is living **inside** us, don't you agree?"

"Well, now that you put it that way, I have to say YES, I agree. I wonder if Jeff and Pete are having this kind of conversation in their room. Gloria, I must have an outlet for all this excitement."

The phone rang.

Gloria answered. "Hello. This is Gloria….. Oh, Pastor James. I am surprised to get your call. Of course, we four are planning to be at Adaton on Sunday morning….. Come early, did you say? Ten o'clock? …. (Gloria's voice got louder.) Of course, I will ask the others, but I know they feel just like I do and would consider it an honor to teach a class. Thank you, Pastor James. We love your church, and if I don't call you back, I can assure you we will arrive at 9:45 on Sunday morning. See you then. Shalom." Gloria hung up the phone and sat on the side of her bed, trying to catch her breath.

Sarah's eyes got big. "I had **just** said I needed an outlet for the excitement in our lives together, and the phone rang. Now, Gloria, you know that was God answering me, and He did it so quickly."

"Another God incidence!" the girls exclaimed together. Now Sarah started crying, and Gloria was laughing.

"I will call Jeff right now," said Gloria. And then you can talk to Pete, if you want to." Gloria dialed, and Jeff answered. "Jeff, hold your hat. We have just added to our ministry calendar a Sunday School class at Adaton Baptist, beginning this coming Sunday at ten o'clock and continuing every Sunday. I just got off the phone with Pastor James. His members are begging him to let us have a regular time to teach and share. Tell Pete, pray together, and call me back. However, I already accepted for the four of us. If the Lord tells you anything different, then call and tell me. Sarah and I will pray right now. We will also pray about **how** we should teach the class, okay? …. Are you still there? …. Honey, what's happening?"

"Slow down, sweetheart. You knocked me off my feet. But you won't believe this, Gloria. Guess what Pete and I were doing when you called? We were on our knees praying. He is listening to me right now. I'm glad he is on his knees, because I would hate for that lumbering giant of a man to fall and hit his head on something." Jeff got carried away, laughing, and told Gloria to wait while he filled Pete in on Pastor James' phone call. A minute later, Jeff came back on the line. "Okay, I told him, and he is laughing, too. He wants to talk to Sarah."

Sarah took the phone from Gloria. "Hello, Pete. Before you say anything, I have to tell you that right now my heart is bursting with love for you. In my mind I am in your arms, loving you with all my might. Feel it? …. I knew you would, but go ahead. I want to hear your reaction to Gloria's message."

Pete could hardly talk through the tears. "Sarah, you are going to be amazed to hear that Jeff and I were praying specifically about our ministry together and asking God to screen any requests we have to go places to speak and pray for people. We were both blown away with the reception we got tonight at the BSU, and we have been refilled with the Spirit once we got back to the dorm and started our prayer time together. For the first time, we got on our knees. That's good for me, because heretofore I have definitely not been a humble person. Anyway, we prayed in the Spirit before we prayed in English, but our basic petition was that God would give us some ministry appointments that HE wanted us to accept. As people hear about our story, we may get a lot of calls, but we want to accept only those we are sure that HE is setting up. And no sooner had we voiced that request than the phone rang with Gloria's message. Jeff and I agreed this is a huge God incidence!"

"Of course it is, Pete. This is our divine destiny. If our lives are already so meaningful **before** we are married, I can't imagine how meaningful our life together will be **after** we are married. Well, let me ask you to go back to prayer with Jeff. Gloria and I are going to pray also and try to get God's answer on HOW we are to teach the class. Okay?" Pete agreed, and both couples were soon praying fervently.

The phone rang.

"My turn, Gloria, I will get it. Maybe it is another answer to prayer. Hello, this is Sarah.... Chaya! It's wonderful to hear from you. Before you say a thing, I want to ask how you are feeling, and what the doctor is saying about your pregnancy.... Well, hallelujah! So glad to hear that. My little niece or nephew is going to light up my life, and now Pete will be an uncle, too.... But why does it matter that the doctor says you can fly now? Are you and Max going on a trip?.... Whaaaat? HUNGARY?... Wait a minute. I must tell Gloria.... (Sarah fills Gloria in.) Chaya, we have already had a mega-exciting phone call tonight, and now you call and tell me this. Oh, I wish I could go with you. Pete will want to go, too, because he has discovered his family's connection to Hungary. Did you tell Max all I related to you about the astounding revelations from Melvin, Pete's brother, last Sunday?.... Yes, I shared that, too, about **my** roots being in Hungary. I had Great Uncle Boris' diary in my purse, and I read some of it to them. They were astounded.... So, you are going in March? If it's during our spring break, Pete and I must go with you. ... Please tell me the dates as soon as you know. Gloria and I were praying when your call came in. Now we will continue to pray and include a petition for the planning of your trip and that all will go well with you health-wise. I love you. Shalom." Sarah hung up and fell to her knees with a sense of wonder.

Gloria broke in on Sarah's reverie. "Sarah, another exciting phone call. I gathered that Chaya and Max are going to Hungary, and you and Pete may go with them. Is that the essence of her call?"

"Yes, and I can't wait to get the exact dates of the flight. If it hits on the dates for our spring break, then it will clearly be another God incidence. Of course, it is possible Pete may have other plans. Gloria, we just need to pray and try to discern how God is leading us."

"Sarah, you should have told her the dates of spring break, so they can at least **try** to get the flight during that time."

The phone rang.

"A THIRD PHONE CALL! Sarah, this place is popping! What in the world will **this** call be about? I don't think my heart can stand another huge surprise. Pray hard as I answer. Ask God to help me think straight and discern if this is of HIM…. Hello, this is Gloria. Oh, Mama Anna, how fantastic to hear from you. This is a first, for you to call me in the dorm. I hope it is good news…. Whew! You both are fine and healthy…. So, Dad called you and told you that Pete and Sarah are engaged. Yes, it was a glorious day last Sunday when Pete popped the question. Did Dad tell you that Sarah's roots are in Hungary, and that Pete's brother found out that the Carsons have a trace of Jewish ancestry through Raoul Wallenberg's mother?…. Glad he told you. I figured you and Papa Sam would know all about Raoul Wallenberg. Isn't that something? ….Oh, really?…. What did you say? You want us four to fly up to Chicago to celebrate the Passover with you and also my parents? That is awesome! I hope Jeff and I can come, but if it's in March, Pete and Sarah may be going to Hungary with Chaya and Max. We don't know yet. Spring break begins after the last class on Friday, March 13th, and we return to school on Monday, March 23rd. When is Passover?…. Oh, amazing. You say Passover begins Friday night, April 10th? That coincides with Good Friday, with Easter following on Sunday. MSU gives us a holiday that Friday. Praise the Lord! Whether or not Pete and Sarah go to Hungary on our spring break, they could still go with Jeff and me over the Easter weekend…. Yes, it is unusual for Easter and Passover to coincide because of separate holidays for Christians and Jews. I will ask Jeff, Sarah, and Pete and see if the four of us can come. Passover at your house was always a joy to me, and now I can share it with my fiancé and closest friends. How generous of you to invite all four of us."

Sarah had their ministry calendar out and was furiously filling in some dates. She was listening to Gloria's end of the conversation and hoping that Pete, as well as Jeff, would agree. She loved Mama Anna and Papa Sam. She already had extra money from her inheritance, so buying a plane ticket wouldn't be a problem. *However, it could be a problem for Pete, since he will have already had the expense of going to Hungary with us, that is, if he and I get to go with them. I surely hope so. Dear HaShem, what surprises you have in our lives. If this plan is yours, I have confidence every detail will work out. I love you with all my heart.*

Gloria was concluding her conversation. "It will be wonderful to be with you. And while we are there … Wait, please forgive me for **assuming** Jeff, Sarah, and Pete will agree to it, and **assuming** that they will have the money to do it. I know Mom and Dad will pay my way. But if it all **does** work out and we come, I am eager for you to tell us about your plans to make aliyah…. Oh, good. But you can't leave until you attend our wedding. I know you wouldn't do that, however. I can't wait to tell you about a possible double wedding. …. What? You already thought we would do that? Mama Anna, how will I ever get to sleep tonight? The four of us have already had some astounding news earlier. I need to get to bed, but I will call you in a few days, I promise, and tell you all about this other good thing that has happened to us. Maybe by then, Sarah and Pete will know if they can join us for Passover in Chicago…. I love you, too, with all my heart. Shalom, now." Gloria turned to Sarah and grabbed her hands.

"I think I understand all about your conversation with Mama Anna, so let's just pray now," said Sarah, pulling Gloria to her knees.

They prayed for about five minutes. Then Gloria lifted Sarah to her feet. "Roommate, you know we will never get to sleep tonight unless we expend ourselves physically. Otherwise, these exhilarating emotions will keep us wide awake. Let's go walking down the halls and up and down the stairs for about ten minutes."

Sarah agreed, and they took off walking at a brisk pace, smiling at each other but not talking.

CHAPTER TWENTY-FOUR

LOVING YOUR ENEMIES

Sarah and Gloria awakened at 7:00 o'clock, quickly dressed, straightened up their room, and bounded down the stairs. They had a sound sleep and felt motivated to get on the 'education track,' fulfilling their responsibilities as students, which was part of being good witnesses for Yeshua. In their zeal, they were about to brush past Jenny Simmons and Rebecca North, their former roommates, in the lobby, when simultaneously, they slowed down. "Hi, Jenny and Rebecca," greeted Gloria. "I have missed seeing you around since Christmas break. I hope you enjoyed your vacation and everything's going well for you." Gloria stopped and pulled Sarah down on the sofa across from their former roommates. *Of all people, Jenny and Rebecca need Yeshua. Help me, Lord, not to be a stumbling block to them. I guess some Christians would say we shouldn't cast our pearls before swine, but I refuse to think of them as swine. They probably had a terrible home life growing up. Only God knows what is in their hearts.*

Sarah reluctantly sat down beside Gloria and greeted the girls, too, trying to sound sincere, although inside she cringed. "Yes, I also hope you had a great time at Christmas and on New Year's Day."

With a smirk on her face, Jenny said, "We had a ball. My parents were all for me spending the break with Rebecca, and her parents were gone most of the time. Yesiree, we had a good ole time with the run of the house, inviting our girl friends over for parties. One of our rich friends brought cases of beer and even some whiskey. We laughed, danced, drank, and did pretty much what we wanted to. Rebecca's parents have money, and they left a lot of food in the house and told us to help ourselves. Yep, we cleaned the place out!" Rebecca joined Jenny in laughing. But to Gloria, their laughter sounded diabolical.

Gloria was praying silently, seeking how she should respond. "Well, girls, Sarah and I and our fiancés had a glorious time. Pete proposed to Sarah, and you already knew that Jeff and I are engaged. We really would like to have you attend our weddings." Gloria prayed hard she could withstand a mocking response from them.

Rebecca had a surprised look on her face. "Well, Jenny and I appreciate the invitation. Just let us know in plenty of time when the big event will be, so we can save up our money to buy new dresses. I assume it will be formal." Gloria was amazed that there was no hint of scorn in Rebecca's voice.

"Oh, no, I don't think so, although we haven't gotten that far in the planning. Actually, I may be premature in inviting anyone, because we aren't positive of the location, whether New York or down here. But we surely do want our college friends to be able to attend, so most likely we will have it down here in Mississippi. We will let you know as soon as we can. I am thrilled that you want to come. Also, I want to invite you both to our new Sunday School class at Adaton Baptist Church at 10 o'clock. The four of us will be teaching about our Jewish roots and about Israel. If you are not interested in that, it's okay. I understand. But you are invited nonetheless." Gloria smiled and stood. They needed to get a bite to eat in the cafeteria and go on to class.

Sarah felt like her contribution to this encounter with their former "enemies" would be a smile and a few words. Yeshua's command to love your enemies was a brand new concept for her. "Yes, I do hope you can attend our weddings and also our new class at Adaton Baptist Church. You girls have a good day."

Jenny was dumbfounded and couldn't give a reply, but Rebecca managed a smile and said, "Thank you. We hope you have a good day, too."

Jeff and Pete found Gloria and Sarah in the cafeteria, got their food, and sat down with them. Jeff squeezed Gloria's shoulder. "I bet you girls are half-asleep after that exciting phone call last night. Pete and I figured we would never get to sleep, so we both did push-ups for about fifteen minutes. After all the rich food over the holidays, we were huffing and puffing. We fell in the bed exhausted and had a great night's sleep. I didn't even dream. Neither did Pete."

Sarah responded. "You don't know the half of it. We haven't even told you about getting a second and then a third phone call last night. Gloria and I were so hyped up, we had to walk the halls and up and down the stairs until our bodies begged for rest. Then, like you guys, we fell in the bed worn out. The four of us need to do some sharing big time. So many decisions have to be made concerning these phone calls. I am filling up our calendar fast. When can we devote a big block of time in person to go over all this? The sooner the better. This is Thursday. What about tonight, or is Friday night better? That's Shabbat. I don't think this should be shared over the phone. The four of us need to be together when important decisions have to be made. Don't you agree?"

Everyone was in enthusiastic agreement. "Unless one of us has a test tomorrow to study for, I say we make it tonight," urged Jeff. "Is the Chapel a good place? It is usually vacant."

Again the friends were in agreement and expressed that they didn't need to study much. Gloria voiced what the others were thinking, "So, let's do it. And then on Friday night we can meet and pray together about our class at Adaton. I suggest that before we meet, we each write down some of the things we want to include in our forty-five- minute class. We are getting busy, aren't we? But we can't rush our devotional time with the Lord each day. Sometimes

Sarah and I spend that time together and sometimes separately. We both keep a journal and jot down what we think God is saying to us and record insights in Scripture."

Pete was impatient to share his thoughts. "Holy Rollers, I think we need to remember to take care of our temples. Remember, our bodies are the temple of the Holy Spirit. We need to get physical exercise on a regular basis. Since we don't play sports at MSU, we have to find another way to stay in shape. We could buy memberships at the gym, but I suggest that be an individual decision. It's worth the expense to me, and Jeff might be interested. You girls, however, have a good thing going, just walking fast in the halls and on the stairs of your dorm. That's my two-cents worth," Pete smiled.

"Oh, my he-man. You already look like Superman, but if you want more muscles, then join that gym. As for me, until warmer weather, I am content to do what you said about fast walking in the dorm," said Sarah.

Gloria agreed with Sarah. "Speaking of physical exercise, I want to share that in my study of Hebrew I have found a way to develop our strength, and that is to **praise God.** 'The **name** of the Lord is a strong tower; the righteous run into it, and they are safe.'[74] The Hebrew word for 'strong' is *oz,* and it's not pronounced like the *oz* in The Wizard of Oz, but with a long o. Listen to this – God's name is *oz,* meaning 'security' and 'majesty.' But guess what – *oz* also means PRAISE. If we praise God a lot, we are going to be strong. 'The secret of true strength is not exercise or willpower, the secret of strength is given to those who praise God… And the **name** of God is a strong tower – a tower of praise.'[75] I love to sing this verse from Proverbs. Go ahead, and do your pushups, Jeff and Pete, but if you add singing praises to God throughout the day, you will be strong men through and through. Tell me if you like this song." Gloria sings, "*Blessed be the name of the Lord; blessed be the name of the Lord. Blessed be the name of the Lord Most High…. Glory* to the name of the Lord… The name of the Lord is a strong tower. The righteous run into it, and they are saved…."[76]

"Gloria, I love to hear you sing that. Next time you sing it, I will sing with you," said Sarah. "But I want to make a request before we go on to classes. Pete and Jeff, please pray for our former roommates, Jenny and Rebecca. You won't believe what Gloria did this morning. She invited them to our weddings!"

"Whaaaat?" snarled Pete. "I'm sure they mocked you and Gloria for even thinking they would be interested. You better stay away from them."

"Calm down, buddy. I think that was a magnanimous thing for you to do, Gloria. And what did they say?"

"I was surprised, but I really believe they are seriously considering it, if we get married down here and not in New York. I told them we would have more definite plans later and would give them a date," answered Gloria. Looking at her watch, Gloria exclaimed, "Oh, the time passes fast when I am looking into your deep brown eyes, honey. I have **got** to get to class. I dare say, we all do. Shalom. See you tonight. Call and tell us when you are meeting us." Gloria blew kisses to Jeff as they all hurried out the door.

CHAPTER TWENTY-FIVE

PLANS SETTLED

J eff, Gloria, Pete, and Sarah met in the Chapel at four o'clock and sat on the front row. Jeff took charge. "Come to order, Holy Roller Ministry. I am electing myself to be President." Jeff stood up, took on a dictatorial persona and shouted, "Sit down and be quiet!" He observed three shocked faces and then continued, stifling laughter, "I demand to know what the other two phone calls were, and I will decide what we should do. You will obey my decrees."

Pete caught on to the charade, tackled Jeff, held him on the floor, and demanded, "You are no longer in power. Relinquish your office immediately. You are exiled to Cuba with your consort, Gloria Sondheim. I am taking over the reins of government with Princess Sarah Bernstein, and we will be co-rulers of the Holy Rollers, now reduced to two people, Sarah and me!"

Jeff began crying alligator tears. "I didn't mean it, I didn't mean it. Please don't put me away. I will be good, I will be good."

Gloria got into the act, comforting Jeff and drying his tears with a tissue. "Oh, Jeff, it was fun while it lasted, being the monarchs of the Holy Rollers. Now we must leave behind living in the lap of luxury. Bread and water won't be so bad. Maybe we can escape in a boat. Someone will have pity and take us back to America."

Sarah was laughing so hard that the paper crown Pete had put on her head toppled off. All four went into paroxysms of laughter, until they could hardly catch their breath.

Pete stayed in charge. "Okay, roommate and fiancées, parliamentary procedure is done with. We now have a fresh perspective to discuss the two phone calls. For heaven's sake, spill it, girls!"

Gloria began the discussion. "Yes, I knew Sarah and I were *meshuganah*, but now I see that y'all are also *meshuganah*. I love you anyway. I will let Sarah tell about her phone call first."

"Getting right to the point, Max and Chaya are going to Hungary in March. Right before Gloria and I left the room a few minutes ago, Chaya called and said they made reservations for her and Max from New York to Budapest for March 16th to 20th. That's Monday to Friday. Pete, can you believe it? That is during our spring break. I want to meet them in Budapest. Can we fly out of Golden Triangle Airport together? Will your parents pay for your ticket? I have money I inherited from my parents' estate. I hope you don't have any other plans for spring break."

"I can't believe it! This is an answer to prayer. After Melvin told us about Raoul Wallenberg rescuing the Jews of Hungary from the Nazis, and then his finding out that the Carsons are kin to Raouls' mother through her great-great grandfather, Michael Benedicks, a Jew from Sweden, I have prayed that I could visit Hungary. Yes, by all means, Sarah, I want to go with you. Mom and Dad will surely pay my way."

Sarah squealed, "Praise the Lord! Now Gloria, tell about your call. This involves the four of us."

"My grandmother, Mama Anna, called and invited all of us up to Chicago for Passover. Mom and Dad will be there, too. It is amazing that this year Passover and Good Friday coincide on the calendar. That is perfect for us because MSU gives us a holiday on Good Friday, which is April 10th. We could get a flight out of the Golden Triangle Airport that morning, and we could return on Sunday, so we can be back in class on Monday. Isn't that great? Can any of you think of a reason that you won't be on that plane? Again, money is involved, but all our parents are very generous, and Sarah has her inheritance money. What do you say?"

Pete looked puzzled. "Wait, we would be in the air on Easter Sunday for our return flight. Since I am a full-fledged Christian now, I hate to not be with my family in church. We make a big deal of Easter dinner. After all, that day we will be celebrating the most important event for a Christian, the resurrection of our Lord and Savior Jesus Christ."

No one had an answer for Pete. Gloria prayed silently for a minute, then reached out to Pete. "Yes, Pete, I loved the Easter services at First United Methodist Church in Port Jefferson. The choir always made the hairs on my arms stand on end with their loud singing, celebrating Jesus rising from the dead. Those are good memories. Also, even as a twelve-year-old I loved the Easter egg hunts. However, my parents drew the line with the Easter bunny delivering candy to me. I went to church with my friends, but Mom and Dad didn't go on Easter. When I questioned them about it, they said it seemed like a betrayal of their Jewish heritage, but they didn't explain why."

Sarah's face became hard. "Pete you need to know this, so I am going to tell you, and I won't spare your feelings. In 1903, there was a pogrom. That word means 'organized massacre of an ethnic group, particularly the Jews.' It happened on Easter Day in Kishinev, a capital city of the Russian Empire. People were killed. Women were raped. Homes and businesses were damaged. The most popular newspaper in Russia regularly published headlines like 'Death to the Jews' and 'Crusade Against the Hated Race.' Before the pogrom, a Ukrainian boy was found murdered, and a girl killed herself by poisoning. The newspaper insinuated that the Jewish Community had killed them for the purpose of using their blood to make matzo for the Passover. These allegations sparked the pogrom which went on for two days. It started after Christians were dismissed from the Easter Sunday service. They became a mob led by the priests. The general cry, 'Kill the Jews,' was taken up all over the city. The Jews were slaughtered like sheep. Babies were torn to pieces by the bloodthirsty mob. The local police did nothing to stop it. At sunset the streets were piled with about 120 corpses and 500 wounded. Those Jews who could escape fled, and the city had hardly any Jews left in it."[77] Tears rolled down Sarah's face. Pete looked at her. He felt ashamed.

Gloria didn't want Pete to feel guilty about his love for Easter Sunday, but she knew now was the time for the truth to be told from Scripture, as well as from history. "This is a heavy subject, friends, but since we are already talking about it, we might as well see what God says about observing the Resurrection. I was on the phone with Papa Sam during Christmas break, and he pointed out some things to me. Please sit back and try to absorb this. We really need our Bibles and paper and pen, as well as tables to sit at. Since this isn't a classroom, I will just hit the highlights, and we can go in depth later. But first, to explain more on what Sarah just told us, I think you can get a good idea of Jewish life in Russia in those days when lots of pogroms took place by seeing the movie, 'Fiddler on the Roof.'"

Jeff and Pete smiled. "That was a great musical," said Pete, and Jeff agreed. Sarah had a blank look. "Oh, honey, we will have to watch it together sometime. It is really funny but serious, too. And the music is outstanding. Have you heard of it?" Sarah shook her head.

"To continue," Gloria said, "God gave His feasts to the Israelites in the wilderness to show His great plan of redemption. Try to remember Leviticus, the 23rd chapter. You can read about the seven annual feasts, all agricultural feasts with lots of sacrifices and rituals. But the chosen people were to faithfully observe them later in Jerusalem three times a year. Each one portrays a part of the gospel – the death, burial, and resurrection of Yeshua, the pouring out of the Holy Spirit, the second coming of Jesus, the national salvation of Israel, and the reign of Messiah Yeshua over all the world from His throne in Jerusalem."

Jeff's mouth was wide open, drinking in every word Gloria said. "Oh, my goodness, I have never heard any of this. You mean all those strange customs of the Jews are **describing** what Jesus did for us on the cross, being buried, then rising from the dead, sending the Holy Spirit, and coming back the second time to rule and reign? I am floored!"

"Yes, honey. This is our heritage. Aren't we Jews blessed that God chose us to reenact these feasts and show the Messiah to the world? Three of the seven feasts are in the spring, beginning with Passover. Then fifty days later comes Pentecost, when the church was born. Then the last three feasts are in the fall. These feasts are 'appointments' with God. They are prophetic, and they are rehearsals of our salvation. Isn't that exciting?" A collective gasp went up from Jeff, Pete, and Sarah.

"I never have heard this either, Gloria," marveled Sarah. "Please go ahead and teach us."

"Okay. When Christians celebrate Easter, they include pagan customs, such as eggs and bunny rabbits. The name 'Easter' comes from the pagan fertility goddess Ishtar. The story of this pagan religion is absolutely filthy,[78] but most Christians have no idea whatever about it. Anyway, if you accept Mama Anna and Papa Sam's invitation to come to Chicago and celebrate the Passover with them, you will learn how it shows Yeshua's death, burial, and resurrection. Passover week includes the second feast of Unleavened Bread, representing the burial of Messiah, and the third feast, Firstfruits, representing the Resurrection. So we **do** have a biblical date for celebrating when Yeshua rose from the dead. It is the date of the Feast of Firstfruits, the third feast of the seven, and the THIRD DAY of the Passover week. Yeshua is the firstfruits from the dead, rising on the third day, making it possible for US to have a resurrection. He is the first, and we follow. I will conclude with this. The early Christians celebrated the Passover and Unleavened Bread and Firstfruits up until the fourth century. It was when the leadership of the church shifted from the Jews to the Gentiles that the Church's Jewish roots got cut off, and Easter was observed instead of Passover. Papa Sam will teach it much better than I can.

But I hope you have more understanding now. And please say you will go to Chicago to my grandparents' house."

Jeff, Pete, and Sarah looked at each other. "Chicago, here we come!"

CHAPTER TWENTY-SIX

TEACHING JEWISH ROOTS

Jeff and Pete picked up Gloria and Sarah at Hamlin Hall on Sunday at 9:15. They only waited a minute until the girls came down the stairs. Priscilla greeted them, saying she and Gary were looking forward to the Sunday School class, and that he would pick her up at 9:40. Gloria and Sarah were not dressed to 'the nines' this time. They wanted to blend in with the more casual dress of the church goers.

"Here come our girls, always a vision of loveliness. Let me help you carry your materials, little teacher," offered Jeff. Sarah's two Bibles were all she brought.

"It's easy to see who is more prepared," noted Pete as he pointed to the stack of materials that Gloria transferred to Jeff. "That is a welcome sight. You have no lack of material for the first class, Gloria. I am here for moral support."

"Oh, no, you are not. Be alert. I may call on you, Pete. Let's get in Jeff's SUV and practice our theme song on the way to Adaton." As soon as Jeff cranked up, Gloria handed out song sheets to Pete and Sarah and held up a copy close to Jeff, so he could glance at it as he drove. "We are going to teach 'Days of Elijah' to the class. Just like the Holy Spirit anointed this song in Israel, I know He will fill our classroom with His presence today as we sing. What a prophetic song with which to prepare the way of the Lord. From the conversation I hear at Adaton and the hymns and praise songs they sing each Sunday, I can see this song is right in sync with everyone's expectation that Jesus is coming soon." The others heartily agreed. Gloria led out, and the powerful presence of the Lord filled the vehicle as they sang at the top of their lungs.

"That took me back to Israel, Gloria. Thank you so much," exclaimed Sarah. "I wonder who will attend our Sunday School class today. I hope we have a lot of college students, but I want the old people to attend also."

They pulled up in the parking lot of the church, and Pastor James greeted them. After unlocking the doors and showing them to the classroom, he went back to his study. The room had rows and rows of chairs and plenty of wall space for Gloria to display the maps and other illustrations she had brought. The four helped Gloria prepare the room, placing a song sheet in each chair, tacking up the maps, and deciding how they should sit at the long table at the end of the room. Jeff would be on one end and Pete on the other with the girls in the middle. They had already decided that Gloria would lead the first class. Then Sarah, Jeff, and Pete would each take a class, rotating back to Gloria on the fifth class.

Pastor James came back and went over to Pete to ask how he had been doing since the time he and Jeff met with him in his study. Pete grinned from ear to ear. "Pastor, I have been free as a bird, thanks to you and also to Jeff that night. And you will be happy to know that I proposed to Sarah last Sunday at my parents' house." The pastor gave Pete a bear hug and congratulated him. Then he walked over to Sarah to congratulate her also.

Looking around the room, Pastor James was visibly pleased. He took Gloria aside. "I can't thank you enough for teaching this class. I understand all four of you will teach, but you are the leader. Is that right? I want to sit in. I hope that won't be a distraction for you, but I need to learn all I can. I am planning a trip to Israel for our members."

"Oh, Brother James, that is fabulous! Since you are going to Israel, would you mind if I include some teaching of the modern Hebrew language that is spoken there today? I am trying to learn it, and I have already begun teaching a few phrases to Jeff. Nobody knows it yet, but I am also learning some Hebrew **songs.** It really excites me and makes the Bible come alive, singing and speaking Hebrew."

"The answer to your question is 'Yes,' Gloria. Jeff bent my ear about your marvelous talent, playing the piano, as well as singing. You may have noticed that we have an excellent grand piano on the stage. It would be our great joy for you to play during a worship service. Also, Jeff said one of the key reasons he came to believe in Jesus was when you first met, and you sang a song to him, seemingly out of the blue. When he told me the name of it, I said that it was my absolute favorite hymn, 'The Love of God.' Would you do me the favor of singing it next Sunday morning in the worship service? We can put a microphone for you at the piano, so you can sing and accompany yourself. How about it?"

Gloria's heart was beating fast. "Oh, my, teaching a class and then singing a solo? Ooh, I am such a new Christian, but if this is God's plan, I will do it. Let me pray after I get back to the dorm, but if you don't hear from me, you will know God says 'yes.' What a compliment, Brother James. Thank you so much for asking me." The pastor left, and Gloria went back to the table to tell the others that he would be sitting in on the class to learn because he was taking his members to Israel. Everyone was excited.

Jeff reached out and held Gloria's hand. Pete and Sarah held hands and closed the circle. "Let's pray," said Jeff. "People will be coming in any time now. There is no telling what the Lord might do today. We need Him to put the words in Gloria's mouth. All four of us need the anointing of His Holy Spirit, and we have to pray for the individuals in this room today…. Dear Yahweh, You are the God of Abraham, Isaac, and Jacob, and the God and Father of our Lord and Messiah Yeshua. We call You 'Abba,' and we love You. Use us as Your vessels to make disciples for Yeshua. Please fill this room with Your Holy Spirit. Change us all, we ask. May Your love and truth pour out over these people today. Give a special blessing to Pastor James. We thank You for Him. In Jesus' name. Amen."

As the group echoed Jeff's "amen," the door opened and in walked Gary Grayson and Priscilla Caldwell, followed by Grace Thomas and several others from the Baptist Student Union. Jeff was glad to see Walter Sessions come in and rushed over to shake his hand. "It's great to see you, Walter."

Walter said, "I heard about this and had to come hear y'all teach. I know I will learn a lot. I can't wait till you come to **my** church and speak to us. I have it on the calendar, Wednesday night, January 28ᵗʰ." Jeff and Walter talked a few minutes. Then Jeff walked to the classroom door to close it. The big clock on the wall said it was 10:00, and Jeff wanted to start on time. He looked around and was surprised to see that nearly all the chairs were taken.

As soon as he reached for the door knob, he saw Rebecca North and Jenny Simmons down the hall, headed for the classroom. Jeff said a quick prayer, put a big smile on his face, and extended his hand to them. "Welcome, Rebecca and Jenny. We are so glad you are here for our first lesson. Make yourself at home." Rebecca and Jenny saw chairs on the first row right in front of Gloria and Sarah at the table, and they noisily pulled the chairs out and sat down, giving a half-wave to the girls.

Gloria had red flags go up in her spirit and silently claimed God's promise from Isaiah 54:17 – *No weapon formed against you shall prosper, and every tongue that rises in judgment you shall condemn. For this is the heritage of the servants of the Lord, and your vindication is from Him.*" Gloria smiled at Rebecca and Jenny. She knew what to do. She heard the Lord plainly say, "Sing the song first."

Gloria took a deep breath, stood up, and looked out over the room. Almost every seat was filled. She saw the pastor in the back corner and smiled at him. Then she greeted the class. "Shalom, everyone. We are so glad you have come to our Jewish Roots class. Today is Sunday, the Christian Sabbath. I want you to learn the first Hebrew greeting that Israelis say to each other on Friday night, which begins **their** Sabbath – 'Shabbat shalom!' It means 'Perfect peace.' Say it with me – SHABBAT SHALOM!" The class copied Gloria's enthusiasm and repeated the Hebrew phrase eagerly. Gloria was surprised that Rebecca and Jenny joined in. "Most of you know us, but I want to make a formal introduction. I am Gloria Sondheim from Long Island, New York. My fellow teachers are Jeff Quentin from Tupelo, Sarah Bernstein from New York, and Pete Carson from Columbus. I am happy to announce, and some of you know, that Jeff and I are engaged, and as of a week ago, Pete and Sarah are also engaged." The class applauded. "Jeff and Pete are roommates. Sarah and I are roommates. By the way, our **former** roommates are here today, Rebecca North and Jenny Simmons. They are new to Adaton, so please welcome them." Rebecca and Jenny stood and smiled at the class. Pastor James walked up and shook their hands. Jeff secretly squeezed Gloria's hand. She felt power go out from him, and she knew God was pleased.

"Without further ado, I want to open up our teaching with this powerful song that became our theme song in Israel. You all have a copy. The four of us call ourselves the Holy Rollers because we are set apart for God's purposes, which is the meaning of 'holy,' and we are always rolling down the highway or traveling on the airways. We loved singing this in Israel. Follow us. You will learn it in no time. It is a prophetic song, drawing from the Old and New Testaments and is about preparing the way of the Lord. We will sing about Elijah, Moses, Ezekiel, David, and, of course, our Lord and Savior Jesus Christ. One day soon He will split the eastern sky. He will ride on the clouds and come back to be the King over all the earth. Just think, we who believe in Him will rise to meet Him in the air and be with Him forever! Let's sing."

The class was a great success. Some of the oldest members of the church attended, as well as high schoolers. Many commented to Pastor James that they had an interest in going to Israel. The Minister of Music had chosen for the worship service hymns and choruses appropriate to what the new class was covering, such as "He is Jehovah,"[79] a newer song, and "All Hail the Power of Jesus' Name," an old hymn. The second verse of that hymn underscored the church's Jewish roots – "Ye chosen seed of Israel's race, ye ransomed from the fall. Hail Him who saves you by His grace, and crown Him Lord of all." The four friends had separate conversations with individuals in the class who had questions, both before and after the worship service. Pastor James stood with them at the front door until the last person filed out. They looked in vain for Rebecca and Jenny and wondered how they missed them. Gloria made a mental note that the four of them needed to pray and see what God would have them do to reach these two lost girls. Jeff offered to treat Pastor and his family to Sunday dinner at Harvey's, but they had made other plans. The Holy Rollers began talking up a storm when they got in Jeff's vehicle.

Sarah couldn't wait to compliment Gloria on her presentation. "Roommate, you are the greatest! No wonder you have spent so much time at the library these last two days. When you said you were meeting Jeff there, I thought it was mainly a chance to work on wedding plans. I didn't realize the magnitude of your project for our class. What a pleasant surprise to see that you worked up an outline with Scripture references for all of the sessions of our Jewish Roots class, and you didn't even show it to me until this morning. Did you know about it, Pete?"

"No, I did not. I thought the same thing you did, Sarah. We had our own little meeting going on in the Chapel, babe, and it had more to do with the heart rather than the head, if you know what I mean," laughed Pete.

Sarah continued thanking Gloria. "It is straining my brain to catch up with what most Christians already know about the New Testament. However, not many Christians know about the Church's Jewish roots in the Jewish Messiah. The course title you picked is perfect, 'Why Study Jewish Roots?' Your answer is great, 'You Are Heirs.' You wrote, 'According to Galatians 3:26-29, Gentile believers belong to Yeshua, so they are the seed of Abraham like the Jews and heirs of God's promises to Israel.' Then you listed the **Benefits** of the heirs: blessings, land, the Spirit, the Scriptures, and the Messiah. The second part I love, and I look forward to the time this is taught. You all have a copy, but I want to read it aloud - **Responsibilities** of the heirs: 1. Provoke to jealousy, 2. Fullness, 3. Evangelism, 4. Support and Comfort, 5. Assist Aliyah, and 6. Prayer. Oh, how I wish all the churches would teach this. And I want to share it with Chaya. I hope she will listen."

Gloria was elated that her outline was well received by her friends. "Okay, Jeff and I have to confess that this material is not original with us."

Pete was slightly shocked. "What? You didn't plagiarize it, did you? From something you found in the library?"

Jeff explained, "Pete, this course outline was faxed to us at the library. It was freely given, and the Christian lady who wrote it for Gentile believers urged us to teach it without cost. Hold your hat. This material came from **your brother** Britt and his wife Camille. Since we last saw them, they started attending a Jewish Roots class taught by this lady at your church, First Baptist….. Well, here we are at Harvey's. But let's sit out here a few more minutes. I want to read the **third** part of the outline after the Blessings and the Responsibilities. Here it is - **Results**. This is exciting, and it's what the Holy Rollers **must** participate in. 1. All Israel saved! 2. World-wide Revival! 3. Inheritance of the Land! 4. God's Name Glorified in All Nations through Gathering of Jews back to the Land and HIS Fighting for Them! 5. Church and Israel ONE! 6. Return of Yeshua HaMashiach! It's amazing, friends, that we are in possession of a masterpiece outline. I want to make a declaration. This is the Operational Manual for the Holy Roller Ministry. Agreed?" The couples cheered and gave each other high fives.

CHAPTER TWENTY-SEVEN

PRAYER TIME

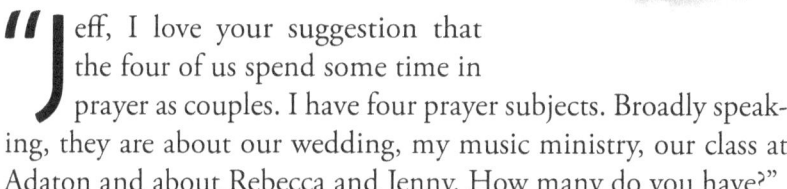

"Jeff, I love your suggestion that the four of us spend some time in prayer as couples. I have four prayer subjects. Broadly speaking, they are about our wedding, my music ministry, our class at Adaton and about Rebecca and Jenny. How many do you have?"

"My Gloria, I love praying with you, and I agree with your prayer subjects. Maybe that is enough for tonight. I need to focus spiritually and not get in the flesh, being this close to you in private. Yes, it was my idea for Pete and Sarah to pray separately from us. Then we can come back together and share what God shows us about getting married and about our class. I tell you what, let's pray fervently for thirty minutes. Then let's show our affection for each other. Then let's go eat supper at the Union. Does that sound good?"

"Jeff, you think I don't have trouble focusing on spiritual matters when I'm around you? Well, I am telling you, I certainly do. My heart is racing right now. Maybe the next time we pray we can get in a **semi-private** place, like in the Union building when the food bar is closed or in the lobby of our dorm very early in the morning. But here we are tonight in the Chapel with **no one around**. Okay, we can be honest with God. He knows what we are thinking anyway. Our love for Him has to be stronger than the love we have for each other. And speaking of love, I will start right off, asking you to pray with me about my first solo at Adaton next Sunday. You will be happy to know that I am singing your favorite, "The **Love** of God." Pastor James asked me. He said you told him I could play the piano and sing. I love the way you build me up to others."

"That's an easy prayer request, babe. We will see the answer to that prayer next Sunday. Before we pray though, I want to ask you if you are going to say anything to introduce the song? I don't mind if you tell them you first sang it to me, and it wasn't long afterward that I gave my life to Jesus."

"Well, I called Pastor and told him I would do it, that God showed me He wanted me to sing that particular song. Yes, I will make an introduction. I have found out that Frederic Lehman, who wrote the first two verses was a German immigrant who came to America as a child in 1872. He became a Nazarene preacher but mostly wrote songs. Once he was at a camp meeting and heard the evangelist quote what became the third verse of the hymn. That evangelist said that those lines were found scratched on the wall of an **insane asylum**! Later it was found that the scratched lines came from a Jewish poem of ninety couplets written in Aramaic. It was called the *Hadamut*. A Jewish rabbi, Meir ben Isaac Nehorai, had composed it in 1096 in Worms, Germany. That was the same year that the Crusaders came to the city and murdered all the Jewish people, probably including the Rabbi! Isn't that awful? The whole poem, the *Hadamut,* is a beloved song of the Jews, which some synagogues chant during the Feast of Shavuot.[80] It touches me to think that a Jewish person – me – will be singing those words next Sunday.

"What a story! And did you have any idea at the time you sang it to me that the third verse was written by a Jewish rabbi?"

"No, I didn't Jeff. I did some research and found out these things."

"Well, it is obvious to me that this is another God incidence, the fact a Jewish girl unknowingly sang to a Jewish boy a Christian hymn with a verse written by a Jewish rabbi! Evidently, those beautiful words about the extreme width, depth, and height of God's love had deeply touched that insane person, and he wanted the next person in the cell to be blessed like he was. It almost makes me want to cry. Yes, it is a story worth telling. I feel sure Pastor won't mind if you take more time than he anticipated. And the congregation will be so blessed. Sing that third verse for me again, my sweet songbird, and right after, I will pray."

"Okay, Jeff. It really moves me."

Could we with ink the ocean fill, and were the skies of parchment made,
Were every stalk on earth a quill, and every man a scribe by trade,
To write the love of God above would drain the ocean dry.
Nor could the scroll contain the whole, though stretched from sky to sky.
O love of God, how rich and pure! How measureless and strong!
It shall forevermore endure the saints' and angels' song. [Listen][81]

Jeff prayed, "Dear Father in heaven, You gave us music, and what a gift it is. I can't thank You enough for blessing Gloria with a beautiful voice and a talent for playing the piano. Combined with the anointing of Your Holy Spirit next Sunday, I know You will use Gloria to impart the knowledge of Your unconditional love to every person listening. Please do it, Lord. Thank You in advance. In Jesus' name."

"I agree, Father, with Jeff's prayer. Also, I ask you to help me prepare the piano pieces that I will play for Mrs. Pagani's television program in February. I know the beautiful music surely came from You. I ask that my performance will not just be received by the hearers intellectually, but that Your Spirit will impact them and stir their hearts, causing them to realize Your greatness and goodness. In Jesus' name I pray. Amen."

Jeff felt empowered by the Spirit to continue praying. "Lord, thank You again for using Gloria to launch our new Bible study on Jewish Roots at Adaton. Thank You for giving us favor with Pastor James. Please use this study to help the class to understand why it is important to love the Jewish people and the Jewish nation and to learn these things in order to prepare the way for the coming of our Jewish Messiah back to earth. Thank You for the kind lady who has shared her study outline with us through Britt and Camille. Bless her, and help her to reach a lot of church members at First Baptist. Lord, please empower Sarah, Pete, and me to also teach with excellence as Gloria did, and may Your purposes be realized. Kindly give success to Pastor's plans to take his flock to Israel. In Jesus' name. Amen."

Gloria reached out and grasped Jeff's hand, feeling the need for His strong agreement. "Dear God of Israel, I can't praise You enough that Rebecca and Jenny came to our class. Only You know their hearts and the reason for their attendance. Please give Sarah and me sensitivity to Your Spirit as we interact with them on campus. Put Your words in our mouths when we encounter them. Oh, Lord, save their souls! And help them to live holy lives, to realize that their life-style now is self-destructive. Keep Sarah and me safe from any plans the devil may have to use them against us. We need the gift of discernment, O Lord. I know You will protect us and also use us in their lives. In Jesus' name I ask this. Amen."

Jeff took Gloria's face in his hands. "Don't worry about Rebecca and Jenny. Pete told me that Jenny is in one of his classes, and he intended to keep an eye on her. He even followed her after one class, but he stayed far back, and she didn't see him. Nothing irregular so far, he said. And would you believe it that Rebecca is in one of **my** classes? From now on I plan to pray in the spirit when I see her. Maybe they came to church out of curiosity, or maybe the Lord drew them there. Of course, there is always the possibility that Satan sent them there for his purposes. I have peace about it. I want to think the best of them, not the worst. So pray for me on that score."

"I will, honey. And now can we pray together about our marriage plans? You know what, I love our little church so much, and we already have a history there. Has it entered your mind that maybe Adaton Baptist Church is the place He has picked out for us with Pastor Jeff James marrying us?"

"It **has** entered my mind. Also, you do remember that conversation we had with Sarah and Pete after Pete proposed, don't you? We agreed we had double destinies and we could have a double wedding. Also, you said when you told Mama Anna about that plan of a double wedding, she had already thought of it! I remember you drove me past First United Methodist Church in Port Jefferson, Long Island, and said that was where we would be married. Of course, things have really changed since then. We now have a ministry with Sarah and Pete. As for me, I think a double wedding is the way to go, and yes, Adaton Baptist is the place, with Pastor James doing the ceremony.

"Remember I told you that after we came back from Israel, Mom and Dad and I attended a watchnight service at the Methodist Church in Port Jefferson, and the pastor's message was great. The Holy Spirit used him, and Mom and Dad squirmed in their seats. Although I loved it, I think the message may have caused Mom and Dad to change their minds about having our wedding there. Now maybe they would be more open to having our wedding in Starkville at Adaton Baptist. I am on board with what you are saying about Adaton and Pastor James. Now let's pray about having a double wedding with Pete and Sarah."

"Okay, Jeff. I really want to have a double wedding, but it is such a radical thing, I need to be sure it is not only **our** idea, but it is **God's** idea. I will lead the prayer. Then let's be silent and try to HEAR what the Lord will answer, okay?"

"I agree with you one hundred per cent."

"Dear Lord, you chose the Garden of Eden, the most perfect place on earth, to bring together in marriage the first man and woman, Adam and Eve. You stood back and looked at all You created and said it was 'good,' but **after** You created the man and woman You said it was '**very** good.' Oh, Lord, You delighted in uniting Adam and Eve in marriage, and I can feel Your delight in Jeff and me as we plan for marriage. You have the perfect plan. We think that we should have a double wedding with our best friends who are not only friends but partners in Your ministry. Please show **all four of us** if that is what You truly want and if it is **You** putting Pastor James and Adaton on our hearts to be the person and the place where You will join Jeff and me together and join Pete and Sarah together. We know Jesus said, 'What God has joined together, let not man put asunder.'[82] We await Your answer." Jeff and Gloria held hands and remained silent before the Lord.

Gloria was the first to speak after five minutes had passed. "Jeff, what came to my mind is the word 'double' in relation to the prophet Elisha asking his mentor Elijah for a **double** portion of his spirit.[83] After Elijah was taken to heaven in a whirlwind and chariots of fire Elisha began to do some of the same miracles that Elijah did, but Elisha's miracles were **double** that of Elijah's! I guess the synergy of our partnership with Pete and Sarah is indicative of a double wedding. Don't you think so?"

"Well, if I knew what the word 'synergy' is, I could answer you, babe."

"It means that the cooperation of us two couples will produce a combined effect greater than the sum of our separate effects. It was only a few weeks ago that I discovered that powerful word, 'synergy.' It fits us, doesn't it?"

Jeff teased Gloria. "Hmmm. Let me see. I think you are telling me that us two couples getting married at the same time means God will tie the knot tighter and fill us with more love than we had ever dreamed of. Our embraces and kisses will be more scintillating, and our honeymoon will break a record for romance! Also, we will be **very** fruitful, like Elisha was." Gloria blushed, and Jeff reached over and drew her in his arms. "Well, let's see what Pete and Sarah say about it. I propose this plan – if they say that they are for sure planning on a double wedding, and they think God wants it for us, let that be our answer."

"Yes, Jeff, I think you are right. I agree. And now let's seal it with a kiss."

CHAPTER TWENTY-EIGHT

A MUSLIM'S LIFE CHANGED

Pete was eager to attend his Criminal Justice class on Thursday, especially because the topic would be terrorism and the complications of court cases involving terrorists. This drew his mind back to the 1993 bombing of the World Trade Center in New York City, and Sarah's father, Dr. Nathan Bernstein, being a witness in the trial. He also remembered what Max told him at the airport before they departed to Israel, how the organizer, Ramzi Yousef, had written letters to the New York Times before the bombing, making demands that the U.S. end all aid to Israel because Israel is a terrorist country.[84] Max had said it was only **last year** that Yousef was convicted! Memories of the way Gloria led the five of them in prayer before he, Jeff, and Max aborted the terrorist attack on Sarah sent chills down his spine. Then Pete was also reminded how he promised Sarah to be her shield following her first attack by a terrorist on campus, a man who likely was connected to that bombing in New York. The expression of fear on Sarah's face was vivid in his memory. Added to that, Pete had been seeing more foreign students on campus this semester. Worst of all, last Saturday he had noticed Jenny and Rebecca in the Union Building, talking to two students who appeared to be Arabs from the Middle East. Pondering this, Pete decided to ask his brother Britt to come to the campus and help him develop a surveillance plan. After all, what Britt did in his job at Columbus Air Force Base was to provide antiterrorism protection and investigate criminal activity on the base. Pete was excited that his own brother could be the source of aborting any possible evil plan against Sarah. He had to admit that there was nothing else suspicious about Jenny other than that one time she and Rebecca had talked to those Arabs. Also, Jeff hadn't mentioned anything going on with Rebecca that looked shadowy. He decided to call Britt and also to talk to Jeff about a surveillance plan. That night in their dorm room Pete filled Jeff in on what he was thinking. Jeff closed the textbook he had been studying and gave Pete his full attention.

"Okay, I am ready to talk, bro. To tell the truth, even though Jenny and Rebecca appeared to be interested in our Jewish Roots class, I had a nagging doubt inside that they were acting. We need to pray for the gift of discernment. When we prayed in the Chapel, Gloria especially prayed for them to be saved and live holy lives. Did you see them leave the church? I didn't, and I don't think they were in the worship service. Evidently, they only attended our class and then sneaked out."

"My thoughts, too, Jeff. I am going to call Britt right now."

"Go for it. I am eager to see if he will help us."

Pete punched in the number, and Britt answered. "Hey, Britt, this is your younger brother Pete calling for help. Is there any way you could come to the campus this weekend and use your expertise to lead Jeff and me in a surveillance project? You may remember that I told you Sarah had been attacked on campus by a guy last October who was likely linked to the terrorist group in the World Trade Center bombing in 1993. This seems way out, and we are not sure, but we suspect that Gloria and Sarah's former roommates may be plotting to harm our girls in connection with some Middle Eastern types whom they met with last Saturday. I saw them talking together in the Union Building. You and I both know that things like this need to be checked out, even though it could be a wild goose chase.... What? (long wait of ten minutes).... You don't say! That is another God-incidence. Wow!.... I will fill Jeff in. This is amazing. Okay, we will look for you on Saturday morning at the Union Building. We won't let Gloria and Sarah know what we are doing…. I can't thank you enough, Britt. You are a godsend. Jeff and I both love you and Camille. Bye now."

Jeff was attentive to Pete's end of the conversation, and he was eager to hear what Britt said. "I heard your excitement, and if it's another God incidence, whatever it is, it will surely work," declared Jeff.

"God's divine orchestration of our lives never ceases to amaze me, Jeff! Guess who Britt is bringing with him Saturday to help us with surveillance? Ahmad Hafeez, the Muslim guy that got saved after Britt got rid of his demons!"

Jeff's mouth dropped open, and his eyes were wide. "We will fight fire with fire, right?"

"And get this, bro – Ahmad knows how to lip read. He can lip read conversations in Arabic and can do it at a distance. How perfect is that? Of course, it would be a miracle if we could catch Rebecca and Jenny talking to those two Arab guys within the time frame that Britt and Ahmad will be here on Saturday."

"No problem, Pete. If God is orchestrating all of this so far, why not? Miracles are the modus operandi of our mighty God. But I have questions. The last thing I heard about Ahmad was that he was attending his wife's Bible study with other couples. If Britt thinks he, as a former Muslim, is now trustworthy in a possible situation of apprehending Muslim terrorists, then he must have come a long way in the Christian faith in a short time."

Pete was so excited he could hardly talk. "I feel like shouting hallelujah about now. Whoo, hallelujah!" Before he could go on, Pete had to let the laughter roll. "What is that verse? Oh yeah – 'A merry heart doeth good like a medicine.'[85] It really does. God is on this case, Jeff! No doubt about it."

"Hurry up and tell me what makes you shout hallelujah and laugh so hard, roommate." Jeff was impatient.

"Okay. Britt said that he and Camille invited Ahmad and Fadwa to their Jewish Roots Bible study at First Baptist. As you know, the teacher is the lady who gave us the outline for our class.

Her name is Mrs. Lorene Murphy. Britt said that Camille prayed silently non-stop as Ahmad and Fadwa listened to the teaching. The topic was the Land of Israel, and Mrs. Murphy covered the Bible evidence of God's covenant with Abraham, Isaac, and Jacob, giving them the land of Israel from the Mediterranean Sea to the Euphrates River in Iraq.[86] She also talked about God's promise to Abraham's son Ishmael, the father of the Arab people, that He would make his descendants a great nation, starting with twelve princes.[87] But she made a point of saying that Isaac was the child of promise, and the covenant would pass down through him and his descendants, the Jewish people, not through Abraham's older son Ishmael by the slave woman Hagar.[88] Here's the thing that rang my bell – In Britt and Camille's car on the way back to the base to take Ahmad and Fadwa home, Ahmad made a startling statement. He said, 'I was taught to hate the Jews and the nation of Israel since I was a child. I had friends who joined terrorist groups, who trained to attack Jews and kill them. I hated the Jews, but I didn't want to kill them, even though the Quran calls them 'descendants of apes and pigs,'[89] and killing Jews can get you a special place in Paradise.[90] I hated Israel, which Muslims call 'Satan,' but I didn't hate America, which Muslims call 'the **Great** Satan.' I always admired America, and I grew up, wanting to live in this nation. But tonight, hearing that **Jesus Himself** was Jewish and died for all people, loving and forgiving even those who tortured and killed him, I felt my heart get completely cleansed of hate. And now I can say that I actually **love** Jewish people, and I believe they really did suffer in the Holocaust, even though my friends said that is all made up. Also, I have stopped hating Israel.' Jeff, do you see that what happened to Ahmad at that Bible study is HUGE? It's a **radical** change for a **Muslim**. Does that blow you away?"

"Oh, Pete, how can the Christian life get more exciting than to see a Muslim's life changed by the power of God? And also to see how the teaching of God's Word is so relevant to the world scene **today** and impacting enough to change a **lifetime** of wrong thinking. Aren't we privileged to have Mrs. Murphy's study course in our hands? If her teaching could be used to change Ahmad from hating to loving the Jews, then we should expect He will change hearts when **we** teach."

"I agree, even though I have never considered myself a teacher. Well, I never considered myself a 'one-woman man' either, until I met Sarah, and then we both were touched by His Spirit in Israel. Tonight I feel powerful in the Spirit, but allow me to change the subject, bro. My **physical** body needs to be exercised as the Holy Spirit's **temple**. Okay, I am coming back down to earth. Let's go running, what do you say?"

"Great idea, Pete. I think we should keep up our prayer meetings with the girls and also our exercise program. That song that Gloria taught us has been going over and over in my head – *'Blessed be the name of the Lord…. The name of the Lord is a **strong** tower; the righteous run into it, and they are saved.'* When I am at the gym and out walking and singing the song in my head, I really do feel stronger. I like that Hebrew word meaning **strong**, *oz*. And we need to build up our muscles to apprehend terrorists."

Pete laughed. "I agree, but can you guess what I was thinking about, **another** reason we need to stay in shape?"

"No problem reading your mind, roommate, because I was thinking the same thing. We need to build up our bodies to continue being 'Greek gods' in the eyes of our future wives. Sex appeal is part of it and also the ability to shelter and protect our gorgeous girls. Let's go. Bet I can outrun ya to the Union!"

189

CHAPTER TWENTY-NINE

A PLOT UNCOVERED

Britt and Ahmad arrived at the Union Building at 9:00 on Saturday morning. Jeff and Pete were sitting in a far corner with no one else around. Pete stood up and waved to Britt, and they went over and sat down. Pete and Jeff brought pictures of Jenny and Rebecca to give to Britt and Ahmad. Pete told them that this was the place where the girls had met with the Arab guys. They all expressed the hope that another meeting would happen sometime during the day. The plan was for Britt and Ahmad to hang around until they saw the clandestine meeting, let Ahmad use his lip-reading skill, and then separate, with Ahmad following the Muslim guys and Britt following the girls. Bringing whatever information they gathered, they would meet back at Suttle dorm at noon and go up to Jeff and Pete's room to tell them. If nothing happened, Britt and Ahmad would go back to the Union and remain there until 5:00 p.m. if necessary. If they completed their mission before then, they would meet again at Suttle dorm. It seemed like a good plan, but it would be useless unless the Lord orchestrated everything. So the four of them prayed together for a successful outcome, whichever way it went – either finding nothing to be alarmed about or discovering an evil plot.

Jeff and Pete decided to go to the library following their meeting with Britt and Ahmad and get the books they needed for their homework in history. They had already told Gloria and Sarah that they would be studying in their room most all of the day. Pete knew Sarah had plenty to do, getting ready to teach her lesson on "The

191

Land of Israel" for their Jewish Roots class the next day. She said it was a great way to spend Shabbat, and she felt HaShem's joy. Gloria was using her time to practice the piano. At noon Pete and Jeff heard a knock on the door. It was Britt and Ahmad. Unfortunately, nothing had happened, but they did see some students who looked like they were from the Middle East. Ahmad said he got some practice reading lips, and he found several Arabic speakers. Nothing in their conversation was alarming, however. They all appeared to be genuine students and not intruders. The four men prayed together again that the afternoon surveillance would yield positive results, one way or the other. Then they went to lunch in twos back to the Union Building. Ahmad and Britt remained. It was a good thing they both had brought reading material while on watch, or they may have dozed off.

Part of their surveillance was walking around the large room. Ahmad went first while Britt stayed seated. When he noticed that Ahmad had been gone for about twenty minutes, Britt became alert and prayed silently in his prayer language. He craned his neck to see if he could spot Ahmad. In the meantime, back in the dorm Pete remembered that HE was the only one who saw the Arabs talking to Rebecca and Jenny, and he thought he could recognize them, if he saw them again. So he took the chance of scaring off their "prey" and ventured over to the Union Building about 3:00 o'clock. Britt saw him come in the front door but did not acknowledge him. Pete noticed that Ahmad was not at the table with Britt, so he nonchalantly walked toward the back of the room. Sure enough, there was Ahmad, sitting at a table about two tables away from the very same Arabs he had seen talking to Jenny and Rebecca! *Oh, Lord Jesus, please, please help Ahmad to get every word they are saying, every word. Oops, I see he notices me. I am going back to sit with Britt and pray with him while Ahmad "listens in" on the conversation. Then I will go back to the dorm, and Jeff and I will wait for the report.*

In about thirty minutes, Britt and Ahmad knocked on the dorm door. Pete and Jeff had been doing some serious praying.

Pete opened the door. "Come in, come in. We can hardly wait to hear what you have to report. Jeff and I will sit on the bed. You two sit in the chairs."

Britt was all smiles. "Well, the hard part is accomplished. You were right to suspect Jenny and Rebecca. After you hear what Ahmad heard, we will talk about a course of action. Tell them, Ahmad."

Ahmad cleared his throat. "The Lord Jesus has blessed me. I now realize HE is the One who gave me the ability to lip read. I caught almost all the conversation between the two Muslim men. Yes, they are Muslims, and they are not students. They live in New York, but their origin is from the West Bank in Israel. They are in a Palestinian terror group. Their names are Nasir and Omar. When I heard them mention 'Rebecca and Jenny,' I knew I had to get every word they were saying."

Pete and Jeff gasped. "But you didn't see Rebecca and Jenny meeting with them, did you?"

Ahmad continued. "No, the girls were not there. It seems they had met and made plans together last night. I figured out from their conversation that these men had come to the campus, looking for Sarah. They were asking around, and it so happened that they picked out Rebecca and Jenny and asked them if they knew a student named Sarah Bernstein. Jenny said that Sarah was once her roommate. The Muslims told the girls that Sarah owed them thousands of dollars in legal expenses because of her father's false testimony in a New York court. They needed to find a way to talk to Sarah. I heard them say that the girl named Jenny had suggested they come to Adaton Baptist Church at 10:00 in the morning because Sarah, as well as **two more Jews**, would be there, teaching the class. Any time in their conversation the name 'Jews' was mentioned, their faces were contorted with hate, and Nasir spit on the floor. Here is their plan. They will go to the church and wait until the class has started. Then they will come in the back door. They talked about their knives and how they would injure Sarah and the other two Jews. If they saw it would be possible to kill them, as well as a lot of Christians and Jew lovers in the room, they would be glad to die as shaheeds![91] Their faces lit up as they thought about being shaheeds. Then they talked some more about how they would escape. It wasn't money they were after. Their foremost objective was to seriously injure the girl Sarah or possibly kill her. Then they would leave the campus and report to a man named Malik. They knew that Malik would be happy, if they even injured the girl, and he would reward them greatly. If their mission was successful, Malik would not have to come back to the campus. They said that the first time Malik attacked Sarah was unsuccessful, and he was arrested in the JFK Airport when he tried again." Ahmad thought a minute to see if he had left out something. "Well, that's about it, as far as their plot. They said some other things about what was going on in Israel, and several times they expressed their hatred for the Jews everywhere, especially the ones in Israel."

Pete and Jeff were astonished, as was Britt also. After a few minutes went by, Pete had regained his composure enough to thank Ahmad for his help and for his amazing ability to lip read. But he was still angry and had to express himself. "So who are the **real** 'descendants of apes and pigs'? It's people like these Muslim terrorists. I know the Bible says that it is **God** who will take vengeance on evil doers, but I am offering myself as a **willing** instrument for His use." Pete's voice got louder and louder. "I am so angry, I could bite a nail in two! That Malik they mentioned who has tried to hurt Sarah **twice** is the one I would like to get my hands on. And this happens just as I was beginning to have a little bit of hope that Rebecca and Jenny would soften up and come to Jesus, but now they have conspired with these evil men to hurt my Sarah. How could they do that? Maybe they are demon-possessed. And what do they get out of it, if Sarah is hurt or even killed? It makes no sense. It's obvious from what you heard, Ahmad, that these girls would be happy if Jeff and Gloria are also hurt simply because they are Jews. Rebecca and Jenny are not dumb. Surely they could sense that these men are terrorists and intend to do physical harm to Sarah, as well as to Gloria and Jeff."

Jeff was angry, too. "Rebecca and Jenny are like a time bomb about to go off. And they only live a few doors down from Gloria and Sarah in the dorm. But I have faith that our mighty God is going to intervene tomorrow, and this horrific terrorist plot by two Muslims, aided by two hateful girls, is going to have a surprise ending. Our God is well aware of what is going on, and I believe He will cause all this to come out for our good and His glory."

"Jeff, I like your faith. And little brother," said Britt in a conciliatory tone, "You heard me tell how Ahmad went from being demon possessed to being Jesus-possessed in a matter of **hours**, so nothing is too difficult for the God of Israel. And speaking of the human instruments God uses, you two don't have to defend your girls alone tomorrow. Ahmad and I will be back for that class. We will bring our weapons, too, but I doubt we will have to use them. We are experienced in martial arts. Also, if you have male friends who are attending the class that are strong enough to help, contact them ahead of time. Their services may be needed."

"I will contact Walter Sessions. He is a tall, muscular guy and is already coming to the class," offered Jeff.

"And I will contact Gary Grayson. He and Priscilla were here last Sunday. It will thrill him to be in on this action," said Pete. "Of course, we must swear him and Walter to secrecy."

"I don't know how we are going to hide this from Gloria and Sarah," said Jeff. "But I think it is best for them **not** to know, especially Sarah. She will be a nervous wreck, trying to teach the lesson. I will contact Pastor James. I definitely think he should know what's up, don't you guys agree?"

Pete's mind was running ninety miles an hour. "Oh, I just thought of something. If we tell the Pastor, he is going to immediately think of all his flock in the building, and I bet he will ask if we have called the Oktibbeha County Sheriff. Should we notify him, Britt? Nasir and Omar will have to be put in jail and charges filed. Man, this thing is much bigger than I envisioned at first. Then we have to consider that Rebecca and Jenny are accomplices. Help me, Britt. Am I right about this?"

"Yes, Pete, you have stated it well. Evidently, your Criminal Justice class is part of your preparation for this takedown tomorrow. I will be glad to contact the sheriff. He will have to drive up in an unmarked car and be dressed like he's going to church. That should be no problem. Of course, he needs to join the class. No more than he and one deputy should come. I suggest the four of us have a meeting with Pastor James right away. Ahmad and I won't go back home until the plans are put in place. Then we will drive up to the church about fifteen minutes early tomorrow and take our seats at strategic places in the room. Jeff and Pete, when you call your two friends, tell them to come early and pray about where to sit. Ahmad and I will go see the sheriff now and go over the entire plan with him. After that, the four of us can talk to the Pastor. Will you set it up, Jeff?"

"Yes, I will. I think we should tell Gloria and Sarah ahead of time that Britt is attending and bringing Ahmad, so they won't be spooked when they see them and think something is going on. Pete, we can tell them that Ahmad and his wife have been attending the Jewish Roots class with Britt and Camille, and Ahmad wants to hear that second lesson on the Land of Israel **again** after he heard Britt's future sister-in-law would be teaching it." Jeff thought that was a pretty good idea, and maybe the Spirit gave it to him.

"Good idea, Jeff," agreed Pete. "I know we have to get moving and get everything set up, but the greatest concern I have is that Gloria and Sarah may have a meltdown when those two terrorists enter the room. Because they have the Holy Spirit living inside them like we do, they will definitely sense the evil in those guys. Maybe when they come in the room, we can whisper to the girls that it looks like they have followed Ahmad, maybe some of his friends from his old life. Is everyone in agreement?"

Each one agreed. Britt gave their plans closure. "Jeff and Pete, remember the lesson on spiritual warfare that Camille and I taught you at our house that night? Be sure you have the 'armor of God' on. And remember we don't war against flesh and blood but against the evil spirits inside these terrorists. Okay, everyone. Let's do our tasks. See you at the church shortly." But no one made a move until they held hands and prayed for the wisdom, knowledge, and power of the Lord to carry out these plans. They already understood that God was orchestrating all that had happened thus far, and they vowed to stay in a spirit of prayer and thanksgiving that God would make their plans successful. They encouraged each other to sing praises to the Lord and not let worry and fear get a foothold in their minds.

DRAMA IN THE CLASSROOM

Gloria and Sarah awoke on Sunday morning, refreshed and eager to see their men again and to go to Adaton for their class and the worship service. Both had been very busy the day before, and they were tired, but before they went to bed, they prayed together and took time to sing several songs to the Lord. Rebecca and Jenny had come by the room and asked if they wanted to watch a movie with them in the third-floor lobby. It was the old classic, "Gone With the Wind," but they politely declined, saying they wanted to have a devotional time and get to bed early. Gloria smiled at them and made small talk a little while, but it was obvious that Jenny and Rebecca were uncomfortable. Jenny said, "See you in the morning for class at Adaton."

Sarah could discern that Jenny was hiding something, but she didn't know what. Truly, it was a real mystery why those girls were attending their class. Since she and Gloria had been praying for them, Sarah believed that God would eventually grant them repentance and draw them by His Spirit to belief in Yeshua. As she and Gloria were getting dressed, Sarah said, "Gloria, I have a feeling that Jenny and Rebecca are going to encounter real suffering, but it will cause them to realize they need a Savior. We can't stop praying for them. Do you sense something evil around them? I do. Maybe they need deliverance like that Muslim man Britt told us about."

"Yes, they have indulged in gross sins, and maybe it has opened them up to demonic activity. Anyway, God told us to love them and pray for them. Oh, speaking of Britt, I got a call from Jeff, and he said Britt was coming to the class today and bringing that Muslim man with him. Isn't that great? His name is Ahmad Hafeez, and his wife's name is Fadwa, but she won't be with him today. They have been attending the Jewish Roots class with Britt and Camille. The last lesson was on the Land of Israel, the same lesson you are giving today, and Ahmad wanted to hear it again, Jeff said."

"Oh, my. I hope he won't be offended when I teach that Ishmael, the father of the Arabs, did not inherit the covenant for the Land from his father Abraham, but it was Isaac, the child of promise. And then the covenant was passed down through Isaac to Jacob, whose name God later changed to Israel. Muslims in general hate Israel. We Jews alive today have inherited that covenant. But when God called Abraham and told him that through his seed, meaning his descendants, all the families of the earth will be blessed,[92] God was not referring just to the Jews as Abraham's seed. He was referring to THE Seed, our Messiah Yeshua. And the **Gentiles** who believe in Yeshua are grafted into the Jewish olive tree and adopted into God's family. The Gentiles are the ones I will be speaking to at Adaton. **Besides you and Jeff and me, everyone in our class, including Ahmad, is a Gentile, and they all can share in God's promises to Abraham.** I guess Pete could be considered a Gentile, but he does have a trace of Jewish blood. Oh, my goodness, I think I am going to **love** being a teacher today. You know what, I could never in a million years stand up in front of a room full of people and teach from both the Hebrew Scriptures and the Brit Hadasha, if it was not for Yeshua living on the inside of me."

"Sweet roommate, be assured I will be praying for you the whole time you are teaching. And I also ask that you pray fervently for me as I play the piano and sing a solo in the worship service. I haven't told you yet, but the third verse of the hymn I'm singing was written by a **Jewish rabbi** in Germany in 1096. Isn't that awesome? When I sang it to Jeff right after we had met, he was deeply moved, and that hymn played a part in his salvation. So, this is a powerful song. I am believing it will move hearts at Adaton, and someone could even be saved. Help me believe for that, Sarah."

The Holy Rollers pulled in the church parking lot promptly at 9:30 a.m. Pastor James greeted them, and they went to the classroom together, held hands, and prayed for the Spirit of the Lord to be present in a stronger way than ever before. The Pastor brought Sarah a glass of water. She arranged her papers and put a big illustrated book of the Land of Israel on the table and tacked up a bigger map of the Land of Israel than was already on the wall. Pete took her face in his hands and said, "Darling, you are stunningly beautiful today. I can hardly wait to hear truth pour from your lips. I am right beside you, my insides cheering you on. Remember, I have pledged to be your shield at the risk of my life. No demon spirit can put fear on you today, no sirree. You are going to do great!" Then Pete encircled Sarah in his arms warmly and hugged her tight. Sarah looked up into his face, love shining from her eyes.

"Here they come," said Jeff. He went to the door and greeted Britt and Ahmad, then took them over to introduce Ahmad to Gloria, Sarah, and Pete, who pretended he had not met Ahmad before. All shook hands, but Sarah hesitated slightly. Jeff went over to greet Walter and Gary. *Now I will look out the back door to see if the terrorists have arrived. I haven't seen them before, but I know I will be able to recognize them. Oh, I see the sheriff and his deputy. They are pretty big guys. That must be them. Now it's time for me to be at the other door when Jenny and Rebecca come in. Lord, please help me to show love toward them and the other class members and be prepared to speak faith-filled words when the action starts. But keep me centered on my part of foiling the attack on Sarah and Gloria and myself. Pete is probably not a target, since he looks non-Jewish.*

Gloria looked out across the room. It was time to begin. She felt like the Lord was directing her to lead the class in singing "Days of Elijah" before Sarah started teaching. But she would welcome everyone first and then lead in prayer. Almost every seat was filled. She decided not to make introductions but would say what was burning in her heart. "Welcome to our second class on the Jewish Roots of the Church. I want to emphasize the most important fact of this course – Jesus Christ, or as we call Him in Hebrew, Yeshua HaMashiach, WAS and IS JEWISH. The very last title He gave Himself in Scripture is found in the final chapter of the Bible, Revelation 22:16 – 'I am the Root and Offspring of **David**, the Bright and Morning Star.' King David was the greatest king Israel ever had. Yeshua was also called 'the SON of David.' King Jesus is returning to Jerusalem, the capital city of Israel, to set up His throne and rule over the whole world. So you see, our roots as believers in Jesus are very, very Jewish, and we should never forget that. Now, let us bow our heads and pray for the Holy Spirit to be welcome here, to anoint Sarah as she teaches and to fill this room with His presence."

As Gloria prayed, people spontaneously reached out and held hands in the room. No one suggested it. It just happened. Jeff kept his eyes open, especially watching the back door. He noticed that Jenny and Rebecca refused the hands offered to them. Gloria was about to end the prayer, when Nasir and Omar came in and quickly found a seat. Jeff watched them intently. He saw Pete watching also. Nasir and Omar were sweating profusely, Jeff noticed. Their eyes were filled with fear as they looked around the room. They must have noticed quite a few brawny men. Gloria closed the prayer. Heads were lifted, and tears trickled down cheeks. Gloria told the class to get their song sheets, and she began to sing in a strong, steady voice "Days of Elijah." Pretty soon, the volume was increased as the newcomers caught on and joined in the singing. Jeff heard the Lord say, "The attack will happen about ten minutes into Sarah's teaching. Be ready."

Pete introduced his brother Britt and his friend Ahmad. He wanted to be sure no one would mistake Ahmad as one of the terrorists when the action started. Then he introduced Sarah as his fiancée and told a little bit of her background, how she and Gloria became roommates, and then how he met her. Sarah was grateful to have a few minutes to stand by Pete, drawing strength from his presence. Then Pete sat down, and she began her carefully prepared teaching on the Land of Israel, using the large map to point out the original size of the land that HaShem, the heavenly Father, had given to Abraham by covenant to be passed down through his descendants, Isaac, Jacob, and the twelve tribes of Israel, culminating in the Jews of today. Jeff noticed Nasir and Omar's faces change into hateful stares at the mention of the word 'Jews.' Sarah taught about God calling Abraham to go to the land of Moriah and sacrifice his only son Isaac. She read the whole chapter of Genesis 22. Everyone was amazed when she said that God had painted in advance a picture of Yeshua's sacrifice on the cross in this historical event, and she proved that the well-loved verse of John 3:16 in the New Testament was the fulfillment of Genesis 22.

Sarah explained, "God stopped Abraham from sacrificing his son Isaac and provided a ram instead. The ram was caught by its horns in the thicket. Verse 14 says, 'And Abraham called the name of the place, *Yahweh-Will-Provide*; as it is said to this day, 'In the Mount of Yahweh it shall be provided.' You see, God DID provide the sacrifice, not only in the case of a substitute for Isaac, but in the case of every one of us who will accept Yeshua as **our** substitute sacrifice for sin and be saved. The Hebrew name for that mountain is Yehovah Yireh. A thousand years later, King David bought with money that very piece of land on Mount Moriah,[93] and it became the site of his son Solomon's temple. Yeshua was crucified on the cross very near the spot. Yahweh said He would provide the sacrifice, and **He did**. And WHY did he? John 3:16 tells us – 'For God so LOVED the world that He gave His only begotten Son, that whosoever believes in Him should not perish but have eternal LIFE.' Yes, Isaac was a foreshadowing of Yeshua. He lay down willingly on that altar to be slain and then sacrificed as a burnt offering."

Suddenly, Nasir stood up and stomped his feet. Fire was in his eyes, and he was gesturing wildly as he shouted, "NO! IT WAS NOT ISAAC! IT WAS ISHMAEL![94] And it was NOT the Jewish temple that stood on that spot. What you call the Temple Mount is Haram Esh-Sharif, the Noble Sanctuary of Jerusalem.[95] And the Dome of the Rock is our beautiful gold-domed shrine that covers the rock where Allah commanded Abraham to sacrifice **Ishmael**, not Isaac! There have never been any Jewish temples on OUR mount! Palestine is OUR land. The Jews must get out! You Jews are liars! The mouth that teaches such lies must be STOPPED!"

Nasir, with lightning speed, drew out his knife and threw it at Sarah! Pete grabbed the large book on the table and raised it in front of Sarah's face. The knife hit the book at an angle and ricocheted off in the direction of Jenny. She moved her body quickly, but it stuck in her shoulder. She screamed, "Help! I'm wounded! Help! It's bleeding!" Her face was filled with terror. Blood was soaking her blouse. Rebecca ran from the room, screaming. Walter Sessions climbed over chairs to get to Jenny. Jeff shielded Gloria, and Pete shielded Sarah. The four ducked under the table. The Sheriff had grabbed Nasir the minute he threw his knife, and the deputy handcuffed him. Britt tackled Omar, who had already drawn his knife and was lunging at Gloria. Ahmad wrested the knife out of Omar's hand and helped Britt hold him on the floor until the deputy came over and handcuffed him. The Sheriff and the deputy marched Nasir and Omar out the back door and took them to the county jail. Britt and Ahmad sat down, breathing heavily.

Many in the class had knelt on the floor and were holding notebooks or purses up in front of their faces. Some had run out the hall door. Pastor James called for people in the room to be calm. "People, you are safe. Please sit in your chairs and try to calm down. The two terrorists are no longer a threat to any of you. The Sheriff and his deputy have them in custody and are now on the way to the County Jail. It is regretful that one person has been wounded. She is Jenny Simmons, a student at MSU. Her roommate, Rebecca

North, has left the room. Would someone go find her and tell her it is safe to come back in? We need to pray for Jenny, and ask God to heal her wound and give her peace. Walter Sessions has graciously offered to drive her to the hospital. I want all of you to know that four men here today were prepared for this attack. Stand up, men. Let me introduce these visitors again – Pete's brother, Britt Carson, and his friend, Ahmad Hafeez from Columbus Air Force Base. Because of a surveillance project, these men, together with Jeff and Pete, learned of this plot and worked out our response to the attack you just witnessed. The four of them met with me yesterday and warned me that our Jewish friends, Jeff, Gloria, and Sarah, would be attacked in this class, but Sarah would be the main target. To keep all kinds of rumors from circulating, I will tell you why these two Palestinian terrorists from the West Bank in Israel – their names are Nasir and Omar – wanted Sarah either dead or injured. Sarah's father, Dr. Nathan Bernstein, was a witness to the 1993 World Trade Center Bombing in New York City. His testimony helped to convict some of the terrorists that perpetrated the bombing, but the network of terrorists they belonged to are still active. These two that came here today to harm Sarah are a part of that network. Their motive was primarily vengeance. But also they fear that others in the network will be exposed and prosecuted. Perhaps they think that through harming Sarah, her family members will be terrorized and will surrender to them Dr. Bernstein's written documents concerning the 1993 bombing in exchange for the family being taken off the terrorists' hit list. Sarah has already been attacked on campus back in October, and we have discovered that the one who attacked her then is the same one who sent Nasir and Omar here. His name is Malik, and he attempted a second attack on Sarah in the JFK Airport in December. Now that I have given you three names of terrorists, I want you to be praying for them to be brought to justice. However, they are people for whom Jesus died, so pray for their salvation."

Everyone in the room was stunned. It was as if they were shell-shocked and needed some time to process what had happened. Gloria was well aware of this, as she heard the Holy Spirit prompting her to lead the class in singing. She stood up at the table and smiled at the people, allowing several minutes to pass, as the room fell completely silent. She just kept smiling. Then she began to sing very softly, *"He is here, let's celebrate the presence of the Lord. He is here, the Holy One, oh let Him be adored. He is here, to worship Him is such a sweet reward. He is here, in our midst, He is here."*[96] Most of the room had joined in at the end of the song. Gloria smoothly transitioned into singing, *"Oh, the blood of Jesus, oh, the blood of Jesus, oh, the blood of Jesus, it washes white as snow."* Then she raised the volume and indicated everyone should stand, continuing to sing: *"Oh, the blood has POWER, oh, the blood has power, oh, the blood has POWER to wash me white as snow."* Everyone's voice had a note of victory. Gloria said, "That was beautiful. The Lord gave me a verse while we were singing, and He said to take it to heart. He wants us to know He is leading us in victory. Our faith is the victory. Jesus said, 'In the world you shall have tribulation, but be of good cheer, I have OVERCOME the world.'"[97]

Gloria sat down. Jeff put his arm around her shoulder and whispered in her ear, "You are magnificent!"

Pete had already been holding Sarah in his arms as she cried and cried. Pete soothed her, and she gradually regained her composure and entered in the singing. Now she was smiling broadly, and inside she was praising HaShem with all her might.

Pastor James had greatly enjoyed the singing and felt completely refreshed. Now it was time for him to assume the mantle of authority the Lord had given him and lead the class in prayer, which included thanks for the wonderful lesson Sarah taught and the things they had learned. He asked that Jenny would be healed and have peace. He gave thanks for the men who had acted with courage to protect them and stop the terrorists. He specifically thanked God for giving Ahmad the ability to lip read and discover the plot. He asked the Prince of Peace to let His peace reign in the hearts of all the class members and to draw everyone close to Him in worship as the service was about to begin in the sanctuary.

CHAPTER THIRTY-ONE

ALL THINGS WORK TOGETHER FOR GOOD

The Adaton worship service ended right at twelve noon. Pastor James, with Gloria, Jeff, Pete, and Sarah standing by his side at the front door, shook hands and conversed with the people as they filed out of the sanctuary. Almost every person profusely thanked Gloria for playing the piano and singing that beautiful hymn, saying that they never understood or felt the love of God stronger than when Gloria sang those majestic words. Many remarked that the circumstances surrounding the writing of the third verse and its impact on the life of a person in the insane asylum made the hymn even more endearing. Several people had tears in their eyes and reached out to hug Gloria and then thank the Pastor for requesting that she sing.

Jeff leaned over and whispered to Gloria. "Honey, you are a celebrity now. That long line of people waiting to touch you and speak to you resembles autograph-seekers!"

Gloria whispered back, "Oh, Jeff. I want God to get the glory. Yes, I like to be appreciated, but surely it is obvious that the music and the story behind it came right down from His throne."

Sarah gave Gloria a fierce hug. "Roommate, you are my hero! Not only did you establish Yeshua's authority when you led our class both at the beginning and at the end with your soothing singing, but you knocked it out of the park with your piano playing and singing in the worship service. The fear that threatened to engulf me was driven far away, and I felt the Holy Spirit massaging my

209

heart. Thank you, dear friend." Gloria hugged Sarah back, and the love that flowed between them spilled over to the others.

Pete spoke up. "Pastor James, I want to congratulate you on the way you calmed our class members after the terrorists tried to sabotage Sarah's teaching and do her bodily harm. I am one sheep who felt secure under your leadership as our shepherd. Also, the sermon topic you picked could not have been more appropriate, and you were anointed with the Holy Spirit as you preached."

Pastor James smiled. "You Holy Rollers, as you call yourselves, must know that my sermon was entirely unplanned. This was the first time I did not preach what I had prepared. I simply spoke out of my heart what I have found to be true in my own life. In a time of danger and desperation what people need most is HOPE and assurance that whatever bad things God allows in our lives, it will ALL work together for **our good**. There is one condition, as you heard me say. The promise applies to us, if we love God and are called according to His purposes. That is probably my favorite verse, Romans 8:28."

"It did my heart good, Pastor," said Jeff. "Well, I guess we better be on our way. After a meal at Harvey's I plan to get me a good nap. I need it. When your adrenaline is pouring, it wears you out. Oh, wait, Pastor, let me tell you that Britt and Ahmad had to hurry home. Camille is keeping their dinner warm. They both said to tell you that they admire you for the way you preached the unadulterated truth of the Scriptures and also the way you handled the class in such a highly-charged atmosphere."

They could hear the phone ringing in the church office. The pastor said, "Let me go get that call, but don't leave yet. I have one more thing to say."

Pastor James was back in five minutes. "They got me in time before we all left. It was Walter Sessions. He wants you four to come to his house for lunch. As you probably know, Gary is his roommate, and they have gone to pick up hamburgers and French fries. They will probably be back by the time you arrive. Priscilla is with them. Together they took Jenny to the hospital. Walter said the waiting room was empty, so Jenny got immediate attention. Thankfully, it was only a flesh wound. The doctor stitched up the cut, cleaned it and dressed it and gave her a mild sedative. Then they took her to the dorm. They saw Rebecca's car there. Priscilla took Jenny to their room. Okay, that was the message. I have written down his address for you. Wait. I wanted to say one more thing to you all. I am SURE that the Lord has called you four to minister together. I think the Lord told me to tell you this – 'The bad things that may happen to you will all work TOGETHER for your good, as you minister TOGETHER.' But I, not the Lord, say to you, I think it would be a splendid idea if you have a DOUBLE wedding! You can pray about that, and see if the Lord agrees."

Jeff and Gloria looked at each other and grinned, thinking, "For sure, that is our sign." The pastor handed the note to Jeff, and he hugged them all goodbye and drove off. "Let's go," said Jeff, leading the way to the SUV. I think I can find Walter's house. It's on North Jackson Street. Oops, I didn't even ask y'all if you agree to go to Walter's for lunch. You probably were looking forward to a mouth-watering meal at Harvey's. But I think that fellowship with our friends should take precedence over food. What do y'all think?" All agreed and got in the SUV, as Jeff drove toward Walter's house.

Pete took a deep breath, trying to control his temper. "Yes, fellowship with friends is a good thing, but I think we should first report Jenny and Rebecca to the Sheriff. Ahmad can witness to the fact that they conspired with Nasir and Omar against Sarah, as well as you, Jeff and Gloria. Those girls were **accomplices** to the terror attack in our class today. And if the terrorists had succeeded, Sarah might be severely injured or not even be with us today!"

Gloria and Sarah looked at each other. "Wait a minute, wait a minute," said Sarah. "I am confused. Just HOW did Jenny and Rebecca play a part in the attack?"

At that point Pete realized the girls needed to be filled in on the whole story, so he recounted everything that had transpired since he first saw Rebecca and Jenny talking to the two men who turned out to be Nasir and Omar. Sarah's heart was racing. Gloria's anger was beginning to match Pete's. She moved away from Jeff on the front seat. "Jeff Quentin, how dare you hide this plot from Sarah and me! Can't you trust me? Do you think I am a fragile flower that will wilt at the first sign of trouble? Sarah and I didn't even have a chance to pray against the evil attack!"

Sarah also removed herself from Pete's embrace. "Pete Carson, I don't think you have any idea how tough I am. Yes, I have been glad to have you as my shield, but my trust is in HaShem, not in **you**! He may choose you to protect me, or He may choose another way to protect me. Don't get such an exaggerated idea of your importance!"

Jeff was praying silently with all the spiritual strength he could muster. He decided not to answer back. Walter's house came in sight, and he saw his vehicle, as well as Gary's in the driveway. "Well, here we are. Please, Holy Rollers, let's remember what the pastor said to us, 'The bad things that may happen to you will all work TOGETHER for your good, as you minister TOGETHER.' Let us all present a united front to Walter, Gary, and Priscilla. After we eat, I am going to ask that we have a little prayer time about the things that upset us. Is that agreed?"

Gloria took a deep breath and managed a half smile. Sarah wouldn't let Pete hold her hand, but she also agreed that prayer was needed.

Walter met them at the door, while Gary and Priscilla got the table set with their fast food and drinks. "I have good news. Come right in. Let's eat. Then we can talk." The four friends were grateful they could be with others, which would help them to cool off and find healing in their relationships.

Walter, Gary, and Priscilla couldn't help but notice a coolness between the two couples, but they determined to provide an easy and light atmosphere which might dispel the tension. After the small talk and the eating was finished, Walter said, "Let's go in the living room and get comfortable. I want to tell you the good news."

The countenances of the four friends displayed a skeptical attitude. Pete replied, "I think we all could use some good news after what happened in class today. Thank the good Lord we had some inspiration from Gloria's music and Pastor James' preaching, but the four of us need some healing from the trauma of the attack."

"Okay, here goes. Don't interrupt me. I will tell the whole story. First, you guys may not know that I have had my eye on Jenny Simmons this semester. For some reason, she appeals to me, and I had planned on asking her out. When she was stabbed in the shoulder today, I felt like I had been stabbed in the **heart**." Shock registered on everyone's face except for Gary and Priscilla. "I wanted to be sure I got her to the hospital as fast as possible. Gary and Priscilla followed us in Gary's car. Driving there, she started to cry. As I reached over to pat her arm, not the injured one, she looked at me with puppy-dog eyes, as if no one had ever shown her any concern. Anyway, that's how it felt in my gut, and I myself was almost moved to tears. Then she started crying harder and harder, until it looked like Niagara Falls. I offered comforting words. Again, she looked at me with sorrowful eyes, and torrents of words poured from her mouth. She was heaving so much, it was hard to make out everything she said. But I did understand this much – she was deeply sorry that she ever talked to those terrorists and kept saying over and over that Sarah did not deserve to be hated and attacked. Then she surprised me by saying, 'Oh, God, save my soul! I am wicked! I am wicked! I don't want to be the way I am any more. Please, please change me! And help me to make it up to Sarah. As a Jew, she has suffered enough hate and persecution. Help me get over this wound. I promise I will believe in Jesus like Sarah and Gloria do, I promise!"

It felt like a bombshell had been dropped in the room. Sarah was the first to speak. "Oh, Walter, thank you for caring for Jenny. When I was her roommate I saw how miserable she was. Of course,

I was disgusted with her relationship with Rebecca, but more than anything I felt sorry for her. To be honest, there were also times I hated her, especially when she and Rebecca both attacked me the day I moved out and moved in with Gloria. Jenny tripped me and I bumped my head on a chair. They made it look like an accident when a pile of books fell off the desk on me, and then Jenny crushed my hand with her big foot. But Gloria has been teaching me to forgive my enemies like Yeshua said. So, I want to say right now in front of all of you that I do forgive Jenny. Yeshua died for all those sins she confessed."

"Wait a minute," continued Walter. "There is more. Jenny also said that the two terrorists approached **them**, not the other way around. However, she admitted that she and Rebecca have had a prejudice against Jewish people. It's the way they were brought up. Jenny swore that she never dreamed these two men would actually try to **kill** Sarah, but she was sorry that she should have realized what they were up to. She and Rebecca told them that there would be three Jews in the class. Jenny really cried hard when she told me that she was jealous of Sarah and Gloria because they had attracted such good-looking men. After the doctor bandaged her up, he told her she would be very sore, but the wound would be completely healed in two weeks. Finally, Jenny got a smile on her face. She couldn't wait to get back to the dorm and tell Rebecca that she was going to be a follower of Jesus from now on."

All the anger drained out of the four friends. Jeff and Gloria looked at each other with unabashed longing. Pete and Sarah looked at each other the same way. And the two couples embraced and held on for dear life. Sarah was the first to speak. "Oh, I praise Yeshua. It was all worth it. It was worth it. The terrorist attack must have been HaShem's plan! Who would ever have figured it out? Thank you, Pete, for not telling me. I love you, I love you!"

Gloria was next to speak. "Jeff, how could I have ever doubted you? I trust your judgment, and I know you trust me, too. Jenny was a hard case but not too hard for our mighty God. She is saved, and Walter was privileged to witness it. Glory! I am so happy. I love you, Jeff, I love you!"

Gary and Priscilla were not going to be left out. They also flew into each other's arms and kissed passionately.

Walter grinned from ear to ear. "My day is coming. But my joy today has been sharing this good news with you friends. Right now I declare this house to be holy ground. Instead of going to movies or other places of entertainment, you all have a standing invitation to come here for fellowship, food, fun, sharing, and prayer. Who knows but what Jenny may be here in the near future."

Pete was beaming. "Our pastor is a smart guy. What he preached on today has been dramatized in our lives, proving that God's Word is true. 'And we know that all things work together for **good** to those who love God, to those who are the called according to His purpose.'"

Gary had been thinking. "And that is not the **only** Scripture that describes what happened at Adaton Baptist today. I was impressed that Pete raised that huge book in front of Sarah just in the nick of time, because Nasir's knife was on a trajectory to take her out! And then to see the knife deflected by the book made me think of the 'shield of faith' that is part of God's armor we wear to protect ourselves against the wiles of the devil. The Bible says the shield of faith will 'quench all the fiery darts of the wicked one.'[98] If that knife wasn't a fiery dart, then I don't know what is," declared Gary. "Pete was exercising his **faith** like a shield when he raised up that big book."

"That's the truth, Gary," exclaimed Pete. "I did something I had NOT planned to do. Grabbing Sarah, shielding her with my body, and ducking down under the table was the most logical thing to do. Ahmad had told us the terrorists would likely use knives, not guns, but I was expecting the terrorist to try to **stab** Sarah, not THROW a knife at her. The second I saw Nasir unsheathe his knife, I grabbed the book. It looks like God allowed the knife to wound Jenny, causing her to face her mortality and repent of her sins. Now that's something, isn't it? Sure does prove that God's ways are not our ways, nor are His thoughts our thoughts, as Isaiah says.[99]

"I am sorry Jenny was hurt, but if that's what it took to cause her to get right with God, then it was a good thing. And you know, it's really strange, but my book was barely scratched," marveled Sarah. "Remember, Gloria, we bought that book at the Christian book store next to the post office in downtown Jerusalem. Pete and Jeff were buying stamps for our postcards, and you and I were urgently looking for a bathroom! Thank goodness, there was one in that store. The man was so nice to us. He could tell we were believers, he said, because our lights were about to put out his eyes! Ha! And that illustrated book of the Land of Israel is such a treasure to me. Who would have ever thought that it would be a means of saving my life?"

"Sarah, I wish you had told the class about the maps in our Bibles being wrong, but you can tell them next Sunday. In your new book, the map of Israel in the days of Jesus is correct. I was glad to see that," said Gloria.

Everybody in the room began to thumb through their Bibles to the back. Pete said, "Okay, I am looking at my map. It is titled 'Palestine.'"

"Yes, that's the problem," answered Gloria. It should be titled 'Israel.' That was the name of the land in Jesus' day. I will prove it to you. Turn to Matthew 2:19-21. It reads, 'Now when Herod was dead, behold, an angel of the Lord appeared in a dream to Joseph in Egypt, saying, 'Arise, take the young Child and His mother, and go to the **land of Israel**, for those who sought the young Child's life are dead.' Then he arose, took the young Child and His mother, and came into **the land of Israel**.' You can see that **ISRAEL** was the name of the land in Jesus' day, NOT PALESTINE."

Jeff was really interested now. "So why are our Bible maps titled 'Palestine'?"

Gloria was eager to answer. "Sarah and I didn't know about this until the man in the Jerusalem book store told us. He said that it wasn't until A.D. 135 that the name of Israel changed to Palestine. It was after the Romans defeated the Jews in their second revolt, called the 'Bar Kochba Revolt.' Emperor Hadrian renamed the land 'Syria Palaestina,' which was later changed to 'Palestine.' The man — he must have been the owner of the book store — recommended this large book of the Land of Israel which has beautiful pictures along with the history of the Holy Land. It was expensive, but he gave us a free book in Hebrew. It contained testimonies by Jewish people who had met their Messiah. We went back to the post office and found Jeff and Pete talking to a security guard who knew a little English. It was obvious they were telling him about Yeshua, so we walked up and handed our free book to them. They gave it to the security guard. His name is Uri, and we have been praying for him ever since."

Priscilla got excited. "You girls make me want to go to Israel. I love our Jewish Roots class. I have a question which may seem dumb to you. But please tell me WHY it is important to know the land in Jesus' day was not called Palestine."

Jeff spoke up. "I think I can answer that. This fact is just symptomatic of the failure of the Church to recognize its Jewish roots and to remember that God made a unilateral and everlasting covenant with Abraham and his Jewish descendants for the land of Israel.[100] Most Christians think the Church has replaced Israel as the recipient of God's promises, and they completely forget that Jesus was and is Jewish. That is the very reason we are having this class. Do y'all mind if I pray? So many awesome things have happened today that my heart is overflowing with gratitude to God. Let's make a circle, holding hands, and each one of you pray whatever is on your heart. I love every one of you, especially my beautiful fiancée and songbird. Let's pray."

Bonds of love tightened their circle of friendship as prayers were spoken out of hearts full of faith and love. It was a time they would never forget.

CHAPTER THIRTY-TWO

FRUIT

Rebecca was asleep when Jenny got back to the room on Sunday afternoon. Jenny wanted to talk to her, but also she needed a nap. The mild sedative was doing its work, and it was easy to switch off her mind and yield to the spirit of slumber. Two hours passed before Jenny awoke. Rebecca wasn't there. Groggy from her deep sleep, Jenny sat on the edge of her bed, mulling over the life-changing events she had experienced a short time before. Thinking of Walter and his caring actions, she smiled. In the midst of her pain in his car and at the hospital, she also felt something else, and it was a good sensation. This man made her feel like a woman, a normal woman. She looked around the room and suddenly stood up. There was no sign that Rebecca had lived here. Didn't she see her in the bed when she came in two hours ago? She began opening drawers and opening the closet. It suddenly hit her. Rebecca had moved out! Then she heard a knock on the door. She unsteadily walked over to open the door. It was Sarah, of all people.

"Come in." Jenny's voice was full of wonder.

Sarah could see the puzzled look on Jenny's face. Taking a deep breath, Sarah began, "May I sit down?"

"Sure, take that chair over there."

Help me do this, HaShem. Please put words in my mouth. "Jenny, I came here to say how sorry I am that you were wounded this morning. I want you to forgive me for hating you. I don't hate you any longer, and I want to be your friend."

Jenny was wide awake now. "What? I can't believe what you said. I was the one hating **you**, and I didn't even have a reason. But **you** have a reason to hate **me.** I will admit it. Rebecca and I talked to those terrorists a week ago. They were looking for you, Sarah, saying you owed them money. They asked how to get in touch with you. I said the first thing that popped in my mind, that you would be at Adaton Baptist Church on Sunday, and I even added that there would be two more Jews with you. Sarah, I am so ashamed. Can you ever forgive me? I must have wanted you to be hurt, or I wouldn't have said what I said. Really, I didn't expect them to try to **kill** you though. Please **believe** me. But, most of all, please **forgive** me!" Jenny grabbed Sarah's hand as she knelt in front of her.

Sarah's heart was moved and she put her arms around Jenny. "Oh, Jenny, I love you, and certainly, I forgive you. Will you forgive me for hating you?"

"Yes, yes! That's easy. I **deserved** to be hated. I wish Rebecca were here. I want her to find the freedom and the love I have found in Jesus. But I don't know where she is. It looks like she has moved out," said Jenny, sadly. "Well, maybe it's for the best. I know we cannot continue the ungodly relationship we had. Actually, it makes me sick to even think about it. I feel the air in this room is entirely different now. And I am determined to find a godly roommate, if Rebecca isn't coming back. I don't want her coming back, until she knows Jesus like I do."

"Do you mind if we pray about that right now, Jenny? By the way, you probably didn't know, but Gloria and I have been praying for you and Rebecca to be saved for a long time. God answered our prayer for you today. I have faith He will also draw Rebecca to Himself. And don't worry about living here by yourself for a while. Rebecca has already paid the fee, so you can take your time about finding another roommate. Gloria and I will pray for that, too."

Sarah and Jenny held hands and talked to the Lord, expressing their thanksgiving for a tragedy being changed into a triumph, petitioning for a speedy healing of Jenny's arm, asking Him to direct her life step by step and cause her to grow in the faith, and then asking Him to save Rebecca. They prayed for Sarah's protection against another possible attack and for the Lord to bless Gloria, Jeff, Pete, Walter, Gary, Priscilla, and Brother James. Sarah and Jenny lovingly embraced, shedding tears, and speaking words of encouragement.

After Sarah left, Jenny pondered all the things that had happened to her in a few short hours. *Oh, Jesus, I love you for hearing my prayer and forgiving me. Thank you for the gift of a new relationship that is healthy and godly. My feelings toward my new friend Sarah are pure. I will never go back again to the impure and wicked relationship I had. I feel like You have cleansed me on the inside. Thank You, thank You. I can't wait to see how you will change my whole family through me, Your child. I think I love Walter. Is this Your idea, putting us together? These new feelings are very refreshing, Lord. You are first, but I do love Walter. Thank You.*

Sarah couldn't wait to report to Gloria about her visit with Jenny and that they were now friends. Gloria received the news with joy, and in her usual ebullient expression, she danced Sarah around the room. "Oh, Sarah, the Holy Rollers have produced FRUIT! God has used you and me, our prayers, but most of all, the ministry of the Holy Rollers as we held a class today that was popping with all the elements of high danger, which He used for His divine purposes. And He brought calm out of chaos and good out of evil and **fruit** out of barrenness. Whee! I feel the Holy Spirit infusing me with greater joy than ever. I remember this verse from a Bible Study at BSU. 'Jesus said, 'You did not choose me, but I chose you and appointed you so that you might go and **bear fruit**—fruit that will last—and so that whatever you ask in my name the Father will give you.'[101] I am really excited about how the Lord is using us to change lives!"

"Didn't you say you have a tough assignment in English, due tomorrow, and you also need to get over to the music building and practice, practice, practice? My wise fiancé said we are here at MSU for an education, dear Gloria. I have been praying for you that your piano performance in February will give glory to HaShem, so I want you to be well prepared. As for me, I don't want to put off preparing for my teaching at Adaton next Sunday. As you know, I was prevented from teaching the whole lesson. We had a 'little distraction,' didn't we?" Gloria and Sarah did their happy dance again, and Gloria picked up her music and English book with notebook and headed for the music building.

CHAPTER THIRTY-THREE

BEAUTY

FEBRUARY 10, 1998

Jeff and Gloria met in the lobby of Hamlin dorm to talk about their parents coming for the weekend. "Valentine's Day is coming up, babe. Do you want me to get you candy? Or am I sweet enough?" joked Jeff.

"A tiny little box of candy would be fine, but what I want most of all is for you to be on the front row at the Buttersworth Auditorium in Lee Hall, cheering me on when I am playing the piano Saturday night. And your prayers for me that I hit the right notes, and my heart doesn't beat out of my chest will be much appreciated, too."

"You bet I will be there. What an appropriate date for the concert, February 14th. I have been spreading the word, so the auditorium will be full."

"Now that's really funny. Have you been inside it? It is humongous – 1,000 seats! I don't understand why Mrs. Pagani picked that location. I certainly am not a famous pianist, and neither is Amy Rosenberg, who will be playing the duet with me." She will also play a Beethoven sonata, and my other piece is by Chopin. It is like a mini-concert with only two, possibly three, of us."

"I am all ears. Give me the details, sweetheart."

"Well, Amy will start out with the Beethoven number. Then I will play "Fantaisie-Impromptu in C# Minor" by Frederic Chopin. There may be another number by another student of Mrs. Pagani. I am not sure. But Amy and I will play "Hungarian Rhapsody No.

2 in C# Minor" by Franz Liszt at the end. It is a real crowd pleaser. You will probably recognize some of it, because the music has been used in animated cartoons. I get the biggest kick out of playing it. Mrs. Pagani gave me the treble part, and Amy has the bass part. My fingers really do get a work out. Please pray that I don't stumble. The cadenza is optional, but I am going to try it. One thing that thrills me is that I will get to play on a ten-foot Steinway concert grand. The tone is unbelievable. Oh, Jeff, I've been over there practicing, and I especially get carried away with the mellow tones when I am playing the middle section of 'Fantaisie-Impromptu.' That pretty melody was used as a popular vaudeville song, 'I'm Always Chasing Rainbows.' When you hear it, I know you will recognize it. The first part of the Chopin piece is really difficult because of the cross-rhythms. My right hand is playing sixteenth notes against the left hand playing triplets. I have to play it really fast to fit them together, but it is so fun to play."

"And I want you to have fun performing it. Just pretend it is only me listening. In my eyes you are perfect, and your playing is perfect. I love you so much, Gloria. And I am super proud of you and can't wait for my parents and your parents to hear you. With Dad being a descendant of Felix Mendelssohn and having those music genes, he will be knocked off his rocker! Mom and Dad have only heard you play one time, and it was nothing fancy, just a hymn."

"What do you mean JUST a hymn? I remember playing 'It is Well with My Soul' at your house. Our awesome God inspired that hymn at the lowest point in Horatio Spafford's life. His family was on an ocean liner, got hit by another ship, and his four daughters drowned. The music and words are Holy Spirit-anointed. He was comforted, and God uses that hymn to continually comfort others. Let me tell you something else. In my music appreciation class we have been studying the Romantic composers. You probably don't know, but there are different 'periods' in music history.

For instance, Mozart was in the Classical Period. Bach was in the Baroque Period. But my favorites are all in the Romantic Period."

"Hey, I am with you. Any kind of romantic music is my favorite, too. Come here, and let me show you just how romantic I can be, you lovely thing," Jeff cajoled.

"Jeff! We need to save that for a more private place. Now let me continue. Learning about Franz Liszt, Frederic Chopin, and Felix Mendelssohn, who were contemporaries and friends, I suddenly realized their first names all start with the letter F – Franz, Frederic, and Felix. Ha! It got me to wondering if maybe they were all Jewish, since we know Mendelssohn was."

"Hmm. That's interesting. I think a lot of the great composers were Jewish. And I know that some of the best popular music we have today, especially from Broadway musicals, was written by Jewish people. One example is Rodgers and Hammerstein. Yes, God has certainly gifted us Jews with musical talent. You, my dear, are proof of that."

"Something has been bothering me, Jeff. I had an assignment to study the lives of Liszt and Chopin, and I found that, although they were geniuses and composed and performed such beautiful piano music, there was much sin in their lives. Chopin was raised in a loving and religious family, but he drifted away from his faith while making his career in the salons of Paris, a horribly wicked city. When he met the infamous novelist who called herself George Sands, he was at first repulsed because she smoked cigars and wore men's clothing. But he lived with her for eight years in her country home, and they had a stormy romance.[102] Nevertheless, privately he was a man of prayer and knew the Scripture, as his friend Liszt and his servant attested. Right before his untimely and painful death at the age of thirty-nine, he finally returned to God. For four days his beloved Abbe heard his confession of sin. It was a bittersweet ending. He talked about being happy and how good God was to punish him for his sins.[103] Chopin was Poland's greatest composer, and thousands attended his funeral.

Let me tell you about Franz Liszt. He was the most famous concert superstar of the nineteenth century. As a child he begged his parents, unsuccessfully, to enroll him in seminary. All his life he was a fervent Christian, but he was also an incorrigible womanizer! He never married, even after living for years with one lover or another and fathering several illegitimate children![104] He was tall and handsome, and at his piano concerts women fainted and mobbed him. They called it 'Lisztomania.'[105] But can you believe that at the end of his life he became a monk? And he was the greatest composer of religious music, was a philanthropist, and was so loved for his unselfishness. What an enigma Liszt was. He and Chopin created music of great beauty, and yet their lifestyles betrayed that beauty. When I play Liszt's gorgeous piece, 'Liebestraum No. 3,' meaning 'Love Dream,' it moves my soul. It is sheer beauty. And I have learned a lot of Chopin pieces. They are **all** beautiful. But **how** can that beauty come out of people who have so greatly indulged their fleshly lusts? Help me understand, Jeff."

"That's a hard one. But think of how Solomon indulged his fleshly lusts with 700 wives and 300 concubines![106] And even King David committed adultery with Bathsheba and murdered her husband.[107] Maybe this verse will help. I memorized it. 'Finally, brothers and sisters, whatever is true, whatever is noble, whatever is right, whatever is pure' – now get this – 'whatever is LOVELY' – in other words, whatever has BEAUTY – 'whatever is admirable, if anything is excellent or praiseworthy, think about such things.'[108] So it is entirely fitting for us to praise and admire this classical music even though it was written by worldly people. Listen, we are getting a **secular** education. After all, we are not attending a seminary. And that's okay for us at this stage of our lives. Remember that the prophet Daniel was given a Babylonian education,[109] and it was useful for him in the position of influence God gave him with King Nebuchadnezzar…. Wait…can you believe I said all that? God showed me that on the spot!"

"He surely did. You sound like a sage, Jeff. And what you said really helps me. Thanks. While you were talking, God reminded me that we humans, all of us, good or bad, were created in His image. And He calls us His 'workmanship.' He is proud of what He has made, and that includes Chopin and Liszt, whose music He has used to bless others. And we are proud of what **we** make. As children, when we did a good job coloring a page in our coloring books, we considered it a masterpiece and showed it to everyone."

"Yeah, I was even proud of my mud pies." Jeff laughed and reached over to tickle Gloria. It was all she needed to dispel her melancholy. She got so tickled, she could hardly stop laughing.

"We've got to get serious, Gloria. We are supposed to be planning the weekend for our parents. They both will get here Thursday. We've got to pick up your parents at the airport that morning and take them to the Holiday Inn. Pete said that his dad will be happy to show them possible venues in Columbus for the wedding reception. There are quite a few, including ante-bellum mansions. My parents will drive here on Thursday and check into the same motel. All of us, including Pete, his parents, and Sarah, can go to The Veranda that night for dinner. Isn't it neat that your parents and my parents are talking to each other and planning the wedding?"

"Yes, I heard from Mom that she really likes Leah, and they think alike. Mom has not at all been disappointed that the wedding is not in Port Jefferson. On Friday, Mom and I are going to look for my wedding dress in Columbus. Then they have made an appointment with Pastor James on Saturday morning for the ten of us, Pete and Sarah, his parents, you and your parents, and me and my parents. I wish that Chaya and Max could come, but Chaya will be doing good to make the trip to Hungary in March at seven months pregnant, much less coming here at this time on an airplane. I refuse to be worried about the logistics of a double wedding. Our heavenly Father is our event planner, and He will take us through the planning as smooth as glass. I know it. It is a load off my mind that we finally settled on the date of the wedding – Shabbat, June 13th. Chaya and Max's baby should be a month old by then, and they can travel. Oh, by the way, for the concert on Saturday night Mrs. Pagani said that she has seats reserved for our families. She asked how many seats to reserve, and I guessed about fifteen. The seats will be on the very front. Ooh, Jeff, please, please keep the prayers going up for me."

CHAPTER THIRTY-FOUR

MRS. PAGANI'S PROTÉGÉ

"How do I look, Sarah? Do you think this dress is appropriate for the concert? I have only worn it one time because it is floor length and obviously for a formal occasion. The deep teal color is really pretty, don't you think? And I like the long sleeves and high scooped neckline. My pearls will look so good on it. Well, you haven't said anything. Am I overdressed?" Gloria fidgeted nervously, arranging her hair out of the way, so the drop pearl earrings could easily be seen. She looked at Sarah and saw that she was crying. "Oh, Sarah, please tell me what is wrong. I have been totally consumed with my appearance and didn't even notice you are upset."

"I am not upset. I am so happy. My heart is overflowing. Your beautiful appearance has made me realize afresh how blessed I am to have you as my closest friend and as my roommate. I couldn't find the words to tell you how angelic you look. If you play the piano as well as you look, there will be a standing ovation!" Sarah reached out and hugged Gloria tightly.

The phone rang. Gloria answered. "Oh, Mrs. Pagani. I am surprised to hear from you. The concert is only forty-five minutes away.... What? Amy is sick?..... Oh, no! What can we do?...... You really mean it? Wow! What an honor for me, and what a blessed bonus for the audience in person and the audience on T.V.... Really? That blows me away. You played it in Hungary?.... Oh, that's good. Amy will have another chance in April.... No, I'm sorry I will be in Chicago then, but I am honored you want me to play in another concert…. Oh, Mrs. Pagani, I don't think I am ready to do the Liebestraum. Would you allow me to substitute a hymn, maybe 'It is Well With My Soul'? I could even sing as I play, if there is a microphone on a boom stand available…. You will make it happen? Oh, that is fantastic. Thank you so much. My parents and my fiancé's parents will be in the audience. I know they will thank you. You are the greatest. And I can't wait to hear you play two numbers in place of Amy. In the meanwhile, I will pray for Amy to be healed, and I will pray for you and me to flow together like we've played the Hungarian Rhapsody duet hundreds of times…. Okay, see you soon."

Gloria hung up the phone and plopped down on her bed, her mouth hanging open. Sarah squealed with delight. "Oh, roommate, after tonight you will be famous. I understood the conversation. You and Mrs. Pagani will be playing that duet, and she even played it on a stage in Hungary! I want to talk to her and tell her that my family and I and my fiancé are traveling to Hungary during spring break. She can give me the name of the concert hall and also tell us places we should go see. I am more than excited, and I can't wait to hear you play tonight. Let me pray for you right now, and then you need to leave. Jeff is surely downstairs and getting nervous for you to appear, so he can get you to Lee Hall."

AFTER THE CONCERT

The audience was on its feet yet again, wildly applauding with shouts of "Bravo! Bravo! Encore! Encore!" They wanted a third encore. Mrs. Bianca Pagani led Gloria and her accompanist, Mr. Arturo Zappala, to the front of the stage. The three bowed deeply and received the avalanche of applause. Girls in bright dresses came onstage and presented Mrs. Pagani and Gloria with several bouquets of long-stemmed red, yellow, and white roses. Gloria looked out at her family, fiancé, and friends at the front and threw them kisses, smiling and shining with God's love.

Jeff had his arms waiting. If Gloria didn't come off the stage quickly enough, he would go backstage and grab her. He couldn't stand still much longer, and then, suddenly, she was right in front of him. Gloria eagerly flew into his arms, and they kissed without embarrassment. Gloria reached out to embrace all of hers and Jeff's family members, Sarah, and all the Carsons, which included Lars and Elsa, Britt, Camille, Melvin, Carola, Edward, and Elinor. Mrs. Pagani was right behind Gloria, waiting somewhat impatiently, and there was a white-haired man in a tuxedo with her. He was smiling broadly and extended his hand to Gloria. "Oh, Bianca's protégé is **much, much** more than she told me. My darling, I will make you the sensation of Europe. Please let us talk. I am Edsel Gruber, Bianca's concert manager."

Gloria shook Mr. Gruber's hand. "I am so glad to meet you, Mr. Gruber. I want to introduce all my family and friends to you and Mrs. Pagani. My parents and my fiancé's parents are here. Jeff Quentin is my fiancé. Please meet Alvin and Sylvia Sondheim and Jeffrey and Leah Quentin. Jeff's roommate is engaged to my roommate. Meet Pete Carson and Sarah Bernstein. His parents are here, Lars and Elsa Carson, and the rest of their family. Jeff and I are planning a double wedding with Sarah and Pete in June. So, I would like us to talk right here, and all can hear what you have to say. Your words have startled me."

Jeff spied two folding chairs and quickly brought them over for Mrs. Pagani and Mr. Gruber to face the family on the front rows. "Please sit here, Mrs. Pagani and Mr. Gruber. We are very happy to meet you, and we can't thank you enough for having Gloria in your concert. We all knew Gloria was musically talented, but we truly did not know HOW talented until tonight! And Mrs. Pagani, you were awesome on the piano, too. You must be the one who got this big audience here. We don't know how you did it, but we really thank you. And it's wonderful that this performance was also on television. Now please tell us what you want to say."

Mrs. Pagani spoke first. "Gloria, forgive me for not telling you beforehand that you would have an accompanist. When we spoke on the phone before the concert, and you wanted to sing and accompany yourself to fill in the gap from Amy's absence, I knew immediately that you should **stand** to sing. The audience could enjoy the full effect of your wonderful voice, as well as your commanding stage presence. You seem to have a flair for the theatrical. Your voice teacher has been telling me for weeks that I should hear you sing, so after I hung up the phone, I called Arturo Zappala, my colleague at the college, and asked him to hurry and come accompany you. He can sight read anything, so, of course, he could play that hymn for you that you planned, as well as the one you sang for an encore. Do you forgive me?"

"Of course, Mrs. Pagani. It was a real treat to have an accompanist. I am so used to playing for myself to sing. Mr. Zappala is quite accomplished. And I loved your playing the duet with me. What a virtuoso you are! I kept up with you though, didn't I? And what did you think of the cadenza?"

"Well, my dear, you had played it for me once, but you said it was too difficult to play for a performance. Actually, I was surprised you managed it beautifully."

Jeff had to comment. "Mrs. Pagani, you have taught Gloria well. The Hungarian Rhapsody blew me away. I'm glad you played it again for an encore. That music is the definition of 'happy.' I could go on and on. You may be surprised, but this is the first time I have been to a concert of classical music. I loved it!"

Mr. Gruber wanted to get down to business. "Yes, Jeff, as a concert manager, I make sure that popular tunes, crowd pleasers, are included in the program. We seek for both the heart and the head to be moved. Now, I want to talk business. My dear Gloria, you have no idea how far you can go on the concert stage, both as a pianist and as a vocalist. I have already arranged a concert in Central Europe for several outstanding artists, including Bianca, and I would like you to join them with at least three or four numbers, both piano and voice. Is there any way you can do that? Bianca says your spring holidays are beginning on Friday, March 13th, and going through the next week. It is that very week that I have the concert scheduled in three venues – Budapest, Vienna, and Prague. I appeal to you, Mr. and Mrs. Sondheim and Jeff Quentin to allow your Gloria to travel with Bianca for these concerts."

Mrs. Pagani interrupted. "Wait, Edsel. We must first ask if Gloria and Jeff have planned anything for the spring holidays. If they have not, or if they are willing to change their plans, I suggest Jeff accompany Gloria. The University has a Young Artists program, and they will pay all expenses for one of their students to travel to a foreign country for an artistic performance. Also, expenses will be paid for one person to accompany Gloria. The only stipulation is that they must share a hotel room. What do you say to that, Jeff and Gloria?"

Jeff gritted his teeth. He wanted to make sure he gave the correct response, so he paused for a few seconds, sending up a silent prayer. "This is a fantastic offer for Gloria. Actually, we had not yet made any plans for spring break. I think Gloria should do whatever she thinks is right. I myself cannot share a room with her until we are married, but I would be glad to pay my own expenses for another room. An option would be for Gloria's mother, Miss Sylvia, to accompany her. She has always had dreams of her daughter's success as a pianist."

Gloria's heart was beating fast. *Is this what you have for me, Lord? Can my light shine for You by playing the piano and singing in these concerts? Please give me an answer. I can tell that Jeff is a little unsure. But this may be a once-in-a-lifetime opportunity before I am married and have children. Should I seize the moment and step out in faith? I may be able to reach a lot of people for You, Lord, by appearing in these concerts.*

Sylvia was waiting for Gloria to say something. She was sure that her daughter should not let this opportunity pass her by. "Mr. Gruber, if Jeff is willing to go, I think that is the best option. But if he does not choose to, I will be glad to accompany my daughter. I was so thrilled tonight to hear her perform. Gloria and Jeff, what have you decided?"

Gloria whispered to Jeff that she felt this was God's plan for them. "Mr. Gruber, I am honored you think me worthy of appearing in concert in Europe. I gratefully accept your offer."

Jeff felt like he was backed in a corner, but he would open his mouth and trust God to put the words in it. "Yes, I agree to accompanying my fiancée. Mr. Gruber, if you will give me the itinerary, I will book a separate room for myself in each hotel. Thank you for asking Gloria to do this."

Mrs. Pagani and Mr. Gruber were ecstatic. They both talked at the same time, loudly expressing their gratitude to Jeff, Sylvia, and Gloria for agreeing to this concert tour.

"Leave it to me," Mrs. Pagani said. I will arrange everything, the flights, the lodging, the rooms. Gloria, we must coordinate with your voice teacher to prepare the solos, and you and I will decide on the piano numbers. You must practice, practice, practice between now and March 13th, a month away. I am very excited. Also, I will make sure Arturo Zappala can go along as your accompanist. Ah, Europe, here we come!"

Edsel Gruber and Bianca stayed behind to make plans for the concert tour after the auditorium was cleared out. "I knew you would be amazed, Edsel, at that girl's talent. This is her second year with me. She had a good background in high school, but she has progressed leaps and bounds with my teaching, especially in this her sophomore year. Also, her love affair with Jeff seems to give her more passion in her playing. But I don't know what to think about her desire to sing religious numbers. That is something new to me. Do you think that will go over with the European audience?"

"No, my dear, it will not. But we mustn't tell her that until we have left the States. You should prepare her with extra vocal numbers. Granted, she is an excellent pianist, but since she is so beautiful and very poised when she sings, the audience will prefer the vocal numbers. When you go shopping, please outfit her in colorful gowns that have more sex appeal than the one she wore tonight. I would say to use that one for the opening concert. After that, you make the decisions. Also, I can't help but say that she and Arturo looked especially handsome together on the stage. It's too bad she is engaged, and he is married. I had hoped they could share a suite at the hotel. It never hurts for the performers to be in love."

"Edsel! You shock me, and I am not easily shocked. I will not have a part of corrupting this naïve and beautiful girl. All you care about is large audiences and money, you old reprobate!"

"You didn't call me that when I rolled out the red carpet for YOU on the concert stage in Budapest last summer. I don't call it 'corrupting' a young and naïve person; I call it 'educating them in the real world.' As for Arturo, he and his wife are getting a divorce. You see he is not wearing his ring any more. Arturo is an outstanding artist, too. I concede that Jeff is a fine young man, but he is more naïve than Gloria. He turned down an opportunity to share a room with the girl he is going to marry. No one back home would ever have to know. Anyway, I am more interested in her talent than in her personal life. Thank you again for having me fly down here for this outstanding concert. Bianca, you yourself are quite a performer. This old man was thrilled with both of you ravishing women."

CHAPTER THIRTY-FIVE

CHANGE OF PLANS

GOLDEN TRIANGLE AIRPORT
FEBRUARY 15, 1998

Alvin and Sylvia had a hard time leaving their daughter, knowing they would not see her again until Passover in April at Papa Sam and Mama Anna's house. Their hearts were warmed, thinking of all that had transpired in three days. They had fallen in love with Leah and Jeffrey, the pastor and people at Adaton, the Carson family, and the South in general as represented on the Mississippi State University campus. They were aglow with visions of their outstanding daughter sharing her musical talents in Europe. Deep down they realized that these feelings had a lot to do with their new outlook on life since they had begun to read the Bible together. They loved the New Testament and had more telephone conversations about spiritual matters with Alvin's parents than ever before. Romance had come back into their lives, too. Now it was time to go home. Many hugs and endearing words were exchanged with Gloria and Jeff before they boarded the plane back to New York.

Gloria had tears as she fiercely hugged her mom and dad one more time. Then she and Jeff walked slowly to his SUV and sat there a while. "Oh, Jeff, this has been the most glorious Valentine weekend a girl could ever experience. Having our parents here to plan the wedding together, meeting with Pastor James, my concert, the offer to perform in Europe, and having our parents attend the Jewish Roots class and the worship service today makes my heart burst with gratitude to our heavenly Father. We could finally announce the wedding date in church today, and we can tell our friends at BSU on Wednesday. What a heart-stopping blessing it is that Walter and Jenny are now faithful members of our class. I love to see them holding hands and looking like they are in love almost as much as we are. We are coming right along on our outline, 'Why Study Jewish Roots?' The lesson today on 'Provoking the Jews to Jealousy' was excellent, and it was appropriate that Pete taught it, his being a Gentile. I am so glad his parents heard him. Romans 11 is certainly the most important chapter on that subject, and yet we rarely hear a sermon on it. It is smack dab in the middle of the book, and with chapters nine and ten, is the centerpiece of Paul's theology. I do love teaching the Church about its Jewish roots. Whew! I am so hyped up, I am just a little chatterbox."

Jeff took Gloria's face in his hands and looked deep into her eyes. "Little chatterbox, watching your lips move has excited me to the core. Just keep on talking. The sound of your voice mesmerizes me. One day I will own those beautiful lips. I am counting the days until June 13th. But to respond to your long monologue, I will say that I don't consider what you said 'chatter.' I agree with every word. Yeshua, our Shepherd, has led us this weekend, and the wedding is going to be His masterpiece. I am also looking forward to accompanying you to Vienna, Budapest, and Prague. I can't wait to get the itinerary, so we can compare it to Pete and Sarah's itinerary in Hungary. For sure, they must come to your concert in Budapest. Won't that be something? Maybe we can go with them to an important tourist spot that is connected to Pete's or Sarah's ancestry. They will have a lot to tell us, and we will have a lot to tell them about our separate adventures after we return to MSU. You know, we live a most unusual and rare, not to mention exciting, life since we met Jesus. I love Him so. And I am praying that you don't let the world's applause capture your heart, but you will love Jesus more and love me more than fame. I know it will be a great temptation, when they fall at your feet in Europe, and they WILL.

Maybe I better get your autograph NOW before your hand falls off from writing so many autographs in Europe," Jeff joked.

"Honey, I am announcing right now that Jesus is first in my life, and **you** are second. That is not going to change. But I do want your prayers."

TUESDAY, MARCH 10TH

Jeff called Gloria to meet him at the Chapel at 7:00, saying he had important things to tell her. Gloria hurriedly finished off her meal in the cafeteria and walked to the Chapel. Jeff was waiting on the front row, and the building was empty as usual.

"Well, what's up? I bolted down my supper, and I am anxious to hear what you have to say. You sounded very worried on the phone."

"I **am** worried. It's about my mother. She called me last night. Last week she went for a routine checkup with the family doctor. After she told him the pains she had been having in her neck, shoulder, and around her heart, he sent her to a cardiologist in Memphis. He wants her to have a heart catheterization at Methodist University Hospital. She found out today it is scheduled for March 16th. Her doctor is pretty sure she needs heart bypass surgery which would take place the next day. Gloria, I am her only child. I need to be there with Dad, and I need to stay at the hospital and then stay with them at home until she recovers. It's a good thing I will be out of school on spring break. I am very sorry I will not be able to go with you on your concert tour. You told me that Mrs. Pagani already booked our flight. Please tell her to cancel my reservation, and then make a reservation for your mother. You need to call Miss Sylvia and find out if she can go. If not, I guess you and Mrs. Pagani will have to room together, or you will room alone. Oh, babe, I hate I can't be with you. It breaks my heart, but it's clear to me that my mother comes first at this time."

"Sweetheart, you are right. You need to be with your mother. It breaks my heart, too. I will have to be brave. If it were possible,

I would back out of the tour and go with you to Tupelo and then to Memphis, but I have already signed the contract. I am forced into it now. Aw, shucks, I hate it!" Gloria started to cry.

"I knew you would respond this way. That's the awesome girl I am marrying. You would give up the opportunity of a lifetime to be with me and my family. But even if you wanted to break the contract, I would not let you. No, I would not. I don't think God would honor that. Well, I have a silver lining to this cloud. I bought a present for you, and it certainly tops a bouquet of roses at a concert. Close your eyes, and hold out your hands." Jeff put a small gift bag in Gloria's hands. "Now open your eyes."

Gloria was expecting an expensive gift of jewelry, but her eyes got big as she pulled a little phone out of the bag. "Is this a cell phone?"

"Yep, it sure is. Up until now, I couldn't afford one, but the price got low enough that I bought one for you and one for me. It's a Nokia 6110 and costs $900, but a two-year contract with a service provider brings the cost down to $200. My dad found out about it and bought himself and Mom one. Do you know what this means? We can stay in constant touch with each other across the ocean. I haven't checked to see what international calls cost, but it doesn't matter. I can afford it, but the one thing I cannot afford is to be out of contact with you an entire week. Do you like it?"

"Here's my answer, husband-to-be." Gloria grabbed Jeff and kissed him passionately. "Now all I have to do to be a success on the stage is hold this memory of you in my mind as I play and sing the romantic songs Mrs. Pagani is preparing me to sing."

"Ooh, your gratitude is overwhelming, babe. I want to know the names of the songs you are preparing, so I can find them at the library or on the internet and listen to them. I can then pray for your performance in a specific way."

"Well, I am going to the Buttersworth Auditorium right now. Mrs. Pagani said to be there at 8:00 for my practice. Do you want to go with me? I hope you aren't bored."

"That is a no-brainer. Of course, I want to go, and I will love it. But let's have a quick prayer for my mother first." Gloria reached for Jeff's hands, and she prayed that the Lord would cause the catheterization to show that no surgery was needed after all. Jeff squeezed her hands tightly in agreement. Their faith was strong. Then they prayed that Sylvia would be able to make the concert tour with Gloria and that Gloria's performances would glorify the Lord.

Jeff not only got a musical education at Gloria's rehearsal, but the different songs found a way into his heart. He remembered their conversation about the great composers most often having lifestyles that did not reflect the beauty of their musical creations. He observed Arturo Zappala at the piano and wondered what kind of person he was. It was evident that his talent was equal to and maybe surpassed Gloria's. He was skilled in following her at any tempo she chose. He never lagged behind or got ahead of her. The Italian music was something Jeff had never heard before, but it immediately impressed him as the 'plumb line' of classical songs. Without any previous knowledge of classical music, he somehow knew that the selections were perfect for a sophisticated audience. Mrs. Pagani handed him a printed program. It was good to see the English translation printed for 'Caro mio ben' by Giordani, composed in the 1700s. The translation was 'Thou, all my bliss (an arietta).' The most demanding of the songs for Gloria to sing was 'One Fine Day' from the opera, *Madame Butterfly*, by Giacomo Puccini. Jeff was relieved it was in English, so he could get involved in the story. He wondered if Gloria would wear a Japanese dress. Surely not, for just that one song. Besides, she didn't need anything but her voice to immerse the listener in the heartbreaking story, and Jeff could feel his **own** heart breaking as the song was finished. It was obvious the girl's lover would never return, and Jeff almost wanted to cry. But as Gloria began to sing "Let My Song Fill Your Heart (Viennese Waltz)" by Ernest Charles, Jeff's heart, which had been in the depths, now reached to the heights. What a happy and victorious way to end a concert. He assumed that was the finale.

Mrs. Pagani walked over to Jeff. "Well, what did you think?"

Jeff stood, tears streaming down his cheeks. "Mrs. Pagani, I am so proud of my girl I could burst. I know you call her your 'protégé,' but I have to tell you something she confided in me. She said that she knew she could sing well, and she enjoyed it, but after she met Jesus, her singing changed altogether. She feels like God gifted her with musical talent when she was born, but after she invited Jesus into her heart, He now **anoints** her singing. She wants to bring joy and blessing by playing the piano and singing. She wants the glory to go to God. She has told me that many times."

Mrs. Pagani didn't know what to say. "Well, she **has** brought joy to me, and I look forward to introducing her to the world. A talent like that cannot be hidden in a small southern town. I am looking forward to showing you and Gloria around Vienna, Budapest, and Prague." Bianca handed Jeff his and Gloria's tickets and the concert itinerary.

Gloria joined Jeff in the audience. Together, they broke the news to Mrs. Pagani that Jeff would not be accompanying Gloria, and they hoped Gloria's mother would take his place. Right there Jeff decided to call Mrs. Sondheim on his new cell phone. Jeff punched in the number, and in a few seconds Sylvia answered. All three of them were on tiptoe to see what the answer would be. The conversation was short. Jeff hung up with a big smile on his face. "She said her schedule was cleared for her to make the trip. Mrs. Pagani, will you please confer directly with her? You will need to cancel my reservation, and then have the University buy a ticket for her. I apologize for this inconvenience, but I **must** be with my mom and dad during her medical emergency. Gloria and I are both believing she won't have to have surgery. Nevertheless, I can't leave the country, not knowing what will happen to Mom. I'm sure you understand."

Gloria thanked Mrs. Pagani for this great opportunity and for her excellent teaching. For the first time, Gloria reached up and hugged her teacher. She wanted to say, "I love you," but she felt like a warm hug was enough. Jeff shook her hand and thanked her again for handling everything. He praised her ability as a teacher and also as a pianist.

CHAPTER THIRTY-SIX

VIENNA

I t was 11:00 p.m. in Vienna on Monday, March 16th, so it would be 4:00 p.m. in Memphis. Gloria couldn't wait any longer to call Jeff and find out how his mother was doing, if she had already had the heart catheterization, and if she got a good report. She took her cellphone in the bathroom, so she and Jeff could have a private conversation. Her mother was almost ready for bed.

"Jeff, can you hear me? Where are you? I have to know what the status is on your mother. I kept thinking about it all night, even while I was onstage singing. It's 11:00 p.m. here, and Mom is about to turn in for the night, but I wouldn't have been able to sleep a wink until I heard your voice, beloved."

Jeff was sitting in the waiting room with his dad, so he walked down the hall, looking for a private nook. "Hey, babe. Your voice is like an angel, and I know your **singing** voice wowed them tonight. I want to know every detail. However, we would spend a fortune if we talked that long," Jeff chuckled. "The nurse came out to tell us that Mom was resting well after the catheterization. She said the doctor would be here soon to say whether or not surgery was needed. Keep lifting her up in prayer. However, the night we prayed for her I seemed to hear the voice of the Lord telling me He heard and was already healing her."

"That's great! I felt the same way. I had a calm in my spirit. Now, let me quickly tell you how it went tonight. The Lord was with me on every piano piece and every song. I could feel His presence. But one thing wasn't right. I didn't get to sing the two hymns I was supposed to sing, and they were in the printed program. Mrs. Pagani said that Mr. Gruber insisted that Arturo and I play the popular piano duet, 'Malaguena,' by Ernesto Lecuona in place of the hymns. We had practiced it for a possible third encore, but I didn't expect we would get to play it. Mr. Gruber knows his business, because it brought down the house! We got more applause on that one than the Hungarian Rhapsody that I played with Mrs. Pagani. Jeff, please pray for me about Arturo. I think he is flirting with me, and when we played that duet, he kept glancing at me with a seductive expression. Also, he tried to press his body too close to mine. It was all I could do to keep playing and not miss notes. Oh, well, I don't want you to worry. I will get Mrs. Pagani to speak to him. I have one more prayer request, and then I must stop running up your phone bill. Mrs. Pagani took a tape measure to the dress I wore that night in Starkville, and she measured **me**, too, last week. I wore that dress tonight. But she shopped in Tupelo and bought me two more gowns, which she didn't show me. As soon as we arrived in Vienna, she took them to a seamstress that is employed by the concert hall and told her to tailor them to the measurements she took. They would be worn for the concerts in Budapest and Prague. I don't trust her. There's no telling how sexy they will be. The reason I think that is because she herself wore a very low-cut gown tonight, and it also had a split up the side almost to her waist! I am going to go looking for some safety pins at the hotel desk, just in case." Gloria couldn't help but laugh, wondering how she sounded to Jeff.

"This would be funny if it were someone else telling me this. But it is not funny when it's my girl they are trying to use as a sex object. In fact it makes me mad. If I hear a good report about my mom, and they say she can go home in the morning, I am flying to Budapest as quickly as I can. You can count on it!"

"Oh, honey, that would be wonderful! Maybe you can find where Pete, Sarah, and her family are staying. I think they arrived today. We will be in Budapest tomorrow, but the concert isn't until

Wednesday night. Then we go to Prague on Thursday and have the concert on Friday night. You saw the itinerary. We fly back on Sunday, and I should be at GTR in the evening. That's another thing I don't like. We flew into Vienna on Saturday, but I didn't get to go to church on Sunday. However, it was good to rest up from jet lag, and we had rehearsal that night, too. I will miss being at Adaton two Sundays in a row. Y'all keep our class going strong. I know you will. It's your time to teach, sweetheart. I'd give anything to be able to hear you. Please show me your notes when I get back. Oh, wait! You may be flying to Budapest today or tonight, your time, and will follow me to Prague and then back home. If you do, **you** will miss the class, too. I wonder when Pete and Sarah will be back. I know what we can do – ask Pastor James to take over the class that one Sunday. He could stay with our outline or he could give a bonus teaching. Be sure to call and ask him, if you do come to Budapest. I just know your mother won't need that surgery, and you **will** be coming. It's fun singing onstage to a huge audience and receiving wild applause, but still it doesn't match the **thrill** I feel being with you, Jeff."

"Okay, I will call Pastor. I know the doctor will give us a good report. In fact I already packed my bag before we left Tupelo. As soon as I got here I booked a flight to Budapest. I also got in touch with Pete for the name of the hotel, and I booked my room. The minute I hear the doctor's report, and if it's good news, I will get my dad to drive me to the airport. I'm so excited. I love you with all my heart, little songbird. Keep blessing the Europeans, and also insist on singing those two hymns. If Arturo won't play for you, just sing them a cappella. That's the way I first heard you sing, just your voice, no instruments. But I think you had an angel choir backing you up. I will absolutely never forget that life-changing experience, hearing you sing 'The Love of God.' I am kissing you goodbye. Call again whenever you want to. I do not mind the expense. You are definitely worth it. Did I say I love you? Here it is in Hebrew: **Ani**

ohev otakh." Jeff heard Gloria chuckle. "Pleased with me? Well, I prefer English – I LOVE YOU!"

Two nurses walked by Jeff as he finished the conversation with Gloria. They covered their mouths and giggled.

Sylvia shook Gloria. "Get up, Gloria. It is 6:00 a.m. in Vienna on Tuesday morning. We only have an hour or two to explore the 'musical capital of Europe.' It's cold, but I want us to walk to Stadtpark on the Ringstrasse. I hear there are gorgeous statues of the great musicians, like Johann Strauss, Franz Schubert, and Amadeus Mozart. Strauss, the 'Waltz King,' has a golden statue. You will love it. Get up, Gloria!"

"Oh, Mom, let me sleep thirty more minutes. I was up very late because Jeff called me back last night. Mom, he is coming to Budapest! Miss Leah is fine! But I wish he could see Vienna with us, the 'City of Love.' They say there are places all over the city for waltzing. And Beethoven had a house on the Ringstrasse. I will go to the park with you, but we won't have time to see the gorgeous Schonbrun Palace, the Hofburg Imperial Palace, or St. Stephen's Cathedral that I have read so much about. At least our concert took place in a landmark place, the Musikverein. How opulent it is. Mom, it is absolutely **cruel** to whisk us away from here at 10:00 this morning for the train ride to Budapest. I certainly hope that Jeff and I can come back. However, let me say right now, no city in the world is more important to us than Jerusalem, the Holy City. Jesus will return there and reign over the world as **King**."

"Honey, I think you are right. Your dad and I want to travel there soon. I hope you and Jeff have planned your honeymoon carefully, so you can do all the things you didn't have time to do last December."

"Yes, Mom, we will start planning in earnest after we meet you and Dad in Chicago at Papa Sam's and Mama Anna's for Passover. That reminds me, you and I have not had a real devotional time yet on this tour. Can we read some Scripture and pray together right now? And then I will dress and get a cup of coffee and a sweet roll, so we can be on our way to Stadtpark."

Sylvia turned to the Book of James where she left off reading a few days before and read aloud the first chapter. When she got to verses 14-15, Gloria stopped her and repeated the verses. "'But each one is tempted when he is drawn away by his own desires and enticed. Then, when desire has conceived, it gives birth to sin; and sin, when it is full-grown, brings forth death.' Let's pray right now, Mom. I hear God speaking to me. There is something He wants me to do."

Gloria led the prayer, first thanking the Lord for the perfor-mance last night and then asking for courage to do the thing He wants. Gloria could feel the Holy Spirit, and it was obvious her mother could, too, because she was trembling. "I have to go see Mrs. Pagani. She will be in her room because the Lord told me so, and He gave me something to say to her. It won't take me long." Gloria got dressed in a flash, walked a few doors down, and knocked on Mrs. Pagani's door.

Her teacher came to the door and invited Gloria in. It was a surprise to see Arturo there. They were having coffee and sweet rolls. The three of them sat down in the plush chairs. Gloria didn't want to take time for small talk, but she was reminded that she did owe Mrs. Pagani a lot for her excellent teaching and also giving her this opportunity to perform, which she expressed first. Then she took a deep breath, looking straight at Mrs. Pagani, and delivered God's message to her. "Mrs. Pagani, I don't know how far along the seamstress is with my gowns for the other two concerts, but I have to warn you that I may not wear them if the necklines are cut too low, or if there are any slits up the sides of the skirts. To be clear, I do not want to look sexy. I am sorry if the sewing has been in vain, but I may have to wear my own gown the other two nights. I have given my life to Jesus Christ, and I want to glorify Him in my appearance, as well as in my actions."

Mrs. Pagani was taken aback. "My child, you cannot dictate to me. You have signed a contract, and the terms are to be under my instructions and provisions, along with Mr. Gruber's. But I do not want to be harsh with you. You are unlike any student I have had before. I guess I should have realized from our previous conversations that you and Jeff are very religious and out of step with the rest of the world. Anyway, it's good you have come to me early. I will go back to the seamstress and have her modify the gowns. I hope she can finish by the time we have to depart. Edsel will be upset, but if you perform in Budapest and Prague like you did last night, he will be glad that I gave in to your eccentric request."

Gloria smiled big and put her arms around her teacher. "I love you, Mrs. Pagani, and I wouldn't trade you for any other teacher in the world!" Bianca was shocked at this display of affection but welcomed it. They knew all was well. Arturo had sat and observed this odd behavior with his eyebrows raised. He stood and nodded his head as Gloria smiled at him and left the room.

CHAPTER THIRTY-SEVEN

Together Again in Budapest

BUDAPEST – MARCH 17TH

Checking into the hotel in Budapest, Edsel Gruber casually mentioned to Bianca that they must be at the Vigado Concert Hall[110] that night to rehearse at 8:00 p.m. "What? Oh, Edsel, it cannot be! I am ecstatic! How did you do it? We will be performing at the Vigado Concert Hall on the Danube River? But you know that Gloria Sondheim and I are not equal to the task. This is like a fairy tale. Miss Sondheim will faint, and I myself am not sure my heart won't stop. If you have done something illegal to get us on this amazing concert stage, I don't even **want** to know about it. HOW did you do it, Edsel?" Mrs. Pagani began to laugh hysterically and smothered Mr. Gruber with kisses.

"My dear Bianca, you act like a teenager. I can see that you do not realize my stature in the music world in Europe. You see, there are powerful people who owe me favors. Please, do not act like a Mississippi country bumpkin. You were born for this stage. Remember your Hungarian roots. And your protégé has done something to my heart. I am an old man, but I have fallen in love with her. I do not mean romantic love, but her singing and playing have won my heart. If it's the last thing I do, I will make her famous. You watch. Coach her well tonight. And you also are star material, Bianca."

"Wait a minute. The Vigado Concert Hall is not what you had printed in the itinerary. I hear that Jeff Quentin is flying over here. I hope he finds us."

"Well, maybe he won't. He and I may be working at cross-purposes anyway. You know what I mean."

"Edsel, I will not hide this from Gloria. I am going to tell her right now. She said their roommates who are also engaged, will be at the concert tomorrow tonight. Do you remember Pete Carson and Sarah Bernstein? They are touring Hungary with Sarah's sister and her husband. Gloria wants to spend some time with them. You know the two couples are having a double wedding in June, don't you? Together they have a religious ministry, unfortunately. I don't want Gloria to be distracted from her music career. I am warning you, Edsel, if we don't let her sing the religious numbers, we may lose her. She can be stubborn."

"Well, wasn't I right about substituting the Malaguena duet for her hymns? I could tell she really enjoyed playing it. Maybe I will let her do the two hymns tomorrow night, but I have to think about it. Another thing you must emphasize to Gloria is to remember that Franz Liszt is greatly revered all over Hungary. He held many concerts in the Vigado Concert Hall. She must put her heart and soul more than ever into playing 'Liebestraum.' Also tell her not to be surprised if a few people in the audience get so bold as to start dancing during the 'Hungarian Rhapsody!' I love it when they do that. And Chopin's 'Fantaisie Impromptu' will likely not elicit as much applause in Budapest as it did in Vienna. Tell her not to worry about it, but she could put more passion into the middle section, as well as the final page. Tell her, Bianca. This old man has been around."

"Of course, Edsel. I always try to please you. You have opened many doors for me, and you have forgiven me for settling on a position at Mississippi State University instead of trotting the globe with you. I do love you, my friend." Edsel kissed Bianca on the cheek.

Gloria and Sylvia walked into the lobby of the beautiful Ritz-Carlton Hotel. They were at the desk checking in, when Gloria felt strong hands on her shoulders, turning her around to look into the laughing faces of Pete and Sarah. "Oh, you are staying at the Ritz Carlton, too? How fantastic! I have really missed you two and Jeff." Gloria got them in a group hug. Then Pete and Sarah hugged Sylvia.

Sarah explained that due to the family inheritance they could afford to stay in this expensive hotel, and she had prayed it was the same one in which Gloria and her mother would be staying. "My prayer was answered. Another God incidence for the Holy Rollers. Yea! As soon as you get settled, you and Miss Sylvia meet us back here in the lobby at 1:30, and we can get started on our tour. Chaya feels like all the walking involved would be too much for her with the baby coming in only two months. She and Max are in their room. You will get to see them later."

In about twenty minutes, Gloria and her mother met Pete and Sarah back in the lobby. "Sarah and Pete, let me tell you first that Miss Leah is okay. I talked to Jeff at 11:00 last night. He called an hour later and told me that the doctor found she did not need surgery after all. Jeff and I spent five precious minutes on the phone, thanking and worshiping the Lord. And Jeff should be in the air now. In faith that his mother would not have to have surgery, he packed his bag before he left Tupelo. He was so sure of it that he went ahead and booked a flight at the Memphis Airport. After the good report from the doctor, he left last night. Can you believe it? He is supposed to arrive here tonight. He will miss the sightseeing today, but he can go with us again tomorrow morning. Isn't that great?"

Sarah said, "Yes, the Holy Rollers will roll again in Budapest. Ha! I have already called the taxi. Let's go outside and wait. We are going to see the Raoul Wallenberg Holocaust Memorial Park. Here is the description in the tour I have planned for us today. Listen. 'This memorial park pays tribute to Raoul Wallenberg, a Righteous

Among the Nations. It is located at the back side of the Great Dohany Street Synagogue and features the Tree of Life, a haunting weeping willow sculpture with the last names of Jewish victims. The synagogue is the largest in Europe and one of the biggest in the world. It has twin onion-shaped domes.' But first we will eat a late lunch there in the Jewish Quarter. I am so excited! Well, here is the taxi. We will be there is no time, so let me quickly read you something from Great Uncle Boris' diary about Raoul Wallenberg. Remember, I already read you some of it that day at Pete's house when he proposed to me."

Sylvia looked confused. "Wait, Sarah, I haven't heard all this. Gloria, you should have told me."

"Mom, I apologize. My life is going so fast I forget to call and keep you up to date. I did tell you that Sarah's ancestors came from Hungary. Her Uncle Boris was among the Jews in Budapest that were saved from the concentration camps by Raoul Wallenberg. And then we had the surprise of our lives when Pete's brother revealed their genealogical link to Wallenberg!" Sylvia squeezed Gloria's hand and assured her she understood.

Sarah continued, "Listen up. This part precedes what I read you at Pete's house. Uncle Boris wrote, 'We were in a train full of Jews on the point of leaving for Germany and the death camps. The officer of the guard did not want Wallenberg to enter. He then climbed up on the roof of the train and handed in many protective passports through the windows. The Arrow Cross men fired their guns and cried to him to go away, but he continued calmly to hand out passports to the hands which reached for them. I believe that the men with the guns were impressed by his courage and on purpose aimed above him. Afterwards, he managed to get all Jews with passports out from the train.'"

"Here is another excerpt from the diary: 'On November 4, Arrow Cross goons were called, and they held several hundred Jews at Dohany Synagogue.' **Hey, we are going there now**. To continue, 'Wallenberg burst into the temple and stood himself in front of the altar and made this announcement: 'All those who have Swedish protective passes should stand up.' That same night a few hundred of us Jews were freed, and we returned to our houses under the protection of Hungarian policemen.' Amazing, isn't it? Oh, don't you love Raoul Wallenberg? I am going to get on the internet and read all I can about him. Just to think, Pete, you are actually kin to that heroic man."

"Yes, Sarah, my bashert, and you will soon be kin to him, too, when we get married in June. Well, here we are."

As they were getting out of the taxi, Gloria said, "I don't want this tour to be cut short, but I must be back at the hotel by 3:00, because my new gowns require a final fitting, as well as the Japanese costume Mr. Gruber requires for my solo, 'One Fine Day' from *Madame Butterfly.* But you can drop Mom and me off and continue on. Mrs. Pagani insists I get a good nap after the fitting, and then we will rehearse at 4:30. I believe **my** bashert will be here in time to have dinner with us. Then I have to get to the second rehearsal at 8:00 p.m., which will be a full dress rehearsal. I am not inviting you two and Jeff because I want you to see the real performance fresh. I will have two changes to make while Mrs. Pagani is onstage, playing her pieces. As you can see, this is a 'working vacation' for me. But I am not complaining. I have to admit, I love performing. The concert hall tonight can seat 700 people, and Mr. Gruber assures me it will be full. He said he had 'an ace up his sleeve' to draw the cqrowds. I have no idea what he meant by that, but these worldly people God has put me in the midst of bear close watching. All of you, please help me pray that God will be glorified, no matter what Mr. Gruber has plans for. As for the sight-seeing, save something special for Jeff and me tomorrow. I will have the entire morning and a few hours after lunch. Now let's go see our Jewish heritage here in Budapest."

At 3:00 Gloria and her mother were dropped off at the hotel. Sylvia decided to go to their room while Gloria had her fitting in Mrs. Pagani's room. Her teacher had brought the gowns that the seamstress in Vienna had finished, and when Gloria tried them on, it was obvious they needed no further alterations. The seamstress in Budapest had received the measurements from Mrs. Pagani the day before from which to make the Japanese costume, and it fit perfectly. However, it wasn't easy to put on and take off. There were several zippers to maneuver. It shouldn't be a problem though because the wardrobe lady in the dressing room was experienced and came highly recommended. Gloria was pleased with the other two costumes. As she had requested, the necklines were high enough, and there were no slits up the sides. She breathed a sigh of relief. She and the teacher were ready to go to the concert hall for rehearsal, when they heard a knock on the door. It was Mr. Gruber.

"Bianca and Gloria, I have a surprise for you. Look at this!" exclaimed Mr. Gruber, holding out a newspaper.

Mrs. Pagani squealed with delight. Halfway down the front page of the Budapest newspaper were these bold headlines: "AMERICAN TEENAGE SINGING SENSATION GLORIA SONDHEIM APPEARS TOMORROW NIGHT AT THE VI-GADO."

Gloria felt like she was going to faint. It was several seconds before she could respond. Finally, she said, "I must show this to my mother," and she quickly hurried from the room, her heart beating wildly.

Sylvia had just awakened from her nap and was sitting by the window, holding a cup of hot tea, when Gloria burst into the room. The newspaper was thrust in her hand, and she read the headline, threw down the paper, and embraced her daughter excitedly. "Oh, my talented, beautiful daughter! This is one of the happiest days of my life. Gloria, you are taking Europe by storm with your musical talent. I am so grateful to the Lord God. Please let me use your cell phone so I can call Alvin right now. I hope he doesn't have a heart attack!"

Gloria picked up the newspaper and read the entire article. She could see that Mr. Gruber had stepped over the line of truth with his exaggerations about her training, experience, and ability. On every point it was not really true. This was the world scene she had been thrust into. She wished she could talk to Jeff. While her mother was on the phone, she prayed silently. *Dear Lord, is this what you want for me? I remember that the Jewish girl Hadassah became Queen Esther of Persia. The young Jewish boy Daniel, in captivity in Babylon, became a ruler there because of his gift of interpreting dreams. I am a Jewish youth also. You have given me the gift of musical talent. What use do you have for it? Is my transformation from an unknown college student to a singing star in Europe part of your plan for me? When I perform tomorrow night, I want you to give me some kind of sign. I will not go a step further if you show me I have gotten out of the center of your will. I will not go on to Prague in that case. But, oh Lord, Jeff, Sarah, and Pete will be in the audience tomorrow night. I ask you to bless them and bless my mother, whichever way you show me your will. In Jesus' name. Amen.*

At 6:00 that night Gloria, Sylvia, Pete, Sarah, Chaya, and Max met in the hotel dining room and ordered their food. Everyone was chattering about their experiences in Budapest that day except Gloria. She was silently praying that all went well with Jeff's flight, and he would soon arrive. The waiter brought their food, and Pete led the prayer. He thanked God for the food, their wonderful tour, and for giving Jeff a safe flight. As Gloria picked up her glass of water, she noticed that everyone at the table had bright smiles, and they were staring at her. Then she felt her neck grow warm. Jeff had come up behind her and gently kissed her on the neck. She jumped out of her chair and into Jeff's arms. They unashamedly hugged and kissed. The dining room erupted in laughter and applause. Eating was suspended as Jeff told his table partners how the Lord opened the Red Sea for him to get from Memphis to Budapest in record time. He also told them the hotel gave him a room only a few doors down from Gloria and her mother. The conversation flowed.

Sarah tapped her knife on her glass. "Attention! We must recognize one of the Holy Rollers who has come to a milestone in his life. He is blazing a trail for the four of us, leaving the life of a teenager. Tonight Pete Carson is twenty years old! Look, here comes his birthday cake." The waitress walked to their table on cue with a small cake topped with twenty blazing candles. Jeff pulled Pete to his feet to receive loud congratulations from everyone. Gloria led the 'Happy Birthday' song. Then all in the dining room applauded.

Pete dutifully bent his tall frame over the cake and blew out the candles. He chided Sarah, "I told you not to tell, my bashert. I see I have to start now training you to be a submissive wife." Sarah bowed her head in mock repentance.

Max extended his hand in congratulations. "Good luck with that, future brother-in-law," he joked, as he looked at Chaya. Hearty laughter erupted at the table.

CHAPTER THIRTY-EIGHT

HIS NAIL-PIERCED HAND

The night of the concert had come. Gloria, Mrs. Pagani, Mr. Gruber, and Arturo Zappala were backstage at the Vigado Concert Hall. It was 8:00 p.m. Mr. Gruber walked onstage to introduce the program. The others looked through the curtain to see a packed audience. Gloria was glad that seats had been reserved for her mother, Jeff, Pete, Sarah, Chaya, and Max right at the front. She saw Jeff looking at the curtain intently. She knew he was praying, and so was she. It would be time for her Budapest debut after Mrs. Pagani played her first two numbers. At that point Gloria felt like she was on auto-pilot. Each piece she played, and each song she sang was greeted with enthusiastic applause. She could feel the Holy Spirit's hand on her, and her heart filled with love as she played Liszt's "Liebestraum" and Chopin's "Fantaisie-Impromptu." Whatever the composers felt like when they wrote that gorgeous music did not matter to her now. She only wanted to glorify God and communicate His presence as she played. But it seemed the Lord had put her in a bubble during the whole concert. Everything was almost like a blur. It transpired so quickly up to a point.

While Mrs. Pagani played her third and fourth numbers, it was time for Gloria to change into her second new gown. She loved the first one. It was made of shimmering white satin with touches of lace and sequins. If the style had been different, it would have looked like a wedding dress. It exuded purity and innocence. The second one was a pale rose color, and its lines made her appear taller than she was. This brought to her memory how Mrs. Pagani

259

had said she had a commanding stage presence when she sang and that she had a flair for the theatrical. Gloria had no fear. It was like she was floating.

Her performances of 'Caro mio ben' and 'Let My Song Fill Your Heart (Viennese Waltz)" were greeted with thunderous applause. Now it was time for the climax of the concert, Liszt's duet, "Hungarian Rhapsody No. 2," with Mrs. Pagani. For some reason, Mr. Gruber decided that she should end the concert with the *Madame Butterfly* aria. She would have plenty of time to change into her Japanese costume after the duet, while Mrs. Pagani played two more solo numbers. Gloria had been promised that she could sing the two hymns, "The Love of God" and "It is Well with My Soul," as encores. Her whole focus was on the hymns, as her time on the stage progressed. She did not know that Mr. Gruber had persuaded the head of an opera company in New York to come to the concert and give his assessment of Miss Sondheim's chances of becoming an opera singer at the Metropolitan.

Gloria was backstage, changing into her Japanese costume, her arms still covered with chill bumps from the prolonged standing ovation for the Hungarian Rhapsody duet. Some in the audience had indeed danced in the aisles, and this was an added ingredient of entertainment for those who could see them. Enthusiastic concert goers had thrown flowers on the stage in raucous approval of the outstanding performance of Liszt's famous folk music. Gloria had worried that the hair and makeup artist would be making her over as a Geisha girl, but the woman did not change her hair style and only put a few upward lines from her eyes to give her an Asian appearance. She looked like herself. And she was thankful the dress only had a Japanese "flavor" and was not like the clothes worn in the opera. Gloria's mind was on Jeff now, as the concert was drawing to a close. She had not noticed that the wardrobe lady was looking sick, until she heard her cry out and run from the room. *Oh, no! I don't think she is coming back. I hear the bathroom door slamming shut. She must be really sick. And it's almost time to go onstage. Oh, my goodness! I can't get this thing zipped up. It's hard to reach all the way up my back…. I've got it now…. No, I don't. Durn it! It's stuck. What can I do, Lord? I can't go out there with the back hanging open. Mrs. Pagani is receiving applause now. Should I wait for her to come backstage?*

Gloria came all the way back down to earth. She had been immune to fear the entire night, but now it was raging in her. She looked, and no one but Arturo was standing in the wings. *Where is Mr. Gruber? I can't believe Arturo is the only one around. I have no choice. I will have to ask him to get this zipper to work. How humiliating.*

"Arturo, I am having a problem with this Japanese dress. It has several zippers. I think I closed them all except this one long one that goes all the way up the back. I could barely reach it, and now I've got it stuck. Could you please get it loose and zip me up? I don't want to make the audience wait after Mrs. Pagani comes off the stage. I want to go right out there like we have rehearsed."

Arturo grinned from ear to ear. "Our beautiful little songbird who never has a problem now needs my services. I don't know what happened to the wardrobe lady, but lady fortune is smiling on me to allow me to take her place. Just turn around, Gloria. I will be glad to assist."

Gloria cringed, but she had to have his help. As Arturo was working to unstick the zipper, Gloria said, "Arturo, I am really grateful for you as a talented accompanist, and now I am grateful for your help in this emergency."

No sooner were the words out of her mouth than Arturo had zipped up her dress and grasped her shoulders tightly, turning her around to face him. He was determined she would not escape, and in a flash he pressed his lips tightly on hers, and he pulled her whole body close to his. Gloria began to struggle to get away, but he only renewed his kissing and embracing more forcefully. They could hear the applause dying down. Mrs. Pagani was about to discover them.

261

Gloria wrenched free and slapped Arturo as hard as she could. Then she broke down crying, falling into Mrs. Pagani's arms. Arturo looked on helplessly, finally deciding to confess his trespass. "Bianca, I could not resist this little beauty any longer. She needed my help getting her zipper unstuck, and I did what any red-blooded young man would do in proximity to such a ravishing diva – I kissed her. That's all."

Gloria dried her tears and faced Arturo with fire in her eyes. "That's all? If no one had been around I dare say you would have raped me! I could literally **feel** the lust driving you. Arturo, my Lord and Savior revealed to me last night that you are a married man. He warned me to keep my distance from you."

"Married man? How did you know that? Bianca, you must have told her. But did you tell her I am getting a divorce?"

Mr. Gruber had now come backstage to see why the audience was having to wait for Gloria's next and final number. Bianca quickly apprised him of the situation. He was livid. "Arturo, how dare you upset our singing star?" Patting Gloria on the hand and taking her face in his hands, Mr. Gruber looked lovingly at Gloria as if she were his daughter. "My dear, you were right in slapping this insolent young man. He knows you are engaged. Besides, he is not worthy of you." Turning to Arturo, Mr. Gruber demanded in his harshest voice, "Now I am telling you, Arturo, to go to the piano and try to redeem yourself, accompanying Miss Sondheim with the best you have ever done."

Gloria assured Mr. Gruber she would do her best also and asked if she might say a few words of introduction. He replied, "My precious star, you may have the liberty to speak what is in your heart."

Gloria paused momentarily, making sure she heard what the Lord was saying. *Yes, Lord. The performance of this song is for You more so than all the others.* Before she went back out on the stage, she looked at her accompanist and said, "Arturo, I forgive you. And I pray that you and your wife will try again. If you ask the Lord,

He will redeem your marriage. He has told me she will forgive you, if you ask. As for me, from now on, I am forgetting this incident tonight, and I only expect the best from you going forward." Gloria smiled at him. He lifted his head and smiled back. Mr. Gruber looked at Mrs. Pagani with wonder on his face.

Gloria could see Jeff in the audience and focused her attention on him, as she introduced "One Fine Day. "It has been a great pleasure to play the piano and sing for you tonight. You are a wonderful audience. Please forgive me for singing this famous aria in English, not Italian, but my fiancé and friends from America are in the audience, and I want them to understand the message of faith, hope, and love in these words. I am sure most of you know that in the opera little Butterfly is betrayed.[111] All will agree that it is better to have loved and lost than never to have loved at all. But that is a small consolation. As a Christian I can identify with Madame Butterfly up to a point. Her beloved had left her but promised to return. She was waiting for him, never wavering in her faith, hope and love. However, the opera ends tragically. I cannot help but compare it to the Christian's waiting for Jesus Christ to return as He promised. But this is where I can NOT identify with Madame Butterfly because my Lord and Savior IS coming back! I will be rewarded for my faith, hope, and love, because Jesus WILL return!"

Gloria had the audience in the palm of her hand as she sang "One Fine Day" from the depths of her being. After the last note the audience was on its feet, shouting "Bravo! Bravo! Encore! Encore!" Gloria and Arturo took several bows, then returned backstage. Mrs. Pagani reached out her arms to her protégé and hugged her furiously. Mr. Gruber had gone to sit by his friend from New York. The applause would not abate. The usual "Bravo!" and "Encore!" shouts changed to "Gloria! Gloria! Gloria!" Mr. Gruber hurried backstage to tell Gloria that now was the time to do the religious numbers. He must reward his prized songbird. "Go back out, and do the religious numbers, both of them, Gloria," he encouraged. She went back onstage to even more resounding applause. Her heart was moved as she looked over at Arturo, patiently waiting to play for her. She went to him and shook his hand. Together they bowed deeply several more times. When Gloria went to the front of the stage, the audience grew quiet.

Gloria made introductions for both the hymns, telling how each one was written. A hush fell over the audience. She was filled with God's love anew as she sang "The Love of God." After the last note Gloria put up her hand to indicate the audience was not to clap, and she began to introduce "It is Well with My Soul." Beforehand she had instructed Arturo to begin playing it **while** she was introducing it. At its conclusion, the audience stood and applauded enthusiastically. Mrs. Pagani came onstage. The three performers joined hands and bowed deeply several times. Mr. Gruber was in the wings, joyfully clapping his hands and shouting "Bravo!" The three performers came backstage, and the four celebrated, complimenting each other. After several more minutes, the applause had not stopped. The audience still wanted more. It was 11:00 o'clock, and no one wanted to leave. The shouts changed from "Encore, encore!" to "Gloria, Gloria!" yet again. Mr. Gruber looked at Gloria. He actually looked helpless. He did not know of another number that Gloria could sing.

Gloria silently prayed. *Do you want me to sing again, Lord? What would You have me sing? Lord, you know that Arturo and I have not practiced the hymn that I am thinking of. You know my heart, and this hymn's message is exactly how I have been feeling tonight, especially after Arturo violated me. Yes, I will do it, if Mr. Gruber agrees. Thank You, Lord, for this awesome ministry you have given me.*

Applause and shouts of "Gloria! Gloria!" continued. Gloria swallowed hard and approached Mr. Gruber who had a look of astonishment on his face. "Mr. Gruber, I believe the Lord has instructed me to sing another hymn. Would you permit it? And may I introduce it? I desire no accompaniment."

Mr. Gruber realized he had been drawn into what he perceived as a "playing it by faith game." He took a deep breath and answered,

"Miss Sondheim, I see that you have won the hearts of the people, and they will eat anything you feed them. I have to concede that you drive a hard bargain." He laughed and hugged Gloria. Now she was HIS protégé.

Gloria made a brief introduction of her song, saying, "Recently, I have memorized this classic hymn. I am sure you all know of Billy Graham, the man whom God picked to take His message of salvation in Jesus around the world. Maybe some of you have heard him preach. Anyway, his soloist, George Beverly Shea, has made this hymn famous, and I want to sing it for you now. I didn't write the words, but I have adopted them as my own declaration of faith." Gloria's eyes filled with tears as she sang in a steady, powerful voice:

> *I'd rather have Jesus than silver or gold;*
> *I'd rather be His than have riches untold;*
> *I'd rather have Jesus than houses or lands.*
> *I'd rather be led by **His nail pierced hand***
>
> *Than to be the **queen** of a vast domain*
> *Or be held in sin's dread sway.*
> *I'd rather have Jesus than anything*
> *This world affords today.*
> *I'd rather have Jesus than **men's applause**;*
> *I'd rather be faithful to His dear cause;*
> *I'd rather have Jesus than **worldwide fame**.*
> *I'd rather be true to His holy name*
> *Than to be the **queen** of a vast domain*
> *Or be held in sin's dread sway.*
> *I'd rather have Jesus than anything*
> *This world affords today.*[112]

Gloria bowed her head and lifted her hands in worship. The audience stood, many with tears running down their cheeks, their eyes closed, but with faces lifted upwards. A few people silently filed out, but the majority of the audience was obviously moved and did not want to break the silence. They continued to stand. After several minutes Gloria lifted her head, smiled broadly, and blew kisses to the audience. Then she looked toward Mrs. Pagani and Arturo backstage, and they came out to take bows for the glorious concert that had ended on a reverent note. The audience then began to applaud loudly. No longer calling for another encore, they were satisfied with this extraordinary evening of musical joy, praise, and even worship.

Sylvia, Jeff, Pete, and Sarah had tears in their eyes as they went backstage to hug their now famous daughter, fiancée and friend. Chaya and Max tried to stifle their emotions, knowing that the hymns they just heard should have no meaning for Jews. But despite their best efforts, tears spilled from their eyes, too, and they could do nothing but fiercely hug Sarah's close friend, complimenting her on her beautiful singing and playing. They, along with Pete and Sarah, would remain in Budapest until Saturday, so they would miss the Prague concert. Backstage, the warm embraces continued for some time.

Gloria lay in bed that night, marveling at how she had fulfilled Jesus' words concerning His disciples, as He prayed to the Father for them on the night He was arrested – "They are not of the world, just as I am not of the world. Sanctify them by Your truth. Your word is truth. As You sent Me into the world, I also have sent them into the world."[113] Jesus had sent Gloria into the world, and she felt His pleasure. He had led her through Europe by His nail-pierced hands.

CHAPTER THIRTY-NINE

LEAVING PRAGUE

The concert in Prague was a roaring success, not an anti-climax, as Edsel had feared. He did not dream that the glorious performance at Budapest could be topped, but it was. More than ever, he felt affirmed as the consummate concert manager. Never before had he pulled strings with newspapers the way he did for the Budapest and Prague performances. But it paid off. He wanted to share his darling protégé with the world. He purposed that Gloria would not know about the Prague newspaper headlines. He would give her mother a copy and let it be a surprise **later**. This would cause Gloria to keep him in her thoughts. Maybe she would let him groom her music career after college.

After the final curtain call, Jeff, Mrs. Sondheim, and Mr. Gruber rushed backstage to shower Gloria and Mrs. Pagani with compliments and affectionate embraces. Sylvia would be flying out that night, but the rest would board their flights early Sunday morning. Gloria took her mother aside to express her deep gratitude for her accompanying Gloria and witnessing her daughter's musical success, which was due in part to Sylvia's grooming. "Mom, one of your dreams for me has been fulfilled. Thank you and Dad for sending me to Mississippi State University, where I would receive a wonderful music education under Mrs. Pagani and my other teachers. You gave me security here in Europe, a strange place, by being at my side and cheering me on. I love you. Oh, how I look forward to seeing you and Dad in just a month at Papa Sam's and

Mama Anna's house. Take care. I am praying for your safe trip home. Give Dad a big hug and lots of kisses from me."

Mr. Gruber was having a hard time getting Gloria off by herself. The others realized he needed to talk to Gloria, so they stood back. "My teenage sensation, I hate to let you go. You have not only exceeded my expectations as a pianist and a singer on these stages in Europe, but I have been touched by your strong expressions of faith onstage and also in private with Bianca and me. You have stood your ground for what you believe in, and I respect you for it. I don't know what your future plans are, but if you decide to pursue a music career in Europe or in the concert halls of America, I will be proud to be your agent. I let Bianca slip out of my hands, but now I see it was for a purpose. Her teaching career at your college has borne fruit and produced another star – YOU, my child. Before we part, I want to say one more thing. I am not a religious person, and I have not been inside a church since I was a young boy. All that has changed now, and it's because of you. I am beginning to pray and ask for direction in my business life and personal life. Already I have vowed I would buy a new Bible and begin reading it. Thank you, Gloria. Please let us keep in touch." Mr. Gruber warmly hugged his protégé. Gloria assured him she loved him and would keep him in her prayers constantly. As she walked away, her heart was doing flip-flops, and she couldn't wait to share with Jeff that she had borne fruit, the fruit they asked for back when they were on the Golan Heights!

The flight departure for Jeff, Gloria, Mrs. Pagani, and Arturo was scheduled for Sunday morning in order for them to do some sightseeing in Prague. What a reward it was to sleep late on Saturday, eat a leisurely breakfast in the hotel, and then get a taxi to the Old Town Square. They got quite an education in church history when Jeff pointed out the monument to Jan Hus, a reformer of the Catholic Church who was inspired by John Wycliffe. He in turn inspired Martin Luther. Hus was burned at the stake in 1415. Arturo wanted to know why Jan Hus was the focal point of the

Old Town Square. He really preferred seeing other sites in Prague. Jeff had done some reading on his flight to Budapest, wanting to know more about that city, as well as the city of Prague. He then could tell the others the significance of the memorial. He said, "Jan Hus wasn't afraid to speak out about the abuses of the church in his day, the same as Martin Luther later did. When <u>Czechoslovakia</u> was under Communist rule, sitting at the feet of the Jan Hus memorial became a way of quietly expressing one's opinion and opposition against the Communist rule.[114] I felt inspired, just reading about this brave man. Today, Christians must be faithful, even if it costs us our lives."

Gloria had to add, "We can't expect our lives to be a bed of roses when we accept Jesus as our Messiah. Hard times may be ahead for us, but we have to stand strong and not deny the One who laid down His life for us. I am looking forward to Passover, when Jews all over the world will rehearse what their ancestors had to suffer under Egypt's rule, but then how their great Deliverer took them out of slavery. It will be a great blessing to be at my grandparents' house to celebrate Passover."

Flying back to the Golden Triangle Regional Airport, Gloria's seat was beside Mrs. Pagani. She would have to wait to be **alone** with Jeff after they landed and pour out her heart about all that had transpired in Europe, plus all their plans going forward. Her emotions had fluctuated wildly the whole week, and she longed for the tranquil, secure feeling of being alone in Jeff's presence once again. But now she would enjoy sitting by her teacher.

After the takeoff, she and Mrs. Pagani soon fell asleep. When the flight attendants nudged them awake for a meal, they gradually began their conversation. Mrs. Pagani surprised Gloria with her first words. "Gloria, you are the best student I have ever had in my ten years at MSU. It is my delight to teach you, and I am already thinking about the new pieces I will assign you. I realize that you and Jeff have a Christian ministry, so you must help me plan your new repertoire. Together, we will choose pieces from all the periods of music that will harmonize with your Christian calling. Of course, there are some classics that won't fit that description but must be included in your education for you to be well-rounded musically. But let me stop and say right now, and it is humbling for me to say it, I was moved spiritually by your performances, Gloria. Your sincerity and deep faith have affected me. As you know, I have been divorced since before I came to MSU. I will confess that over the last few months I have been considering having an affair with a married man in the English Department. But that is no longer a temptation. I hear that you and Jeff and your roommates are teaching a class at the little country church, Adaton Baptist. I hope to attend, maybe not regularly, but I want to see what it is all about. I have not been a church goer. However, now I am genuinely interested. And do you know the reason I did not accept Edsel's offer years ago to let him make me famous on the concert stage in Europe? It's crazy, but I felt a 'pull' to teach college students, and 'something' told me to try to get on the music faculty at Mississippi State University. What do you think of that?"

"Oh, Mrs. Pagani, I think it is absolutely wonderful! You didn't even know that the Holy Spirit was tugging on you, maneuvering you into His plan for your life. And I am so blessed to be a little part of that plan. The 'pull' you felt to teach college students, and the 'something' that told you to come to MSU, it was God! It was His Holy Spirit wooing you. He loves you so much and wants to shower you with His blessings. This concert tour is part of the blessing, seeing the fruit of your labors in me, your student. And also your own performances are used by the Creator of music to bless people. Music is His gift to all people, actually. But the ones who use His gift to glorify Him are the ones who receive His best blessings." Gloria hardly noticed her food, she was so full of the Lord's presence. And she could tell Mrs. Pagani felt His presence, too. They chatted a while about the three exciting performances in Europe and all that happened in the three cities. Sleep soon overtook them until a short while before the plane landed in New York. On the connecting flight to Columbus, Gloria and Bianca again sat beside each other. They continued to share about their common experiences at MSU and in Europe until the plane landed at the Golden Triangle Airport in Columbus.

Mr. and Mrs. Quentin had left Jeff's SUV in the airport parking lot. Jeff and Gloria said goodbye to Mrs. Pagani and Arturo at the luggage carousel and then drove back to the campus. After unpacking, they met up with Pete and Sarah at the Union Building. The Holy Rollers were together again, and they shared their separate adventures, including the sight-seeing in Hungary and Prague. Gloria told about Mr. Gruber and Mrs. Pagani both being touched and changed by the Lord's Spirit. She related the conversations she had with them, and they rejoiced together in the fruit of her music ministry.

Gloria said, "This is your fruit, too, because my mother and you three have been 'the wind beneath my wings.'"

CHAPTER FORTY

MAKING WEDDING PLANS

CHICAGO, GOOD FRIDAY, APRIL 10TH

After a quick lunch at the Chicago airport, the Holy Rollers got a taxi, and Gloria gave the address of her grandparents' home to the driver. They were soon at the Sondheims' front door, and Mama Anna opened the door before they even knocked. "Oh, children, come right in. At last you are here. Chag Pesach Sameach! Happy Passover!" Mama Anna reached out and hugged each one.

Papa Sam came to the entry hall and heartily greeted them. "It is so wonderful to see you four again. You make me feel young. I will never forget our time together in Port Jefferson at Alvin and Sylvia's house last Thanksgiving. Oh, the excitement when you announced your engagement, Gloria and Jeff. We all had such enriching conversations about Hanukkah in the midst of your planning to be in Israel for Hanakkuh and the 50th birthday of the nation. Five months have gone by, and you four have had even **more** adventures, having just come back from Europe. Gloria, we were elated to hear that you wowed the concertgoers in three cities with your musical gifts, and you made the headlines twice! Sylvia has told us all about it. May I have your autograph?" Papa Sam laughed, and Gloria fell into his outstretched arms. Oh, how she loved her grandparents.

"Sweet daughter, come here and hug your Daddy." Alvin came out of the kitchen with Sylvia following behind. "I could not be prouder of you. Your mother has been walking on air ever since she got home. She has bought CDs of the songs you sang and listens to them all the time. Of course, none of the pianists or singers on the CDs sound as good as you!" Gloria felt deeply loved as she always had in the arms of her dad and then her mom.

"Mom, I didn't know I made the headlines twice. Was the second time **after** the concert in Budapest or is it in the Prague newspaper?"

"It was in the Prague newspaper **before** the concert. You will find it in your room later, and you can read it at your leisure. I am so proud of you, darling. I have to hug you one more time." Gloria let her mother hold her as long as she wanted. It felt so good.

Alvin and Sam helped with the luggage. Mama Anna led the way upstairs and showed the four to their bedrooms, one for each pair of roommates. Jeff noticed that the wall décor and other decorations included many verses of Scripture with the Messiah's name prominent. The entire house seemed to exude the personality of the owners. It felt cozy and peaceful. Jeff could smell the fragrance of holy anointing oil. He knew that Papa Sam and Mama Anna had applied it throughout the house in preparation for this family gathering at the sacred feast of Passover. The roommates got settled in, and then it was time to gather in the living room. The main topic of conversation was their upcoming double wedding.

"I had a call from your father this morning, Pete," said Alvin. "You were in the air by then. He was very upset to have to report to us that the venue where we had planned to have the wedding reception in Columbus is no longer available. The owners of the antebellum home had an opportunity to sell the house and property, and they couldn't turn it down. The new owners will take possession by the first of May. They will immediately start major renovations, and it will not be ready for our reception by June 13th. We must quickly find another venue. I have already contacted the companies who are providing the food. Of course, Sylvia and I will be bringing many items. Your parents, Pete, said they would take care of the decorations, the serving dishes, et cetera."

Pete knew the Lord would have a solution. "Jeff, why don't you lead us in prayer? It's nothing the Lord can't handle. And boy, do I know that to be true these past few months."

All reached out to hold hands. Jeff remained silent a few seconds to seek the Lord's presence. "Dear Father God, You are not surprised at this development. You must have a better place for us to have the wedding reception. Please reveal whom we should contact. Help us to hear Your voice now. In Jesus' name, amen." Jeff indicated all should be quiet and wait.

After some minutes had passed, Jeff spoke up. "I just had a surprising idea. Surely it came from the Lord. He has already said, 'Ask, and ye shall receive.' Do y'all remember that Walter Sessions offered us his house for our meetings any time we wanted to come together for the Lord's work? You know, his house used to be a fraternity house, so it is really big. It has also served as the type venue for which we are looking. I think it's perfect for the reception, especially because it is right there in Starkville. Knowing the kind of guy Walter is, I bet he will be thrilled to let us use it."

Pete wasn't so sure. "But that house is in a run-down condition. Didn't you notice that time we were there? It was all grown up outside, and only Walter's and Gary's bedrooms, the kitchen, bathroom on the first floor, and the living area had been cleaned up."

Gloria and Sarah looked at each other. Gloria spoke first. "God's ways are not our ways. That house has been set apart for the Lord's use. Walter said so. Can we pray again?"

Gloria led the prayer. "Lord, is this your answer, Walter's house? Could you give us a sign that it's the place?" The prayer was interrupted by the phone ringing.

Mama Anna was sitting beside it and answered. "Yes, they are here. Who should I say is calling?" Mama Anna's voice got louder. "Did you say **Walter Sessions**? Oh, I am glad to meet you. I am

Gloria's grandmother, but you already know that because you have our number. Bless you, Walter. I think you are the answer to our prayers." Mama Anna handed the phone to Jeff.

Jeff's countenance lit up. "Walter! It's good to hear from you. I hope nothing is wrong. We were just talking about you. Why did you call? …. Whaaaat? I can't believe it! You and Jenny? Man, you move fast, Romeo. …. You are getting married? …. Did you say Saturday, May 16th? You don't mess around, friend. School will be out, and it's only a month from now. Then a month later the four of us are getting married. …. Yes, of course I am happy for you! This blows me away. I have never seen anyone so quickly transformed by Jesus as Jenny. I can tell from your voice you are really, really in love. Congratulations, man! ….. What, you want the four of us to be in the wedding? Well, I will have to ask them, but I am looking at them right now, and they are nodding their heads with their mouths wide open! So, tell me the details – the church, where the reception will be, the honeymoon, everything…. Oh, I see. Well, that doesn't surprise me. Adaton is where y'all met, isn't it? And Pastor James has agreed? Of course he would…. Now that surprises me the most of all – Rebecca is going to be a bridesmaid! Later, you have got to tell us all about that. It looked like Rebecca was a lost cause, but our God is full of surprises, isn't He? …. Okay, what else? …. Oh, Gary is moving out, and you are having your house renovated for your residence. That's great, but will it be ready in time to host the reception there?"

No one in the room could comprehend the magnitude of what Jeff was hearing on the phone. They kept shaking their heads in wonder. Soon Jeff had finished his conversation with Walter, but not without asking if Walter would let them use his newly-renovated house for **their** wedding reception. Everyone in the room heard Jeff's words, "Thank you!" repeated over and over again before he hung up.

"I am ready for a happy dance," exclaimed Pete. "You are all teenagers, and I am your elder, having just turned twenty, so follow me." Pete began a line dance, but Sarah shook her head. She didn't know it.

"Wait, I have also left teenage-hood," proclaimed Jeff. "I didn't tell you, but my birthday was on April Fool's Day! Ready, everybody? Pete and I will lead this line dance."

Gloria took charge. "Let's wait on the line dance. Happy birthday, Jeff! Here is my present to you. I am teaching you, as well as everybody, the Hora, because it's the Israeli national folk dance, and Passover is all about Israel! Not only that, but after the reception at Walter's house, we four will be going on our honeymoons to Israel." Gloria demonstrated. Sarah excitedly joined in, and soon the four of them had it mastered. Alvin and Sylvia shyly joined in, too. Papa Sam and Mama Anna stood and sang "Hava Nagila," as they clapped to the rhythm. "Israel, here we come!" shouted Gloria. It wasn't long before the happy dancers were winded and sat down, breathing hard.

Papa Sam was ecstatic. "Dear family, and I include Pete and Sarah, I prayed that miraculous things would happen in our home during Passover, and what just transpired on the phone call is the first installment, I believe!" He chuckled and clapped his hands, as excited as a child. "The prayer that Jeff led us in was immediately answered, and **my** prayer was answered, both of them miracles! Passover is a time of miracles. Tonight we are going to reenact the story of the Exodus, the greatest miracle in history except for the resurrection of our Messiah. It was a mighty deliverance from slavery that God performed for His people, the Israelites, the night they killed the Passover Lamb. They spread His blood over the doorposts of their homes, and the death angel PASSED OVER them. The firstborn sons of the Egyptians were slain, and the Pharaoh finally let his slaves go. There were probably two or three million Israelites who departed from Egypt as Moses led them. God parted the Red Sea, and they escaped from the Egyptian soldiers on chariots who pursued them. When the people were safe on the other side, God brought the waters crashing back down on Pharaoh's army and drowned them. It was a HUGE MIRACLE, but it was only the **first of many** miracles God did for them as they went through the wilderness to the Promised Land. We will learn more about it as we partake of the Seder, beginning at sundown."

Sarah was beside herself. "I am SO EXCITED! Papa Sam and Mama Anna, Mr. Alvin, and Miss Sylvia, I have thought about being with you last Thanksgiving so many times. All the things I learned from you about the Messiah from Isaiah 53, the New Testament, and Hanukkah have stayed with me. When I finally was born again in Israel, I felt gratitude to you for planting those seeds in me. You were like midwives sort of. What masterful teachers you are, Papa Sam and Mama Anna. I feel honored to be in your home and to be a part of the Seder tonight. My heart is full of joy!" Sarah looked at Pete as he drew her close. He was excited because she was excited.

"And we are honored to have you here, Sarah, and all of you." Mama Anna glowed. "Children, you go on upstairs and have a nice nap. Then come in the dining room a little while before sundown. Lighting the candles signals the beginning of the Pesach Seder. My sweet husband will be the host."

After they napped, the four met in the girls' room and discussed wedding plans. They prayed for Walter and Jenny and the success of **their** wedding plans and gave thanks for the answer to prayer about Walter's house as their reception venue. Then they began to make a guest list. Gloria made sure that Mrs. Pagani, Mr. Gruber, and Arturo Zappala were on the list. Of course, everyone at Adaton Baptist would be invited, as well as everyone at the Baptist Student Union. Pete wanted Bryan Green and his parents on the list. Jeff said he would get his parents to make a list of their friends from Tupelo. That would be a short list, but Pete's list would be very long, considering the large Carson family and their friends. Ahmad and Fadwa Hafeez would be invited. Laura Henderson should be on the list. Gloria had high school friends from The Knox School she wanted to invite. Sarah had friends from Yeshiva High School and University she would like to be on the list. She hoped all her siblings and their family members would be coming. Gloria was writing on a pad of paper. Suddenly, she laughed. "My pen has run out of ink!"

Jeff exclaimed, "Halt! We can't get married in a small church. We need a stadium!" They all threw up their hands in utter frustration. "WE NEED TO PRAY. This is a problem with no human solution. But we have seen God do the impossible, so I know He won't refuse now. Let's ask."

Pete led the prayer, feeling the Holy Spirit stronger than ever before. He made the request in simple words, and they waited for an answer. Gloria got excited. "I am sure the Lord just said to call Pastor James and tell him we have an impossible situation and ask for his advice. This is Friday night. They may be going out to eat, but I bet we can catch him, because the Lord said to call him."

"I'll do it," offered Jeff. He dialed the number, and Pastor James answered. First Jeff thanked him for teaching their Jewish Roots class while they were in Chicago, especially since it would be Easter, the most important day of the year for the church, and he would be busier than ever. Then Jeff laid out their problem in a brief statement. There was a pause, and Jeff silently prayed.

The pastor said, "I have an idea. Yes, it will work. I know it. I think I can be of real help because I will be brimming over with resurrection power after preaching the sermon the Lord has given me. You will have my plan by Sunday night."

Jeff replied, "Thank you so much. We will be flying back on Sunday and can meet with you Sunday night. Chag Pesach Sameach! Happy Passover!" Jeff hung up and told the others what the pastor said. They praised the Lord, knowing everything would work out beautifully. Then they discussed honeymoon plans. The wedding would be on Saturday. They would spend Saturday and Sunday nights at the Shadowlawn Bed and Breakfast in Columbus and leave for Israel on Monday. Jeff volunteered to make the reservations for the flight to Israel on June 15th, returning June 22nd.

"I found a duplex apartment for us off campus," said Pete. The others gasped to hear this news. "It will be available on May 30th, so we can get a lot of our stuff moved in before the wedding. I know all of you will love it. My mom came over and helped me find it. Also she promised to help us clean it up. Knowing her, she will do extra stuff, like having a cake on the table in both apartments when we return from the honeymoon. Jeff, you and I need to go to the rental place and pay the first month's rent as soon as we get back, so they will hold it for us. Agreed?"

"Agreed. I'll take it, sight unseen," declared Jeff. "Bro, I am proud of you for taking the initiative. Now I have a question. What do we do between Walter's wedding and ours? We can't stay in the dorms, unless we sign up for summer school, I guess."

Gloria advised, "Guys, I think we have made enough decisions for today. With Yeshua in charge we don't have a care in the world. He will bring all things to mind that we need to take care of. He is really working through both you men."

They were thankful when Mama Anna called up the stairs to come to the dining room. "Talking about the duplex got my imagination stirred up," murmured Jeff in Gloria's ear. "Lord, lead me not into temptation." The two couples separated from their embraces and started down the stairs.

CHAPTER FORTY-ONE

Passover Seder

Mama Anna indicated where each person should sit and began to explain the table arrangement, first noting the small booklet at each plate. She held up one. "For those who do not know – I think that would be Jeff and Pete – this is called a 'Haggadah,' Hebrew for 'the telling.' It is the program booklet for tonight. It is different from what you are used to, Sarah, because it is a **Messianic** Haggadah and shows Yeshua in the Passover. 'Seder' simply means 'order of service.' This large plate in the center of the table has all the elements that are included in telling the story of the Exodus. Everything we do here tonight can be found in Scripture. Yahweh told Moses to instruct the Israelites to have a spotless lamb for each family. They were to slaughter it on the evening of Nisan 14. Not a bone was to be broken. Then they would put its blood on the doorposts and lintel of each home. They were to roast the lamb and eat it with unleavened bread and bitter herbs, to remember the bitterness of slavery. The death angel would pass over the homes of the Israelites when he saw the blood. But the firstborn sons of the Egyptians would die that very night. The Israelites were to be ready to leave Egypt immediately. Their bread dough would not have time to rise. It would be unleavened bread, and they were to eat it for seven days. Yahweh wanted them to always observe this event every year, so the children would never forget their history. You can find this in Exodus, the 12th chapter.

"It is customary for the woman of the house to light the two candles, but I am going to break tradition because I believe Yeshua

281

told me to ask Sarah to light the candles. I also want her to say a blessing for this occasion. Sarah, do you have your tallit with you?"

"Yes, Mama Anna. I wear it when I pray each night before going to bed. I will run upstairs and get it. I am honored that you asked me." Everyone was silent until Sarah returned with her tallit. "Okay, I am ready now. I will also break tradition and not read what is in the Haggadah. May I pray first and then light the candles?"

"Surely, child. I knew you would be led by the Spirit," said Mama Anna.

Sarah's heart was overflowing with joy as she prayed. "Dear HaShem, it was in the presence of these dear people that I first began to realize the great love You have for us, Jew and Gentile. Your holy Presence at the Sondheims' home in New York touched me deeply. It was a milepost for me on my journey into the full revelation of Your love as shown in Your Son, the Lamb of God who takes away the sins of the world. I thank You for the teaching I have received and am still receiving tonight from these friends. I thank You for the sacrifice of Yeshua as He shed His blood to forgive our sins. Please, Lord, reveal Yourself to my family as they partake of the Passover meal, and may the day soon come when all Israel shall be saved, as You promised. I thank You for this Seder, and I ask that You bless our hosts and each one of us around the table. May we see and hear You in all Your glory tonight. I love You. Amen." Sarah's last few words were spoken with great difficulty as she tried to keep from crying. But now she let the tears flow.

Pete drew her in his arms. "Babe, no one could have said a better prayer."

Sarah smiled through her tears. "And now I will light the candles. If you don't know Hebrew, just say the English words in the Haggadah." Sarah lit the two candles with her head covered, and she waved her hands above the flames to spread the light throughout the room. She spoke the Hebrew first. Then the others repeated the words in English. "Blessed are You, O Lord our God, Ruler of the universe, who has set us apart by Your Word, and in whose Name we light the festival lights."

Papa Sam continued, "As light for the festival of redemption is kindled by the hand of a woman, we remember that our Redeemer, the Light of the World, came into the world as the promised seed of a woman. Genesis 3:15." Papa Sam continued to guide everyone through the Haggadah, step by step, with their spoken responses.

Sarah was on the edge of her seat, as she clearly understood for the first time what the Passover service was really all about. The different parts of this reenactment of the Exodus story came alive for her: the cup of sanctification, which was the first of four cups of wine; washing of hands; parsley; the four questions; the four answers; the matzah or unleavened bread; the bitter herbs represented by spicy horseradish spread on the matzah; the charoset, representing the mortar for the bricks made in Egypt; the story of their slavery and the call of Moses as deliverer; the cup of plagues, the Passover lamb, the singing of 'Dayenu' about God's goodness that was more than sufficient; the actual Passover supper, the afikomen; the cup of redemption; the prophet Elijah; and the cup of praise.

After the ceremony ended, the four friends complimented Mama Anna and Miss Sylvia for the tasty meal. Then everyone wanted to talk about the matzah and the afikomen. They expressed that it was amazing that the Jews had been observing the Passover for nearly 2,500 years, and the great majority of them had never seen Yeshua, their Messiah, depicted in this interactive program of the Exodus. When Papa Sam held up a piece of matzah and showed them how it represented Yeshua, they marveled. First of all, it was flat. There was no leaven in it. Leaven depicts sin, the way it puffs up the bread. Jesus was sinless. Then the stripes on Yeshua's back by the Roman whip were depicted in the brown stripes on the matzah caused from baking it. Papa Sam held the matzah up to the light. There were holes it. This represented the piercing of the nails in Yeshua's hands and feet. The lamb was absent from the Seder and was only represented by a shank bone. The Lamb was not there because Yeshua rose from the dead and went back to heaven!

Papa Sam was really in his element, explaining everything. "The mysterious word, 'afikomen,' is the only Greek word in the Seder. It means, '**I came**.' This piece of matzah, the afikomen, represents the Messiah. He is speaking to the Jews, telling them He already came! The **Greek** indicates that it is through the **Gentiles** that Yeshua will be revealed to Israel. Paul wrote, '...because of their transgression, salvation has come to the Gentiles to make Israel jealous.'[115] It is right under their noses at the Passover table. Yeshua says to His beloved Jewish children that He has already come. This part of the ceremony also shows His **second** coming. As you read in the Haggadah and saw me as the host demonstrate it, three pieces of matzah were inserted in the three compartments of the cloth matzah tash. We Messianic Jews can see this as the Father, **the Son**, and the Holy Spirit. The host takes out the **middle** piece of matzah and **breaks it.** Why the middle piece? Who can tell me what that represents?"

Pete spoke up. "I think it stands for the body of Jesus that was broken on the cross. Is that right?"

"Yes, it certainly is, Pete. One half of the broken matzah is called the 'afikomen.' The host wraps it in a white linen cloth. He has the children close their eyes, and he **hides** it in the room. What do you think that represents? I know I already told you, but I want to imprint it in your minds."

Jeff answered, "It stands for Jesus' body being wrapped in the burial cloth and placed in the tomb."

"Right answer, Jeff. This happens at the beginning of the Seder. Later, after supper the children go search for the hidden afikomen. The one who finds it brings it to the host, and the host pays the child ransom money. This is a Jewish custom. We don't have children here tonight, but if we did, I would have given the child some gelt. That is chocolates wrapped in gold foil, looking like gold coins. Jesus was sold, not for gold though, but for twenty pieces of silver.

Then, you remember, I unwrapped the afikomen, signifying the grave clothes were removed. You can see as plain as day that this is the **resurrection!** Yeshua has come out of the grave. The afikomen was hidden in the room, and Yeshua has been hidden from the Jews. Yahweh Himself blinded them, so the Gentiles can get the gospel. Paul said, 'For I do not desire, brethren, that you should be ignorant of this mystery, lest you should be wise in your own opinion, that **blindness** in part has happened to Israel until the fullness of the Gentiles has come in. And so all Israel will be saved…'[116] The unwrapping of the afikomen also represents the **second** coming. John said, 'Behold, He is coming with clouds, and every eye will see Him, **even they who pierced Him**. And all the tribes of the earth will mourn because of Him. Even so, Amen.'"[117] Every eye will see Him, especially the Jews.

"I broke the afikomen in small pieces, and shared it with you. This part of the Seder has become what Christians call 'Communion' or 'the Lord's Supper.' Churches forget that it was a full Passover service that Yeshua led that night before He was arrested. He said, 'With fervent desire I have desired to eat this Passover with you before I suffer.' Of course, you know what the cup of redemption represents. Jesus inaugurated the New Covenant in His blood as they drank the wine. The wine represented His blood shed for them to REDEEM them. I wonder what they thought? He had not yet died on the cross! He shared the unleavened bread with them, calling it His body that was broken for them. You can read about it in the first twenty verses of Luke 22. Did you realize that partaking of the body and the blood of Yeshua is taking HIS LIFE into you? You have eternal life because of that broken body and poured out blood." Papa Sam paused to let his words sink in.

Alvin and Sylvia were agitated at this point. Sylvia leaned over and whispered to Alvin, "Do we have eternal life, Alvin? I can see how much Sarah has changed since she was at our house last Thanksgiving. She said she was born again. I want to talk about this with you when we say our bedtime prayers." Alvin nodded his head and gripped Sylvia's hand.

Mama Anna wanted to speak. "My dear family, we are brothers and sisters in the Messiah. We have been adopted into His family. But there are many of my people, the Jews, who are still blind. Paul said he would give up his own salvation if they could be saved. He loved them that much. We must also love the unbelieving Jews. King David said to 'pray for the peace of Jerusalem.' What that really means is to pray for the **salvation** of the Jewish people. Sarah prayed for that in her opening prayer. Now we need to close our Seder with all of us interceding for them. Don't you agree?" Everyone expressed their agreement.

Mama Anna led them into the living room. She prayed a heartfelt prayer for the Jews in Israel and around the world, as well as the Jews in their own neighborhoods. She mentioned the names of some she knew and prayed fervently for all of Sarah's family to come into a knowledge of their Savior and Lord. At the close of her prayer, all said a loud "Amen!"

Papa Sam said, "Young people, it is time to turn in for the night. We old people are going to clean up the table and kitchen and get things in place for tomorrow. Alvin and I have planned a special Jewish breakfast. I will be calling you downstairs at 8:30. Lila tov!"

"I have heard Gloria say that. It means 'Good night.'" Jeff explained.

"I am glad she is teaching you, my grandson-to-be," chuckled Papa Sam.

"LILA TOV!" Everyone echoed the Hebrew *good night,* and the young couples scampered upstairs.

CHAPTER FORTY-TWO

JEHOVAH JIREH

PASTOR JAMES' OFFICE
SUNDAY NIGHT

As soon as they got off the plane in Columbus and loaded their luggage in Jeff's SUV, the Holy Rollers made their way to Adaton Baptist Church. Pastor James was waiting for them. "Come on in and have a seat. Well, the Lord has been up to His same old tricks. When you asked my advice about the seating of such a huge crowd for your wedding, I consulted the top Wedding Planner immediately. He told me to call the Young at Heart prayer group and ask them to meet with me this afternoon. You know them because they attend your class. They never miss a Sunday or Wednesday service, and they have regular prayer meetings in their homes, rotating homes every month. Some people think they are gossips or busy-bodies, and it delights them no end. That's their cover, but they are fierce prayer warriors. Being nosy is simply the way they develop their prayer agenda. The things they discover in their covert operation are held in strictest confidence. Miss Lizzie is their chief, and there are four others. They fast for two or three days on occasion, if it's a hard case. Sometimes they go on prayer retreats to this cabin in the woods that Miss Lizzie's deceased husband used as a hunting lodge. Prayer is not their only activity. About two or three times a year they take up a mission project. Everybody calls them the Young at Heart prayer group, but I call them 'Miss Lizzie's Swat Team.' Last year I had a bad case of insomnia that lasted about six months. I refused to take sleeping pills, but I finally decided I had no choice. I bought the most potent kind, almost like narcotics. One Sunday before church about three weeks ago, Miss Lizzie came in the office, looked straight into my eyes, and said, 'The Lord told me you can't sleep at night. My ladies and I started praying about it yesterday. We met early this morning again and prayed. The Lord said you wouldn't have any more trouble. Don't take the pills.' And I have been sleeping like a log ever since."

They had been hanging on every word out of the pastor's mouth. Pete started laughing. "God uses the most unlikely people, but nothing surprises me any more about His orchestrating things. It's just like Him to use some old ladies to fix our problem. Before you even tell us how they are going to help, I know it will be spectacular. Praise the Lord!" The other three were in agreement and breathed a sigh of relief.

The pastor continued. "I laid out the whole scenario before them and said I would be meeting with y'all tonight to tell you the solution. Here's what Miss Lizzie said: 'Pastor, please leave the room. Della, Ruby, Lena, Pearl, and I must prevail in prayer for about ten minutes. You can come back in, and we will have an answer for you.'

Gloria chuckled. "I can just picture that. As I keep saying, 'God's ways are not our ways. His thoughts are not our thoughts. They are so much higher!'"

"So I left the room and came back in ten minutes. Miss Lizzie laid out the plan. They heard from the Lord four phrases – 'sturdy chairs, a wedding tent, and parking attendants outside with men in charge, Leon leading; Claude with videographer and Back Stage Music store setting up sound and video system with screens, outside and inside; wedding canopy and poles, kneeling cushions, and two glasses to be smashed arranged by Josephine; solos by Lee Ann Williamson and music for organist and pianist coordinated by Hilda.' I was writing as fast as I could, and I volunteered to do the printed programs. Miss Lizzie started chuckling. She said, 'Preacher, the minute our group heard about a double wedding at

Adaton Baptist, we got on our knees. We knew this little church could not withstand the onslaught of hundreds of people. Also, we knew that those four precious young people had bitten off more than they could chew. But since they have been coming to our church, the Lord has piped in His Holy Spirit all over the place. Our group knew we had to do something to show our gratitude. We love the Jewish Roots class, and we love it when Gloria sings and plays the piano. The only recompense we are seeking for our labors in prayer is that after they are married they continue to be a part of the Lord's body here at Adaton, taking time off for the honeymoon, of course. We have heard a lot of our members say the same thing. So, you see, our prayers have brought about this meeting with you today. We will be glad to contact these four people supervising the four tasks the Lord outlined to us. Della, Ruby, Lena, Pearl, and I will provide prayer cover for each person and each task going forward, and that includes you, Pastor James, and the young people, of course. Now will you please anoint us with oil and lay your hands on us for this prayer ministry that is the engine behind the task force for the wedding?' And I did just that. The Holy Spirit almost knocked me down! I'm telling you, those ladies look so harmless, but they are tigers!"

"God surely does provide, doesn't He?" exclaimed Gloria, clapping her hands and the others joining in. "And, of course, my parents are providing the floral decorations and candles."

Sarah had a look of wonder on her face. "Yes, He provides. I love that word, 'provide.' I remember when I taught my first lesson for the Jewish Roots class. I talked about Abraham binding Isaac on the altar on Mount Moriah. Yahweh had told him to sacrifice his son, and he lifted the knife to slay Isaac. The Angel of Yahweh – that's Yeshua – stopped him. Yahweh was pleased that Abraham obeyed Him and was willing to kill his beloved son Isaac. This proved that he loved Yahweh more. But Yahweh showed him a ram caught by its horns in the thicket, and the ram was sacrificed instead of Isaac. 'And Abraham called the name of the place, *Yah-*

weh-Will-Provide; as it is said to this day, 'In the Mount of Yahweh it shall be provided.' And you know what? Right this minute I just realized that this story told in **Genesis 22** was fulfilled in **Luke 22**, when Yeshua celebrated the Passover with His disciples the night before He was arrested. Everything that happened at the Passover table pointed to the SACRIFICE He would make the next day on the cross. What happened in Genesis 22 foreshadowed what happened in Luke 22. **Yahweh provided the sacrifice!** It was the **ram**, Isaac's substitute, in Abraham's case, and it was **Yeshua**, **our** substitute, in the Father's case. Do you see it? Yahweh always **provides**! That is what He has done for us concerning our wedding. People who don't know Hebrew say 'Jehovah Jireh,' meaning 'God provides.' Hebrew has no Js. It really should be pronounced 'Yahweh Yireh,' However, the important thing is YAHWEH PROVIDES. And that is what He has done for us. He has provided Miss Lizzie's Swat Team!"

Pete was proud of his girl. "Sarah, thank you for reminding us of that Scripture. I love the song my parents used to sing around the house, 'Jehovah Jireh,' written by Merla Watson.[118] We can see the message, Yahweh provides, is for us today. Pastor James, I want you to pray for us, especially Jeff and me, as we are coming into our roles of providing for our wives' needs. We can't expect our parents to keep underwriting us, although they are glad to do so, and we won't reject their help from time to time. However, Jeff and I need steady income. I haven't told ya'll yet that a door has opened for me. I need prayer about whether or not I should walk through it. My criminal justice professor told me that I had promise as a private investigator, and he has given me the phone number of a P.I. firm in Memphis to contact. He heard they had need of a P.I. in our area."

Jeff interrupted, "And I haven't told y'all about my dad's offer. I am excited about it. I need prayer in the same way Pete does." All eyes were on Jeff. "As you know, Dad had high hopes that I would live in Tupelo and join him in his wholesale grocery business. When he gets ready to retire, he will turn it over to me. After I told him that Gloria and I, as well as Pete and Sarah, may be making aliyah to Israel at some point, he and Mom started praying in earnest about my need to earn a living around here at the present time. He called me recently and said he is trying to set up an extension of his business in the Golden Triangle area of Columbus, West Point, and Starkville. He is looking for property to be used as a distribution point. He told me that he had already found a promising site close to the campus! Can you believe it? I think the classes I am taking now in business have prepared me to administrate this extension of Jeffrey M. Quentin Wholesale Grocery Company. Can I hear a cheer?"

Pastor James shouted "Praise the Lord!" louder than the others. "Jeff, you have been in my thoughts lately, and I have prayed that you could be 'making tents' like Paul right here, so you and Gloria can finish your college education before you move to Israel. Now I will pray your office can be built speedily and the business set up in record time."

Sarah added, "And if you need me to continue as your book-keeper, Jeff, I know Pete will agree that I can do it. I have worked for you gratis up to now, but I will soon have my hand out for monetary rewards." Everyone laughed. "Pastor, pray that Pete gets that job or another job close by. With both our incomes, we will even be able to save for the move to Israel after graduation."

"Well, that makes three of you who already have possible jobs. But what about me?" Gloria asked.

"Honey, you could have taken in thousands of dollars in Europe in those concerts, so I know there will be no problem making money here with your training and talent," Jeff answered. "Mrs. Pagani could get you set up as a top dollar piano teacher, I bet. God will open a door for sure. Mrs. Pagani may even get you a paying job as an adjunct teacher in **both** piano and voice at the University. Hey, how did I ever think of that?"

"Young people," cautioned Pastor James, "Don't forget all these jobs must be part-time if you want to continue your education toward a four-year college degree. My goodness, I have a lot to pray about. Let me throw something else into the mix. Gloria, the church would be glad to have you use the sanctuary for your piano and voice lessons. And Jeff, I can put out the word that you could deliver a great message as a lay preacher in our district. I have been impressed with your Jewish Roots lessons. Our district churches always give good-sized honorariums. Pete, if the private investigator job doesn't turn out, there's a man in our congregation who may be able to get you a job at the local police department or even with the campus police."

Pete put up his hand. "Enough talk. I love all these ideas. My head is swimming with the massive input from this meeting, but nothing will happen unless we pray. We want GOD'S will to be done, not ours. I think we should have Pastor lead in prayer for God's consideration of all these possibilities and ask Him to open and close doors, so that we fulfill our **divine destinies**, both together, then as couples, and also as individuals. We ourselves must continue to pray and **believe** that God's clear directions are forthcoming."

"And I have one more idea, people," exclaimed Jeff. "If we ask Miss Lizzie's Swat Team to take this on as a prayer project, there is no telling how many God incidences we will see. Let's start thanking God for the answers right now."

Pastor James took out his anointing oil and touched each forehead with it. Then he asked each couple to put their heads together. He laid his right hand on Gloria and Jeff and his left hand on Pete and Sarah. The couples began to sway, as the power of the Holy Spirit enveloped them. Pastor James anchored his feet, opened his mouth, and the most beautiful prayer they had ever heard was spoken over them to the Father. God's love filled the room, as the five people embraced each other. The couples kept thanking their pastor as they left the church.

CHAPTER FORTY-THREE

MORE FRUIT

OKTIBBEHA COUNTY JAIL - APRIL 15ᵀᴴ

Pete was worried. "Sarah, are you sure you heard from HaShem? He told you to take me and go visit those two terrorists in the Oktibbeha County Jail? Are they still there? It was on January 25ᵗʰ that they were arrested. That has been three months since the Sunday in the classroom when they tried to kill you. Surely they have already been transferred to Parchman Penitentiary. But if they are still at the jail, we can't stay long because we promised to be at BSU tonight to talk about Passover and our visit with Gloria's grandparents in Chicago."

"Yes, Pete. HaShem spoke to me in the middle of the night. I told Gloria, and she is praying for us. Neither one of us has a class this afternoon, so this is the perfect time to go. I feel at peace about it. HaShem gave me something to say to them."

Pete gave in, and they prayed as he drove to the jail. They were still praying as they pulled into the parking lot. When they told the deputy at the desk what they wanted, his face registered surprise. "Do you young people realize these two men are terrorists?"

Sarah tried to look as confident as she could. "Yes sir, but God told me to bring my fiancé and come visit them." Pete nodded his head to support Sarah.

Reluctantly, the deputy led them down a long hall to the adjoining cells where Nasir and Omar were housed. He saw that Sarah had two small sacks, so he opened them for inspection. Two items were in each, a Gideon New Testament and a wrapped sweet roll. "Okay, you can visit these men, but keep your distance from the bars. I will hand them the sacks. If you need me, call out for Deputy Sanderson. I will keep the hall door open, and I will be alert to hear your call." The deputy kept looking back as he returned to his desk.

Sarah began the conversation. "Nasir and Omar, I know you recognize me, Sarah Bernstein. I was teaching the class that day at Adaton Baptist Church, when you came in the class room. When you threw the knife at me, fear and hate rose up in my heart. I was hoping the sheriff and the deputy would kill you. I rejoiced that they arrested you and took you out of my sight. I have come here today to ask you both to forgive me for hating you and wanting you dead. I do not feel that way now."

The snarl on Nasir's face suddenly turned to confusion, and hateful words he was about to say at the sight of Sarah would not come out of his mouth. Omar wished he could see how Nasir had reacted to these surprising words from the Jew they had tried to kill.

Sarah continued, "I am Jewish, as you know. My ancestors two thousand years ago killed a Jewish man who loved them and came with a message of life and forgiveness. Your religion, Islam, knows this man as 'Isa,' but you do not believe he died on the cross to forgive the sins of mankind. Your Quran considers Him to be a great prophet, and you honor Him, but you don't follow Him and His teachings. I call this man by His Hebrew name, Yeshua, and our Bible, both Old and New Testaments, prove that He is the Messiah of Israel and of the whole world. I have brought a New Testament for you both to read." Handing a third New Testament to Nasir, Sarah said, "And here is a New Testament for Malik, your leader who attacked me at the beginning of the school year. I have no hatred in my heart for any of you now. Because Yeshua has forgiven me of my many sins, it is easy to forgive you. I want everybody to know the love and peace and joy I have now, ever since I was born again. I invited Yeshua to come into my heart and save me. Please tell me you will read the New Testament. You

294

can decide for yourselves if it is true. None of your people back in the Middle East will know that you have read it. Again, let me say that I forgive you, and I love you. Will you forgive me?" Sarah extended her hands through the bars to Nasir and Omar. Pete was alert, holding Sarah tightly in case either man tried to hurt her.

Sarah waited a few minutes, but Nasir and Omar did not speak and did not take her hand. She smiled at both men and said, "Pete and I have to go now, but we will be praying for you and for God's will to be done in your court cases. If you want to talk to me, just tell Deputy Sanderson. He will have my phone number. The last thing I want to say is, 'There is nothing too hard for our God.'"

Pete and Sarah talked on the way back to the campus. "Sarah, I was really proud of you. You didn't flinch when you saw those terrorists' hateful stares. I watched their faces as you talked, and it was amazing how their expressions changed from hate to puzzled looks. Then it appeared that they had let their guard down. As we walked away, I looked back. I couldn't actually see them, but I heard the rustling of the paper sacks and knew they were looking to see what you brought them. One of them sort of laughed, and then I heard them chattering in Arabic. I think they were enjoying the sweet rolls. At least they didn't tear up the New Testaments or throw them against the walls. I would have heard that for sure."

"Of course, they are going to read those New Testaments. Why else would HaShem have told me to take them? They have plenty of time to read. You know what, Pete? The Lord has been showing me that since I was born again, I have produced fruit for Him. Look at what has happened to Jenny! And now God is using me to get His message of salvation to these Muslims, all three of them. Can you believe it? I never would have had such boldness if I had not been filled with the Holy Spirit."

"Babe, you were amazing back there. As for fruit, I have produced a little for the Lord, too. If He had not empowered me, Laura Henderson would still be a lost, drug-addicted and promiscuous girl. Of course, it took both Camille and me, with Jeff helping, to birth her into the Kingdom."

Sarah clapped her hands. "All four of us Holy Rollers have produced fruit. Jeff was the first, when he prayed for Gary Grayson at the accident scene that night. Gary was saved and healed at the same time. And Gloria won souls on foreign soil, both Mrs. Pagani and Mr. Gruber. Wow! I bet Arturo Zappala will be ripe for the picking, too, before long. Oh, Pete, you and I and Gloria and Jeff are fulfilling our **double destinies**! I am on tiptoe to see what HaShem does next."

"Yes, I wonder what He has in store for us tonight at BSU. He needs to put the words in my mouth for our report on the Chicago trip, because right now I don't have a clue what I'm going to say," worried Pete.

"You know you don't need to worry. Remember what Gloria always says from the Scripture, 'Open your mouth wide, and I will fill it!'[119] The Lord will orchestrate everything. Things always fall into place. As for the wedding party, Gloria said she would be getting an answer tonight from Grace Thomas about being her bridesmaid. Priscilla Caldwell has accepted. Camille accepted being my bridesmaid. I hope she is not prettier than me. My sweet sister has graciously consented to being my Matron of Honor. And I can't get over how unselfish it is of Celeste, the pastor's wife, to volunteer to keep Chaya's baby the day of the wedding and even the night before when we have the rehearsal and go to The Terrace for dinner."

"Well, I got a yes from Britt and your brother-in-law Max about being groomsmen. Jeff said that Gary Grayson and Walter Sessions are happy to be his two groomsmen. I know we made the right decision about two attendants each, due to the size of the church. Chaya and Max are coming anyway. The others live close by, except for Grace Thomas. I hope she will say yes.

Sarah reached over and kissed Pete on the cheek. "We have got to do something special for the two couples who agreed to move out of our duplex two weeks early, so we can move in when the dorm closes. Of course, Gloria and I will still be roommates in the duplex until the big day, June 13th. And you and Jeff will be roommates until then, too. We have to use the honor system, you understand." Sarah laughed and laughed.

"As gorgeous as you are, I will be severely tempted, babe, but I will restrain myself until the evening of June 13th. Then I will love you to my heart's content!" Pete squeezed Sarah's hand. "Just like Gloria said, everything has fallen into place. I guess God has a special love for double weddings."

CHAPTER FORTY-FOUR

WALTER AND JENNY'S WEDDING

S arah had flown to New York two days before the arrival of
her infant niece Estelle on May 14th, and she wouldn't return
until May 22nd. She was very disappointed she had to miss
Walter and Jenny's wedding. But she bought a special present for
them, an illustrated book of the Land of Israel, and gave it to Jenny
and had a wonderful visit with her before she left for New York.
They expressed their gratitude for each other as friends.

On the way to the wedding Jeff, Gloria, and Pete expressed
how incomplete they felt without Sarah. Gloria said, "At least Sarah
will be spared from moving our stuff to the duplex. Mrs. McClen-
don is a jewel for allowing Sarah and me to pile our belongings
in the middle of the floor in our room, so the cleaners can clean
around it until the move. And Mrs. Pagani is a blessing for letting
me spend a few nights with her until Monday. Pete, your mother is
an angel sent from heaven to allow us to store the wedding presents
at your house. And isn't it neat that the Dillard's bridal registry on
the internet will take the gift orders and ship them directly to your
house?"

"Yes, my sister Elinor has cleared out half of the dining room
and set up tables for the gifts. She has even decorated the room,"
marveled Pete.

Gloria laughed. "I don't even know what we got! Practicing for
my piano and voice recital and studying to teach the Jewish Roots
class, not to mention preparing for finals last week, has taken up
most of my time. At least I have been constant and true with our

dinner dates, Mr. Quentin. Nothing can tear me away from **you** on Friday nights. That's what puts 'steam in my engine' to do all the other stuff. Tell me honestly, you guys – I mean y'all – what do you think of the blue and white color scheme for our wedding? I am not going as far as to have Israeli flags all over the sanctuary, but the blue satin dresses with white sashes for the bridesmaids is perfect, don't you think?" Gloria didn't wait for an answer. "And the blue bow ties and cummerbunds with white tuxedo coats and navy blue pants for the groomsmen and you, Jeff, carries out the theme. Miss Lizzie said we would love the chuppah. She is so adorable saying it – CHuppah, like 'CHeese!' She can't make the guttural sound. I told her to just say 'wedding canopy,' but – bless her heart – she is trying to be as kosher as possible. I love, love, love her and her swat team. This is all going so smoothly because of their prayers."

"I think the master touch for our wedding ceremony is the Aaronic benediction spoken over us in Hebrew by Max and Chaya in unison," said Jeff. "I can say it in English, but I want to learn it in Hebrew, too."

"Well, they will also repeat it in English. Otherwise, the guests won't know what is being said. Let's say it together now before we go inside the church. We have arrived." Gloria led them: "The Lord bless you and keep you; the Lord make His face shine upon you and be gracious unto you. The Lord lift up His countenance upon you and give you peace. Amen. Numbers 6:24-26."

SESSIONS MANOR AFTER THE WEDDING

"What a transformation!" Jeff exclaimed as he, Gloria, and Pete drove up to Walter and Jenny's residence on North Jackson Street for the reception after the wedding. "This old fraternity house has seen several makeovers in its time, so I have heard. I thought Walter had money, and now I am sure of it. The name is fitting,

'Sessions Manor.' And we will have **our** wedding reception here in less than a month. Gloria, I know Mr. Alvin will be beside himself when he sees this mansion. His cuisine will be fit for a king and have the royal ambience in which to display it."

"You got that right. My dad has catered in all kinds of places, but I dare say Sessions Manor will be in his top ten venues. Well, let's get on inside. And let's all pray we don't spill anything on these gorgeous wedding clothes, especially you men. You have to return your tuxedos on Monday. Jenny told us bridesmaids we could keep our dresses. Her mother is a top notch seamstress, and I love this dress. Jenny said I may have need of it for a musical concert. Wasn't that thoughtful?"

Pete answered, "Yes, she has really changed since that day the terrorist's knife wounded her. I've thought about it a lot. It was like the Spirit 'circumcised' her heart. The day Sarah visited her in the dorm was entirely planned by Yeshua. Sarah said He gave her the words to say, and they are now the best of friends. Gloria, I am really glad you asked her to be a bridesmaid when Grace Thomas couldn't do it. And what do you think about the big change in Rebecca?"

"She is totally different. I didn't hear the whole story, but she must be born again, too. Back when we were roommates, she had a rotten attitude about everything, but now she is a classic optimist. And she smiles continually. She hugged me warmly at the rehearsal, and we had some really good conversation at Harvey's afterward. She didn't just talk about herself. She wanted to know all about my concerts in Europe and about our plans for a double wedding. She expressed her regrets that she wouldn't be able to attend but that she would be praying for us. That definitely wasn't the 'old Rebecca' speaking. I can't wait to talk more to her tonight and get her whole story. Oh, wait, I must tell you one thing she said last night. She said, 'Gloria, back when we were roommates I noticed that you were happy all the time, and the way you read your Bible faithfully and talked about God made an impression on me.' We got interrupted, so I didn't get to hear the whole story, but she surely has changed."

"Let's go inside and keep our antennae up," said Pete. There are probably a lot of people here seeking what we have found. We need to go plant some seeds for Jesus."

Walter met them at the door. "Greetings to my dearest friends. You were the greatest tonight! Jenny and I were honored to have you in our wedding party. What do you think of Sessions Manor? Quite a change, huh?"

"You bet, bro. It's totally transformed into a majestic mansion," answered Jeff. "We are more than grateful that you are allowing us to use it for our wedding reception. I guess you and Jenny will set up housekeeping right here when you get back from your honeymoon. And later on I hope we can have Bible study and prayer meetings here like you envisioned when we first visited you."

"Oh, yes. Jenny and I have been talking about it. We really are sorry that Sarah had to miss our wedding. We wanted to tell her, too, that you four have been models for us. We want to let our lights shine for Jesus like y'all do."

Jeff, Gloria, and Pete moved around the room, doing just that. It was not a front they put on, but they simply yielded to God's Spirit, allowing Him to draw others to Himself through them.

CHAPTER FORTY-FIVE

DOUBLE WEDDING

"**B**oker tov, Sarah! Good morning!" Gloria looked over at Sarah, her head buried under her pillow, stirring ever so slightly. *Oh, Yeshua, You are the most marvelous Shepherd. You are Jehovah Jireh, providing every detail of our double wedding. I praise You for this wonderful duplex apartment, the place that Jeff and I will continue our ministry for You, but with a double anointing. I want to sing my heart out to You for the glorious anticipation of our becoming one tonight in every sense of the word,* **echad, one**. Gloria sat up in bed to raise her arms to Yahweh and sing. "This is the day, this is the day that the Lord has made, that the Lord has made. I will rejoice, I will rejoice and be glad in it, and be glad in it...."

Sarah sleepily dragged herself out of bed and joined in with Gloria singing. "Yes, this is the day!" Boker tov, Gloria. Yom tov. Good morning on this good, good day! My bashert and I are becoming one **today** as Pastor James declares us man and wife, but Pete says he can hardly wait until **tonight**. To be honest, I am a little bit scared, but after I prayed last night the Lord assured me I would be equal to the occasion." Sarah giggled.

"Yes, my dearest friend, since Adam and Eve, couples have made it through the consummation, and I am sure you and I will pass with flying colors. I am not ready for the babies yet though. Yahweh told Adam and Eve to multiply, but He didn't say how long they could enjoy married life before the first pregnancy. I have put in my request for two years, maybe three, if He wills it. We need to graduate and then get established in Israel first, don't you think?"

303

"That occurred to me also. As I told you before, barrenness plagued Chaya for four years, so I don't think I will be getting pregnant right away. But I will petition HaShem like you did."

"You know, Sarah, this double wedding is a piece of cake since the four of us turned it over to the Lord. Right away He sent Miss Lizzie's Swat Team, and He gave us a Wedding God Squad made up of mine and Jeff's and Pete's parents. Instead of us directing people in their jobs, the Lord is using **other** people, and I trust all their decisions, don't you?"

Sarah had bittersweet thoughts. "Yes, I do, but I have to confess it hurts me that only one of my siblings is coming to the wedding, Chaya, and, of course, Max. And it is a hardship for them, with a new baby. It helps that Hannah, the oldest, and her husband Avi are planning a reception for Pete and me at Stony Brook in July, especially so they can meet Pete, and he can meet them. Chaya and Max will co-host, and every single member of my family will be there. We hope Pete's family can come, too. Of course, you and Jeff are invited."

"Well, I have a surprise for you. Mom and Dad said they want to have a reception for Jeff and me at Port Jefferson in July also! Let's get our families to coordinate, so both our receptions will be within a day or two of each other. Won't that be great?"

"Thank You, Lord! That really helps my feelings. Just pray for me. So few of the guests will know me today. There is one consolation – I have two friends from Yeshiva University who said they would be here, but I haven't seen them yet. I do hope they are here."

"Sarah, don't feel bad. You are already a part of Pete's family and mine, too. And add to that all the precious people at Adaton. We are rich with relatives in the family of God."

"Gloria, you know just how to perk me up. I'm so grateful you are my soul sister. And my heart is flowing over with gratitude for Walter and Jenny giving us Sessions Manor, their own residence, for the reception. Jenny has two rooms prepared for the men and women to change clothes. After that we start our honeymoon, and we won't see this duplex again until we return from Israel. Miss Elsa and Miss Sylvia and Miss Leah are going to have everything exchanged from a women's apartment and a men's apartment to married couples' apartments. Remember Pete chose the right side for us. I hope that's okay. You and I had so little to do to furnish this duplex. Jeff took charge, and I love the furnishings he and Pete selected with only a little input from you and me. Oh, glory! How I love the Lord!"

Parking attendants at Adaton Baptist Church did a masterful organization of directing parking for the wedding, even though some vehicles were parked at a distance on the roadsides. The church had every seat filled, and the number of chairs outside proved to be sufficient for the overflow crowd. It caught everyone's attention that it was mostly young people who made the choice to sit outside, giving preference to older people sitting inside the church. The day was sunny but the temperature never reached 80 degrees, surely a miracle in June. Beautiful music came over the speakers, and the video on the huge screen had perfect color and clarity. Elinor and Julie were whispering to each other, but when Mrs. Pagani began her musical prelude at 2:30, they hushed. It wasn't customary, but they determined to lead the clapping outside for each beautiful number she played. If anyone near them started to talk, they shushed them. Elinor was thankful for the printed program with names of the musical numbers, musicians and their bios, bridesmaids, groomsmen, parents and grandparents of the brides and grooms and directions to the reception venue. Nothing was left out. Both girls were mesmerized with the singing of Lee Ann Williamson, a world evangelist, whose ministry was headquartered in Starkville. It was stated in the program that her father Cecil had passed on his global ministry to her, and that she also gave concerts in the United States.

The first number Bianca Pagani played was "Liebestraum No. 3 (Love Dream)" by Franz Liszt. Edsel Gruber was sitting close to the front by Arturo Zappala. They gave each other knowing looks, reflecting on the beautiful concerts in Europe. Bianca played more well-known romantic piano classics, typical wedding music. But they were very surprised when Bianca played an arrangement of the hymns Gloria had sung in Europe. Outside, Julie led the enthusiastic applause.

After Leah and Sylvia were seated, Mrs. Pagani began the introduction to "Sunrise, Sunset" from *Fiddler on the Roof.* Lee Ann Williamson came to the front of the stage and looked at the parents and grandparents sitting on the front rows. Elinor and Julie drank in Lee Ann's gorgeous singing. Her voice was rapturous and poignant. The accompaniment by Mrs. Pagani could not have been better. *Is this the little girl I carried? Is this the little boy at play? I don't remember growing older, when did they? When did she get to be a beauty? When did he grow to be so tall? Wasn't it yesterday when they were small? Sunrise, sunset. Sunrise, sunset, swiftly flow the days. Seedlings turn overnight to sunflowers, blossoming even as we gaze. Sunrise, sunset. Sunrise, sunset, swiftly fly the years. One season following another, laden with happiness and tears.*[120]

Lee Ann then continued in a somber tone a solo no one was familiar with. It was a song about the suffering of the church as she anticipated the Lord's return, "The Bride of Christ," recorded by Patti Roberts.[121] *Shrouded in sorrow, sometimes dressed in shame. Through the ages she stood it all for the honor of His name. There were times she watched her children perish in the martyr's flames, while remembering purity is sometimes won through pain. Slowly she shakes herself as His strength pours through her veins, and He whispers, "I've trained you well. Now the time has come to reign. So arise, dress in royal robes, prepare yourself for Me. Come My bride, come My love, let's share the day of victory. (Chorus): Here He comes, the King of Glory is coming for His bride. And she rises to meet Him through the fire purified. Oh, Church, the day is coming, perhaps the day is here, when*

306

the skies will break open, and Jesus will appear! ....Come My love, let's share the day of victory. Melvin and Carola were especially moved.

Sylvia, Leah, Mama Anna, and many of the guests, had begun to shed tears during "Sunrise, Sunset," and now some were sobbing. Gloria and Sarah, standing in the wedding tent outside, were visibly moved by the two powerful songs describing their coming of age, now about to be joined together with their divinely chosen mates, and then going forth with divine power to fulfill their divine destinies. Jenny took a tissue and wiped away Gloria's tears. Chaya did the same for Sarah.

Lee Ann's next solo was a familiar praise song, "I Worship You, Almighty God."[122] She indicated that the guests should join in. Everyone who knew the song, including the wedding party, sang with all their hearts. Gloria had requested the song and prayed that it would give pleasure to the Lord.

Samuel Sondheim, Gloria's grandfather, had stepped up to serve as Sarah's escort. He took the chance at the rehearsal to ask that she let him do this. Sarah had put off asking anyone, continuing to pray that HaShem would provide an escort in the place of her father. At Papa Sam's offer, she burst into tears and fell into his arms. He prayed for her and wiped her tears. Sarah felt a deep peace and knew her parents were smiling down from heaven.

Now it was time. In the wedding tent Sarah took Papa Sam's arm, and Gloria took her father Alvin's arm. Pastor James, Jeff, and Pete came out from the stage door and stood behind the altar railing as Mrs. Pagani began to softly play an arrangement of "Jesus Loves Me (based on *Clair de Lune* by Claude Debussy)."[123] Sarah's bridesmatrons, Camille and Chaya, walked slowly down the aisle on the arms of their husbands, Britt and Max. Next in line were Gloria's bridesmaids, Jenny on Walter's arm and Priscilla on Gary's arm. The pastor, grooms, and attendants stood in place at the front and looked in anticipation toward the open door of the church, as Mrs. Pagani in concert with the church organist played the famous "Wedding March" by Richard Wagner at full volume. Heads were craned to see the two beautiful brides walk with their escorts very slowly to the front, Sarah with Papa Sam first. The guests stood. As the "father-daughter" pair walked down the aisle, the processional music peaked in volume and then diminished. Papa Sam brought Sarah next to Pete. A dramatic pause ensued. Mrs. Pagani and the organist then gave the maximum volume to the music as Gloria on the arm of her father Alvin glided down the aisle to the front. The oohs and ahs had reached a crescendo at this spectacle of beauty. Arturo elbowed Mr. Gruber in the side. Their faces glowed with admiration.

At the altar Papa Sam answered the customary question, "Who gives this woman to be married to this man?" He said, "Her father and mother in heaven, and I and my wife on earth do." The guests' sniffling became audible as tears flowed. Papa Sam lifted Sarah's veil and put her hand in Pete's.

Gloria's wedding dress was a regal style. It had a modest scooped neckline just low enough to display the gorgeous short string of real pearls Jeff gave her. The fabric was silkened taffeta with lace motifs and sequined butterflies. Her waist-length veil of silk illusion fell from a petal bandeau outlined in seed pearls. After Alvin was presented the customary question, he answered, "Her mother and I do." Then he lifted Gloria's veil and put her hand in Jeff's. The groom could not stifle the gasp escaping his lips as he took time to gaze at his bride's beautiful face. Both their hearts were thumping in their chests, drinking in the sight of each other.

The modified Jewish wedding ceremony began. In the program bulletin all the participants were listed by name and connection to the brides and grooms. There was an insert with information about a typical Jewish wedding, followed by a Scriptural teaching of the Messiah and His bride, the Church, drawn from the Gospels, Ephesians 5, and verses from Revelation. The guests who had come early would have had time to read it, while Bianca blessed them with the musical prelude. The wedding party was amazed at the breathtaking beauty of the chuppah on the stage that Miss Lizzie and her ladies had provided. It resembled a Jewish prayer shawl, symbolizing the house the couple would live in, and it was large enough for the pastor and the two couples to stand under for the ceremony. The brides walked seven times around their grooms, as seven blessings were pronounced. A deviation from the usual ritual was inserted, when the couples knelt on cushions, heads bowed in prayer. At that moment Lee Ann sang the timeless classic arrangement of "The Lord's Prayer" by Albert Hay Malotte. All four of them felt the Holy Spirit so strong they began to weave from side to side. Jenny and Chaya, Matrons of Honor, steadied them. Then they arose and faced the audience as Chaya and Max draped a tallit over each couple and pronounced the Aaronic blessing, first in Hebrew, and then in English. Chaya and Max stepped back in place. The brides also stepped aside, and Jeff and Pete each smashed with their foot a crystal glass wrapped in a white linen cloth, symbolizing the destruction of the temple in Jerusalem.

Pastor James referred to the bulletin insert and asked the guests to read it after the wedding was over, if they had not yet read it. Then he completed the ceremony with the traditional ritual of the rings, the vows, and the final direction, "Now you may kiss your brides, Jeff and Pete."

Due to the temperature in the sanctuary and the awareness of the rising temperature outside, Pete whispered in his bride's ear, "This is just a sample." Sarah felt drunk, the same way she felt at Pete's house when he proposed to her. She looked at Gloria, and they both broke into laughter. The guests didn't know what was happening, but they loved it and joined in the laughter. Pastor James presented the married couples to the guests as Mr. and Mrs. Pete Carson and Mr. and Mrs. Jeff Quentin.

Mrs. Pagani and the organist surpassed the volume of Wagner's wedding march with the exploding, majestic music of Felix Mendelssohn's "Wedding March." Jeff whispered to Gloria, "My ancestor knew he would bless us one day." The couples and attendants wasted no time in grabbing their partners and joyously marching down the aisle to the yard. The newlyweds stood waiting for thirty seconds outside until their limousine appeared from its hiding place nearby and whisked them away to Sessions Manor. Mischief makers had fully decorated Jeff's Ford SUV and Pete's yellow Chevy, so they felt cheated that the savvy couples had foiled their scheme.

CHAPTER FORTY-SIX

Honeymoon

Everything at the reception could not have been more perfect, the newlyweds thought. After pictures were made, the two couples were thronged, but they had supernatural energy to converse and hug and treat each one special. Lee Ann couldn't wait to tell them what she observed in her ringside seat on stage and while standing to sing. She told them of the touching scenes of Sylvia, Leah, and Mama Anna weeping copiously when she sang, "Sunrise, Sunset." And she saw what appeared to be a Muslim couple in the far back, turning their heads to stare at the wedding party as they stood in the vestibule. Also, Lee Ann said there was a group of ladies close to the front who kept their heads bowed and apparently were storming the gates of heaven for blessings on the wedding. She asked Sarah if the two girls who were wearing prayer shawls were related to her. Sarah beamed and answered that those two must have been her friends from Yeshiva University.

Mr. Gruber, Arturo, and Mrs. Pagani took Gloria aside to tell her that she had changed their lives. Arturo said his wife was allowing him to return, and they would begin again to make their marriage work. Mr. Gruber said he found a church to attend when he was home in New York, and that he had started reading his new Bible. Gloria praised her piano teacher for the awesome music she played, and Mrs. Pagani said she was excited about teaching Gloria and helping prepare her for a possible music career in Israel after graduation.

Bryan Green and Laura Henderson made a point of speaking to Pete and Sarah to tell them they would be praying for their safety in Israel. They were rejoicing in the new friends they had made in Columbus, friends who attended First Baptist Church with them. Pete and Sarah turned around to talk to Jeff and Gloria but saw them going upstairs to change into their "going-away" clothes. They excused themselves and followed.

Edwin and Elinor were responsible for cleaning up Jeff's and Pete's vehicles and bringing them around to the back of Sessions Manor. As the two sets of newlyweds exited the front doors, Julie carried a message to Edwin and Elinor that it was time to drive around front. Jeff and Pete ushered their wives to the Ford and the Chevy. Gloria and Sarah laughed and waved from inside, safe from the rice shower that pelted Jeff and Pete as they pressed twenty-dollar bills in the hands of Edwin and Elinor, gave them quick hugs, then joined Gloria and Sarah and speeded away. "Mazel tov" and "Have fun in Israel" was shouted by the wedding guests until the newlyweds were out of sight.

Jeff breathed a sigh of relief. "I love you, Gloria Quentin. It was a beautiful wedding. And your dad's food at the reception can never be surpassed. At the church Pastor James outdid himself, and Pete and I gave him $200 each. He told me we were now brother preachers, and he would call me when we return from Israel to give me my first preaching assignment in another Baptist church."

"Oh, honey, that's wonderful. I hope I can miss our class that day and go with you. I must fulfill what Pastor added to the ceremony, the passage from the Book of Ruth. It was spoken by her to her mother-in-law, but it is God's instruction to **me** as your wife – 'wherever you go, I will go; and wherever you lodge, I will lodge; your people shall be my people, and your God, my God. Where you die, I will die, and there will I be buried. Yahweh do so to me, and more also, if anything but death parts you and me."[124]

Jeff grinned. "Wherever I go, you will go? I like that. I'm glad God instructed you to do that."

Jeff pulled Gloria close to him on the front seat, and she moaned in pleasure. "I feel so safe with you, honey. Now let's talk about the wedding and the reception. At the reception Mr. Gruber and Arturo thanked me for changing their lives. Oh, Jeff, it warms my heart to know that God helped me make a difference in Europe."

"Babe, I'm not surprised at all. You are totally magnificent!"

Gloria became alarmed. "I know I said I would follow you anywhere, but you are going the wrong way. You said we were spending two nights in Columbus at the Shadowlawn Bed and Breakfast. You aren't going toward Columbus. Jeff, I trust you, but I really loved that ante-bellum place that is so regal and part of the Columbus Pilgrimage every year."

Yes, my adorable wife, I loved showing it to you. I pictured how we would begin our married life in that plush old bedroom. Actually, it was Pete's idea, and that's where he and Sarah are checking in right now. But I have a much more beautiful place, deserving of my Queen Gloria. After I prayed, the Lord showed it to me. Nobody knows where we will be, not a soul. Talking about privacy, whoo hoo! I can't wait. But don't worry. Dad has my cell phone number, and he will only call in case of an emergency. He is in touch with Mr. Alvin, and they can be trusted. Pete has the number, but I threatened him not to call me on pain of death. Don't worry, my bashert."

Gloria took a deep breath. "Well, married life has begun, and I know what the Bible says about wives being submissive to their husbands. Okay, I might as well be blindfolded. I would go with you, handsome hunk, to the ends of the earth."

"Well, you passed the test. You are allowing me my little surprise, so I'll tell you. We are headed toward West Point, and we will be there in a few minutes. Our destination is the Old Waverly Golf Club on the site of the historic Waverly Mansion. I reserved us a cottage. It overlooks the golf course and Lake Waverly. There is not a tournament going on now, so it's practically deserted except for the staff in the lodge who know they will be serving a honeymooning couple. They even brought in a romantic four-poster canopied bed for us. How does that sound?"

"Oh, Jeff, it sounds perfect! I love it that you wanted to surprise me. I know our marriage is going to be filled with one adventure after another. Marrying Jeff Quentin is the smartest thing I have ever done, except for 'marrying Jesus.' He is my **first** love, and I know He is yours, too. And He wants nothing more than that we be fulfilled in each other on this honeymoon night. In fact He actually told me that!"

"What? Are you saying Jesus talked to you about tonight?"

"He surely did. It was in a dream I had several nights ago. I was sitting on His lap, encircled in His arms. He stroked my hair and kissed me on the cheek. Then He looked me straight in the eyes, and in the most loving voice imaginable He said, 'My beloved, I chose your husband for you. Tonight you will become one with him. Much joy awaits you, and it is My will that you and he rejoice in your union. He is the gift, but I am the Giver. Always remember, beloved, that I am jealous, and I must be your **first** love.' Then He hugged me tight, and I woke up. I was overcome with His love, and I knew He would always have first place in my heart."

"Oh, honey, that is awesome! I want to say it right now that I, too, vow to keep Jesus first place in my heart. And you know what? This made me think of a dream I had several months ago. Before I fell asleep that night I was thinking about our double destinies with Pete and Sarah and the way we both had been bearing fruit for the kingdom. Then I dreamed, and I was sitting at a campfire with Jesus, like Peter and the others did on the shore of the Sea of Galilee after Jesus rose from the dead. Jesus took my hands, and we walked away from the fire. He said, 'Jeff, you are my disciple like these others. You are a leader like Peter. I can see in your heart a faithful love for Me, but your love for Gloria is as strong as your love for Me. I must be **first** in your affections. You are to feed and care for my sheep, **especially Gloria**. She is My gift to you. Be tender with her."

"Oh, Jeff, my heart is about to burst! Both our dreams confirm that truly our marriage was made in heaven!"

"No doubt about it, little wife. Well, here we are at our divine destination." Jeff thought he had been displaying remarkable self-control, but as he turned the key in the lock of the columned cottage, he was counting the minutes until he and Gloria became one. With Gloria's permission Jeff took the luggage inside first, along with a cooler and a box of food.

She marveled at Jeff's forethought of having her dad pack for them two-day's worth of food, although West Point restaurants were only three miles away, and they could also get meals at the Clubhouse. He had thought of everything. Jeff picked up his wife and carried her across the threshold of their luxurious brick cottage. Looking around, Gloria gasped at the grandeur and romantic ambience of Jeff's chosen place for their love nest. It had three bedrooms and baths and every amenity. It was for groups, so Jeff must have paid a lot to reserve it. The bed in the master bedroom equaled any of those in antebellum mansions. She continued to wander throughout the spacious cottage, while Jeff positioned their suitcases outside their bathrooms, hung up their clothes, and organized their food in the refrigerator and on the counters. It was a glorious beginning to their honeymoon.

Gloria emptied the contents of her tote bag on the table near the large-screen television set. "Jeff, come here, and let's select a good movie before we go to bed. I brought these new-fangled DVDs, and I see they have a player here by the T.V. Also, I have board games. Do you like Scrabble?"

Jeff recognized Gloria's delaying tactics. "Do you really want to watch a movie or play a game? I thought those would be better activities for tomorrow morning."

"Okay, in the morning it is. Now don't you think it's time to have our devotional together before we retire for the night? It would be perfect if we read the Song of Solomon together," cooed Gloria.

Jeff grinned. "Babe, someone told me that is x-rated literature. You are not old enough to read that in mixed company," he joked. Gloria nervously laughed, but she knew the inevitable was coming. She turned around and saw Jeff, already dressed in his bathrobe and holding out his arms. "There is only one thing I would like to do before bedtime," he said, "And that is to go sit outside in the moonlight, look at the lake, and you let me whisper sweet nothings in your ear. Also I made sure they have a stereo system here, and I brought some romantic music CDs we can dance to. We didn't do the customary 'first dance' at the reception, little wife."

Gloria could resist no longer. "Ooh, dancing with you would be heavenly. But, honey, it is beginning to hit me. I am so tired." She went into Jeff's arms. "I see you are ready for bed, too. Lila tov, my husband."

Monday morning dawned too soon for the honeymooners. They could not bear to leave their love nest. Food and entertainment had no allure for them. They expressed their desire to stay another week, wrapped in each other's arms. But they had to make their 5:00 p.m. takeoff for Israel. The plane tickets had been purchased, and hotel reservations had been made. Kelila had been engaged as their guide, and she had booked the various sites all over Israel. Besides that, Rabbi Leonard and Miriam Katz were expecting them in Katzrin at their Kehilat with the four giving testimony of their ministry.

But the dreamy couple still had a few more leisurely hours before they packed to leave. Gloria took her Bible outside, and Jeff followed for their morning devotional time. "Honey, I am going to open the Bible and read at random. I know Yeshua will speak to us." Jeff watched intently. "Oh, Jeff! Look what it fell open to!

I'll read it. 'My beloved spoke, and said to me: Rise up, My love, My fair one, and come away. For lo, the winter is past, the rain is over and gone. The flowers appear on the earth; the time of singing has come, and the voice of the turtledove is heard in our land.' Jeff, that is King Solomon speaking, and he is talking about the **land** of Israel. Our Beloved Yeshua is calling us to rise up, get on our airplane, and come away, fly to His land of Israel! Could it be any plainer? He just touched my heart. I did not want to leave here, and now I do. I am ready to pack and meet Pete and Sarah at the GTR airport. And don't forget, my bashert, there are exquisite hotel rooms in Israel. Gloria looked adoringly at Jeff.

"Whoa! I love your enthusiasm, babe. You are wholehearted about everything you do. That's one of the reasons I fell in love with you. And I totally agree with you. But do you realize it will take us only minutes to get to the airport? Our love nest is paid for. And King Solomon also said, there is a time for all things. I will leave on time, I promise. But right now you must relax and enjoy our honeymoon in this beautiful place." Jeff picked up his mate and took her over the threshold a second time.

"You are the head of the house, so lead the way. And I am so glad you are a descendant of Felix Mendelssohn. Didn't his wedding recessional music thrill your heart, my wonderful husband?" Gloria continued to talk until Jeff's lips covered up the sound.

END NOTES

1. http://www.johnstonsarchive.net/terrorism/terrisrael-6.html
2. Psalm 81:10
3. https://askdrbrown.org/library/users/michael-l-brown
4. Michael L. Brown, *Our Hands are Stained with Blood: The Tragic Story of the "Church" and the Jewish People* (Shippensburg, PA: Destiny Image Publishers, ©1992).
5. https://www.christianbook.com/the-hiding-place-corrie-ten-boom/9780553256697/pd/56696?event=Homeschool|1012903
6. https://www.amazon.com/Operation-Exodus-Gustav-Scheller/dp/185240454X
7. https://www.amazon.com/Appointment-Jerusalem-Lydia-Prince/dp/0800790901
8. Matt. 18:20.
9. Col. 2:12.
10. Amazing Grace by John Newton, former slave trader (1779) https://hymnary.org/text/amazing_grace_how_sweet_the_sound
11. "The Rose" by Amanda McBroom & Vince Gill, Warnerchappell.com - https://amcbroom.com/about/the-rose/
12. Matt. 16:18, NLT.
13. Matt. 16: 13-19.
14. Matt. 26:69-75.
15. John 21: 15-17.

[16] Gen. 35: 22-26.

[17] https://en.wikipedia.org/wiki/Mendelssohn_family

[18] https://www.loc.gov/item/ihas.200156430/

[19] https://www.snopes.com/fact-check/harry-truman-middle-name/

[20] https://www.womansworld.com/posts/entertainment/michael-j-fox-middle-name-165119

[21] https://en.wikipedia.org/wiki/Felix_Mendelssohn

[22] Ibid.

[23] *Tallit* is the prayer shawl that religious Jews wear; plural is *tallitot*

[24] https://www.goodreads.com/book/show/17878647-shock-absorption

[25] Matt. 6:34 (NIV)

[26] I Sam. 16:7.

[27] I Cor. 12:8.

[28] These words were uttered by a woman to whom my husband was ministering. I was a witness. He cast the demons out of her. Afterward, he prayed for her to be saved and filled with the Holy Spirit. It was quite a dramatic scene.

[29] https://www.bible-knowledge.com/deliverance-system-for-casting-out-demons

[30] Ex. 19:14-15.

[31] John 12:31.

[32] Rev. 12: 4, 7-9.

[33] Acts 11: 27-30.

[34] Acts 21: 10-11.

[35] Acts 5: 1-10.

[36] Luke 10:17-20.

[37] Luke 8:2.

[38] Mark 16:9.

[39] John 20:11-18.

[40] Luke 8:1-3.

[41] This fictional account contains much of the true story of my husband Curtis preaching in a crusade in the Philippines. He and the team prayed for people, and there were some miraculous healings. A Muslim man came in the back of the tent, holding up a Bible and a Quran and shouting the same words in this fictional account. There were manifestations of demons with the tent flaps

making noise and the wind whipping up, as the man fled. The next day my husband and his team were called to the man's house by his wife. The man was lying in a catatonic state on his bed. After he was prayed for, he awoke. They prayed for him to be saved, and he became a vibrant Christian. The next time my husband went back to the Philippines that man was pastor of a new church! Glory to God!

42   Mark 5:1-13.

43   John 20:16.

44   https://hymnary.org/text/i_come_to_the_garden_alone.

45   "Little is Much When God is in it" by Kittie L. Suffield, (1924) - https://hymnary.org/text/in_the_harvest_field_now_ripened

46   "Days of Elijah" by Robin Mark   https://youtu.be/ca9LnzJnpjQ.

47   "Cares Chorus" by Kelly Willard   https://youtu.be/zn7RHpQ6ots

48   Mark 12:41-44.

49   Luke 12:48.

50   Matt. 5:27-28.

51   Col. 3:9-10.

52   Prov. 20:27.

53   Rom. 12:2.

54   I Cor. 15:51-52; I Thess. 4:16-17.

55   Gal. 5:22-23.

56   I John 1:9.

57   I Cor. 10:13.

58   Rev. 21: 9-21.

59   https://www.goabroad.com/articles/language-study-abroad/what-is-the-difference-between-yiddish-and-hebrew

60   https://www.jewishvirtuallibrary.org/marriage-in-judaism

61   I Cor. 3:17.

62   John 8:36.

63   John 14:1-3.

64   Mark 13:32.

65   *Lost Hero* by Danny Smith (London: Harper Collins Publishers) ©2001, p. 92; first published as *Wallenberg: Lost Hero* (Great Britain: Marshall, Morgan and Scott Publications LTD) ©1986.

66   https://www.amazon.com/Our-Hands-Are-Stained-Blood/dp/1560430680.

67   Ibid, p. 97.

68 https://raoulwallenbergww2.weebly.com/
69 http://wallenberg.umich.edu/raoul-wallenberg/the-story-of-raoul-wallenberg/
70 http://www.jewishanswers.org/ask-the-rabbi-category/jewish-history/post-biblical-history/?p=3072
71 https://www.jta.org/archive/authors-claim-wallenberg-family-assisted-nazis-in-banking-deals
72 https://en.wikipedia.org/wiki/Raoul_Wallenberg
73 https://en.wikipedia.org/wiki/%22Pimpernel%22_Smith
74 Prov. 18:10.
75 "The Oz Connection" from Message #986 – Inside the Tower, Sapphires devotionals, September 29, 2021, Hope of the World, by Rabbi Jonathan Cahn.
76 https://youtu.be/bYrcrP1ysjw "Blessed Be the Name of the Lord (The Name of the Lord is a Strong Tower) by Clinton Utterbach, ©1989.
77 https://en.wikipedia.org/wiki/Kishinev_pogrom
78 https://thetruthersjournal.home.blog/2020/02/20/the-babylonian-origins-of-easter-ishtar/.
79 "He is Jehovah" by Betty Jean Robinson, ©1982
80 https://hymnstudiesblog.wordpress.com/2017/11/20/the-love-of-god-is-greater-far/ and also https://israelmyglory.org/article/the-love-of-god-is-greater-far/
81 https://youtu.be/k6B_jYtjvME - Bill & Gloria Gaither, November 1, 2012 performance
82 Mark 10:6-9.
83 II Kings 2:1-15.
84 https://en.wikipedia.org/wiki/1993_World_Trade_Center_bombing
85 Prov. 17:23.
86 Gen. 15.
87 Gen. 17:20
88 Gen. 17.
89 https://www.jewishvirtuallibrary.org/muslim-clerics-jews-are-the-descendants-of-apes-pigs-and-other-animals
90 The Islamic paradise is described in great sensual detail in the Koran and the Traditions; for instance, Koran sura 56 verses 12 -40 ; sura 55 verses 54-56 ; sura 76 verses 12-22. I shall quote the celebrated Penguin translation by NJ Dawood of sura 56 verses

12- 39: "They shall recline on jewelled couches face to face, and there shall wait on them immortal youths with bowls and ewers and a cup of purest wine (that will neither pain their heads nor take away their reason); with fruits of their own choice and flesh of fowls that they relish. And theirs shall be the dark-eyed houris, chaste as hidden pearls: a guerdon for their deeds... We created the houris and made them virgins, loving companions for those on the right hand..." https://www.theguardian.com/books/2002/jan/12/books.guardianreview5

[91] Martyrs.

[92] Gen. 12:3.

[93] I Chon. 21:18-28; II Sam. 24:18-25.

[94] https://answering-islam.org/Morin/ish.html

[95] https://en.wikipedia.org/wiki/Temple_Mount

[96] "He is Here" by David Baroni & Niles Borop, sung by Alvin Slaughter on Hosanna! Integrity's album, "Revive Us Again," released in 1995.

[97] John 16:33.

[98] Eph. 6:16.

[99] Isa. 55:8-9.

[100] Gen. 15.

[101] John 15:16.

[102] Patrick Kavanaugh, *Spiritual Lives of the Great Composers* (Grand Rapids: Zondervan, 1992, 1996), pp. 83-86.

[103] Ibid, pp. 90-91.

[104] Ibid, pp. 94-95.

[105] https://www.factinate.com/people/franz-liszt/

[106] I Kings 11:3.

[107] II Sam. 11:12

[108] Phil. 4:8, NIV

[109] Dan. 1:4.

[110] http://budapestconcert.com/vigado-concert-hall-budapest

[111] https://www.metopera.org/discover/synopses/madama-butterfly/

[112] "I'd Rather Have Jesus" by Rhea F. Miller (words - 1922) and George Beverly Shea (music) https://hymnary.org/text/id_rather_have_jesus_than_silver_or_gold

[113] John 17: 16-18.

[114] https://en.wikipedia.org/wiki/Jan_Hus_Memorial

END NOTES

[115] Rom. 11:11.

[116] Rom. 11: 25-26.

[117] Rev. 1:7.

[118] "Jehovah Jireh" by Merla Watson, 1974 - https://youtu.be/SSDByrcWQV8

[119] Psalm 81:10.

[120] "Fiddler on the Roof" musical by Jerry Bock and Sheldon Harnick ©1964.

[121] "The Bride of Christ" by Patti Roberts, Word Music ©1984.

[122] "I Worship You, Almighty God" by Sandra Corbett, Integrity's Hosanna! Music, ©1983.

[123] "Jesus Loves Me (based on Clair De Lune by Claude Debussy)" arranged by Fred Bock, Fred Bock Music Co. ©1975.

[124] Ruth 1: 16-17.

Also by Nancy Petrey

Jewish Roots Journey

Why Christians Should Care About Their Jewish Roots

Habitation of Honey

The Honeycomb Is Waiting

Letting My Light Shine

www.energiondirect.com

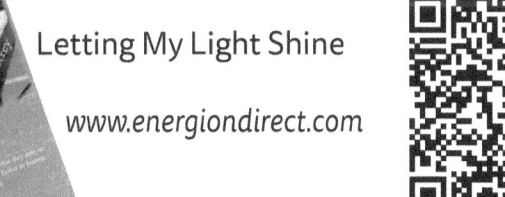

Learn how it all began in *Family Secrets - Divine Destinies*

https://www.energiondirect.com/product/family-secrets-divine-destinies/

Also by Nancy Petrey for Amazon Kindle:
https://amzn.to/2J5AI3B